# Soul Shot Skirmisher

# Soul Shot Skirmisher
## Book 1

### Cullen Spurr

To "AlsoJohn" who commented that Kaleb doesn't sound English enough because when his cousin visited we sounded different…

# Chapter 1
# There Are No Palm Trees in England

I woke up face down in the dirt. I could taste the musty earth grinding against my teeth as I moved my tongue and lips around as one often does after waking up in a strange place with no recollection of how one got there.

I didn't expect to wake up face down in the dirt by the way. I don't usually make a habit of waking up in weird positions and unfamiliar places. Well…there was that one time on my eighteenth birthday, but the less said about that the better.

Nope, there was no reason I could think of as to why I'd woken up in a weird place. The previous night I'd run out of driving hours, I was a truck driver, so I'd parked up in a safe location, called my wife, gotten into my sleeping bag and fallen asleep in the cab bed.

So then how the hell did I end up here?

I pushed myself up from the ground and looked around. I was surrounded by palm trees. Now I know for a fact that there are no palm trees in England, which is where I'm from, so either this was some kind of oddly specific dream, or I'd been kidnapped. Well, there was also the chance it was an acid trip but that was unlikely.

What was weird about the palm trees was that they were clustered together in such a way that it felt like I was in a jungle. A palm tree jungle? *Wait no, that can't be right.* I thought as I began rubbing my eyes vigorously.

I stood up and felt a warm breeze between my thighs. *Wait, am I naked? How cliché.* I thought as I looked down to see that I was wearing nothing but a pair of worn grey socks.

To be fair, I did fall asleep naked in the truck last night… with my socks on. Hey! Don't judge me, my feet get cold ok.

I could hear an incessant chirping sound, probably birds. I still couldn't understand how and why I was here. Then it happened.

Time seemed to freeze, and by that, I mean the gentle breeze that was causing the palm trees to sway stopped and so did the swaying. Then an overly happy voice filled my ears and words appeared in my vision, almost like a notification in a game.

**Welcome players, to Celestia!**
**It's your lucky day! You get to be the newest residents**
**of this little slice of heaven.**
**This is a world filled with peoples of all races, monsters,**
**magic and even the odd dragon or two.**
**How great does that sound? It's literally every nerd's**
**dream come true right?**
**So, what's the catch?**
**You're being hunted!**
**That's right folks, all 10,000 of you have been gifted a**
**brand-new tattoo, completely free of charge. Each tattoo**
**is a wholly unique and different part of a map. The**
**Celestial Map to be precise, not that I expect you to**
**know what that means.**
**Gods, cultists, kings, crime syndicates and… well**
**basically anyone with power in Celestia, are oh so very**
**eager to put that map back together again, piece by**
**agonising piece.**
**They see you when you're sleeping. They know when**
**you're awake. They want to skin you all alive so run or**
**you'll get flayed!**

**The map is on your skin and starting now, the hunt is
on.
Good look out there, players. We hope you enjoy your
stay in the idyllic and welcoming world of Celestia.**

Time unfroze and the voice and floating words disappeared as
suddenly as they'd arrived.

"What the shit," I said aloud, looking around for some kind of
PA speaker, or maybe a camera crew that were about to tell me I was
the victim of a televised practical joke.

Sadly, I saw neither of those things.

*Did she say I was being hunted?* I thought.

Before I had time to properly think about that my vision flashed
for a moment and a heads-up display appeared. At first, I thought I
was looking at something held statically in the air, but no matter
where I looked it was still there. There were four parts cluttering my
vision:

**Level: 0**
**HP: 10/10**
**Stamina: 10/10**
**Options**

Level and HP? This really was just like a game. Though 10 HP
seemed awfully low. Also, my level being 0 seemed a little off. I was
28 years old, surely that should have gained me at least a few levels
from life experience alone.

The whole system seemed odd. It spoke like it was alive, like it
had a personality.

*I wonder what options means?*

As I had that thought the options menu opened before my eyes.
It was long, listing things from stats to inventory and even plenty of

other things. As interesting as that was, I decided to ignore it for now.

The announcement said something about being hunted and also about a tattoo. I quickly checked my skin. I already had tattoos so it might be hard to tell if a new one had appeared… wait.

"Where the hell are my tattoos!" I shouted out loud.

I had a full sleeve when I fell asleep. Ink was expensive and I'd spent years getting it done piece by piece. Yet, as I stared down at my arm I saw unblemished skin. No tattoos.

Putting my outrage aside for a moment I continued to check for this *free gift* tattoo the announcer had mentioned. I couldn't see it, maybe it was a back piece? I tried to look over my shoulder but ended up spinning in a circle with no luck.

I sighed, then another thought hit me. 10,000 other people. The announcer had said there were 10,000 of us being hunted. Where were they? Who were they? Was my wife one of them? I hoped not, she was pregnant and the thought of her being stuck in a place like this, whilst with child, chilled my blood.

I began breathing heavily, my mind clouded with racing and spiralling thoughts. I didn't know what to do, I knew I needed to get my mind in order. I needed to focus.

I thought back to something my mother once told me. She said that when a task seems insurmountable, just focus on one thing at a time and eventually the rest will fall into place. I only needed to focus on one thing. I took a deep breath and let it out slowly.

*Just one task at a time.*

Just as I had that thought another notification flashed on my HUD.

**New Quest: Rock Out *Without* Your Cock Out.**
**They say that the body is a temple and you should be**
**proud of it. Well, I say stop flashing everyone and get**

**some damn pants you reprobate! Seriously no one**
**wants to see that.**
**Objectives:**
**Cover your manhood 0/1**
**Reward: A bit of fucking dignity.**

That was certainly odd. I didn't remember quests usually being that aggressive in the games I'd played before. I wondered who came up with them. This one seemed unique to me unless the other players were also all naked.

Considering that I was wearing exactly what I had on when I went to sleep last night though, I doubted it. Some were probably in PJ's.

The opening announcement said that there were 10,000 people transported here. So, I wasn't the only one who had been isekaied, at least that was something.

Huh, a truck driver in another world. Sounds like an anime title. Wait…does that make *me* truck-kun?

My stomach rumbled loudly interrupting my train of thought. It was then that I realised I hadn't eaten since yesterday afternoon. I needed to find some food. I couldn't fight off hunters *and* find pants on an empty stomach after all.

I looked around and a thought occurred to me. *I'm surrounded by palm trees; I should eat a coconut!*

I took a few steps forward towards a palm tree and looked up. Nestled at the top of the trunk, below the leaves, was a single coconut. It looked a little larger than the ones I'd seen on holiday before. It was green and hairy, shaped like an oval and it seemed to be attached to the tree by a thread.

*Must be a ripe one.* I thought. *If I'd have arrived a day later, it might have already been on the ground.*

How could I get it down though? Using precisely no brain cells, I did the first thing that came to mind. I grabbed the tree trunk and tried to shake it.

Nothing happened.

I stepped back and kicked the tree.

Nothing happened.

*Dammit, how am I going to get it down!*

I took a few paces back and placed my hand on my chin like some kind of philosopher. Then I heard a low thud. I looked back towards the tree and as if by magic, there was a green, hairy coconut on the ground.

*Perfect.*

I took a step towards it when words appeared on my HUD again.

**You have discovered a new monster!**
*Loconut*
**These little cuties are mostly harmless. They live inside the husks of coconuts, hanging out on palm trees. Their diet consists of coconut milk and human organs. They mostly keep their distance from people, preferring to live the quite life out in the tropics. However, if you attempt to shake their tree, they will fuck you up.**

"Well shit."

I stared at the Loconut for a moment. It still just looked like a large coconut to me. That was, until it stood up. Two small, stumpy legs protruded from the husk, followed by two small, stumpy arms. There was no head, just eyes that looked through holes in the coconut's husk. Just underneath the eyes, the danger appeared.

A set of razor-sharp teeth shaped like perfect isosceles triangles began gnashing together. It locked eyes with me and I felt my blood run cold for the second time in a matter of minutes.

I was having a bad motherfucking day.

The Loconut rushed at me without warning. It was surprisingly fast for a creature with the legs of a dachshund. It waddled and bobbed more than ran, but with those devilish teeth taking pride of place I had little time to be amused.

As it closed in on me, I gave into my baser instincts. I didn't have time to formulate a plan. I had no weapons, no armour. Hell, I was naked apart from a pair of old socks. So, I did what any rational person would do in the same situation.

I kicked it like *Harry Kane* in an England quarter final.

I pulled my leg back, gritted my teeth and punted the little fucker as hard as I could. It was a lot lighter than I expected, but it still felt like stubbing my toe. I hopped around a little, clutching my hurt toe as the Loconut crashed into the tree trunk. Its husk shattered and blood, gore and what I thought might be an overused liver, sputtered out from inside.

*I take that back; Harry Kane would have missed the tree.*

The smell was vomit-inducing.

I don't know if you've ever smelt a rotting carcass before, but it smelled like that. Overpowering, thick and musty with a hint of gangrene mixed in for good measure.

*So much for my diner.*

I guess Loconut was off the menu. On the upside my stomach wasn't growling anymore. Watching a midget in a coconut cosplay explode in a cacophony of guts and gore would be enough to put anyone off their food.

I turned around and a series of notifications popped up on my HUD.

**You have defeated:**
**Loconut (lvl: 1)**
**You have gained bonus experience for defeating an**
**opponent above your own level.**

I guess it made sense that the Loconut was only a level 1. In most games the noob isn't able to one shot monsters, even if they are weak.

**Congratulations! You have advanced to lvl 1**
**Ah level 1, the first step on a spectacular journey. And where does that journey lead, you ask? Most likely to you being skinned alive by the hunters. I can't wait.**

I was beginning to get the impression that this system was a bit of a dick.

Going up a level was cool and all, but what did it mean? Before I had a chance to check my options screen to find out, another notification popped up. This time though, it seemed to hover over the Loconut's corpse.

**Loot Loconut?**
**Y/N**

# Chapter 2
# You Have Created a New Item!

I looked suspiciously at the hovering question above the smashed Loconut. Mentally I clicked yes but nothing happened. Maybe I needed to be closer?

Holding my nose and trying not to vomit from the horrid stench I stepped within touching distance and tried again.

## Loot Loconut?
## Y/N

*Yes.* I thought, mentally affirming my choice. Immediately the corpse burst into silver glitter and apparated into the air. The smell went with it, leaving behind the much more neutral odour of grass and hot air that one might associate with a tropical climate.

Another text box appeared in my vision. This one was more in line with the ones I had experienced previously, appearing on my HUD rather than hovering in a physical place.

## New Item Received:
## *Loconut's Hair:*
The *Loconut* is famous for its scraggly strands of coarse, pubic like hair. This hair doesn't really do anything special, but it is a known ingredient in certain potions and I guess it could be used as string. Though it isn't too durable so maybe not.

The notification struck me as being a little odd. It was much less aggressive than the previous ones. All in all, I was quite disappointed. I'd learned that potions existed in this world, but I didn't know how to make them.

The part about using it as string stuck me as an odd addition, but after a few moments of melancholy, it gave me an idea.

As if I had some inbuilt knowledge of the HUD that I didn't fully realise was there, I mentally clicked options. From there I scrolled down to the inventory tab and found the only item.

I mentally clicked on *Loconut's hair,* and it appeared in my hand. I had no idea how I knew to do that, maybe it was part of the system design for the user interface. Pushing that thought aside I looked at the hair in my hands.

There were multiple stands of thick, coarse hair. It looked identical to the kind found on a regular coconut except it was significantly longer. I took all the strands and wound them around each other, creating a medium thickness string. As I finished my task another notification appeared on my HUD.

**You have created a new item!**
**Loconut String**
**This is string created from *Loconut's Hair*. Its use is limited. I know what you're thinking and don't you fucking dare!**

Frowning at the notification a thought occurred to me. It was like the system was alive. That definitely wasn't a pre-made message. It was speaking directly to me. That revelation felt important, but for the time being I had bigger fish to fry.

I smiled up at the sky, like an insane person, and said:

"Oh, I do dare."

Then I took off one of my old grey socks. I used my teeth to create a small hole in each side of the top. I then threaded the string though each side and knotted it, leaving room to put something else inside the sock.

I then slipped it over my manhood, looping the string around my waist and covering myself up…kinda.

**Quest Completed: Rock Out *Without* Your Cock Out.**
**They say that the body is a temple and you should be**
**proud of it. Well, I say stop flashing everyone and get**
**some damn pants you reprobate! Seriously no one**
**wants to see that.**

**Objectives:**
**Cover your manhood 1/1**
**Reward: A bit of fucking dignity. Not that you deserve**
**it you degenerate. I wanted you to find pants!**

I chuckled triumphantly to myself as two more notifications appeared. The first was a nice surprise. I'd received experience points and advanced to level 2. Not that I really understood what that meant yet, but it had to be something good.

There was a lot less fanfare this time. The notifications simply said that I was now level 2, unlike the level 1 notification which came with an ominous paragraph attached.

The second notification was a little more off putting.

**You have created a new item!**
***Cock Sock:***
**An underwhelming item of clothing designed to cover**
**one's manhood, giving the appearance of an inadequate**
**baby elephant. This is no substitute for pants.**

I got the impression that the system wasn't too happy with me. However, I'd completed the quest and gained a level for my trouble. That was one task down and countless more to go. Hooray.

I didn't appreciate the jibe about inadequacy but, assuming this system was what brought me here, at least it didn't kill me.

I swallowed at the thought of what it *might* do to me later down the line if I pissed it off enough though.

Next thing on the old to do list was to find some food, find shelter, hopefully find some actual clothing, and figure out what the hell was going on.

*All in good time Kaleb. One thing at a time.* I thought to myself in an attempt to calm my racing heartbeat.

My name is Kaleb by the way, I probably should have mentioned that earlier but with everything that was going on I figured formalities weren't high on the agenda.

Looking around the clearing I'd started in; I saw a small trail leading through the clustered palm trees and decided to follow it.

The palm tree jungle, as I'd named it, was a weird place. For starters, there wasn't any foliage. It was a relatively simple landscape. The ground was simple, packed earth and everything else for as far as the eye could see was palm trees.

The trees themselves were clustered tightly together and it felt quite unnatural. In my world, palm trees usually grew a lot further apart than this. The whole place felt alien.

As I trekked along the winding dirt path, I decided it was time to look through the stats section of my options tab.

**Status Sheet:**

**Name: Kaleb Akabane**
**Race: Outworlder**
**Level: 2**
**HP: 20/20**
**Stamina: 14/20**

**Strength: 5**

**Agility: 11**
**Perception: 7**
**Vitality: 5**
**Intelligence: 6**

I guess I should explain about my name. I was born in England and have mostly Caucasian features, but my father was Asian. My mother opted to give me his last name even though she didn't share it herself.

They were never married you see. She met him whilst studying abroad. She didn't realise she was pregnant until she got back home and because all of this happened in the mid nineties' communication was a lot harder than it is now.

She only had the landline number for his dorm room, but he'd moved back home after graduating too so she didn't really have any way to contact him. As such I've never actually met my father. It's not something that really bothered me though, my mother did the job of both parents and I can't really complain.

But enough about all that.

Agility seemed to be my best stat. I wasn't sure why exactly, it's not like I ever really excelled in sports or anything. I had taken a few martial arts classes when I was younger and growing up in England it was normal to play football with your friends. That didn't feel like enough of a reason to make that my highest stat though.

I was pleased that my HP had increased. If my maths was right, which it rarely was, then HP increased by 5 points per level. That was useful to know. It seemed Stamina was the same.

That was the only stat that wasn't filled up, I wondered if it was because I was hungry. Maybe food filled it back up? If so, that was all the more reason to find something to eat.

I wasn't having any luck on that front though. As I continued following the dirt path I just saw more of the same. Dirt and palm trees.

It felt a bit like when you get too close to the edge on a massive RPG game. The kind of area where you can tell the developers didn't put anything important there and just filled it up with trees or something for the sake of it.

If that was the case though, at least I should be relatively safe.

*Famous last words.*

I continued following the trail for what felt like forever, but was probably only half an hour or so, until I came across a clearing.

Inside the clearing was a single, wooden box on a pedestal. Nothing about it seemed special, but I did wonder if it was a trap.

Leaving the path, I circled around the clearing carefully; however, nothing caught my eye. So, when I'd made it full circle and arrived back on the trail I decided to approach the box.

As I got closer a notification materialised over the top of it.

**Open Starter Loot Box?**
**Y/N**

**Starter Loot Box?** The phrasing reminded me of a tutorial from an MMORPG. I needed all the help I could get though, so naturally I mentally asserted that I did indeed want to open it.

The box glowed and began to heat up before my eyes. Then the lid flew open with a pop and confetti spilled out all over my feet and the ground.

Inside the box was another hovering notification.

**You have unlocked a starting weapon!**
**Congratulations on making it this far player! Though**
**only one of the 10,000 brought here has actually been**

**stupid enough to die so far so I guess this is more of a participation medal than an actual award.**
**Before you are three weapons which will help you on your journey, and hopefully make your inevitable death more entertaining for me. Choose wisely, losing your virginity is a big deal after all and I wouldn't want you to regret your actions.**

Someone had already died? I wondered how. If my experience was anything to go by it was possible that everyone who arrived here had to face a monster before getting to this stage. Therefore, it stood to reason that this unknown person was killed by their monster. If that was true though they must have been damn unlucky.

The Loconut, though creepy as shit, was easy to kill. I mean all I did was kick it. Either way, the knowledge that someone had died already really drove home the seriousness of the situation.

As promised, three more hovering notifications appeared in front of me. I felt a little bit giddy at getting to choose a weapon. I guess they do say inside every adult is the heart of a child. I eagerly read each notification in turn.

**You may choose one of the following weapons:**
*Basic Sword*
*Basic Bow*
*Basic Sceptre*
**\*WARNING\* You currently have no mana and will therefore be unable to use the item** *Basic Sceptre*.

"Well, that's a cop out," I muttered to myself as I finished reading the options.

What was the point of offering me a weapon I couldn't use? More importantly if mana existed in this world, then why didn't I have any!

I felt like some kind of lame NPC. Who gets isekaied to a world filled with magic only to find out they don't have any? What a let-down.

I kicked the side of the box in frustration and immediately re-gretted it as I remembered I didn't have any shoes.

After a moment of awkwardly balancing on one leg as I rubbed my sore toes, I took a deep breath and calmed myself down.

I needed to make a choice. I had a sword or a bow to choose from. I'd never used a sword, though how hard could it be to swing a big sharp stick at something? On the other hand, it would mean getting up close and personal with monsters, and whilst I had no clothing or protective gear that might not be the best strategy for the time being.

On the other hand, I had only used a bow a handful of times in my life. All of those times had been on school trips and I didn't feel confident I'd make a good archer. If I missed my first shot and a monster came charging at me, what would I do? Stab it with an arrow?

It felt a little bit like being stuck between a rock and a hard place, but I had to choose one of them. So, casting my longing for the **Basic Sceptre** aside I made my choice.

# Chapter 3
## Stag Party

I sighed and shook my head before mentally clicking on the *Basic Bow*. It was the best option at the time. Someone had already died in this place and that knowledge weighed heavily on me.

Maybe I was just scared, but who in their right mind wouldn't be? Rushing into battle naked and afraid with a sword in hand just seemed too reckless. Like I'd be asking for death.

So, that was that. I chose the bow and once again a notification appeared on my HUD.

**New Item Received!**
*Basic Bow*
**This is a basic bow; I'm sure you don't need an explanation for that. It is a piece of wood with a bow string attached and you use it to shoot things. A cowardly choice in my opinion but it is not my place to judge the choice of feeble-minded newbies.**
**The bow is a skilled weapon, so you best get practicing.**
***Arrows not included***

"Arrows not included. Are you fucking kidding me!" I yelled at the sky like a mad man.

Well, that was it. I'd made the wrong choice. This system obviously didn't like me very much. Maybe I should have chosen the sword after all. At least that was useable, unlike the crappy piece of wood I'd been gifted.

I pulled it out of my inventory to have a look. For a basic piece of gear it actually looked quite professional. It was made of a dark wood and curved nicely. It even had a piece of cloth to cushion my hand and act as a grip.

Despite my misgivings I still felt pretty badass holding it. Though without any arrows it was useless. I considered trying to make some arrows myself, but I didn't have anything to carve them with. Without a knife or at least a jagged rock I was stuck.

The only thing I had that could be of any use was the *Loconut's Hair*. I pulled it out, absentmindedly. They were my only possessions. A bow with no arrows, and hair…and a *Cock Sock* but the less said about that the better.

I messed around with the bow for a little while feeling utterly dejected. In an attempt to cheer myself up with some bad humour I placed one of the hairs on the edge of the bow string, pulled back and let it fly, pretending it was an arrow.

Except something weird happened.

The hair held a sturdy shape when placed on the bow string and when I let it fly it shot across the clearing and embedded itself in a tree.

"Well, that's certainly something," I said, a wicked smile creeping across my face.

It seemed I'd just found a loophole in the system's foul play. A loophole that I was happy to exploit.

I immediately took out another hair. I was getting used to accessing my inventory now and could summon the hair into my hand with barely a thought. It was a quick process, much faster than I imagined a quiver would be.

I stood up, took a deep breath, and focused on a spot on a palm tree at the other side of the small clearing. Releasing my breath, I pulled the drawstring back and let loose.

I missed.

The hair flew straight past the tree and disappeared into the dense palm tree jungle.

"Well shit," I muttered.

If I couldn't even hit a tree that was barely five meters away, how was I supposed to hit a monster? Those things moved after all.

I'd have to practice. So, for the next few hours I painstakingly practiced shooting the tree. At least, I assumed it was a few hours, I didn't have any way to tell the time.

I only had a finite amount of *Loconut's Hair* so every now and then I'd have to walk over to the tree and collect as much of it as I could find. After the tenth or eleventh time of doing that, I found that I'd hit the tree more often than I'd missed it.

I worked out quickly that I was more accurate if I kept my elbow high. It felt counterintuitive but if it worked it worked. I also learnt to only breathe halfway out before firing the hair. For some reason that seemed to steady me a bit.

The main issue though, was my forearm.

Roughly half the shots I took resulted in the bow string striking my forearm and I now had a nasty red welt on it. It had scabbed a little and was oozing slightly. I hoped it wouldn't get infected. That would be a truly tragic way to die in a new world shrouded in magic.

Imagine being isekaied away only to die of an infection a few days later. I'd be the laughingstock of the whole world.

My stomach growled again for the first time since my fight with the Loconut and I realised just how much I desperately needed to eat.

I collected my arrows for the last time and headed out.

There was a second trail leading away from the clearing and I figured it only made sense to keep following it. After all, the first trail had led me to the weapons box so hopefully this next one would lead me to some food.

After a few minutes of walking a notification filled my HUD.

**New Quest: *Bear Grylls***
**You're stranded in the wilderness. You need food and water to survive. Whatever will you do? Well, you could drink your own piss like the famous earth TV personality *Bear Grylls*, or you could try and find something fit for human consumption. It's up to you.**


**Objectives:**
**Eat something 0/1**
**Drink something 0/1**
**Reward: Not dying of starvation. You're welcome.**

*These rewards aren't very helpful.* I thought as I finished reading the new quest.

At least it aligned with my own goal though and hopefully I'd gain another level from it. I needed to remember to check my stats afterwards and see if levels affected anything other than HP and Stamina.

I wasn't sure exactly how I would find food and water, but if it was a quest then theoretically it should mean that there was some out there.

Keeping my bow in my hand I continued to walk along the dirt path. It didn't take long before I came across another clearing though. This one was quite different than the last. I rubbed my eyes thinking I'd gone delirious.

In the middle of the clearing was a stage with a large metal pole in the middle of it. There was a deer dancing on the pole. Yup, that's right. A pole dancing deer.

It moved its furry body like a human. Its eyes had lashes that looked fake, they were curled and long. It had little pink blush marks on its cheeks like it was wearing makeup and, possibly, most concerningly, it was wearing women's lingerie and stripper heels.

Sat in front of the stage was a group of stags, each with long, branching antlers. They also wore human clothes. The one in the middle had a crown on its head and a shirt that said *Pussy Patrol* on it.

It was surrounded on both sides by more stags who all wore the same shirt. One had sunglasses on and another was desperately trying to shove what looked like a dollar bill down the pole dancer's G-string.

Naturally, another notification appeared.

**You have discovered a new monster!**
*Stag Party*
**These rambunctious little rascals are exactly the kind of brain-dead idiots you'd expect to find at a strip club. One of their buddies is about to tie the knot so naturally his friends decided to take him out to see some deer titties, after all, it is his last night as a free man – or deer in this case.**
**You have discovered a new monster!**
*Doe Dancer*
**Oh deer. This poor girl likely grew up craving attention from her inattentive father and now spends her nights taking her kit off in the hopes of getting some attention from creepy guys at a stag party and the one older man who claims he's only there for the free buffet.**
**Now I know you've heard the jokes about how it's ok to kill strippers and hide them in the trunk of your car,**

**we've all seen American sitcoms after all, but don't try
any funny business, like eating her, or you'll end up as
the deerly departed.
Get it?
But seriously, don't eat her. She probably tastes like
gristle and shame anyway.**

I had to rub my eyes after that last pun, I rolled my eyes so hard
I nearly saw my own brain. Dad jokes aside though, this might have
been the chance I needed to get something to eat.

People hunted and ate deer all the time back on earth and maybe
I could even make some clothes from their hides and weapons from
their horns.

The only question now was how to kill them. I didn't know what
level they were at and there were five of them and only one of me.
The odds weren't exactly in my favour and I imagined one good
charge from a stag would rip me in two.

I didn't really have a lot of options. Obviously, I'd have to use
my bow but even if I killed one with the first shot, surely the rest
would charge at me straight after.

Then I had a lightbulb moment. It had been staring me in the
face all along. I knew choosing the ranged weapon was a good idea.

I turned towards the closet palm tree and moved towards it. I
looked around and the *Stag Party* hadn't noticed me yet, they were
too enthralled by the stripper spinning herself upside down and wig-
gling her ass at them.

*Perfect.*

I quickly glanced to the top of the tree. The last thing I wanted
was to be attacked by another *Loconut* as I climbed. Luckily there
wasn't one up there, at least not one that I could see.

I wrapped my legs around the thin tree trunk and began to
climb, and by climb I mean shuffle.

It was a painful ascent. Each time I pulled myself further up I scratched the skin around my thighs. Pretty soon I was leaving a blood trail on the tree trunk and I noticed my HP had dropped to 18/20.

I was determined though. This was the smartest way. Everyone knows that deer can't climb trees. It was a foolproof plan if I did say so myself.

Once I reached a significant height, I squeezed my legs together to hold me in place. Unfortunately, palm trees didn't have strong branches I could perch on, but this should do.

I shifted around a little until I had a good view of the clearing. I pulled out my bow and a hair, took aim, breathed out halfway and loosed it.

The hair soared through the air towards my intended target. The stag in the middle, I'd called him the Groom in my mind to make identifying them a little easier.

I watched with bated breath as my little hair flew gracefully through the sky. I continued watching as it soared right over Groom's head and hit the *Doe Dancer* squarely in the face.

She was still hanging upside down and her limp body left the pole as if in slow motion before landing on the stage in front of the stags. Blood leaked from the hole as the light left her eyes.

An achievement popped up on my HUD, but I waved it away. I'd check it later.

The stags all turned to each other, raising their palms in confusion, and looking around at the others in their group.

"Alright, which one of you idiots killed the stripper?" the sunglasses-wearing one asked.

# Chapter 4
# Why is that Deer Naked?

Whilst the *Stag Party* were busy pointing fingers at each other stumbling around like unattended toddlers at a supermarket, I took my second shot.

I lined up the *Loconut's Hair* and loosed another shot. Once again aiming for Groom. The hair whizzed through the air, aiming for his centre mass – his heart. I realised that going for a headshot was probably a bit above my current skill level.

Naturally it made more sense to aim for the largest part of my prey. He turned to the side as one of the others spoke to him and then yelled in a high-pitched voice as he was hit.

The hair pierced his shoulder and I cheered audibly. My first time hitting an intended live target. What an achievement! It might not have killed him outright, but it must have done some damage.

"What the... hey I think there's someone else here!" the sunglasses-wearing stag shouted. I decided to name him Sunglasses to make it easier.

*Crap, he must have heard me cheer. Rookie mistake Kaleb. Don't be such a noob.* I admonished myself.

Sunglasses began looking around. He raised his hand to his eyes, as if blocking out the sun, and eventually he settled on me.

We locked eyes for a moment and I froze. Who'd have thought *I'd* end up being the deer in headlights. Jesus, now I'm starting to sound like that obnoxious, pun-loving system message announcer.

"Hey look, there's something up there," Sunglasses said, pointing towards me.

"Why is that deer naked?" the podgy looking stag asked. I decided to call him Podge to make identifying them easier.

The only stag I hadn't yet named had no identifying clothing, however, he was the one who was trying to put a dollar bill in the stripper's G-string earlier. I decided to call him Perv. With the naming done I could concentrate on choosing my next target.

"Maybe it's got alopecia?" Sunglasses replied.

"I don't care what it's got, it just fucking shot me!" Groom said, clutching his bleeding shoulder.

Whilst they were busy nattering, I nocked my next hair and took a shot at Groom again. This time it hit him in the neck and the stags screamed as a group.

His neck exploded in a torrent of blood that shot out like a water pistol, soaking Sunglasses. He dropped backwards to the floor and began scuttling away, lip trembling as he half screamed, half cried.

"What the fuck. This can't be happening. He was supposed to get married tomorrow. I've known him since pre-school. Oh my god, oh my god."

I began nocking the second arrow but stopped as I heard his desperate, pleading screams. He sounded human. Was *I* the bad guy here? These deer *were* monsters, weren't they?

"Please Mr Naked Deer, don't shoot. We surrender!" Podge shouted, throwing his hooves in the air.

He looked genuinely terrified.

Perv dropped to his knees, cradling Groom's limp carcass in his arms and crying. He gently closed his dead friend's eyes before placing him on the ground and standing.

Shaking, he began to speak as he too raised his hooves.

"Please don't shoot! We don't want any trouble."

Sunglasses didn't join in. He looked truly traumatised as he sat rocking on the floor and mumbling something about how his friend was supposed to get married tomorrow.

I lowered my bow. I felt awful. This wasn't how games were supposed to be. In games you killed monsters for experience points and they tried to kill you too. It was simple, it was obvious.

Then it finally occurred to me.

*This isn't a game.*

I began climbing down the tree. I didn't know what to do, what to say, but I couldn't bring myself to shoot these creatures anymore. In their eyes I was a cold-blooded murder, a terrorist.

Imagine if I'd started killing people on a stag do in Vegas. I'd become an infamous serial killer overnight. Maybe it was the same here. Maybe here, the deer were just another race of people. I mean, they wore clothes, they seemed to have human sensibilities. They could speak for god's sake.

*What have I done?* I thought as I reached the bottom of the tree.

I walked towards them slowly, struggling to look any of them in the eyes. They looked terrified, stood there with their hooves raised above their heads in surrender.

I was a horrible person. That damned system announcer had tricked me. How gullible did I have to be to think that it was ok to shoot creatures attending a stag party.

That's not ok no matter what world you're in.

As I entered the clearing Sunglasses finally looked up.

His eyes were wide with the thousand-yard stare of a seasoned veteran. Tears streamed down his face.

"Why?" he mumbled with a cracking, pained voice.

"I-I don't know," I replied in a hoarse whisper. "I thought you were monsters. I'm…I'm sorry."

Sunglasses stood up and the other two dropped their hooves seeing that I was no longer a threat. I stood before them with a lowered head. I felt terrible. How would I ever come back from this?

Perv approached me hesitantly and placed a hoof on my shoulder. It was oddly comforting, despite being so heavy. How could he be so understanding when I'd just murdered his friend?

"We are monsters, and you're a gullible idiot," he said menacingly.

Shocked, I looked up to see a devilish grin on his face. His eyes were dark and malevolent, like those of a demon. I felt a sharp pain in my stomach and looked down to see a knife sticking out of it, it was held precariously between the two parts of his hoof.

I looked back up, wide eyed and jumped backwards. I stumbled over my own feet and landed on in the dirt as Prev tipped his head back and began laughing like a maniacal Bond villain.

The others joined in; Sunglasses literally doubled up in hysterics.

"Oh, you were supposed to get married tomorrow," he mimicked his earlier words in a mocking and whiny tone as he struggled to get the words out between laughter.

"Yeah, and you were all like. *Please Mr, we surrender*," Podge joined in; slapping Perv on the shoulder as he doubled up as well.

I watched in horror from my position on the floor. What the hell was this place? This was sadistic, it was horrifying.

*You don't have time to freak out.*

27

I took a breath and tried to get serious. My health was depleting rapidly. It had fallen to 7/20 already. I was going to die if I didn't do something.

Looking down I saw the knife still protruding from my stomach. With a grimace I reached down and gripped it with both hands. I pulled it out with a groan. It was painful as shit. Blood seeped out as I finally yanked it free.

My HP had dropped to 5/20. It seemed to stay there though. Removing the knife had oddly worked. It was a bit counter intuitive though. Back on earth the advice was to keep the knife in so it could plug the hole. Then again, earth logic probably wasn't all that relevant in a world with talking deer and magic sceptres that I couldn't use. I wasn't bitter about that or anything.

I looked down at the knife in my hand and then up at the laughing deer. They weren't paying attention to me. They'd underestimated me. I'd make sure it was the last thing those sadistic bastards ever did.

I stood up, lurching to one side as my stomach throbbed with pain from the stab wound. I didn't have time to use my bow. They'd pounce on me before I got off a second shot. No, I'd have to make do with the knife.

I needed to be fast, catch them off guard.

I began walking towards them, one hand clutching my stomach. I would have liked to charge, but I only had 5/20 HP left and I didn't want to risk losing more health to my unhealed wound.

So instead, I staggered towards them. Trying to look as unthreatening as possible. They'd underestimated me before, surely they'd continue doing so?

I was only a few steps away. When I finally got close enough, Sunglasses looked up. The others were still bent over in hysterics, mimicking each other, and laughing ever harder.

"Oh, you're not dead yet. Good for you little buddy–"

Before he could finish, I stabbed him in the throat and pulled the dagger out, spraying myself with his blood.

He gagged and clutched at his throat as a large piece of gristle flew off the end of the knife. He looked at me with surprised eyes and fell to his knees.

Before the others had time to react, I turned the knife around in my hand and hammered it into Perv's head. He dropped like a sack of bricks, hitting the ground with a thud.

*That's for stabbing me you, dicks.*

Finally, I turned towards Podge. He'd stopped laughing now. He took a step back in horror as I continued towards him and he fell to the ground. He continued backing up, shuffling backwards. He looked petrified. He quickly reached the stage and had nowhere else to go.

He looked up at me with pleading, terrified eyes.

"P-please," he began. "I have a family. J-just let me go and we can pretend this never happened," he stammered.

"P-please I have a family," I replied in a mocking tone, just like the one they had all been using only moments ago. "Fuck you," I added as I plunged the dagger into his neck and twisted.

Podge sputtered and writhed against me as I dopped my knees onto his chest, pinning him down. He took longer to die than the others and I made sure to look him in the eyes as the light finally went out.

"What the fuck is wrong with this place," I muttered, shaking my head.

I rolled off the deer and laid against the stage. I felt mentally exhausted. My stomach twinged as I moved but my health hadn't gotten any lower. I looked down and realised the blood had stopped.

The wound was scabbed over, but it didn't seem to be healing on its own.

Chances were that I'd have to eat something to replenish my health. It made sense with the quest I was given being about food. Everything I'd had to do so far seemed to teach me something about this world, like a tutorial. Though I could have been reading into it too much.

I decided to take a breather for a few minutes before I thought about food and how to heal. I'd gotten a few notifications during the fight so I decided to read them.

**You have defeated:**
*Doe Dancer (lvl 1)*
**You heartless bastard, she was just trying to put her kid through college.**
**Experience gained.**
**You have unlocked a new personal skill!**
*Speak English Damnit!*
**You know how it can get really frustrating when you visit another country and they have the audacity to speak in their own language instead of speaking in yours? Yeah, well that's not going to be a problem for you anymore. You can thank me later.**

Interesting. That would explain how I could understand those annoying stags. That skill was useful, though it wouldn't make me any better at combat.

**You have defeated:**
*Stag Party (lvl 1) 4/4*
**Experience gained.**
**Congratulations! You have advanced to lvl 3**

I was surprised their levels were lower than mine. So much for bonus experience for killing a monster above my own level. Oh well, it was probably for the best. If they were any stronger, I might not have won.

I looked around at the stags and they all had loot notifications above them. I had a couple of other notifications but the lure of potential loot won out. I should have probably eaten them but the idea of eating guys who were that sadistic made me nauseous. I mentally clicked yes on all four loot tags.

# Chapter 5
# I Warned You Not to Eat the Stripper

You have received a new item!
*+1 Sunglasses*
These bad boys give plus one to your charisma, not that
you have any. You should take them; you need all the
help you can get.

That was strange, charisma wasn't even on my stats list. Were there hidden stats that I couldn't track or was the system being literal when it said I didn't have any? Before I had a chance to check, the next notification popped up.

You have received a new item!
*Pussy Patrol T-shirt*
There's nothing magical about it. It's a t-shirt. Better
luck next time.

That was a little disappointing. I needed some clothes but *pussy patrol?* It wasn't my preferred choice, to put it mildly. Not to mention it was probably covered in asshole deer blood.

You have received a new item!
*Antlers x2*

Antlers, they're useful both as a potion ingredient and as an ornament for the hood of your pickup truck.
Yeehaw!
You have received a new item!
*Pervert's Lighter*
You don't need me to explain what this is.

As soon as the notifications had ended the four stags burst into silver confetti and began floating away into the sky. It was just like with the Loconut but without the awful smell.

I was about to try on the sunglasses when I noticed the exclamation mark in the top left corner of my HUD. I'd almost forgotten, I still had more notifications from the battle. It was probably best to open them now before I got sucked into trying out my loot.

You have gained a new combat skill:
*Bow*
*Bow* has advanced to lvl 1
*Bow* has advanced to lvl 2
Due to *Bow* advancing to lvl 2, you can now choose a new combat skill.
Pick 1/3:

*A new combat skill? Now that's more like it!* I thought, pumping my fist in the air, and immediately regretting it as my stomach throbbed reminding me of the wound I hadn't healed yet.

By the sound of it I could choose one, but I had three options. "That's awfully magnanimous of you," I mumbled to myself. Through a grimace, I looked through my options.

Novice Bowman
A novice bowman has more chance of actually hitting what they aim for instead of, say, accidentally shooting a stripper right off the pole. You should pick this one, you reeeaaallly need it.

It seemed the system was back to its old self again. I didn't know why it was so rude to me, but in this case, it was actually kind of right. I'd been aiming for Groom but missed and hit the stripper in the face instead. It was probably right; *Novice Bowman* was a good choice. I kept scrolling anyway.

### Hair Regrowth
**Since you love using *Loconut's Hair* instead of arrows I figured I'd give you a skill for it. Now, if you land a successful hit using Loconut's Hair a replacement hair will appear in your inventory. Like you said, I'm magnanimous.**

Infinite ammo was a pretty good perk, I wasn't going to lie. But I had the feeling that real arrows would be better and surely I'd find some eventually. It was a skill that would help in the short term but would probably become redundant pretty fast.

Also, that last bit at the end of the skill worried me. I'd gotten this achievement during the fight, yet the system mentioned something I'd only said a minute ago, after reading the last notification.

If that meant it could change skills and rewards on the fly then I needed to be more careful with what I said aloud. It was obviously listening. Creepy.

### Heat Seeking Hair-sile
**This one's a personal favourite of mine. What's better than shooting hair at people? Shooting hair that locks onto a target and won't go away until it hits its mark. Like a friendly bumblebee of death.**

That would be useful, especially since I wasn't the best shot. But my accuracy wouldn't improve if I had a targeting system and once again, the skill would be redundant in the long term once I found some arrows. Even though it was the most boring option, it only made sense to go for the first skill on offer.

The idea of playing into the system's hands annoyed me a bit though, considering it advised me to pick that one. Though maybe that'd get it off my back for a little while. Without fanfare I mentally asserted that I wanted to pick *Novice Bowman.* A moment after that another notification appeared and this one caught me by surprise.

**You have gained a new combat skill:**
*Dagger*
*Dagger* **has advanced to lvl 1**
*Dagger* **has advanced to lvl 2**
*Dagger* **has advanced to lvl 3**
**Due to** *Dagger* **advancing to lvl 2, you can now choose a new combat skill.**
**Pick 1/3:**

I was caught off guard by being awarded a dagger skill, though it did make sense. I'd killed three of the stags with a dagger. I picked up the blood-soaked weapon and looked at it fondly.

"We might not have started off on good terms with you stabbing me and all, but you really saved my ass back there," I said, realising soon after how odd I must look talking to a dagger like an utter psychopath.

I put the dagger into my inventory and looked at the skill choices.

*Novice Daggerman*
**It's the same as the bow skill you just picked but with more slicing. You get the picture.**
*Stagger Dagger*
**Slicing an enemy with your dagger has a 10% chance of stunning them. This applies to every hit by the way, so if you cut a single enemy ten times they're gonna get**

**stunned, probably. Also, wordplay, because you murdered all those harmless *Stag Party* guys in cold blood.**

"It was not in cold blood!" I shouted at the sky, causing my stomach wound to hurt again.

Despite the ridiculous explanation, the skill itself was actually pretty good. However, the last one was better.

### Dhampir Dagger
**A Dhampir is the offspring of a human and a vampire. They can't turn into bats or anything but in some earthen mythos they drink blood to gain power, or because they think they're edgy or whatever. Anyway, the point is that the *Dhampir Dagger* will steal HP with every cut you make. That's right, cut them and heal yourself in the process!**
**Gain 10% of damage inflicted by the dagger as HP.**

Without hesitation I picked that one. It was a no brainer really. If I'd had that skill already I wouldn't be sat at 10/25 HP. Oh yeah, I forgot to mention, my health increased by 5 points because I reached level 3 so I had been healed ever so slightly. I figured that was what stopped the bleeding and caused the wound to scab over.

I really wanted to sit there a little longer and go through the loot I'd gotten, but I figured it was about time I ate something, completed that quest, and hopefully healed myself back up.

For all I knew there were monsters roaming around and I needed to be in fighting shape if I wanted to have any chance of surviving long enough to justify picking the most boring bow skill.

I pulled myself up and looked at the *Doe Dancer*.

The system asked me if I wanted to loot her, a hovering notification floated above her corpse. I decided not to press Y or N though. I didn't want to risk her disappearing. Instead, I pulled my new dagger from my inventory and cut into her back. I cut a sizable chunk out of her, gipping as I went.

It didn't smell bad or anything, it was just gross. She may have been a deer but she was wearing underwear and makeup. It felt so wrong to cut her up for food, even if that was exactly what people did back home to the non-stripping deer we had there.

After a bit of messing around I managed to get the chunk free and a notification popped up.

**New consumable received:**
***Stripper Steak x1***
**Restores up to 50 HP and tastes like cigarettes and regret.**

I really hoped that last part wasn't true as I stored the meat in my inventory. Looking back up at the dead *Doe Dancer* I smiled. Not because she was dead, or because she was a stripper, but because the loot notification was still there.

I didn't know yet whether my inventory would keep food fresh so I wasn't about to carry an entire deer's worth of meat in there. Not when there was sweet, sweet loot to be had.

**You have received a new item!**
***Stripper Heels***
**These bad boys will make you look six inches taller and if you don't think that's a lot then imagine how all the women you've dated felt.**
***+1 to sex appeal.***
**Ok that's not a real stat, I made it up.**

Well, that was a waste of time. I should have just butchered her after all. I thought with an audible sigh.

Either way, it was time to eat.

My stab wound wasn't going to heal itself. Luckily, I had everything I needed to get the stripper steak to a nice medium rare.

Grinning, I took out the pussy patrol t-shirt and the pervert's lighter. I placed them to one side of the stage in front of me. Next, I grabbed one of the antlers and the stripper steak.

I stabbed the antler through the steak. Then I lit the t-shirt on fire and began slowly rotating the steak over the fire.

The lighter itself was a bronze colour and it had a motif of a pole dancing deer on it. It was a bit gaudy but I guess that's why it was called Pervert's Lighter.

"I bet you wanna make a spit roast joke right about now don't you?" I said, looking towards the sky.

I didn't know how long I'd been in this new world but it wasn't showing signs of getting dark any time soon. I wondered for a moment if days followed the same pattern I was used to. Maybe it never got dark, or maybe it did but the days lasted twice as long or something. Who knew, but I wasn't too tired either, despite the ridiculous day I'd been having, so it probably just wasn't all that late yet.

As I continued rotating the steak I smiled to myself as I pictured the system announcer, whoever or whatever it may be, cursing to itself as it realised I wasn't going to be wearing the ridiculous shirt it gave me.

Soon the steak was looking good and smelling better. Even without seasoning, the gamey smell made my mouth water. I usually ate deer medium rare, and by usually I meant that one time I had deer in a nice restaurant, but I was so hungry I figured I'd try it rare.

I bit into the steak and it was worth taking it off the spit early. The flavour exploded in my mouth. Fresh game was my new favourite food. Holy shit, no wonder people hunted these things so much.

I ate it like a chicken wing, gorging myself on the succulent stripper meat. I'd known I was hungry, but I didn't realise quite how famished I was. I was so glad that it didn't really taste like cigarettes and regret.

I finished up, tossing the left-over sinew and gristle onto the dying shirt fire. I felt really tired all of a sudden. I guess it made sense, it had been a long day and I'd just eaten. It was normal to want to nap after a big meal and I did eat a lot of stripper steak.

I turned around and laid my head back against the stage. I was sure it would be ok to nap for a little while. Hopefully the smell of cooked meat wouldn't attract the monsters or anything. Honestly, I was so tired I didn't even care if it did. I couldn't fight it; my eyes were drooping whether I wanted them to or not.

Just as I was drifting off a notification pooped up on my HUD.

**\*WARNING\***
**You are being hunted!**
*I warned you not to eat the stripper.*

# Chapter 6
# It Seems Someone Has Been Rather Naughty

I came to in a haze. My vision was blurred and my body was chilled. Out in the palm tree jungle it was humid and warm so I'd never really noticed the weather properly, being naked was kinda nice in that climate.

Wherever I was now it was the opposite. I was chilled through. It reminded me of getting out of a sleeping bag when you're camping. The sweet embrace of sleep is warm, but then you wake up and have to get up and suddenly its cold and no matter how much coffee you drink it's still going to take an hour or so to fully warm up again.

I hated that feeling.

My vision felt fuzzy and unfocused as I tried to look around, then I realised why as my eyes began to focus. My HUD was dominated by warning notifications that flashed like angry wasps in my vision.

*WARNING*
*You have been poisoned with Passout; the effect is
instant.*
*WARNING*
*You have been captured by a hunter. Death is imminent.*

*Well, that's not good.* I read the warnings and mentally clicked on them to get rid of them. The hunters were mentioned in the opening announcement. If I remembered correctly, they were the guys that were trying to skin me for the tattoo I hadn't located yet.

My heartbeat raced as I began to panic. I started looking at my surroundings. I seemed to be inside some kind of stone building, or maybe I was underground? There were no windows or natural light.

The room had a lot of what looked like, medical tools. A scalpel, a bone saw, a syringe with some weird purple liquid inside it.

*Wait, those aren't medical tools. They're torture tools!*

My heart sped up again and I found it hard to breathe. My breathing became laboured as I continued to look around the room. There was a single door on the far side, my only possible escape. There was a cauldron-looking thing in front of me, it was huge. If I was stood up it would easily reach my navel.

Speaking of my navel, I wondered if I was still wounded.

I looked down to see a faint, white scar where the stab wound had been. My HUD said my HP was full, so that was good at least. The deer meat must have healed me.

My hands and feet seemed to be bound. I looked down and saw that it was rope that bound my feet, I couldn't tell with my hands because they were behind my back and they'd gone numb.

I needed to escape, but how?

*Calm down, remember, one small task at a time.*

I took a deep breath, in through my nose and out through my mouth. Keeping it circular, trying to slow my heartbeat. I would not get out of here if I was panicking.

As if the system had read my thoughts, a new quest appeared.

### New Quest: *Sink or Skinned*
**You have been captured by a hunter who wants to take your skin and sew it together with other skins to create**

the map. It's probably in your best interest to not let that happen. This is what you get for ignoring my friendly advice when I told you not to eat the stripper.
Objectives:
Escape 0/1
Free yourself from your binds 0/1
Free or kill the other captive 0/1
Kill your captor (optional) 0/1

What no reward? Cheapskate. I grumbled internally.

It seemed that the quest had multiple parts. I needed to focus on the second objective first, getting out of the rope. However, I couldn't help noticing the third objective. There was another prisoner. Were they in here with me or were they somewhere else?

I began looking around again and noticed a large wooden X on the other side of the cauldron. It was dark in the room so I couldn't be sure, but there seemed to be a human shaped outline strapped to the X. I had to look really hard to notice it though. I needed to raise my perception somehow if I ever got out of this room.

I began thinking of ways to escape my rope binds when a thought occurred to me. I hadn't tried to use my inventory yet. If I could summon my new dagger into my hand I could cut the rope. It would be awkward, but I could try.

I mentally asserted that I wanted my dagger in my right hand. Instead, I got another notification.

#### *WARNING*
*The summoning of weapons is prohibited in this area.*

"Well, that's just great," I muttered sarcastically.

"Hello?" a feeble voice called.

I jumped and looked towards the wooden X. The voice seemed to have come from over there. I guess there was another captive in here with me after all.

"I saw them drag you in, I didn't realise you were awake yet," the voice continued, it sounded strained.

"Where am I?" I asked, saying the first thing that popped into my head.

"I don't know where we are, but it seems to be some kind of flaying room. I've been here for about a day now. Some guy keeps coming and chanting spells at me, they finally tied me up on this cross thing just before you arrived."

If he had been there a full day then either I'd been unconscious for a really long time, or he was captured as soon as he got to this world.

I wanted to ask, but I had more important things on my mind.

"I need to get out of these binds, then we can escape. Got any ideas?" I asked hopefully.

"The stuff in this cauldron thing works like acid, I think. It could melt your rope?" he replied.

Dipping my feet in acid was not high on the agenda. I sighed and began looking around for other options. Then I saw it again, the scalpel.

It wasn't that far away from me; it was just behind the other captive. I began scooching my way towards it like a slug.

My naked body grated against the cold, hard stone floor as I moved. It was uncomfortable, but luckily it didn't seem to be draining my HP.

After a few minutes of what was essentially an intense ab workout, I reached the torture table. I rolled onto my knees and grabbed the scalpel with my teeth.

The next step would be getting it into my hands, which were secured firmly behind my back, and still numb. I moved back towards my starting position and dropped the scalpel to the floor. I then turned around and basically tried to do the limbo until my hands touched the scalpel.

Believe me when I say, that wasn't easy on the core muscles. I felt something brush against my hands. You know, how when your hands are numb you can still feel that you're touching something, it just feels like there's almost a barrier between your fingers and the object even though you can see that you're touching it? Well, it felt like that, and with some effort, and a few times dropping it, I managed to get the scalpel into my hands.

Next, I turned it around and began slicing at the rope. I could vaguely feel that it was working, but it was slow goings. Scalpels were designed for precision, not brute force cutting, but I was making some headway and soon I felt the rope give way and my hands were free.

I dropped the scalpel and began shaking my hands, trying to get a semblance of feeling back into them. Pretty soon the pins and needles came and then I could feel again. I picked up the scalpel and went to work on my leg restraints.

"He's coming," the other captive moaned.

He'd been silent this whole time, I'd almost forgotten he was there. His voice still sounded croaky and feeble.

"Who's coming?" I asked, still battling with the rope restraints.

"The hunter."

*Shit!*

I began cutting at the leg restraints with a new vigour, hoping to free myself before his arrival. I was almost all the way through when the door opened and a crack of light illuminated the room.

I managed to see the other prisoner for the first time. He had untamed, mousey brown hair and was stripped to his boxers. He was strung up on the wooden X, facing forwards. It reminded me of an old history documentary I'd seen once where a soldier got tied up and flogged for disobedience.

He was facing towards me, looking straight down into the cauldron and its acid. His face looked gaunt and his eyes were poofy. His lips were swollen and cracked. He was not in a good state.

As the door continued to open, I did the only thing I could think of and played dead. Or, more precisely, I laid back down in the exact position I'd been in when I'd woken up. I put my hands behind my back as if they were still tied. My legs were almost free, but not quite. I held the scalpel firmly, waiting for a chance.

If I was lucky, he'd leave before I needed to do anything.

The door opened fully and a stout man in a crimson robe entered. He was bald with a tattoo of thorns around his head. He had a wiry build and dark eyes.

He walked towards us, whistling a jaunty tune.

*What a sadist.* I thought as his eyes glistened at the sight of his first captive.

"Today is the day boy," he said in a squeaky, but serious voice. "I can finally remove your piece of the map and move onto my new find."

He looked at me, grinning from ear to ear. I stared back defiantly. I was trying to play dead, be the grey man, push attention elsewhere. But something about this freak really pissed me off.

"Oh, it seems we have a feisty one. Don't worry number two, it'll be your turn to break soon enough," he chortled as he spoke, as if the whole situation was somehow amusing to him.

He walked over to the over captive and ran his slender hands over the man's back. Then, as if catching himself, he jumped a little and moved to leave. He walked towards the door and I breathed a sigh of relief.

If he left then I could finish freeing myself, free the other guy and we could get the hell out of here. Hopefully I'd get access to my weapons again after leaving the room. If it was possible, I wasn't going to leave this place without killing the hunter.

I wasn't quite sure what had come over me. I'd never killed a person before. But looking at this bald fuck, I felt bloodlust.

Just as he was about to reach the door he turned back for a second, as if he'd just remembered something. His dark eyes darted towards the torture table. He was going to notice that the scalpel was missing.

*Goddamn it!*

"It seems someone has been rather naughty."

# Chapter 7
# A Sadist and A Battle Junkie

The moment the robed man looked at the torture table I knew he would see that the scalpel was missing. In that fraction of a second, I knew that all bets were off and I acted without hesitation.

All thoughts other than survival left my mind and I acted on pure instinct, fuelled by fear and adrenaline. As he looked at the table, I stopped pretending I was still tied up.

As quickly as I could, I moved my hands to the front of me and began hastily cutting at the ropes binding my legs. I had nearly cut through them just before the man entered the room so I was confident I could free myself before he reached me.

As I cut, he spoke and turned in my direction. His dark, unfeeling eyes glistened with a sadistic joy to match his ear-to-ear grin.

I could tell he was confident because he didn't panic at all. He walked towards me at a slow and threatening pace. That would be his undoing. I freed myself just as he passed by the other prisoner. He didn't seem to have any weapons which was a bonus for me,

As he reached my position, I channelled all of my power to my thighs and, from a squatting position, I leaped upwards and slashed at his throat with the scalpel. My attack landed, I felt the contact, but it was too shallow.

He struck me in the solar plexus with a powerful palm heel strike and I flew across the room into the wall behind me.

The wind was knocked out of me and all the air emptied from my lungs as I fought for breath. My health dropped dramatically.

"I like a feisty captive. I'm going to enjoy beating that out of you," he said, licking his lips as a look of pure, unadulterated joy spread over his face.

*Oh great. He's a sadist and a battle junkie.*

I struggled to my feet as he stood there, watching me. He wanted me to get back up so he could take pleasure in putting me down again. What a freak. His parents must have been mean to him as a child or something.

I stood before him, panting as my lungs were still in shock. I still had the scalpel somehow, but I knew it wasn't going to be enough. I wouldn't survive another hit from him. As it stood my HP was already knocked down to 8/25. It had been full before. He'd dealt 17 damage with a single palm heel. The man was a damned monster.

I knew I only had one shot, so I followed my instincts and hoped for the best.

I threw the scalpel at the man's face. He blocked it easily, but in that moment he was off guard I charged at him and shoulder barged him with all my might.

He was caught off balance and fell backwards with a splash as he landed inside the cauldron.

He screamed bloody murder as the acid began melting his skin. It stank of sulphur and burnt meat as his wails filled the room. I hoped there weren't any other hunters around to hear it or I'd be screwed.

Soon the lower half of his body had disappeared and all that was left was the upper half of a torso draped over the side like a sock puppet.

"Yes! We're safe now mate!" I shouted as I pumped my fist in the air.

I'd managed to win. I was in a little bit of shock from the whole ordeal. I'd never killed a person before. But I'd won and I would live…for now.

It was strange to me. People back home always said that killing another person for the first time was a big deal. They'd said it made some people vomit, others get depression and feel awful for what they'd done. But in that moment the only thing I felt was absolute ecstasy.

The notifications came pouring in but I ignored them for the time being. I needed to untie the other prisoner.

"Hey, we won mate. I'm gonna untie you, I just need to find the scalpel," I said cheerily to my comrade in capture.

He didn't reply.

I stood up and walked towards him. I hoped he was ok.

"Hey buddy, are you alright?" I said, cutting him loose.

He wasn't the lightest fellow, despite being scrawny. Though maybe I was just weak. It didn't matter, I dragged him off the cross and sat him down with his back against the nearby wall.

His head lolled and he seemed to be a deadweight. I wondered if he'd passed out. He did seem malnourished and frail when he'd spoken.

I figured I'd best check he was still breathing so I tilted his head back.

His face was gone. There was nothing there except for bone and leaking brain fluid. It was revolting. I heard a faint sizzling sound as more of his flesh began to disintegrate and then I realised.

49

When I'd thrown the robed man into the cauldron it must have splashed acid at the other prisoner. He was dead. I'd killed him.

That was the moment when the weight of taking another human life hit me as I vomited over his corpse.

I scuttled back a few paces and looked at him. The man who was my counterpart in this awful, fucked up situation. An innocent human, spirited away against his will just like me. And I'd killed him.

It dawned on me that perhaps the trope of people feeling bad or throwing up when they'd killed someone was more related to innocent life, or at least life they could understand.

In war when soldiers kill each other, they feel something because the people they killed were just ordinary folk doing the same job they were. They could relate to them.

The guy who accidentally kills someone in a car crash is affected by it because that person is innocent, just going about their daily lives, just as he had been.

I didn't feel anything for the hooded man because he was the enemy. He was a sadistic bastard who was going to skin me alive and get off on the act of doing so. I couldn't relate to that. He wasn't innocent. He deserved a painful death.

But this guy? He was a fallen comrade. And I didn't even know his name.

The tears welled up as I sat on the floor for a while with my thoughts.

***

At a guess, I'd let about twenty minutes pass before I calmed down. I felt bad that it took such a short time to move on but I couldn't stay in the prison. It wasn't safe and I wasn't even at full health.

I took a deep breath and looked at my notifications. I needed a distraction.

**Congratulations! You have defeated:**
***Chrysus Cultist (lvl 10)***
*You have received bonus experience for defeating an opponent above your own level.*

Wow, that guy had been 7 levels higher than me. If it wasn't for the acid cauldron I wouldn't have stood a chance. It made sense that his palm heel strike would cause so much damage. The rank disparity alone was probably enough.

As expected, I gained a few levels.

**You have advanced to lvl 4.**
**You have advanced to lvl 5.**
**Advancing to lvl 5 has unlocked the following:**
*Achievements*
*X5 Free Stat Points per level*

That was interesting. Now I had stat points I could start pumping up my stats. I wondered if they directly affected the things like my HP and Stamina.

I didn't know what achievements were but I didn't have to wait very long before I got one. It was literally the next notification.

**Achievement Unlocked!**
*I'm Melting! Melting!*
**You have successfully taken down an opponent more than twice your rank by using the environment. That's a dirty tactic if ever I've seen one, kudos.**
**Reward: x1 Acid Reflux Loot Box**

I'd received a loot box. That was interesting. I hoped it had something useful inside, like maybe pants or shoes. I wouldn't get my hopes too high though, after all the system seemed to enjoy messing with me.

Before I had a chance to stop it, the next notification came up on my HUD. The one I'd been dreading.

**Congratulations! You have defeated:**
*Player - Brad Duncan (lvl 0)*
**I could make this like a memorial and tell you about Brad's life here, but honestly, he was a boring guy. He was captured before getting a single level, how lame is that?**
**Reward:** *PKing Loot Box*
*Do you want to absorb Player - Brad Duncan's Celestial Map piece(s)?*
**Y/N**

I wasn't sure what to do. What was a Celestial Map piece? I wondered if it was the proper name for those tattoos we apparently all had. In fact, I hadn't even checked to see if Brad had one.

I also wasn't thrilled about the idea of being rewarded for killing another player.

I crawled over to the corpse of Brad on my hands and knees. I was only a few paces from him. I gingerly turned over his body to take a look and there it was.

The tattoo looked like a small jigsaw piece in the middle of his back. It was all black lines and remined me of a tiny piece of a tribal tattoo.

It made sense that I couldn't find my own if it was placed right in the middle of my back like his. There was no way I'd be able to see that without a mirror or a camera or something.

I sighed and sat back, leaning against the wall.

It would be a waste not to take the tattoo. I didn't really know what they were used for but I sure as hell didn't want the hunters to have it.

It felt right, like a memorial for the man I'd killed. So, I mentally asserted yes to the question posed by the notification.

Brad's body lit up like a starry sky. The tattoo itself lifted off his body like tiny particles of light. The light pieces looked physical, like I could hold out my hand and touch them.

They moved towards me and I felt a warm glow on the middle of my back, like it had joined on to my own tattoo that I assumed was also there.

I felt a small power flowing through me. It was nice and warm like sitting on the beach in a tropical paradise and letting the sun warm your skin.

**You have assimilated a piece of the Celestial Map:**
**Celestial Map pieces collected: 2/10,000**

10,000 pieces? Jesus. I'd known that the system announcer had told us we all had a piece of this map but it only just dawned on me that someone would have to kill 10,000 people to get the whole thing.

That was insane!

Talk about mass murder. No wonder I disliked the hunter I'd killed so much. You'd have to be unhinged to kill that many people just for some stupid treasure map.

**New Quest: *The Celestial Map***
**Collect all the pieces of the Celestial Map. Upon**
**completion of this quest you will unlock another quest.**
**Objectives:**
*Map pieces collected 2/10,000*
**Reward: Vast Cosmic Power**

"Fuck."

# Chapter 8
# A Pretty Terrible Disguise

The system was trying to convince me to kill the other players. With a quest like that, with that *reward*, it obviously wanted the map to be completed. Apparently, it wasn't particular on who did it either: a player or the hunters.

There was no way I was going to hunt down and kill 10,000 people. Especially not for such a sketchy sounding reward. Vast cosmic power sounded like something out of an anime. What the hell did that even mean.

Maybe I'd turn into a god...or maybe I'd be able to go home. That was the first time I'd thought about my wife since this thing started.

I'd put her out of my mind because everything was so overwhelming and I had to fight to survive. Actually, that was a lie. I'd been enjoying myself. Not all the time, not when I accidentally killed Brad. But, in all honesty, parts of this had been fun so far.

Who could blame me? Back home I had a boring job and a relatively boring life. I loved my wife and I had friends but outside of working and having a drink on the weekend what was there really to look forward to, to strive for?

I felt bad even thinking it but part of me didn't want to go home. Not yet at least. I was a terrible person. My wife was back home probably thinking I was dead. She'd have to give birth and raise our child alone and I had the audacity to be enjoying traipsing round a tropical jungle collecting loot.

I hoped she was still on earth. The thought of her being in this place with child sent chills down my spine.

I looked around the room again as the thoughts slowly settled down and I saw something I'd almost forgotten about.

*Loot Chrysus Cultist?*
**Y/N**

I mentally clicked yes. I needed all the help I could get and the dead hunter was 7 levels above me. Surely he'd drop something useful.

**You have received a new item:**
***Robe of Chrysus***
**Whilst wearing this robe you'll be more likely to loot gold from enemies. You will also look like a member of the *Order of Chrysus* and you won't be naked anymore so that's a bonus!**
**+10 Defence**

The idea of wearing the clothes of a man I'd just killed didn't sit well with me. However, the idea of having a defence stat and looting gold from enemies was overwhelmingly good.

Not to mention looking like a hunter would give me certain benefits. I still didn't know what lay beyond the door to this room. No one had come to check on the screams but that didn't mean there wasn't other hunters out there.

For all I knew the room was soundproofed.

I went into my inventory and selected the robe and like magic it appeared on my torso.

I stood up and it hung down to my ankles, which means it must have resized itself by magic when I looted it because I was a few feet taller than its previous owner.

It was crimson and came with a hood. The material was also soft, like walking around with a freshly washed pillow strapped to your chest.

Overall, I was chuffed with the prize. It was probably the best loot I had. The only real issue was that it didn't come with a belt so I was forced to wear it open.

I wasn't sure that was going to bode too well for me as a disguise considering my chest and cock sock were on full show. It might do the trick from behind though and I could always hold it closed with my hand and hope for the best.

It did strike me as a little odd that the cloak wasn't half destroyed. The one the cultist had been wearing was mostly disintegrated by the acid. Had the system repaired it for me? I couldn't tell, I'd have to file it away as system fuckery for now and move on.

Next, I tried to open my loot boxes but I got a strange error message.

**\*WARNING\***
**Action not possible. Loot boxes may only be opened in a safe area.**

That was odd, but it also confirmed the existence of safe rooms. I wondered where they were. Did this mean there were towns too? I couldn't wait to find out but for now I had more important things to attend to, like not dying at the hands of creepy cultists.

With the loot boxes unavailable for the moment there was just one more thing to do before I could leave the room. Assign my free stat points.

I had 5 of them to distribute and I had a good idea of what I was going to do with them. I needed to gain an idea of what stats affected after all. So naturally, since I had 5 different stats and 5 stat points, I'd put a single point into each stat and see what changes happened, if any.

After doing that I immediately checked my stat sheet.

**Status Sheet:**
**Name: Kaleb Akabane**
**Race: Outworlder**
**Level: 5**
**Map Pieces: 2/10,000**
**HP: 19/36**
**Stamina: 32/36**

**Strength: 6**
**Agility: 12**
**Perception: 8**
**Vitality: 6**
**Intelligence: 7**

**Personal Skills:** *Speak English Damnit!*
**Combat Skills:** *Bow (lvl 2),* **Novice Bowman,** *Dagger (lvl 3), Dhampir Dagger*

The first thing I noticed was that I had three new sections on my stat sheet. The first filled me with dread. The stat sheet now told me how many map pieces I had. *That damned quest.*

I tried to ignore it and move on. The other two sections were more useful. They showed my combat skills and their relative levels and something called *Personal Skills* which currently only showed my language affinity. From that I had to assume personal skills were passive skills and buffs.

The other thing I noticed was the changes that came with the stat additions. When I added a point to my vitality stat my HP went up by 1 point which I guess made sense. In most video games back home vitality related directly to health.

It seemed that the strength stat effected my stamina. I'd have been willing to guess that it also effected how hard I could hit something since that's what logic would dictate, but I couldn't be sure.

Thus far my stamina hadn't ever dropped too low but it was good to know how to increase it. I was certain that I'd eventually need more in tougher fights.

With that out of the way I cautiously exited the room and found myself in a posh looking corridor with a lovely, quilted red carpet. It was the softest thing my feet had touched all day.

The corridor was well lit and only led in a single direction. The room I'd been in was right at the end, which was probably lucky for me since the hunter had screamed bloody murder when I murdered him bloodily.

I chuckled to myself at my own joke as I tried to lighten my bleak mood a little. Then I closed the door behind me. The last thing I wanted was for some nosey cultist to walk past and notice the bodies lying around.

That was another thing. It seemed that humans didn't turn into stardust when I looted them, unlike the monsters I'd killed previously. That was definitely going to be a problem eventually, but hopefully I'd find a way out of the cultist's lair before it mattered.

They'd be sure to ask questions when they found one of their own dead and disrobed and their prisoner equally dead and missing his map tattoo.

The next thing I tried was accessing my weapons from my inventory. As I thought, now I was out of the prison room I could remove my dagger again. I kept it in my right hand, hidden under my robe and used my left hand to keep the robe shut. I also pulled my hood up to hide my face.

It was a pretty terrible disguise but from a distance I hoped it would do the trick.

With those things taken care of I set off down the lush, carpeted corridor. It was only a few short steps before I heard something and my blood chilled as someone rounded the corner.

He had his head down, nose stuffed in a large, black tome. I say he, but his face was covered by his hood so I couldn't tell. He wore the same robes as me.

I took a breath and steeled my nerves as I continued walking. I needed to appear to be acting natural so I also put my head down and attempted to walk right past him.

I succeeded. He barely seemed to register my presence as we slipped by each other in the corridor.

"Is the new captive awake yet?" he asked.

I stopped.

He'd walked past me; I should have gotten away with it. If I spoke he'd surely know I wasn't one of them. He must have thought I was the man I'd killed and if that was so then he'd know that my voice was much deeper than his.

I was also a lot taller so if I didn't say anything and he looked up from his tome then he'd realise something was up.

Putting on my squeakiest voice and trying to mimic the hunter, I responded.

"He's still unconscious. I'll check on him again later."

"Good."

That was all the man offered before I heard his soft steps on the carpet as he continued on his way. I'd done it!

Before I could properly celebrate thought my heart skipped a beat. There were no other doors in the direction he was walking. He was going to enter the room.

I turned around quickly and saw the man approaching the door. He reached absently towards the handle, all whilst still reading his book. I had to do something.

Before I realised what I was doing I found myself walking towards him with my dagger outside of my robe. As he turned the handle, I grabbed his mouth with my free hand and shoved my dagger into his throat. The last thing I needed was him screaming and if he was as high levelled as the hunter I wouldn't win in a straight fight.

The man struggled for a few moments, trying to pry my fingers away from his mouth but I held on. At the same time, I felt warmth flowing into me from the dagger, it must have been the healing effect. I checked my HUD to see that my HP was slowly filling back up.

Then the man went limp in my arms and I got another notification.

**Congratulations! You have defeated:**
***Chrysus Mage Cultist (lvl 4)***

It turned out he was weaker than me, which explained why he'd died so quickly – though most humans died if you stuck a dagger in their throat.

I didn't get bonus experience or a level up from the kill but it didn't matter. I couldn't expect to level up every time I killed someone.

*Every time I killed someone.* The thought came so easily, was this my life now? Murdering cultists and taking names.

I casually dumped the body in the prison room and looted him, gaining a second robe which I kept in my inventory. It wasn't like I could equip two of them at once after all.

Interestingly I also received 10 gold coins from looting him. The effect from the cloak was working and surely if I could loot coins then I could spend them. Though I had no idea where.

My HP had gone up from using the dagger but only by 2 points. The dagger awarded 10% of the damage inflicted in health points so that probably meant the dagger had done about 20 points of damage and the mage only had that much health.

That seemed weak compared to my 36 max HP but maybe it was because he was a mage. I had no way of knowing so I left the room once again, closed the door and continued down the corridor.

When I reached the end, I decided to take a right turn. I had no real reason for it, both directions looked identical. I walked for a short while and luckily I didn't bump into anyone. The lair seemed quite spacious, either that or this cult didn't have many members.

As I walked, I felt something strange in the air. It was hard to explain but it was like some kind of aura calling to me. I followed the direction, perhaps naively, and came to stand in front of an ornate, black door.

The door had a skull and crossbones etched into it in a fine, artistic carving. The aura didn't feel foreboding or anything though. On the contrary it felt welcoming, like it wanted me to enter.

Maybe that was the trap, a false sense of security followed by unknown horrors and death. That would certainly make sense in the lair of an evil cult that wanted to skin me alive, but curiosity prevailed.

Throwing caution to the wind I opened the skull door.

# Chapter 9
# Absolute Lunacy

The welcoming aura I had felt vanished as I found myself in a white room. More accurately, I was in an endless white space. There were no floors or ceilings, no windows, or walls, just the great expanse of nothing.

I turned around to check and sighed in relief as I saw that the door was still there. Oddly, it was open, showing the hallway through it.

*What a strange place,* I thought. *Why would the cultists have a room that's just an empty expanse?*

Without warning the door closed and disappeared and I was trapped in the plain of nothingness.

I turned back around, or at least I think I turned back around. It was hard to tell in a featureless realm. Stood before me was a large man,

He gave off a fearsome aura, but somehow I could tell it was part of the same welcoming aura that I followed. Because of that I was not afraid as I stared at him.

He wore a long, green cloak, underneath it was a barely contained, muscular body with a deep red scar across the chest. His lower torso was wrapped in white bandages and his hood was down revealing a handsome yet serpentine face.

Parts of his cheeks seemed to have scales growing on them and his yellow eyes looked inhuman.

"Kaleb Akabane," he began in a confident, deep voice that didn't match up to his snake-like features. "I am Chrysus, the god of wealth. I have summoned you here to instruct you to worship me."

"Sorry mate but I'm an atheist," I replied cooly.

The god might have thought he was intimidating and powerful but nothing in my instincts told me that he was. His aura felt ferocious now, but only seconds ago it felt warm and welcoming. For some reason, I found it hard to see him as anything but that now.

"An atheist?" he replied slowly. "You realise I'm standing right in front of you?"

"Well, I'm not blind," I replied with a chuckle. "Listen mate, I don't really know what the word god means in this world. But where I'm from it's about blind faith and in my opinion, blind faith is akin to a lack of accountability. That's a dangerous game to play with yourself, and religions are known to have started plenty of wars and committed lots of atrocities. I mean each to their own and all, but I don't want anything to do with it."

"Then why do you wear my cloak?" He asked, folding his arms, and looking at me with a surprising amount of amusement.

I realised that was why I recognised his name; it was the name on the cloak I had looted from the cultist I'd killed. That meant this was his cult. Which in turn meant he was the one behind the attempted skinning of both me and Brad. I felt my eyes turn cold as I defiantly stared at him.

"I don't have any clothes and it's got some good buffs. My turn, why are you and your cult trying to skin people and why the fuck did you think it was ok to have your little hunter abduct me?" My voice felt alien and cold as I spoke. This wasn't a fiery rage like the kind you might see in battle, no, this was cold, hard hatred.

"You dare to question a god? You have got some meteoric sized cajónes my boy." He laughed, which only made me madder. "I just told you I'm the god of wealth, the Celestial Map is the pinnacle of all that I embody. I want it, so I'll take it. That is what it means to be a god, boy, absolute power, no matter how whimsical."

He unfolded his arms and placed them in his pockets. His lips curled into a bemused smile, as if he was educating a small child. It irked me, but my hatred was still cold. I wasn't going to do anything irrational. If he was a god it'd be futile anyway.

"Right...so what are we doing here exactly? Can I go now?" I replied, trying to remain nonchalant to show him I wasn't intimidated.

He sighed and rubbed his hand over his eyes, like he had a stress headache or something.

"You're here because I led you here, to the door. I led you here because I want you to become my vassal, I thought I was clear on that. Listen boy, I saw you take the map piece from the other prisoner. I didn't realise that was possible. Do you know how much easier it would be to put the map back together if all I had to do was bring you people and let you kill them? That's why I want you to be my vassal."

He got more and more excited as he spoke, his eyes lit up. He was obviously passionate about the damned map, not that I really cared.

"So, you didn't know that I could adsorb map pieces? I thought gods were supposed to know everything," I replied with a smirk.

I was playing a dangerous game here but I couldn't help myself. He stared at me for a long moment with a hard glare, then his gaze broke into a momentary look of surprise before he continued.

"Gods in Celestia are not all knowing, well apart from maybe Athena, that woman is truly insufferable, but I digress. We aren't all

65

knowing, we are simply the supreme power in Celestia. Suffice to say, it's unprecedented that a mere level 5 outworlder like yourself can refuse a request from me, let alone that you would. It is most perplexing."

*Athena, as in the ancient Greek god? What the fuck.*

"Yeah, I am a bit of an enigma, so can I go now I've got things to do."

"Yes, yes, very well. But I'll only let you leave here alive on one condition. Refuse it and I will kill you right here and now."

"I'm not being your walking talking map. Just kill me," I spoke arrogantly. I didn't know what had come over me. This was a god I was speaking to, why on earth was I asking him to kill me. I must have had a death wish or something, but I honestly couldn't help myself. The dude was just so flippant about the idea of killing 10,000 people.

He seemed to have no qualms at all about causing all of that death just so he could attain some treasure from a map. It was absolute lunacy.

"No not that, I already know you won't accept that. I want you to accept my blessing." He smiled a predatory grin that gave me chills.

"Why would you want to bless me? You know I don't like you right?"

"Have you ever heard the old proverb, keep your friends close and your enemies closer?"

"Fine, it's a deal," I said.

I felt power flow into me and my HUD felt like it wanted to give me a notification but nothing happened. I wondered if the system was blocked out of this realm. If gods truly were the most powerful in Celestia than maybe the system couldn't affect them.

Though it was much more likely that the system was the true power and this god was just an arrogant tool.

Chrysus gestured and the door reappeared. I opened it and walked through without saying goodbye.

***

Chrysus sank down into his throne, rubbing his throbbing temples. The boy had been so obstinate, yet there was something important about him. For a moment when he stared at him, he'd tried to kill the boy with soul pressure but he didn't even wince.

It was almost as if he hadn't noticed it at all. Chrysus had to know more about him. A power that can withstand soul pressure from a god as easily as a mild breeze, that was a power he wanted.

He was the god of wealth after all and it was his right to claim everything in this world for himself.

"My Lord, that boy was insufferable. Far be it for me to question the wisdom of one such as yourself, but why did you let him live?" his servant, Lucius asked.

"He's interesting," Chrysus replied in a strained voice. "I want to keep an eye on him. He might prove useful to me later."

Lucius furrowed his brow. He had been alive for a painstakingly long time. Not as long as his god of course, but much longer than most mortals.

As the longest reigning high priest of wealth in history, he felt that he knew his god better than most. Yet this behaviour seemed odd to him. The boy was greedy, that's for sure. He seemed to relish loot and that was a quality highly regarded by Chrysus.

However, his blatant disregard for rank disparity and divinity left much to be desired. Lucius had seen good men burnt to cinders for less by the very god who had just blessed this disrespectful boy.

"My Lord, does this boy have your protection?" Lucius asked.

"He has my protection from you Lucius. Don't you dare kill him when I've just blessed him. Do you know how tiring it is to give one of those? If he attacks a member of the order they are entitled to protect themselves though and of course the low rankers currently in the temple can do as they wish.

"If the boy can't best the likes of them, he'll never be of any use to me anyway."

"Understood My Lord," Lucius replied. "I have to ask though; how did he manage to resist your soul attack? I didn't think that was possible."

Chrysus sighed and looked at Lucius with sad eyes.

"Lucius old friend, you've been my longest serving high priest. Do you know why?"

"Because I mostly keep my mouth shut and don't pry into godly matters?"

"No, because I thought you were too stupid to understand my secrets. Apparently I was wrong." He sighed and flicked his wrist.

Lucius exploded into tiny specks of ash and was no more. The high priest likely didn't even know he had died it was so instantaneous.

Chrysus rang a little bell that sat on the arm of his large throne and a small man in crimson robes hurried into the chamber.

"The high priest is dead. Let the order know, I'll be holding a competition to find the next one in a few months."

"Yes sire!" the small man said before running from the throne room.

*Things are getting interesting Kaleb Akabane. I just killed my oldest friend because of you. You better be worth it.* Chrysus thought menacingly, his fanged teeth poking out from his lips as he smiled.

# Chapter 10
# Definitely Not as Good as A Dragon

I stepped through the door and it slammed closed behind me. Before I even had the chance to survey my surroundings a notification popped up on my HUD as if it was bursting to get out. It flashed over and over, blocking my vision until I accepted it.

I sincerely hoped it wouldn't do that during combat or it could get me killed.

**Achievement Unlocked!**
*Holier Than Thou*
**You have met a god. Though not uncommon in Celestia,
it's still an achievement for an outworlder like you.
Gods are the most powerful beings in this world and
you got to meet one, you lucky devil.
Now prostrate yourself and prepare for a divine
dicking!
Reward: *Divine Loot Box***

I was a little shocked that meeting a god was so common in this world. Getting another loot box was cool though, especially considering that all I did was walk through a door.

It felt almost too easy, but I wasn't going to complain.

**You have received a divine blessing:**
*Blessing of Divine Wealth*

> You have received a blessing from the God of Wealth.
> Blessings are rare even in this world which has more
> gods than it knows what to do with. Consider yourself
> lucky mortal, a god is more likely to kill a man than
> bless him.
> You will now be able to loot gold from every kill or
> assisted kill.
> *You can only hold one blessing at a time.*

That was a pretty good perk! It was a shame I had to get it from such an egotistical, maniacal sociopath, but beggars can't be choosers.

It basically awarded the same perk as the cloak did but now I wouldn't lose it when I found better, less dubious clothing. I wondered if the skill stacked. Would I be able to loot more gold whilst wearing the cloak now I had the blessing too?

> **Achievement Unlocked!**
> *Child Prodigy*
> You have received a blessing from a god on your second
> day in this world. That's like a toddler going through
> puberty. I don't know what he saw in you but be
> thankful for it, you lucky sod.
> Reward: *Brown nosers don't get rewards.*

Well, that achievement was a bit pointless. Why give me it if I don't get a reward? I thought.

It was almost like the system just wanted to talk to me, or more likely that it wanted to be a dick. I didn't understand how the system worked fully, but it certainly enjoyed profanity and being a colossal asshole.

Either way though, the meeting with the god worked in my favour no matter how you sliced it. I was still alive, despite being ruder than I usually am and I got to walk away with a nice new blessing.

I could be a full-time level chaser now. I wouldn't need to worry about earning money like normal people. Not that I had time to worry about things like that in this world of monsters and hunters anyway, but it was still nice.

As I clicked for the final notification to go away my vision was finally unobscured.

I hadn't returned to the hallways, but instead found myself in a large room. Turning back to the door I quickly opened it to check the hallway was still there and it was.

I breathed a sigh of relief. I was worried for a moment that Chrysus had teleported me somewhere random.

Turning back to the room I'd landed in I took a moment to survey my surroundings. It seemed to be a library.

There were bookcases on three of the four walls, filled with colourful, hardbacked tomes. The middle of the room was bare, but there was something strange on the floor.

It seemed to be a massive magic circle, for want of a better description. It was etched into the floor in what appeared to be melted gold. So, it was a permanent magic circle.

I wondered if that was rare here. It reminded me of a pentagram, with jagged lines that formed a geometric shape. It was certainly intriguing, though it further reminded me of my lack of mana and how I'd missed out on getting the Basic Sceptre when I chose my starting weapon.

Man, I really wanted that sceptre. Bows were ok and I was growing fond of my dagger, but shooting fireballs from a sceptre was top tier isekai. Everyone knew that.

Bows and daggers and swords existed on earth. They were a little outdated, but they were real things. Magic on the other hand was the stuff of dreams. Only a complete idiot would choose a normal weapon over a magical one. It was just common sense.

But I had no choice in the matter.

This stupid game is rigged! I thought angrily.

Still, my love of magical things drove me forward within the room. Perhaps there were books in here that could help me learn more about it. With a silly grin on my face, I went around the room taking all the books off the shelves and adding them to my inventory.

I didn't know when I'd get the time to read, but there didn't seem to be a weight limit so far in the inventory, so I had no reason not to loot them. Besides, if the cultists wanted these then it stood to reason that I should take them away.

By the time I was done I had over 500 notifications, and 500 new additions to the travelling library of Kaleb Akabane.

I waved the notifications away. I didn't have the time to sift through that many of them and they were only item notices anyway.

After that I decided to take a closer look at the magic circle. As I approached, I felt like there should have been some power coming from it, even a wave in the air would have been enough. I felt nothing.

Feeling a little disheartened I moved into the middle of it. Now, I know what you're thinking; what kind of idiot steps inside an unknown magic circle? Me, I'm that kind of idiot. Curiosity may have killed the cat but so far, it hadn't killed the Kaleb.

As I stepped onto the golden etchings a bright red light filled the room. The gold began glowing as if it was turning molten and a wall of light surrounded me. I still couldn't sense anything magical happening though. If I closed my eyes, I'd have never known any of this was happening.

It was like I was magically blind. I was the Stevie Wonder of wizardry.

As I sulkily looked around in wonder at the light show, a notification popped up.

**You have entered a summoning circle!**
**Summon daemon familiar?**
**Y/N**

A familiar? Like a monster who would fight for me? Hell to the yes!

*Now that's more like it!*

If I can't wield magic, then having a minion do it for me would be the next best thing. Did I say minion? I meant to say familiar of course. I'm not a whacko tyrant or anything.

Also, if I was summoning a demon you could bet it was going to be crazy powerful.

I immediately clicked yes on my HUD.

The red light seemed to glow brighter and soon I was blinded to everything outside the circle. It was like the light was becoming more and more corporeal by the second.

It spun around me, getting faster and faster. I was excited. If the fanfare was this extreme then I must have summoned something powerful. Maybe it'd be a lich, or a succubus or a dragon. I wasn't sure if dragons were actually demons but I still wanted one.

*Please God let it be a dragon that would be the coolest!*

The red light spun and shimmered, dancing across the circle before my eyes until it hit a crescendo. Then the light blinked out. With no further fanfare the light was gone and I was once again looking around the room, dumbfounded.

There was nothing there. Where the hell was my dragon?

"Down here moron."

I looked down, and sat at my feet was a small panda smoking a bamboo pipe. It was about the height of my knee when it was sat

73

down. So smaller than a regular panda, at least by my limited knowledge.

"A panda? How is a panda a demon?" I asked incredulously, taken aback by the sudden appearance of a cute, fluffy animal.

"A demon? Kid, are you illiterate?" The panda laughed. "You summoned a daemon."

"Isn't that just an old-timey spelling for demon?" I asked, raising a single eyebrow as I stared at the creature.

He had sharp teeth and claws, so maybe he wouldn't be completely useless. He was a far cry from what I'd expected though, definitely not as a good as a dragon.

"No. A daemon is more like a guide. We were originally go-betweens for gods and mortals back when the system tried to ban direct contact, but since it changed that rule back in the twelfth century, we now act as guides...sages if you will. Yeah, I like that, I am your sage." The panda grinned, showing me its sharp, fangy teeth, and took a drag from its bamboo pipe.

"Ok," I began. "I could definitely use some help understanding this world that's for sure. You can fight too, right?"

Now it was the panda's turn to look at me incredulously as it raised both its tiny eyebrows and cracked a bemused smile.

"I'm a fucking panda, what do you think? It's a miracle my kind aren't already extinct. We're black and white yet we live in the jungles, I mean what kind of camouflage is that?

"On average we spend sixteen hours a day eating, and literally all we eat is bamboo. That's like you living on a diet of nothing but bread. Hell, the average panda poops 40 times a frigging day. Not to mention the breeding issues. Did you know female pandas are only capable of conceiving a cub for twenty-four to seventy-two hours of the year.

"So no, I can't fight. I can give you advice, I can smoke, and I can sing a mean Elton John cover, but I can't fight."

Shaking its head the panda took in a long drag from its pipe and blew the smoke in my face. It smelled like burnt bamboo.

*Fantastic.*

"I guess that'll have to do then." I sighed, waving the smoke out of my face. "What do I call you?"

"Call me Panda," he said, extending his paw as if he expected me to shake it.

"Panda the…panda?" I asked, taking his extended paw. It was soft and fluffy.

"Hey, it's not like I named myself kid. We've all got parents don't we, mine just obviously wanted me to get bullied in school."

"Fair enough, nice to meet you Panda." I laughed as I took my hand back. "I'm Kaleb Akabane and if I ever end up going home I'm gonna google all those panda facts you just dropped. There's no way you poop forty times a day."

"Those are verifiable facts kid; they don't hand out diplomas for nothing at sage school you know."

"You went to school?"

"Of course I did, we're civilised people us daemons you know. Education is what separates men from beasts and I am most certainly a man. Just ask your mother."

"Nice. We've just met and you're already cracking mum jokes. This is going to be a long isekai," I sighed.

Panda continued smoking his bamboo stick and staring at me. It looked like he was sizing me up. I had an exclamation mark in my HUD's top right-hand corner meaning I'd missed a notification. I opened it.

**Congratulations! You have successfully summoned a daemon!**

**Panda is now your summoned familiar.**
**Daemons are rare as far as summons go, and they can be**
**very useful for outworlders.**
***Familiars cannot die, if they drop to 0 HP you can**
**resummon them in the options menu***

That was useful to know. So even though Panda would be use-less in a fight if he died I could just resummon him. Hopefully it wouldn't be too expensive.

I wasn't sure what to think of my new familiar, but he could be useful. It wasn't like I really knew anything about this world and by my estimations, things were only going to get more complicated.

"Ok Panda since you're my guide now, what should I do next? I've pretty much just been wandering around trying not to die so far," I asked.

"Oh, that one's easy kid. We need to get you a class. I think there's a city not too far from here. I say we head there."

# Chapter 11
# The Height of Daily Office Job Embarrassment

"A class?" I asked the bamboo smoking panda. "As in archer or wizard and the like?"

"Yup," he responded between drags. "In this world you need a class if you plan to fight monsters. Classes unlock more ways to increase your level, offer more stat points and they'll help you hone your fighting technique – which I assume is terrible right now."

"I've made it this far."

"You're only a level 5 kid. You have no idea what kind of powers exist in this world. On a scale of noob to god you're not even old enough to start playing yet. Trust me on this, you need a class and some direction."

It felt oddly emasculating to be lectured to by a talking panda, but he was right. I had no idea what I was doing or how this world worked. I wouldn't say everything that had happened was down to luck, no amount of luck forces you to kill monsters and hunters, but I was fortunate to still be alive.

Panda seemed to know his stuff, though I had nothing to compare him to. I decided to listen to his advice for the time being. First, we'd escape – wherever we were – then we'd head for the city.

"Ok. First, we need to get out of this place," I said, nodding at my little companion guide.

"Agreed kid. Oh, and good job killing that level 10 earlier. That was impressive."

"How did you know about that?"

"As part of the summoning contract I get a glimpse into your life so far in this world. You haven't been here long so I probably saw everything of note. That's why I haven't mentioned your lack of pants." He chuckled, raising his paw to his face.

I turned away from him and opened the door to the hallway.

"For the record I don't want to be wearing a sock down there," I mumbled.

"Oh no, it really suits you kid. I'm sure women will love that whole baby elephant dynamic you've got going on." He sniggered.

Ignoring him I left the room and he followed behind me. Standing on his two back legs he reached my waist. He was small for a panda, but at least he'd take up less room in the inn once we got to town.

I assumed there would be an inn at least. In most of the literature I'd read there usually was an inn in isekai worlds.

The corridor was still empty, to my relief. I followed the lush carpet, continuing in the direction I'd been heading before the wealth god's aura had side tracked me.

We didn't have to walk far before we found something.

The corridor opened out into a huge foyer, it reminded me of a shrine or something. We were on the second-floor balcony looking over the golden railings.

The room was huge. There were six roman columns made of gold on each side of the rectangular shaped room. At one end was a massive door covered in etchings that seemed to depict a big guy holding the world above his head. It remined me of Atlas from

Greek mythology, except the man in this etching had a creepy, lustful smile on his face.

It was obviously supposed to be Chrysus, the wealth god I'd met. It looked just like him and this was *his* cult after all – at least according to the loot drops I'd had from killing two of them.

The huge door was likely the exit, though what awaited us outside was anyone's guess. On the other side of the temple was an unnecessarily huge throne. It seemed to be made of solid gold and cushioned with purple pillows.

*I guess gold is more about showing off than comfort. Tells you everything you need to know about a guy who'd make a throne out of it.* I thought as I lightly shook my head, glanced towards the ceiling, and rolled my eyes. It was Chrysus' temple, it stood to reason that he could see me if he wanted to.

"It doesn't look like anyone's home. Let's get out of here," I whispered, turning to Panda who had jumped up to the railing and was clinging on to get a view. His stubby legs were wagging underneath him as he couldn't touch the floor.

"It's your show kid," he replied. "Just be careful if you're gonna open that big door. It probably makes a lot of noise."

With a nod I moved to my left and down a flight of stairs which led to the ground floor. I quickly glanced around to double check, but there truly was no one else there. I moved towards the large door and pushed.

I really hoped it was a push door. Accidentally pushing a pull door was the height of the daily office job embarrassment.

To my surprise it moved easily, gliding across the floor as natural light began seeping through the cracks. I stopped pushing when it was cracked just enough to peak through.

It seemed Panda was wrong this time. The door was quiet.

I peeked outside and saw a large courtyard. It was filled with cultists. There was an outer wall that stretched past my vision in both directions and trees lined the outside, telling me we were still somewhere in the palm tree jungle.

Almost directly in front of me was a large iron gate that seemed to open onto a dirt road. It was much wider than the dirt path I'd been following on foot prior to my capture. The gate was closed though and guards stood on either side of it.

They wore the same crimson robes as the rest of the cult, but these guys had some kind of armour over the top. It looked like chainmail but it was hard to tell from my position.

The guards also wore helmets and held large spears in their hands. They would definitely be harder to kill than the cultists I'd murdered earlier. I wasn't sure I'd win against people that well equipped.

The rest of the courtyard was divided into two sections with an ornate, circular fountain in the middle separating them.

On the left side there seemed to be training facilities. Cultists practiced with bows on straw dummies and some were sparring with swords. None of the training cultists wore armour but there was about ten of them that I could see.

Way more than I could handle on my own at my current strength.

On the right-hand side there were only three cultists and none of them had weapons. They were unloading crates from a vehicle which looked like an old army truck. It was a green flatbed with a khaki-coloured canopy covering the back.

It reminded me of a WW2 era, troop transport. The right-hand side seemed like our safest bet. Hopefully we could sneak past them, but if not, taking out three unarmed guys and running had to be better odds than facing ten armed ones.

I pulled my face back inside and told Panda what I'd seen and which route I'd planned to take.

"Sounds like the wise choice to me kid. Before we go though, take this."

He opened his paw and a small bottle appeared in it. Inside the bottle was a shimmering red liquid, it was thick and reminded me of a red wine.

"What is it?" I asked, taking the bottle from his paw. It was a stupid question because as soon as I touched it a notification appeared.

**You have received a new item:**
*Inferior Health Potion*
**Restores 20 HP**

Before Panda could answer me, I took the stopper out and downed the drink. I needed all the help I could get. It felt warm and burned a little like a good scotch. It was sweet though, so also not like a good scotch.

In my HUD I could see that my HP was fully restored leaving me with a full 36/36.

"I didn't mean for you to drink it now!" Panda shouted in a raised whisper. "You only got four points out of it! I wanted you to keep it to use in an emergency."

He continued bouncing around as it dawned on me how stupid I'd been to waste the potion. It was the first thing I'd drank since I'd arrived here though and it got rid of that dry, sandpaper feeling in my mouth so I wasn't too upset about the mistake.

It struck me as odd that I'd been able to get away without drinking for such a long time. I wondered if it was the system interfering, or maybe it was the adrenaline form the whole experience.

Before I had a chance to ponder further a new notification popped up.

**Quest Complete!**
*Bear Grylls*
You're stranded in the wilderness. You need food and water to survive. Whatever will you do? Well, you could drink your own piss like the famous earth TV personality *Bear Grylls*, or you could try and find something fit for human consumption. It's up to you.

**Objectives:**
Eat something 1/1
Drink something 1/1
Reward: *Not dying of starvation. You're welcome.*

I'd completely forgotten I'd been given that quest. It was a useless one to pass though, I didn't really get anything from it. Still, I felt a kind of childish pride in completing it.

As I finished reading Panda was still giving me the stink eye and shaking his head.

"Are you happy now? You completed a pointless quest by wasting my potion. Gods! I wish I had a different human…" He huffed angrily.

"You're starting to sound like my parents."

Panda stopped complaining, stifling a chuckle, as I checked my inventory. I decided to go with the same approach I'd used before. I'd put the hood up, hold my knife under my cloak and use my other hand to keep the cloak shut.

It wasn't a great disguise but I hoped it would help enough to by me the time I needed to get away from this place.

I walked back to the door and peered through the crack once more. Everything seemed pretty much the same as it had before.

With a deep breath I turned to Panda, who nodded back at me, and I opened the door just enough to squeeze through.

Or at least that was the plan.

As I pushed the door slightly and began moving through the opening, the door decided it had other plans. With a long and obscenely loud creak it slowly opened all the way.

The sound grated heavily on my ears as the door scraped against the stone paving outside. After a few long seconds the noise stopped and Panda said:

"I told you it looked like a noisy door."

"Yeah, thanks for that sage advice mate," I said harshly.

As I stood in the opening of the door, every cultist in the courtyard turned to look at me. The ten on the left stopped their sparring and target practice and stared at me. The three on the right holding their boxes stared at me and the two armoured guards by the gate turned to look at me.

"Fancy meeting like this," I said, raising my left hand in a wave as my cloak opened to reveal my semi-nakedness.

# Chapter 12
# Call Me Truck-kun

"Blasphemer!" One of the training cultists shouted as he stretched his arm out to point at my junk. "He dares show off *that* in front of the house of our god?"

The courtyard exploded into jeers and insults as I stood, opened robed, before them. I glanced around, I needed to do something and fast.

My original plan had revolved mostly around stealth but that wasn't an option now. I'd have to think on my feet.

I took off running towards the right-hand side of the courtyard. That part of the plan hadn't changed. Facing three guards would be easier than facing ten, it was basic maths.

The difficulty now was that I was on a timer. The guys on the left would reach me in less than a minute once they realised what I was doing. I needed to be quick.

I rushed down the stairs to the right. The door had been situated on a platform that stood about six feet higher than the courtyard itself. It had a small stone railing separating it from the courtyard proper but it was only waist height and it was easy to see through.

There were steps to the left and right which swung around in a half circle and were symmetrical to each other. The whole area kind of reminded me of a drug lord's compound in the tropics.

I hurried down the stairs to the jeers of the cultists as they stood throwing insults at me. I reached the first cultist who dropped his box to the ground as a semi-naked man wearing a cock sock rushed towards him brandishing a dagger.

That would be the last thing he saw as I slashed at his throat, tearing out his jugular. Gristle and blood sprayed out of the man's throat, showering me in his blood. I must have made for a terrifying sight after that.

He dropped to the floor as I waved away the notification that popped up. I didn't stop moving, dashing for the next box carrier.

He had enough time to react to me, seeing his friend get slaughtered first. He threw his box at me and I turned to the side to dodge it. I was too slow and it grazed my shoulder, knocking me slightly off balance as I continued towards the man.

As I arrive within striking distance he squatted down slightly and dived towards me in a tackle. The two of us crashed to the ground, his arms wrapped around my waist as he held me down.

He was on top of me, but I had a weapon and he was unarmed. Without thinking I slammed the dagger into the top of his skull with all my strength. His body went limp and I rolled him off me. I went to pull the dagger out but it was stuck.

I placed my feet on his shoulders, still laying on the ground and heaved. The dagger resisted at first and then slipped free, sending me tumbling back as yet more blood sprayed onto me.

Gasping, I sat up and shook my head. The dagger had a chunk of brain stuck to it but I didn't have time to pull it off. I needed to get up.

As I pulled myself shakily from the ground I heard shouting and looked over my shoulder.

To my horror the ten men who had been training with weapons were running towards me at full pelt. The fastest had already reached the fountain. They'd be here in seconds.

Before I could make my next move, I felt a rush of wind as another box sailed past me, missing my head by inches. I turned to see the third and final box carrier glaring at me and shouting.

I couldn't make out what he was saying above the shouting from the armed cultists behind me, but he was red in the face and he looked angry. I summoned my dagger back into my inventory and replaced it with my bow and a hair.

I raised the bow at the shouting man who went wide eyed for a moment before charging at me. He wasn't fast enough. I pulled the string back and released a hair which hit him in the eye. I didn't get a notification, so he wasn't dead yet.

He screamed and clutched at his bleeding eye with both hands as he doubled up. I took the opportunity to fire another hair which hit him in the head. He dropped to the floor and the notification came.

It wasn't lost on me that my newfound accuracy was entirely due to the *Novice Bowman* skill I'd picked up earlier. The last time I'd used a bow I struggled to hit anything I actually aimed for, but this time it was as if my body moved on its own.

I also seemed to shoot faster than before. Not inhumanly fast or anything, but I felt like a trained, medieval archer and that was no small feat. Especially considering the ability came from a single, seemingly lacklustre skill.

As the third man dropped I turned back towards the charging cultists. They were scarily close. I did the only thing I could think of and began firing Loconut's hairs at them. I hit a few of them but received no new notifications. I missed a few shots as well as I was firing as rapidly as I could.

"Kaleb!" Panda shouted.

I hadn't thought about him once since the fight started. I hadn't seen him following me, so I didn't know where he was. I looked around and he shouted my name again. He was standing next to the truck and waving.

*The truck! Of course!* I thought, like it was a sudden lightbulb moment.

I put my bow back in my inventory, turned and sprinted towards the truck. When Panda saw that I was heading towards him he jumped up and grabbed the door with his paw, wrenching it open.

I reached him and threw him inside as I dived through the open door, reaching back to slam it shut. I was in the driver's side, apparently the driver sat on the left of the truck in this world.

That was a little off putting as we sat on the right side of the vehicle back in England. Not that it really mattered right now.

I began fumbling around for a stop/start button or a key ignition but I couldn't find one.

"What are you doing! Get us out of here," Panda yelled as he stood on the passenger seat next to me.

"I can't get it to start," I yelled back.

"It's a magic transport, you need to inject your mana into it. Theres an interface above you, grab it and put it on your arm."

I looked up and saw a device that reminded me of a blood pressure machine. It was a piece of rubber that looked just big enough to squeeze my arm through and it was attached to a long, see through pipe that disappeared into the dashboard.

"I don't have any mana!" I yelled back.

"What do you mean you don't have any mana?" Panda shouted back in a horrified voice, his eyes widening as he looked out of the driver side window to the side of me.

I followed his gaze just as the first cultist got into striking distance. He shoved his sword through the window as glass shattered and fell all around me. I moved backwards just in time and his blade missed me by a hair.

*That was close,* I thought as I grabbed the hilt of the blade and tried to wrestle it out his hands.

He was stronger than me so it didn't work, but it stopped him from trying to stab me for a second.

With me free hand I reached up and grabbed the magic blood pressure machine and threw it at Panda.

"You use it and I'll drive," I said through gritted teeth as I continued to struggle against the strength of the cultist.

Without a word Panda slipped the armband on and it shrank down to fit snuggly around his arm. White energy began flowing through the tube and into the dashboard and I heard a familiar rumble as the engine roared into life.

Still holding onto the hilt of the sword, I pressed the accelerator pedal with my foot and set off, ripping the sword from the confused cultist's hands.

I cheered and dropped the sword onto my lap as I grabbed the wheel and turned it violently towards the gate.

"How do you know how to drive this thing if you can't use mana?" Panda shouted from beside me.

"I used to drive for a living. Just call me truck-kun cause I'm about to send these fuckers to another world!" I said as I aimed the front of the truck squarely at the armoured cultist blocking the gate.

The armoured cultist looked at me wide eyed as he steadied his spear. There was no way it was going to save him and we both knew it. I swear I saw him mouth the words "oh shit" as I ploughed straight through him.

I felt a slight bump as the vehicle ran over him, first with the front tyres, then the back and I received multiple notifications though I waved them away before I could see what they were.

I drove straight into the iron gate and with a god-awful creak, followed by a crash, it gave way and I continued driving down the dirt road in front of me. In the rearview mirror I saw the remaining cultists chasing us down the road as spears sailed past the cab, one of two sticking into the steel frame.

The road's surface offered no traction and we slid more than we drove, but I needed to put some distance between us and the cultists that were chasing after us in the wing mirrors.

They'd never catch up to a moving vehicle back on earth, but we weren't on earth and I didn't want to take that chance. My HP had taken quite a beating in the fight, dropping down to 28/36. It wasn't dire, but considering I'd only really been tackled and hit with a box it meant that the cultists were strong.

As we drove, Panda seemed to calm down, though he panted like he'd just run a marathon.

"Are you ok?" I asked, not taking my eyes off the twisting dirt road.

"I'm good but my mana's running low. Should be able to last another ten minutes or so though and that should give us the distance we need to make sure we've lost them," he replied through laboured breaths.

"Thanks Panda, you really saved my ass back there."

"Yeah well, if you die, I go back to the waiting room and its boring as fuck in there." He shot me a grin which I just caught out of the corner of my eye.

"What's the waiting room?" I asked, mostly trying to keep his mind off the mana-sucker 3000 he had attached to his arm.

"It's a kind of purgatory where familiars sit around waiting for a summoner to materialise them into reality. It's a boring place, like waiting for a doctor's appointment, but for hundreds of years."

"So, like waiting for a doctor's appointment," I replied dryly.

It sounded awful. I almost felt bad for the little guy if that was what his life had been before I summoned him.

"Also, I've been thinking," he continued, still sounding worse for wear. "I get why you summoned me now. I thought it was strange for someone so weak to be able to summon a daemon but it makes sense if you have no mana."

"I just figured that summoning circle was supposed to summon you," I replied absently as I kept my concentration on the road.

"That wasn't a summoning circle, it was a geometric focuser. Really, you can use them to amplify whatever you want to. Alchemists use them as a place to brew their potions and stuff because it makes the results more powerful.

"Thing is, because you have no mana, when you stepped into it you became a catalyst, setting it off. Nonmagical items are used in geometric focusers to, well, focus them. So, it focused on the only thing a guy with no magic could do. Summon a non-combatant familiar.

"You're lucky really, if you'd have had mana you probably would have ended up with a Loconut for your summon. Either that or it would have exploded. You're a lucky guy, you know that?" He laughed, though it sounded more like a chesty cough.

"My juice is running dry kid. See if you can clear the treeline before we have to stop."

I did as he said and as the truck slowed down to a trundling halt, we cleared the last line of palm trees and I got my first glimpse of a city in another world.

# Chapter 13
# One Desert Short of a Cowboy Cliché

"The cult won't follow us out of the treeline, we should be safe to rest for a minute," Panda wheezed as I fiddled with the magic armband and removed it from him.

I helped him out of the truck and we sat together in front of it, resting against it as we looked out towards the city.

It was still a bit of a walk from the treeline, but it was big enough to take up most of the view; a sprawling metropolis of modern skyscrapers, wizard's towers, and cathedral-like architecture.

It certainly didn't look like the medieval village I'd imagined. It was kind of a mix between Prague and Tokyo. Of course, we weren't close enough for me to make out much more than that. Apart from the moat.

The city was cupped by a wide river that seemed to run in a semicircle, starting in the ocean, wrapping around the city, and ending back in the ocean. It had to be manmade. The ocean itself stretched all the way to the sky, it was hard to tell where the water ended and the sky began from our vantage point.

As we took a moment to rest I decided to look at my notifications and there were quite a few.

**You have defeated:**
*Chrysus Cultist Worker (lvl 5)*

**Experience awarded.**

I had two other carbon copies of this notification, so I assumed it was referring to the box carrying cultists. I was happy at their levels; it would surely mean that I'd get some impressive exp. I wasn't wrong.

**You have advanced to lvl 6**
*+ 5 free stat points*
**You have advanced to lvl 7**
*+5 free stat points*

Two whole levels from killing three guys seemed like a worthy trade off. They weren't the easiest of fights, though I guess I did take them down fast considering I was so hopelessly outnumbered.

During the fight I acted mostly on instinct but my instincts seemed to be right on the money for the actual fighting. It was strange considering I'd barely trained in a marital art and I'd never being in the military or anything.

I wondered if it had anything to do with my dagger combat skill. I'd never received an explanation as to what that meant so it had to be a passive skill. Perhaps it helped guide me in knife fights or something?

**Skill:** *Dagger* **has advanced to lvl 4**
**Skill:** *Bow* **has advanced to lvl 3**

During the fight I had killed the final box carrier with my bow and fired a few successful shots into the crowd of charging cultists. I hadn't killed any of them that I was aware of but I was happy for the level up all the same.

"Panda, do you know anything about skills?" I asked.

"I'm more of a spiritual guide than a walkthrough but I know a little bit, what do you want to know?" he replied, sounding tired.

"I have a skill called bow and one called dagger. They never came with explanations but they seem to level up when I kill things. In that last battle I felt like my instincts had more experience fighting than I did, so I leaned into them. I just wanted to know if that was because of the skills?"

"No idea. Skills like bow and dagger track how good you are with a specific weapon. They're basic passive skills that only hone the technique you already have, they don't impart knowledge though. You could train them up easily if you practiced with them under a tutor and learned real technique. Active skills are the opposite, they come with an inherent knowledge of how to use them and they can be used on command. There are also passive skills that are just on all the time, like your novice bowman skill but you can gain knowledge from them too.

"Because that skill is always active, you'll always be a better shot than you were without it. That's not to say you can't get better by training on a range but if you outclass that skill with your own ability it'll probably upgrade itself to match your ability.

"The system likes things to be in order and it has certain rules it has to follow. At least during the lower levels, and you don't need to concern yourself with what comes after those just yet."

I nodded along as Panda explained. It still didn't answer my question of how I'd done so well in battle though. Maybe it was just luck and adrenaline. After all, I'd fought the box carriers but there was nothing to say that they were trained fighters.

Putting my thoughts aside I continued with my notifications.

**You have defeated:**
*Chrysus Cult Guard (lvl 11)*
*You have received bonus experience for defeating an opponent with a higher level than you.*
**You have advanced to lvl 8**

*+5 Free stat points*
**You have advanced to lvl 9**
*+5 Free stat points*

Two levels for a single kill. I almost cheered as I read it. In that battle I'd nearly doubled my level and I now had 20 free stat points to use. It also meant my HP and Stamina would increase by 20 as well.

I knew I was still a low level in the grand scheme of things, but it felt good to be able to see my progress appearing on my HUD.

I opened the next batch of notifications.

**Achievement Unlocked!**
*Roadkill*
**Who taught you to drive? You used a vehicle to kill an enemy. Poor Timmy, he had a family! He was only two days away from retirement and you killed him with your truck.**
**Timmmmyyy!**
**Reward: *Roadkill* Loot Box**

I had a bunch of loot boxes to open now. I needed to find a safe space, whatever that was, so I could open them. There was bound to be one in town. I was still betting it would be an inn. I really hoped I'd get clothing in some of them.

**Quest Completed!**
*Sink or Skinned*
**You have been captured by a hunter who wants to take your skin and sew it together with other skins to create the map. It's probably in your best interest to not let that happen. This is what you get for ignoring my friendly advice when I told you not to eat the stripper.**
**Objectives:**
**Escape 1/1**

**Free yourself from your binds 1/1**
**Free or kill the other captive 1/1**
**Kill your captor (optional) 1/1**
**Hidden Reward: *1000 gold***
***You have qualified for a hidden reward due to***
***completing all optional objectives****

I expected this notification to pop up. I'd remembered that I still needed to escape to complete it so naturally leaving the compound would meet the requirements.

I was pleasantly surprised that I got a reward after all though since one wasn't originally posted on the quest. I didn't know if 1000 gold was a lot yet, but considering I'd only gotten 10 gold for looting the cultist I'd killed after leaving the prison room I was guessing it was a pretty penny.

That reminded me, I didn't get the chance to loot any of the guys I'd killed during our escape. I cursed myself silently at the potential loot I'd missed. Not to mention to the gold I could have had.

**Achievement Unlocked!**
***Parking Prodigy***
**You've run out of mana and now your car won't work
and to make matters worse you've parked blocking off
the entire road. What a douche. The way you pulled in
makes me wish your dad pulled out.**
**Reward: *Fuck you.***

Well, that was disappointing, and a bit passive aggressive. I really couldn't tell if the system liked me or not. One minute it was praising me for killing folk and the next it was being arsey with me for blocking a dirt road with my truck.

Either way, I had gained some good experience overall and I had a new loot box to add to my growing collection of shiny things I couldn't play with yet.

"Panda, I've gone up a few levels. Got any advice on where to put my free points?" I asked.

"You'd be best saving them until you get your class really, but honestly your stats pretty much do what they say on the tin so there are no bad ways to spend them."

I nodded and dove into my stat sheet to disseminate them. There was no way I was waiting for my class. I knew we were going to get it once I was in town but if there was no wrong answer then why would I hold off?

After a bit of thinking I decided to do something a little odd and put all 20 of them into my strength stat. It'd raise my Stamina but more importantly I needed to be stronger physically.

Thinking back on the fight earlier I'd struggled to get my dagger out of the cultist's skull. I had to literally leverage myself and pull with my entire body. That was no good.

What happened if next time I got it stuck but the guy wasn't dead? I'd be screwed.

So, I put all 20 points into strength and then I read through my upgraded stat sheet.

**Status Sheet:**

**Name: Kaleb Akabane**
**Race: Outworlder**
**Level: 9**
**Map Pieces 2/10,000**
**HP: 41/56**
**Stamina: 53/76**

**Strength: 26**
**Agility: 12**
**Perception: 8**
**Vitality: 6**
**Intelligence: 7**

**Personal Skills:** *Speak English Damnit!*
**Combat Skills:** *Bow (lvl 3), Novice Bowman, Dagger (lvl 4), Dhampir Dagger*
**Blessing:** *Blessing of Wealth*
**Familiars:** *Panda (Daemon)*

My stamina had increased by quite a bit and strength was now my best stat by a country mile. I also noticed that my stat sheet had updated to include a familiar's section which was interesting. The plurality of it made me wonder if I could summon more than one, though that would have to wait for another day.

For now, Panda was right, I needed to get a class. Panda was still worn out from using so much of his mana so I offered to give him a piggyback ride.

He grumbled at first, but soon he was on my back as we walked towards the city. He felt really light for a bear. Perhaps it was my new strength stat but I felt like I could carry him the whole way there with relative ease.

The area I needed to cover between the truck and the city was an open grassland with a few farm-looking buildings dotted around and the occasional windmill. All in all, it was a serene looking place.

After about an hour of walking along the dirt road the sun began to sink towards the edge of the sky, it was mirrored in the ocean as a cascading shimmer of brilliant orange light lit up the plain.

It was one desert short of a cowboy cliché.

Just as the sun had crested the sky and darkness fell, we came across a small house next to the road and decided to approach it. Panda said it was dangerous to be out at night as monsters were higher levels and more likely to attack unprovoked.

I opened a small, wooden gate from the dirt road and we walked towards the little house.

"Do you really think whoever lives here will let a half-naked man and his Panda stay the night?" I asked as we walked up the garden path.

"You won't know unless you ask," Panda replied.

With a sigh I knocked on the door to the house and a little porch light came one. The door creaked open and I could see a bloodshot eye peeking through the crack from behind a door chain.

# Chapter 14
# Why is He Wearing a Sock Over His...?

"Can I help you?" the voice from behind the door said.

All I could see was a bloodshot eye hiding behind a chain in the darkness.

"Hi, sorry to bother you so late. We were looking for somewhere to stay the night," I said, feeling a little awkward about asking and trying to sound as friendly as possible.

"Where are your pants and what's that on your penis?" the voice asked in a monotonous tone.

Before I could answer Panda took over, peaking his large head from around my back. I'd been carrying him since we left the truck. He said his mana still hadn't recovered but I got the impression he was just being lazy. Either way, it wasn't any trouble with my new strength, though my stamina did drain faster whilst carrying him.

"Pardon the intrusion, my friend and I were attacked by monsters and his clothes were ruined in the battle, everything except for his cloak and socks you see. Naturally he decided to use a sock in an attempt to make himself look a little more decent."

"Ah," the voice said, "that makes sense. You can sleep in the barn if you want to."

Before we could reply the door shut and the porchlight turned off. We turned towards the barn.

It was large and covered in hay. Naturally there were stacks of haybales in there too but no horses, at least none that I could see. In fact, I hadn't seen a sign of any animals at all which was a little odd for a house with a barn.

Either way, I guess it wasn't my place to pry. Panda and I entered the barn and chose a corner away from the door.

"This place isn't a safe area but I doubt we'll get attacked in here. The main roads are some of the safest places around and if that little girl can live in a house by herself and be safe then we should be fine," Panda said as he began curling up and padding down some loose hay for his bed.

"How did you know she was a little girl? I couldn't tell at all," I asked as I unceremoniously plonked down onto the hay and placed my arms behind my head.

"Call it sage's intuition."

"Fair enough, but is it really safe for a little girl to live out here?" I asked as my eyes began to feel heavy.

"Probably not but we have bigger things to worry about." Panda yawned.

Up until now I hadn't felt much fatigue even though I'd been fighting pretty much since I'd arrived in Celestia. However, a few moments after my head hit the hay I was out like a light.

The next morning, I woke with the sun's rays as the light shone through a crack in the wooden, barn roof and lit up my eyes.

I sat up feeling refreshed and rubbed the sleep out of my eyes. I hadn't felt refreshed from sleeping in years. I couldn't remember the last time I didn't wake up feeling like a swamp monster in dire need of some coffee.

I was one of those people who couldn't even talk to someone before he'd had his morning caffeine. I was dead to the world for at least an hour after waking up no matter where I was or how much I'd slept.

So naturally, waking up feeling refreshed was a welcome feeling as I stretched and jumped to my feet.

"Come on Panda, let's go," I said, nudging the sleeping furball with my big toe.

"Five more minutes," he moaned, swiping at my foot lazily with his paw.

I decided to have a quick look through my stats to check my hypothesis as he came around and, to my delight, I'd hit the nail on the head. After sleeping both my HP and Stamina were full. That meant all I had to do was sleep after every fight and I'd be fresh for the next one.

I doubted that was going to work out considering how many fights I'd already been in, but it was still useful information.

After Panda came around, we left the barn and little house behind and headed towards the city once more. We weren't far off at that point; in fact the city was closer than I'd realised the previous night when we decided to stop at the house.

The closer we got the busier the road became. Carts trundled past, seemingly pulled by magic and we ran into other people walking in the opposite direction. I kept my hood up and my robe pulled shut to avoid awkward conversations about my sock.

I was weary of the people of this world. I didn't know how many of them wanted to skin me or if they could tell I was an outworlder. At the very least I wanted some proper clothes before I started striking up conversations.

I considered asking Panda how well known the tattoo thing was in Celestia but thought better of it. There were too many people crossing paths with us now and the last thing I wanted was some creeper earwigging and trying to flay me.

Instead, we walked in silence for about an hour, right up to the city gates.

The gates themself were more like a guard post at a bridge than a castle wall gate. The city didn't have walls, likely because of the moat.

It had a few different bridges. The one Panda led me to was supposedly the closest to where I could get some clothes and my class sorted out.

As we approached a tall creature stopped us with an open palm and the shrill sound of a whistle.

"State your names and business for the record please." He spoke in a deep voice.

The creature looked like a man with a wolf's head and fur. His eyes were a piercing blue and his chest muscles popped even through his thick, black fur.

He wore an open, military-style shirt and combat pants but no boots. It was honestly a bit off putting and I found myself at a loss for words.

"Panda and Kaleb and we're here so Kaleb can join the Adventure Society," Panda said politely, speaking up in my place.

"Go on ahead then," the wolf man said and I walked past him, trying, and failing, not to stare.

Once we hit the bridge and were sufficiently out of ear shot I turned to Panda.

"What was that?"

"That is a Lycanid, why don't you turn back and actually look at him instead of staring at him out of the corner of your eye and I'm sure the system will tell you everything you need to know," Panda said, sounding a little annoyed.

"Oh yeah, the passive aggressive *Pokedex*," I replied wearily.

I concentrated on the creature and after a few seconds a notification popped up. It was useful to know that the system would give me information on races too.

**You have discovered a new race:**
*Lycanid*
**Half man, half wolf. The *Lycanid* has existed in various forms and by many names across many universes. They're a common race in Celestia, often used to guard the houses of the rich. Some are even kept as pets and trained to "play dead" or to "fetch".
They love nothing more than chasing sticks and sniffing other *Lycanid's* asses.
They are a proud warrior race.
Racial features include enhanced perception, racial specific skills related to smell and a tendency to get fleas.**

"Panda, I'm not sure how accurate this is. It's mostly just quips about them being like dogs," I complained as I finished reading the notification. "Is the system always like this?"

"Most of the time yeah, but if you ignore its personality issues it'll still give you the information you need most of the time," Panda replied.

"Also, what was that about me being here to join an Adventure Society?"

"That's how you get your class. Celestia's culture is centred around the society system and since you can't use magic and you're new here Adventure Society seems to be the best option for you.

"There are lots of other societies of course, but Adventure Society is the biggest and the easiest to get into. They need all the warm bodies they can get." He chuckled and began to swing his arms as he walked, bamboo pipe dangling lazily from his lower lip as he occasionally took a drag.

At the end of the bridge we reached a sprawling cityscape. It was a hybrid of wooden, medieval style stores and inns and the occasional large, glass skyscraper. Hanging over the edge of the bridge was a sign that was written in a strange language I didn't recognise.

As I squinted at it the letters changed before my eyes and became English. It must have been thanks to my skill *Speak English Damnit!* That was going to come in handy.

The sign said: *Welcome to Havar, a recognised independent port city.*

"Havar," I said aloud, muttering to myself as I read the sign.

"Yup, this is the city of Havar," Panda said as we walked, "It's only a small place but it's the biggest city on the island and the only place on the island you can book travel overseas."

"We're on an island?" I asked.

"Yeah, have you not checked your map?"

"I don't have one."

"We'll get that fixed when we get your class. First though let's think clothes. I know an excellent tailor who has a shop just up here," he said and began trotting off up the cobbled street.

I followed him, delicately weaving past groups of people and creatures, and he stopped outside a wooden store with a green sign on it. The sign had a large pair of scissors painted on it and the words: *Taylor's Tailor* written in fancy, cursive writing.

I opened the door and walked in at Panda's insistence. Inside was a few mannequins dressed in bright colours and a counter with a bright-eyed cat woman stood behind it.

**You have discovered a new race!**
**Catonid**
**Catonid's are a demi-human race that are half cat, half human. With a natural affinity for agility, their cat-like reflexes can leave you utterly Cat-atonic.**

**It's common for humans to find them attractive, honestly a little too common. I guess bestiality is a common fetish for your kind huh? Anyway, stop staring at this notification and go talk to her, what's wrong, *cat* got your tongue? Then again you'd probably like it if she did wouldn't you, you sex pest.**

"I swear, every time I read a notification it gets more and more insulting," I muttered as I approached the desk.

"Good morning! How can I help you?" The Catonid greeted me in a chirpy voice.

Unlike the Lycanid I'd met on the bridge she didn'thave that much fur. She was mostly human, but with a fluffy ginger tail, fluffy ginger cat's ears and yellow feline eyes.

Other than that she had wavy ginger hair and porcelain skin and was wearing a plaid skirt and a button up blouse with the sleeves rolled up.

"Hi Taylor!" Panda shouted, jumping up and grabbing the edge of the counter with his claws, his feet kicking as he struggled to find purchase.

Taylor rushed towards him and scooped him up, helping him onto the countertop.

"Panda! How great to see you," she said, pulling him into a hug. "What brings you back to town?"

"I need to get some threads for my human," he said, nodding in my direction.

"Well, I can certainly see that he needs them. Why is he wearing a sock over his penis?" she asked Panda, as if I wasn't even in the room.

"That's not a sock, it just looks like that because of a vicious bacterial disease."

"Hey!" I shouted, mostly at Panda. "I'm standing right here! It's not a disease and what happened to spending the last thousand years in some purgatory waiting to be summoned?" I asked, feeling a vein pop out on the top of my forehead. "How do you two even know each other?"

"As you can see, he's a little sensitive about his penis issue," Panda said, covering his mouth with his paw as he ignored me and continued speaking to Taylor the Catonid.

# Chapter 15
# You Damned Cat

"Taylor and I met last time I was here which was about five years ago now I think about it." Panda explained whilst we chatted.

I was stood on a small platform as Taylor diligently took my measurements. I felt incredibly awkward as the cat lady measured my inner thighs. I was pretty sure people usually wore underwear for this sort of thing.

"I thought you said you'd been waiting for thousands of years to be summoned?" I asked incredulously, shooting him a questioning stare.

"I have been in the waiting room for thousands of years, just not...concurrently," he answered, trying his best to look away from me. "I'm a very old sage. That's what makes me so wise you see, my wealth of experience. But you're not the first person to summon me. I've had lots of summoners over the years, the most recent one visited Havar with me about five years ago."

"What happened to your last summoner?" I asked.

"Can you unfold your arms please Kaleb, I'm trying to measure your shoulders!" Taylor snapped at me.

"Sorry," I muttered, allowing her to position my arms as she pleased. I still glared at Panda as he squirmed.

"Honestly I'd rather not go into detail, but she died," he answered, staring at the floor and fiddling with his bamboo pipe. "I need a smoke; I'll be back in a minute."

He left before I had time to ask anything else.

"Don't push him. He was close with his master and he probably expected to have more grieving time before he was summoned again," Taylor whispered softly as she continued tying me up with measuring tape.

I stood silently for a few more minutes whilst she finished up. She passed me my stained robe as she disappeared into the back of the store.

Maybe I was a bit too hard on Panda, but I didn't like things being kept from me. It was difficult enough waking up in a new world where I had to fight for survival and try not to get skinned.

Not to mention that I didn't know where my wife was or if she was safe, and she was pregnant. Not to mention my friends and family who may or may not be stuck somewhere in this hell hole too.

It was all a little overwhelming and I think it was perfectly reasonable of me to be a bit more demanding of those close to me than I'd normally be. For example, not lying, manipulating, or misleading me.

I took a breath.

I'd definitely overreacted. Panda had a right to keep his past and personal life, well... personal. I decided I wouldn't bring it up again unless he did. He hadn't steered me wrong so far, even if he was arrogant about it.

"What colours do you want?" Taylor shouted from the back.

"Black please," I replied, raising my own voice to make sure she heard me.

"Black isn't a colour, it's a shade, but alright."

I chuckled at her pedanticism; it reminded me of my wife. She was the kind of woman who would give you the time down to exact minute if you asked her what time it was. I on the other had would round it to the closest quarter of an hour.

The little bell above the door rang as Panda re-entered, trailing a thin gale of twirling smoke behind him.

"I see she's finished then?" he asked, acting as if nothing had happened.

I was happy to play along, ignoring difficult conversations was kind of my thing.

"Yeah. Why are we at a tailor? Wouldn't an armour shop make more sense?"

"It would, but you want armour that compliments your class – which you haven't chosen yet. Also, armour is expensive whereas street clothing isn't."

"We're in a tailor shop, I figured we were getting me a suit for my job interview at Adventure Society."

Panda burst out laughing and slapped his leg as he looked up at me.

"You don't interview for Adventure Society. You sign a contract, they test your stats, you choose a class and then you get a temporary membership.

"You'll have to complete three quests to qualify to take the permanent adventurer exam and then you're in."

That sounded needlessly complicated, but if it was going to make me stronger, and help me survive in this world then I guessed it was worth it.

Taylor returned from the back a few minutes later brandishing some clothes.

"These have the self-repair function and are black. Try them on and let me know what you think," Taylor said brightly, handing me a pile of clothes.

"How did you make these so quick?" I asked, taking the clothing from her.

"It's part of my class skills and I'm pretty good you know," she answered winking at me playfully.

From her reply I assumed the short answer was magic and my jealousy reared its ugly head. I wanted to cast spells and shit!

I held out the clothes in front of me and saw she'd given me a pair of black suit trousers with a white belt, a black suit shirt and shoes. She'd even replaced my old grey socks with fresh black ones. The underwear, however, left much to be desired.

It was a pair of white boxer shorts with the motif of a grey sock over the crotch.

*Very funny you damned cat.* I thought bitterly as a notification popped up.

**You have received a set item:**
*Taylor's Tailor Custom Smart Casual Wear*
**Wearing this will make you look like an office worker who never quite got over his *My Chemical Romance* phase. A white belt? How emo.**
**All you're missing is a dyed fringe and eyeliner.**
*This item has a self-repair function.*

I chuckled to myself as I read it. I did have a bit of an emo phase in high school. Though I'd never dyed my hair, I was fortunate that it was already black and you can't get more emo than that.

Wandering behind the curtained area in the shop I got changed into my new clothes, leaving my cloak and cock sock in my inventory. Good riddance I thought as I finally got to slip on some real underwear.

It felt heavenly, like it was made of silk or something. Having a self-repair function would be useful too, though I still wanted some armour if I was going to be fighting more.

When I walked back into the main part of the shop Taylor practically squealed and told me I looked great. I think she was mostly just admiring her own handywork though.

"So, how much does all this cost?" I asked sheepishly, I still didn't know how much gold was worth in items.

"Twenty gold, it would have been five but I added the self-repair for you. From what Panda told me I figured you'd need something that could last out in the wild." She smiled and I happily gave her the money.

I still had 990 gold left because of the 1000 gold hidden reward I'd gotten from the escape quest and the ten gold I'd looted from the cultist. It felt like a bargain! I thanked her and Panda then I left the store.

"You know she gave you a pretty huge discount, right?" he said, as we walked through the crowd of busy people. "You can thank me later. Come on, the Adventure Society building is right there."

He pointed towards the largest building in the vicinity. It was a huge skyscraper that seemed to be made mostly of glass. It had to be one of the biggest buildings in the city.

Glowing neon letters lit up the side of the building vertically in the local language. After a moment's concentration the letters turned into English and I could see it said *Adventure Society* on the side.

"Cool right?" Panda asked, seeing my gawking face as I craned my neck to try and see to the top. "There's an Adventure Society in every major city in the world and lots of smaller branches dotted around too. This one is the HQ for the archipelago we're in at the moment. Havar is the capital of this group of islands, not that it's an overly big claim.

"The director of this branch is only a jade soul, though he's a gold rank adventurer in his own right which is pretty impressive."

"What are the ranks and you never properly explained the jade *soul*, what is it?" I asked distractedly as I continued to take in the magnitude of the place I was about to join.

"A jade soul is what you'll be once you max out your level, though round these parts most people don't ever come close to reaching it. As for the ranks, they'll explain them to you in due time.

"So, there are more levels after the level cap?" I replied, "that sounds like a bit of a design flaw."

"Well, you've seen first-hand how the system operates, kid," Panda shrugged. "What did you expect? Don't worry about it right now, you'll learn more about it when you need to."

"Fine," I sighed. "I guess I'd better go sign up then."

"Now, before we enter, this is really important," he began, taking on a serious tone and dragging me down to his level so he could whisper. "When you fill out the forms tell them you're human. People around here have only heard of outworlders in legends. The Celestial Map is a fairy tale, but a well-known one. You don't want to attract undue attention. Your life might well depend on staying under the radar, got it?"

I nodded solemnly. I hadn't thought about the need to hide my race, I hadn't really thought about my race at all. I knew it said outworlder on my stat sheet but in my mind, I was a human.

I'd always been a human so I would probably have written that on the forms anyway. Panda's warning worried me though, if the Celestial Map was well known as a kid's tale then did that mean I'd be safe as long as I hid my tattoo?

It could mean the opposite. He didn't say that people didn't believe the story. I needed to know more but I didn't feel comfortable discussing it with all these people around.

I decided I'd sort out my class and then we could find an inn for the night and I could gather more information from Panda in private.

With that decided, I steeled myself and walked through the huge, sliding doors. They opened automatically as I entered. I couldn't decide if that was more magic or if there was a level of technological advancement here that was similar to back home.

The foyer was clean and clinical looking; a far cry from the tavern and billboard setting I had expected. There was a customer service desk at the side and a long line of notice boards on the other wall.

Groups of people were casually milling around the noticeboards, reading whatever was posted. I assumed they were quests.

It didn't matter for me at the moment so I made a beeline for the reception desk. As I began walking towards it a tall man stepped in front of me. He was wearing a suit, it looked similar to a modern suit you'd find back home except it came with a green cape and embroidery. Definitely a modern wizard suit if ever I saw one.

I looked up at his chiselled and bearded face. He had bright eyes and swept back, brown hair.

"I've been waiting for you," he said, leaning in and whispering the last word in my ear, "*outworlder*."

# Chapter 16
# Always a Bigger Fish

Well, so much for staying under the radar. I thought, sighing internally.

This man, whoever he was knew exactly what I was. He asked me to come with him, offering no further explanation as he began walking towards a door at the back of the room.

I shared a look with Panda who nodded grimly and we followed him.

In my mind I was already preparing to fight, just in case. I opened my inventory and minimised the window with my thoughts hovering around my dagger.

Using a bow inside probably wasn't the best idea and the dagger would keep my health topped up. I had no way of knowing how strong the man before me was, but he seemed confident.

I didn't get any feeling that he was planning to attack me but that didn't mean he wasn't luring me into a trap. I'd have to keep my guard up.

As we reached the door he placed his hand on a small magic circle that was permanently etched into the wall in metal, I heard a ding sound as the door opened. He walked inside and beckoned me to follow. I did, with Panda hot on my heels.

The little box room we found ourselves in seemed to be the perfect place to launch a sneak attack on the man, which I seriously considered.

The room began moving and I realised we were in a magic elevator. It was an odd feeling, riding an elevator in another world, but I didn't have the time to think on that at that moment.

The man still hadn't said anything and we rode in tense silence for about a minute until the door opened. He stepped out and I followed him into a huge office space.

There was a massive, floor to ceiling window on the far wall. We were so close to the clouds I felt that if I reached out I could touch them. We must have been high up. Just who was this man?

He walked towards a large, wooden desk and took a seat in a plush, leather office chair. On the other side of the desk was two, equally nice chairs and he gestured for us to sit.

I did as he wanted and Panda copied me, though he had to press the little lever on the side of the chair to lower it first. He looked amused as he pulled the lever again to return to a height where he could see the man properly.

"I'm sorry about all that, I wanted to speak to you but we needed to be in a secure location for it. The last thing you want is the entire society knowing what you are, yes?" When he spoke, he remined me of my old headmaster. His voice was quiet, but I had no trouble hearing him. It was deep and soothing.

"Who are you?" I asked, skipping the pleasantries.

"Oh, yes of course. How rude of me. My name is Lucas Regina and I'm the director of this branch of the Adventure Society. It is a pleasure to meet you Kaleb."

He leaned back in his chair calmly, his dark skin standing in a glimmering contrast to the bright, blue sky behind him.

"How do you know who I am?" I asked slowly, my mind still hovering over the dagger in my HUD.

"My god told me, but don't worry about that. I've brought you up here so you can register with the guild. That is why you came here today isn't it?" He smiled and reached into a drawer behind his desk.

I nearly summoned my dagger right then and there but I still felt no hostility from him and I didn't want to attack someone just because I was getting jumpy.

"Here we are," he said, producing a form and a quill. "I wanted to induct you personally so that we could hide your true race. Our application rooms are a lot less private. Though if I'd have known you had a daemon travelling with you, I might not have bothered.

"I'm sure he's already advised you that it would be in your best interest to hide your outworlder race from other people."

He smiled and placed the form in front of me.

"Why would you help me? Everyone else I've met so far wants to skin me alive, so sorry if I seem a bit sceptical," I replied icily. I kept my eyes on the man, trying to drink in every move he made. If he was going to attack me, I would be ready.

"We at the Adventure Society are not savages Mr. Akabane, nor are we fools. The tale of the Celestial Map is just that, a tale. Everyone with half a brain knows that.

"I'm sorry that you've had to deal with ne'er-do-wells thus far, the cults are... bothersome, but here in Havar we don't put much stock in fairy tales.

"I promise that you have nothing to fear from me. I simply wish to aid a promising new recruit to our ranks and help him submit his paperwork. I understand this must be confusing for one such as yourself with no experience of our world, but I assure you that you are far from the first outworlder to join Adventure Society and you won't be the last." He flashed me a curt smile and held out the quill.

I took it slowly and looked over the form.

"If the general consensus is that the Celestial Map is a fairy tale then why do I need to hide my race from your people?"

"It's just a safety precaution. I can't know every adventurer in the society, I'm only one man, and there are some who take on the occasional outside task.

"I'm sure that certain cultist organisations would pay handsomely to have an outworlder delivered to them and I wish to avoid the political upheaval it would cause if that were to happen to you right under my nose."

He seemed legit, though something about him still bothered me. I looked at Panda who nodded encouragingly and I sighed as I began filling out the form.

"Director?" Panda began, "what is a Regina doing out here in the middle of nowhere? I thought your family were big shots on the continent."

I continued looking at the paperwork but stopped halfway through writing my name to listen to Panda's conversation.

"They are, but I like it here. The tropics aren't a bad place to live."

The two of them continued chatting idly whilst I focused on the registration form. It was simple, mostly asking for my current level, name, and race. It also had a contract on the back which I read through.

By signing I would agree that any wounds or fatality caused by a quest were not the fault of the society. They would pay me in accordance with the sum stated on a quest, yada, yada, yada.

I would agree to only take quests suitable for my adventurer rank and that I acknowledged that a full membership would be given to me on the satisfactory completion of an exam.

I had to complete three quests before I could take the exam to become a full member. I wondered what type of quests I'd be able to get as a temporary member.

Knowing my luck, it'd be something crappy like saving a cat from a tree or cleaning stables, or worse, the dreaded fetch quest.

Most games I'd played back on Earth were full of fetch quests. They were usually boring, poorly thought out and often they were infinite with a low monetary reward or something.

As I finished signing my name I looked up to see the director smiling at me. He really did seem like a nice guy but I couldn't help but think there was something more going on with him.

Still, if he was the power in this place and he liked me that could only spell good things. I needed to level up fast and get more power.

"Ah, I see you're done. Let me have a look… yup, everything seems to be in order. Perfect." He scanned the document and then signed it himself before standing up.

"Right, take the elevator back down and go take this to the reception desk, they'll tell you where to go next to choose your class."

I thanked him and headed back into the elevator along with Panda. It was time to get my class!

\*\*\*

After Kaleb and Panda left the office, director Lucas poured himself a drink and sighed, sinking back into his office chair.

"I've done what you asked," he said to the room. "He really didn't seem like he could sense me. I didn't even know it was possible to be magicless."

It is rare indeed my disciple. Keep a close eye on him and don't let him leave the archipelago. I have need of him yet.

The voice appeared in Lucas Regina's mind as clearly as if he had thought it himself. The voice was dark and commanding. He'd heard it thousands of times and it still sent a shiver down his spine.

This was a perk of being a true disciple, an honour only bestowed on those who have maxed out their rank and gone onto the next phase.

It wasn't possible for gods to speak with rankers like this, after all, they spoke to their true disciples directly through their souls.

"If that is what my master commands then it shall be done," Lucas said wearily before downing his drink and placing the glass down on his desk.

Make sure he isn't killed. There are hunters in the city right now who aren't mine to command. I cannot interfere with them as I'm sure you know so I'll leave that to you.

"No problem. I already have society members keeping tabs on them. Hunters bring problems regardless of whether they're chasing after the map or not," Lucas said aloud to the room.

He'd had his fair share of run ins with hunters throughout his career. Growing up in the vast Regina estate hadn't sheltered him as much as one might think.

His father was a ruthless man who showed his love for his children by properly preparing them for the outside world.

In one instance he had left Lucas in the slums for a month and ordered him to survive as an urchin. The idea was to teach him to be self-reliant, even in the worst kinds of situations. However, even in the slums, Castalor was a Regina city and everyone knew who their rulers were.

Paupers had helped him and he'd spent most of his time with a roof over his head and food in his belly. One might think a rich kid like that would be an easy target for kidnappers but no one dared to incur the wrath of his father.

He was a powerful man after all. Yes, he was the head of the Regina family and had a lot of political sway, but nothing was more important in this world than personal power. Of that, he had a scary amount.

Lucas moved to pour himself another drink, feeling the watchful eye of his god leave him. He felt wrong using the new kid like this but it was far from his place to disobey his god.

He was a coward at heart. He'd been a dutiful son more out of fear of his father than an actual sense of duty. When he'd been forced to take over as director in this backwater, nothing place, he'd at least escaped his father's control. For a few days… before he'd been taken in by the god.

It seemed that no matter where he went, he was always fated to serve the whims of those more powerful than himself.

Even as the highest ranked adventurer in the little pond that was Havar, the old proverb still rang true: there is always a bigger fish.

# Chapter 17
# What's With All the Corporate Propaganda?

After exiting the elevator I once again found myself making a beeline for the reception desk. I hoped no one would stop me this time, how unlucky would I have to be for another person to come over and announce my big racial secret?

Thankfully I reached the desk without being accosted and submitted my form. The desk was manned by a blonde Catonid named Lucy.

"Ah, I see you already have the director's signature. Trying to get into his good graces early are we? That's a smart tactic Mr...Akabane," she said brightly, scanning my form to find my name.

"He's an old family friend," Panda piped up from the floor.

Lucy leant over the desk to see him; she didn't seem to have realised that he was with me.

"Aw what a cute little daemon you have Mr Akabane."

It seemed that everyone, even the receptionist, knew the difference between a demon and a daemon. Apparently, I was the only one in need of a vocabulary lesson.

"Righty then," she continued, wagging her fluffy tail as she stroked Panda's head. "If you follow the stairs to the ninth floor you'll find the administration offices. The class selection room is up there. Just take this ticket to their front desk and they'll show you where to go. Is there anything else I can help you with today?"

"No that's great thanks," I said politely, excusing myself and heading for the stairs.

As we continued walking upwards I noticed that each floor had its own message board with tougher and more well-equipped candidates looking at them the higher we went.

Once we hit the fourth floor there were only a handful of adventures in the room and the fifth floor only had two people on it. The seventh floor upwards was deserted. They each still had a receptionist but the message boards were empty and there wasn't an adventurer in sight.

Panda began to speak, noticing my perplexity.

"Each floor is assigned by rank. The ground floor is for newbies like you who don't have a rank yet. Wandering mercenaries can also take quests from there as long as they pay the charges.

"Then, as you go up floors it goes Iron, Bronze, Silver, Gold, Platinum, Diamond and Mithril. You'll be iron once you pass your exam. Bronze is also a common rank in these parts. The exam for that is harder and more combat dependant but it's still low on the ladder.

"Silvers are pretty much the top dogs around here and there are only a few golds in the entire region. Naturally they're the strongest, but most aren't permanent residents.

"It is possible to reach gold rank whilst on the islands but the monsters around here are so weak there isn't much point sticking around after silver. Most golds head over to the continent or come here for a vacation or to accept jobs working directly for the society as administrators and the like.

"Platinum ranks are rare. The director we met is pretty much the strongest guy in Havar and he's only a gold rank. Diamond rankers pretty much run the show worldwide. Most of the continental directors are diamond rank.

"Mithrils…well honestly I don't even know why they have a floor for mithrils here. There are only a handful of them in the entire world and they sure as hell aren't coming out to the boonies to accept jobs.

"Of course, these are adventure ranks so they aren't level dependant. However, I've never heard of a Platinum who hasn't surpassed the top level and even most Silvers are close to top level in their own right.

Panda finished talking just as we hit the ninth floor. I had so much to ask him but the receptionist had turned to look at us as we approached the administration offices.

I relegated myself to asking a single question.

"What is the top rank?"

"Level one hundred. I know you've blitzed through nine levels already but the early levels are easy. Hell, most kids in town are level tens. You're weak as shit my friend, so make sure you get questing once we're done here if you want to survive." He jumped and patted me on the lower back with a cheeky grin plastered on his round, fluffy face.

"If most kids are level ten then how come the cultists I fought weren't stronger?" I replied, hearing the pout in my voice, and immediately regretting it.

"It was part of the tutorial kid. The system isn't just gonna throw you newbies into the firing line from the off, where's the sport with that? More than likely it imposed a sanction on the gods who run the cults and told them they had to send their weakest guys for a while. I'm sure it'll be open season soon enough though and you need to be ready. The system won't protect you for long."

He kept his voice down as he explained, not wating the nosey and impatient looking receptionist to hear us.

I approached her desk and showed her the ticket Lucy had given me.

She sighed deeply. She was a normal human with mousey brown hair. Her name tag said Tash but she looked more like a Karen to me with her cropped, single mom hair style and her perpetually agitated expression.

"Follow me," she said in an irritated voice as she slumped away from her desk and walked down a hallway.

I followed her past the other offices. They remined me a lot of cubicle-style offices back home. Each room was separated by glass but the office layout of the individual rooms was basically small, partitioned cubicles with about ten occupants per room.

"Imagine living in a world with magic and working a nine to five office job. How depressing," I whispered to Panda as we walked.

"I know right," Panda replied behind his paw, as if that made him any quieter. "Just think, any one of these people could have been an adventurer or a warlord or something."

"Ah yes, warlord or taxpayer it's a fine line to walk these days," I replied just as we reached an unassuming, brown office door.

"In here please," Tash said in a bored, monotonous voice.

This certainly wasn't the exciting and magical experience I had hoped for when I'd been promised a class.

I walked through the door and in the room was a single, large screen which took up most of the far wall. In front of the screen was a beachball sized metal ball on a stand, it had cables sticking out of it that disappeared into the floor.

"When you're ready please place your hands on the ball and follow any and all instructions presented to you. Once you choose your class please exit the room and return to the ground floor for further instructions. Please be aware that you will not be allowed to change your class after this unless the system offers you a different one. This is a rare case so make your choice wisely." Tash spoke in a monotone.

She had been reading from a laminated piece of paper which she put down on a table near the door before she exited.

I was left alone in the room with Panda and without Tash's sparkling personality to distract us, I was actually getting excited.

"Ok kid," Panda said after dragging the table to the side of the ball and jumping onto it to be eye level with me. "Class selection one-oh-one. Everyone gets offered the same basic classes, archer, swordsman, spearman, caster, healer and a few other fighting classes like monk and knight. Ignore them.

"Since you're a you-know-what-worlder you're probably gonna have much more interesting choices. Most people have to start basic and get class upgrades to get something cool. The system won't make you do that…probably.

"So, skip past the crap and let's take a look at the good stuff ok?"

He sounded excited and I had to admit that I was too.

"You know who you remind me of? Danny DeVito, you have the same accent," I said, smirking at the confused giant teddy bear.

"I don't know who that is. Are you gonna grab the damned ball or what?"

Chuckling to myself I placed my hands on the giant, metal ball and the screen flickered into life.

It felt like a mild static shock was racing through my veins as the ball reacted to me. The room lights went out as well, like we were at the movies. My heart raced, party from the static, but also from the excitement. I hoped I got something good.

I knew it was naïve of me, but I really wanted a magic based class. But not healer, no one wants to be the healer in a party of one.

The screen flickered a few times and then it came to life. An infomercial sounding voice blasted out as a little animated movie played. The movie itself was of a cartoon person walking through a wood and being attacked by non-descript monsters.

Suddenly he pulled out a cartoon wand and they all blew up splattering blood on the screen. Then he turned to the screen, gave a thumbs up and the words *Adventure Society – Killing the Monsters Under Your Bed* popped up.

Of course, the whole thing was playing to the backdrop of the infomercial-like voice reading its script.

**Here at the Adventure Society we thrive on making the impossible... possible. If you become a fully-fledged member you'll be able to tell the world that you are working for a company that truly makes a difference. We're a company that truly cares and we put you at the heart of all major decisions. Like choosing our award-winning dental plan and offering unpaid holiday days to all employees who complete their monthly quota early.**
**With branches located in every major city, the world is truly your oyster as an adventurer. From fighting monsters in the forests of Barkesh to fighting monsters in the forests of Sinegaul. No day is the same at Adventure Society.**
**So why not sign up today? Adventure Society – Killing the Monsters Under Your Bed.**

The screen flashed for a moment and it remined me of an old film reel at the end of a movie.

"What's with all the corporate propaganda, I'm already here, aren't I?" I asked Panda as the next part loaded up.

"I think this room doubles as a recruitment office," Panda replied, shrugging his shoulders as the next part started.

The next video showed arial shots of the building we were in, mixed up with cheesy clips of office staff pretending to laugh whilst they did their boring, soul crushing jobs. The infomercial stuff continued but it was basically a rehash of the same stuff from the last video, just a little more in depth about the day-to-day stuff.

Then the screen flashed again, just as I looked at my non-existent watch and realised it was half past a freckle. It's not like I had anywhere to be, but this really felt like a waste of time.

Back on earth I'd chosen to be a truck driver to get away from all this bullshit. I'd had an office job before, a few actually, but they were all hypocritical, soulless companies who had the audacity to demand that you pretend to care about them.

No one, and I mean no one, working in an office gives a flying fuck about the policies and the corporate mission. They do it to pay the bills and that's it. So why did corporate assholes continuously ask me why I wanted to work at their shitty office when I took interviews?

In the end I got so sick of it that I got my class c+e license and started driving wagons. It wasn't a glamourous job but at least I didn't have to pretend to care about whatever crap I was hauling.

Just as I finished internally ranting about my old world a notification screen popped up on the big screen in front of me. It jolted me back into the room and I soon forgot about all the infomercial crap I'd just listened to.

**Do you want to begin class selection?**
**Y/N**

# Chapter 18
# Killing Prostitutes and Abducting Kids

I immediately clicked yes on my HUD and it translated to the screen. From what I could tell the metal ball I was touching was an interface that connected to my HUD and showed it on the big screen.

A new notification popped up.

*WARNING*
*You are only eligible to receive one class.*
*Due to your lack of mana you are only eligible for non-magic class selection.*
*Once a class is chosen, all stat points pertaining to the chosen class will be rewarded retroactively.*
*All classes come with +5 free stat points unless stated otherwise.*

The notification flashed up and I read through the information diligently. This would be an important choice for me, perhaps the most important one yet.

It sucked that I wouldn't be able to choose a magic class but a part of me had already expected that. However, the retroactive stat points would be a huge boost.

No matter what class I picked I'd end up with 9x the stat points it rewarded per level. That wasn't anything to sniff at.

Pressing continue I moved onto the classes themselves. The first few pages showed the basic classes Panda had already told me about. He'd said that everyone got access to archer, swordsman, spearman, knight, caster, and healer among other warrior type classes.

I didn't qualify for caster and healer but I had access to all the other ones and they were exactly what you would expect them to be. They also came with a rating which, in the case of the basic classes, were all common.

My excitement skyrocketed when I scrolled down to see the other classes. A new notification popped up as I scrolled.

**\*WARNING\***
*The following player specific classes are available to you.*
*A player specific class is offered based on complex criteria such as achievements unlocked by the player at the time of class selection.*
*These classes are rarely offered to non-players.*
*These classes may negate skills previously received based on skill type.*

"It's a good job we're in here alone," I muttered as I read the screen and quickly dismissed it.

The last thing I wanted was someone walking in on us and reading the part about me being a player. I didn't know if the people if this world understood that term or knew that it meant I was an outworlder, but I wasn't willing to risk it either way.

Even if they didn't know the specifics, anyone reading the screen would definitely know I was different. Attention like that was not what I needed right now.

From the sounds of it, choosing one of these classes would make me lose my other skills. I didn't have many, just *Novice Bowman, Bow, Dhampir Dagger* and *Dagger*. I'd raised their levels a bit and

*Dhampir Dagger* was useful but the trade-off for a special class would probably be worth it.

"Right kid, good job clicking past that screen quickly. Now, let's read through each of these classes in turn and talk it out," Panda said from beside me.

He was sat cross legged on the table he'd moved with his arms folded and a stern expression on his fluffy face.

As Panda suggested, I read through the offered classes in order.

### Trucker (uncommon)

**A staple in American folklore, the trucker is feared and reviled nationwide. Known for killing prostitutes and abducting kids in the dead of night, these creatures of earthen myth are truly a horrifying breed.**

*Selecting the Trucker class will unlock the following skills:*

**Manaless Driver** *– the ability to drive any magical vehicle without needing mana.*

**Shotgun** *– Whilst riding in the passenger seat of a moving vehicle increase all damage to attacks and combat based skills.*

*Selecting the Trucker class will award the following stat points per level:*

**+2 Strength / +1 Vitality / +10 Perception / +5 free points**

***Other skills will become available through levelling up***

Despite being horrendously offensive to my former career, the *Trucker* class didn't seem half bad. The Perception alone almost made it worth it.

However, I was a little worried that only three stats got extra points per level. It would leave me unbalanced and I'd basically have to put all my free points into agility and intelligence, at least to begin with.

The class also seemed to be designed around driving and I didn't have a vehicle. Also, from what I'd seen of this world, a lot of places could only be reached on foot and I imagined being trapped in a vehicle would limit the types of quests I could do.

I'd basically become the go to guy for fetch quests and that sounded awful.

Also, I'd been a truck driver back on earth. Why would I want to do *that* again?

"Hard pass. Next," I said to Panda who grunted his agreement.

### Merchant of Chrysus (rare)

**Ah, the humble merchant. What young boy doesn't dream of growing up to own his own global conglomerate. They do say money is power after all. With a blessing from the God of Wealth himself you'd be hard pressed to find a player better suited to the lifelong pursuit of greed.**

*Selecting the Merchant of Chrysus class will unlock the following skills:*

*Overtime – after dealing a certain amount or damage to one of more enemies you can opt for overtime. This skill doubles your damage rate for the next thirty seconds.*
*Employee Discount – Negotiate better prices at stores starting at 5% off.*
*O' Captain my Captain – 50% higher chance to persuade others to work for you.*
*Selecting the Merchant of Chrysus class will award the following stat points per level:*
*+15 intelligence / +5 perception / +5 free points*
***Other skills will become available through levelling up***

There was no way I was going to choose a class named after the god whose cult was trying to take my skin. It didn't matter how good it was.

I could see the appeal of the merchant class. It seemed to be based mostly on persuasion and that overtime skill was no joke. Having a double damage output must have made it a rare skill.

It made sense considering the class itself was in the rare category. +15 intelligence was also good but it offered no bonuses to HP and fighting stats and that seemed too important to ignore.

"Nope," I said to Panda who nodded as I moved onto the next option.

*International Man of Mystery (legendary)*
**Infiltrating evil cultist hideouts, stealing their books, and ploughing through their nice shiny gate in a dramatic exit. Sound familiar? Well, it should and the fact that you did exactly that is why you've been offered this legendary class. The only thing you're missing is your very own *Miss Moneypenny* to sexually harass before a mission – but I'm sure we can get you one if you ask nicely.**
*Selecting the International Man of Mystery class will unlock the following skills:*
*Man of Many Faces – Whilst out of combat you can change your appearance at will. Your appearance will revert to normal if you are attacked, attack someone else or choose to end the skill.*
*Mission Dossier – the quest system will evolve into a mission dossier. Completion of missions will unlock better rewards... should you choose to accept them.*
*Selecting the International Man of Mystery Class will award the following stat points per level:*
*+5 Intelligence / +5 Perception /+5 Agility /+2 Strength /+2 Vitality / +5 free points*
*\*Other skills will become available through levelling up\**

"Ok, this one is awesome!" I said, looking at Panda with excitement in my eyes.

I mean what kid didn't want to be a super spy growing up? Not to mention the ridiculous number of stat points I'd earn per level.

Legendary classes really knew how to up the ante. The mission dossier skill seemed interesting, though I wasn't too keen on the face changing thing.

It's not that I was a narcissist or anything but I had the impression that I was going to be fighting constantly in this world. Yet this class was more geared towards hiding. Using the *man of many faces* skill I could potentially get close to an enemy to launch a sneak attack.

However, that was unlikely to work on monsters. It was definitely the best option so far and I was interested, but it still had something missing.

I only had one option left so I hoped it'd be a contender. If not though, I'd be happy with the International Man of Mystery class.

### Apex Predator (unique)

**Well would you look at that, your fighting style has been varied so far I've had to create an entirely new class for you. Before you start feeling too special, I've already had to do this for over 500 of the 10,000 players brought here.**
**You've used a bow, a dagger, a vat of acid and a truck to slaughter your way through the countryside. This class is the amalgamation of those styles.**
**Besides, in the beginning I thought you were going to become a bog-standard stealth archer and that's way too mainstream to entertain me.**

"Is it normal for the system to talk directly to a person like that?" I asked Panda.

He turned back to me with a confused expression on his face.

"It's normal for it to passive aggressively alter notifications to make them more specific to the person receiving them. This, however, is extreme. Also, the only people I've ever heard of with unique classes are all exceptional adventurers, including the mithril class guys."

*Selecting the Apex Predator Class unlocks the following skills:*
*Acid Arrows – Every projectile you shoot from a bow will cause acid damage to the target.*
*Acid Dhampir Dagger – Gain 10% of inflicted damage with a dagger as HP. Daggers inflict acid damage.*
*Environmental Hazzard – Killing enemies using the environment awards bonus experience.*
*Selecting the Apex Predator class will award the following stat points per level:*
*+7 strength / +5 vitality / +3 perception / +3 agility / +1 intelligence / +5 free points*
*\*Other skills will become available through levelling up\**

"Well shit kid. You lucked out," Panda said, turning towards me and flashing me the thumbs up.

He was right. The Apex Predator class was perfect. It was versatile and I'd gain 24 stat points per level. Compared to trucker which was an uncommon class and only awarded 18 stat points, that was quite the bonus.

Doing some quick mental maths I realised that I'd gain 171 stat points retroactively. That was a huge bonus to gain immediately.

Acid arrow sounded cool, though I wondered if I'd be able to shoot accurately if I lost the *novice bowman* skill. Then again, I didn't know if I was going to lose it at all. Apex Predator was kind of like an archer class after all.

Acid seemed to be the hallmark of the damage type I'd get. It sounded like a horrible way to kill but if the hunter I'd melted was anything to go by, it'd be effective.

"I think I'm gonna go with this one," I said, looking towards Panda.

"If you don't choose this one I'll slap the shit out of you," he chuckled.

I asserted that I wanted to choose the Apex Predator class and the screen went blank.

I stared at it for a long moment as a little wheel appeared in the bottom right-hand corner. It reminded me of a loading icon from a game. The screen flashed and an actual loading bar appeared.

I felt my body get uncomfortably hot as I saw that my hands were glowing a sickly green colour. The loading bar advanced across the screen as I began sweating and feeling sick.

My stomach felt full to bursting and my eyes felt so full of pressure I thought they might pop. I felt my muscles bulge through my shirt and then the loading bar finished and a little tick appeared next to it.

I bent over and vomited violently.

# Chapter 19
# You're Weak as Shit

Panda laughed at me and patted my back as the vomit burned my throat. It was over as fast as it began but still, I hated throwing up.

I'd always been jealous of the guys that could go on a night out, head to the bathroom for a five-minute tactical chunder and then come back to the party as good as new.

I'd never been able to do that. Throwing up was a drawn out and unpleasant experience for me. There had been times where I was so paralytic from the need to vomit that I'd laid on the bathroom floor for hours before being able to actually do the deed.

However, this wasn't like that and I was pleasantly surprised, if not a little caught off guard, by the speedy recovery I made post-vomit.

As I picked myself back up and looked towards the screen, I saw only a single word.

**Congratulations!**

It seemed my class selection had taken.

"Don't worry about the sickness kid," Panda said, still laughing slightly. "It happens to everyone. It's a side effect of receiving so many stat points all at the same time. Honestly, you didn't have it that bad. A lot of new adventurers are a much higher level than you when they get their classes."

I wondered why Panda hadn't told me that before. He probably thought it would be funny to watch me get surprise sickness. Normally I'd admonish him in some way but I was too excited about my upgraded class and new stat points to care.

I hurriedly checked my updated stat sheet.

**Status Sheet:**
**Name: Kaleb Akabane**
**Race: Outworlder**
**Class: Apex Predator (unique)**
**Level: 9**
**Map Pieces 2/10,000**
**HP: 101/101**
**Stamina: 1/139**

**Strength: 89**
**Agility: 39**
**Perception: 35**
**Vitality: 51**
**Intelligence: 16**

**Personal Skills:** *Speak English Damnit!*
**Class Skills (Passive) Skills:** *Bow (lvl 3), Novice Bowman, Dagger (lvl 4), Acid Dhampir Dagger, Acid Arrows, Environmental Hazzard*
**Blessing:** *Blessing of Wealth*
**Familiars:** *Panda (Daemon)*

Smiling to myself as I read through it, I noticed a few interesting changes. There was the obvious addition of my class and my upgraded stats. My new skills had also been added and I was pleasantly surprised to see that I'd kept my previous *Bow, Dagger,* and *Novice Bowman* skills.

It must have been because bows and daggers were explicitly included in the skills given to me for the Apex Predator class.

I also noticed another change. My combat skills section had disappeared and all my new skills and the old combat skills had been placed under *Class Skills (Passive)*. I wondered if that meant I'd eventually unlock active skills. Panda had mentioned them before as skills you activate on purpose.

My current skills were on all the time, so I could only assume an active skill would be more powerful. I also noticed that my stamina, though massively higher than before, was currently sitting on 1/139. I did feel exhausted.

A knock at the door stirred me from my racing thoughts and I turned towards it as it creaked slowly open.

"Pardon the intrusion, I heard the retching and thought you might be finished with your selection," Director Lucas said as he poked his head through the door.

He smiled at us and, upon seeing the congratulations sign on the screen, entered the room fully.

"Director, what a pleasant surprise," Panda said, turning to the tall man.

"Think nothing of it, I simply wanted to see what class a fellow such as yourself would select. Call it professional curiosity. As it happens, I can also issue your temporary Adventurer permit whilst I'm here," he said in his silky-smooth voice.

He walked towards the back wall and waved his hand. A small keyboard popped out of the wall and he typed something in. There was an affirmative beeping followed by the kind of sound a cash register makes. He turned and walked towards me clutching a card in his hand.

"Hmm, let me see. An archer, light skirmisher hybrid? Not exceedingly rare but still an odd choice. Very interesting," he began, evidently thinking aloud as he perused the card which presumably had my results on it.

I had planned on keeping my new skills a secret but I guessed if the Adventure Society gave me the class, they also had the ability to look at it.

"You're only a level nine?" he asked, looking between me and the card. "You're weak as shit," he added, his voice going up an octave with his surprised outburst. "I know you're new here but most children are at least level ten."

Panda burst into raucous laughter as he fell off the table and began rolling on the floor clutching his stomach. I felt my face get hot and I snatched the card from his hand.

*Adventure Society ID:*
*Kaleb Akabane*
*Level 9*
*Rank: temp*
*Class: Archer / Light Skirmisher*

It was a simple ID card, not too dissimilar to the kind you'd wear in an office back home. I was relieved as I saw that the class section only gave a vague overview.

I was worried it would tell anyone who saw it all of my fighting tricks. Panda seemed to be of the mind that I should play my cards close to my chest so I'd hoped to be able to follow that advice, for now.

"This card is yours now. Once you add it to your inventory it will bind to your very being so you can never lose it," Director Lucas began, seemingly recovering from his earlier shock.

"As I'm sure you are aware, you need to complete three quests before attempting the adventurer exam. If you come here tomorrow morning I will assign a mentor to help you with the first one."

I opened my mouth to object but he raised his hand calmly and continued talking.

"This is mandatory for all new members. We don't want our new recruits to die on their first quest now do we? You'll need rest after gaining your class so I'd suggest getting a room at one of the inns."

I nodded at him. I was tired and I did need to sleep. It also occurred to me that I'd barely drank or eaten anything since I'd arrived in this world. That couldn't be normal.

"Do adventurers need to eat?" I mumbled, mostly to myself.

"Of course we do, but the higher your rank the less often you need food and water. You'll also find that with a higher rank comes the added benefit of needing less sleep. Each time you gain a rank your fatigue and hunger are also reset. So, you probably haven't even felt it until now have you?" Lucas answered.

"No, I haven't."

"That makes sense considering you've gained nine levels in only a day and a half. I have to say, considering your summoned daemon familiar I was surprised you didn't pick a caster class."

"He doesn't have any magic," Panda said, still giggling a little as he pulled himself from the floor and looked up at Lucas.

*So much for playing my cards close to my chest.* I thought irritably, shooting Panda a deadpan glare.

"Ah I see, low mana wouldn't give you any good magic choices," Lucas said, rubbing his chin between this thumb and forefinger.

"No, I mean he has literally no mana," Panda replied.

Lucas looked up from his thoughtful pose for a moment as if it took a few seconds for Panda's words to process.

"Wait what?" he replied in his higher octave again. "Having low mana is relatively common, but to possess no mana at all, that is completely unheard of!"

"It can't be that rare," I muttered, becoming increasingly more annoyed with the two of them.

"Well, *I've* certainly never heard of a person without any mana. How do you sense the world around you? Mana is integral in assessing the power levels of others at the very minimum. That ability dictates the pecking order of polite society." He sighed and took a moment before continuing. "Anyway, it does not matter for now. I'm sure you're exhausted so allow me to give you a parting gift before you leave."

He handed me a small sphere. I focused on it and a notification appeared.

### HUD Upgrade: Map
### Install?
### Y/N

"It is customary for new adventurers to receive the map upgrade if they don't already have one," Lucas explained.

"Thank you," I said, immediately asserting yes on my HUD.

The map had been added to my option page and I took a cursory glance at it as soon as it appeared. It was probably impolite, but I couldn't help myself.

A large map of the world appeared on my HUD. It appeared to be a facsimile of earth. There were some differences, but for the most part it looked similar.

Using that similarity as a basis, I looked at the small blue dot on the screen. When I focused on it I realised it was me.

I appeared to be on an island somewhere near where the Bahamas would be on earth. We were close to what would be the Florida Keys and the continent of North America. I wondered if that was the continent that had been mentioned earlier with the strong adventurers on it.

Most of the map appeared as a shadow, outlining islands and continents but with no further information. However, if I focused on the island I was on and zoomed in, some of It was in colour. There was a little tag next to a white dot beside my marker.

It said *City of Havar.* So, the map must update based on the places I'd visited. My own experiences must be the key to filling in the colour. How very game-like.

"I take it you're looking at the map as we speak since your face has gone blank." Director Lucas chuckled. "You might want to consider upgrading your intelligence if you want to look at your HUD whilst still engaging in conversation. A high intelligence allows you to multitask quite efficiently.

"It's mostly used to increase mana count and regeneration but as that doesn't apply to you it probably doesn't matter."

I switched off the screen and looked at the director.

"Thanks for the map. I should probably be going now, I'm tired."

*And I have loot boxes to open when I get to the inn. It better be counted as a safe space.* I thought.

***

After Kaleb and his Panda daemon left the room, Lucas stayed behind for a moment with his and his god's thoughts.

*So, the outworlder has no mana. That is very interesting, I knew keeping an eye on him would be fruitful.*

"Yes, it is strange isn't it my Lord? That task you gave me to keep him alive might prove harder than I thought." Lucas replied aloud, pondering his orders.

*I'm sure you'll do fine Lucas.* The god replied exasperatedly. *If he dies completing basic quests then he was never going to be useful to me anyway. I just want you to protect him for the other powers in the city.*

*He might be coasting relatively unnoticed for now, but sooner or later outworlders always make their mark. That is how it has always been.*

"I suppose you're right. I've already instructed *her* to keep an eye on him whilst he's in the city."

*Good.*

With that Lucas felt the presence of his god leave him. He fell back into a seat and groaned, placing his head in his hands.

This was going to be a pain in the ass.

# Chapter 20
# I'm Here for a Good Time, Not A Long Time

As Panda and I left the building, I was exhausted. The stamina stat seemed to have an extreme sway over me. My legs felt heavy, my vision blurred slightly and I wanted nothing more than to fall asleep.

With that in mind I asked Panda to lead me to the nearest inn. I didn't trust myself to find one. Luckily it wasn't far.

We left the building and took a few turns; the streets were still crowded but they seemed less rushed than before. I wondered if most people were at work now and the current street dwellers were not.

That's usually how it went back home. Workers rushed around like bees in a hive and the unemployed and retired lived their lives more slowly, peacefully. Of course that's a sweeping generalisation, but in my experience living in the north of England, it was pretty accurate.

As we moved away from the huge, glass skyscraper that was the Adventure Society building I noticed an architectural shift.

The buildings further out were much more reminiscent of the typical medieval style you'd expect in a fantasy world. Of course this was no fantasy, but it bared a striking resemblance to all the expected hallmarks of one.

The buildings in this new area were mostly made of wood and stone. It was quaint, I liked it. I was too tired to read the signs or take much notice of the locals so I followed Panda in a daze until he stopped.

We were in front of a Tudor style building. It had white outer walls with a thatch roof and wooden support beams. It reminded me of a holiday cottage my mum and I had rented for a weekend vacation when I was a kid.

There was a sign hanging above the door that said *The Sleeping Giant Inn.* Panda pushed the door open and led me inside.

The downstairs interior was basically an old-fashioned English pub. It looked just like a tavern from every fantasy game ever. It had wooden flooring, a few support beams, tables and chairs and tankards of wood. It smelled of ale and stale bread and there was a bar on the back wall.

A burly Lycanid barmaid stood cleaning a tankard with a rag behind the bar. She wore a light cloth strapped to her chest and a skirt, though it looked more like a kilt. Her fur was untamed and hung wildly in white, matted locks.

Panda marched up to the bar and climbed onto a stool.

"We would like a room for the night please," he stated confidently.

Without looking up from her task, the barmaid pointed towards a sign above the bar. It read: *We Don't Serve Familiars!*

"Well, that was rude." Panda complained as he looked at me expectantly.

Snapping myself out of my fatigue induced trance I walked over and asked her myself.

"Hi, can I get a room for the night please?"

She growled, but I think it was more like her races' way of sighing. She looked up from her tankard cleaning and her eyes softened slightly as she saw me.

"Oh, a human. We don't get too many of your kind in here. The rooms aren't much but they come with a bed and breakfast every morning." Her voice was rough but she seemed perfectly polite to me. I wondered what that was all about.

I pulled a single gold coin from my inventory and placed it on the bar.

"That's fine, is this enough?" I asked, flashing a toothy grin at the maid.

I think she blushed slightly, but it was hard to tell underneath all the fur.

"That'll get you a week, with breakfast included." She smiled, at least I think it was a smile, it was hard to tell with all the wolf-like teeth.

"That's perfect, thank you."

She took the coin and placed a key on the bar, then returned to her cleaning duties without any further fanfare.

I took the key and headed towards the stairs with Panda in tow. There was a sign saying that rooms were up there. I barely had to concentrate on signs to read them anymore, they auto translated with almost no lag.

"Wow, cost of living is cheap here. I should have been isekaied years ago," I said idly to Panda as we climbed the stairs.

"I took you to the cheapest inn in town. Demi-humans tend to have the rougher end of it here. That paltry amount of gold you have won't even get you basic leather armour, so don't be too happy," Panda replied grumpily.

"What's up with you. Are you really that upset that they don't serve familiars?"

"It's a violation of my rights kid! The only reason you're not standing up for me is because that bitch had a thing for you," he huffed, folding his stubby arms, and shaking his head.

"I thought I was picking up on something," I muttered.

We reached our room and used the key to open the door, locking it behind me.

It was a modest room with a small shack containing a toilet in the corner, a single window, and a bed with a nightstand. The sheets were white with a weird yellow stain on them.

It looked like it was old, you know the kind of stain that doesn't go away even after a few washes. If we were back home I'd have complained but I was so tired it didn't matter to me.

I fell face first onto the bed and groaned happily. The bedding felt so soft and before my body had finished bouncing from the unceremonious way I threw myself onto the bed, I was asleep.

The next day, I woke with the light from the morning sun. I'd been so tired I'd forgotten to close the curtains. I felt refreshed, which was still a strange feeling for me, and my stamina was full once more.

Panda had fallen asleep using my neck as a pillow.

I sat up and stretched and Panda flopped down onto the bed groaning. He was awake, it didn't matter how, and I had something important to do before heading back to Adventure Society.

*It's loot box time bitches!*

### You are in a safe area. Open all loot boxes?
### Y/N

I'd received the notification the previous night as soon as I entered the room I'd paid for. Interestingly, it didn't seem that the inn was a safe room, just the room.

147

Maybe that was because it was paid for and private? I wasn't sure, but I eagerly clicked yes on my HUD and sat back as the fireworks happened.

### PKing Loot Box
**Do you know what sex offenders, player killers and UK prime minister *Rishi Sunak* have in common? No one likes them!**
**Reward: *Entry to the Morning Star Hotel and Spa.***

The box appeared in front of me. It was only about the size of a small jewellery box and as it opened the notification appeared on my HUD along with a voice narrating it to me.

Panda stirred at this and turned around on the bed to watch.

As the box opened, two sparklers popped out and began fizzing as a black light floated ominously out of the box. It stopped in mid-air as the narrator finished and then flew straight at me.

I fell backwards, causing Panda to squeal as I squashed him. The light shot into my hand and disappeared and my right hand began to burn.

It wasn't the most pain I'd ever felt but it wasn't nice either. My skin started emitting a glowing light and as the light calmed down I realised I had a pentagram tattoo on my hand.

"What the fuck!" I shouted, looking down at my sore hand.

I liked tattoos don't get me wrong. I had a sleeve tattoo back on earth before it disappeared upon arriving here. This, however, was fucking creepy.

I had no choice in the matter and it appeared in moments.

"Oh, I haven't seen a tattoo box in years," Panda said, sitting up next to me.

Before I had time to ask him what that was all about the next box opened.

*Acid Reflux Loot Box*

**You killed a guy by throwing him into a vat of acid. Have you never seen a supervillain origin movie? That guy will definitely be back to haunt you all dressed up in clown makeup.**

*Reward: Boots of Resist Environment*

This time the box was the size of a trunk. The narrator spoke over the notification again but there were no sparklers. Instead, confetti popped out when the lid opened.

A pair of boots floated out of the lid and disappeared into my inventory before I could examine them. Then the next box appeared.

*Divine Loot Box*

**You met a god, wow really!? Get over yourself loser, every man and his nan have met a god in this world.**

*Reward: x5 Basic Health Potion*

**What were you expecting, a Nobel prize? Get over yourself noob.**

The divine loot box looked like it was made of gold and I really got my hopes up until the narrator crushed my dreams. Still potions were useful, I'd just have to use them at the right time this time around.

*Roadkill Loot Box*

**You done killed one of dem cultist with yer truck! Yeehaw!**

**Reward: New Skill: *Eat Anything*.**

The final box came with sound effects. To be precise, the sound of a car screeching to a halt, followed by screaming. Classy.

"That's an… interesting skill," Panda said, giving me a funny look from the side of his eye.

"Oh god, what does it do?" I asked.

"Read it and find out."

**You have received a new skill!**

*Eat Anything*

**It does what it says on the tin. You can now ingest *anything*… anything. Let that sink in for a moment. You don't need to cook it first either.**
**Note: eating anything is not advised by the chief medical officer. The system will not be held responsible for stomach aches, diarrhoea or fatality caused by irresponsible digestion.**

"I don't want it," I said, turning to Panda.

"Look at it this way, if you ever decide to be a cannibal you probably won't get the shakes."

"Aren't you supposed to be a sage?"

Sighing loudly, I pulled the boots out of my inventory and examined them. They were black, leather combat boots. They were quite nice.

*Boots of Resist Environment*
**These boots will keep your tootsies from melting off in the event you step in something nasty like acid or lava. They'll only protect your feet though so don't try walking over a pool of lava, the rest of you will melt.**

**Actually... forget that last part, you should definitely
try walking over a pool of lava!**
**Effects:**
*Protection from environmental hazards (feet only)*
*+10% Vitality*

The boots were amazing. I put them on straight away and felt the warm rush of new stat points. 10% didn't do too much at the moment but that could be a huge boon in the future.

They didn't really go with my office attire look, but it was worth it for the bonuses. I was beginning to get used to the system being a dick all the time, so I wasn't even perturbed by its comments about me playing in lava.

"That's a good item," Panda said, jumping from the bed and moving to stand in front of me. "Now you should find out what that tattoo does!"

He seemed excited. I had to admit, I was curious. I stared at the back of my hand and focused on the ink and like clockwork, a notification appeared and I heard a voice like an old timey radio announcer in my head.

**This tattoo allows entry to:**
**The Morningstar Hotel and Spa**

*Hello player! Do you like murder, debauchery, and
depravity of a sexual nature? Why of course you do!
Just like a mid-noughties tween teabagging a fresh kill
on Call of Duty, you've become a player killer!
Yippee, those are the best kind!
What's the only thing better than a player killer, I hear
you ask? A serial player killer!
So come on down to The Morning Star hotel and spa
and try our... facilities... completely free of charge!*

"What the hell is wrong with this world?" I asked, turning to Panda who seemed to have been able to hear the voice as well.

"I say we go, I'm here for a good time not a long time." He shrugged.

# Chapter 21
# Gonads

New Quest:
*A Good Time, Not A Long Time*

You've been marked as a guest of *The Morningstar Hotel and Spa.* I wonder what mayhem and fun awaits behind its doors.

Objectives:
*Enter The Morningstar Hotel and Spa 0/1*
*Uncover the secrets of The Morningstar Hotel and Spa 0/1*

Reward:
*X1 Skill Upgrade Potion*
*X1 Weapon Upgrade Potion*

"God damn it! Why did you have to go and open your big mouth?" I asked Panda as I read the quest notification.

"Have you not seen how awesome the rewards are? You should be thanking me!" Panda replied, folding his arms in a huff.

He was right. The rewards were a skill upgrade and a weapon upgrade. I didn't need a notification to tell me what those were.

A skill upgrade alone had to be rare as far as quest rewards went. That being said, with a reward that good I had to wonder what the catch was. The hotel must be full of danger, it was the only explanation.

Something else was bothering me too.

"Can you see what's on my HUD?" I asked Panda.

"Not exactly. As your familiar, my HUD is linked to yours. I can't see your health all the time and the things that are always there, but when you check your stats or get a notification it appears on my HUD as well."

That made sense. I had wondered how Panda knew the details of items and quests when I got them. I'd put it down to his role as a daemon granting him insight to the world, but apparently it wasn't that simple.

As it stood, I filed the new quest away with the one that wanted me to kill all the players and steal their tattoos. This one wasn't as gut wrenching as the last but I still had no intention of trying to tackle it just yet.

It could wait for another day.

I had a permanent adventurer exam to qualify for after all. I'd get to this weird hotel thing eventually, but I had some serious levelling to do first.

I explained my intentions to Panda who reluctantly agreed that we should hold off until I was stronger. Then we went downstairs for breakfast.

It was a breakfast fit for a medieval peasant. Hard bread, cheese, and broth. Despite the simplicity it was still the first real food I'd had since I arrived. I *had* eaten the stripper, but that was just a rare chunk of meat I seared on an open flame – and I'd rather forget about the trauma leading up to it.

After breakfast we headed back to the Adventure Society. It was only a short walk from the inn, though it had felt much longer yesterday in my sleepy haze.

The city itself was a vibrant hub of activity in the morning. There were so many people out and about. The city's population seemed to consist mostly of the races I already knew about; humans, catonids and lycanids.

However, there were a few weird looking people I didn't recognise. I tried to identify them but the system wasn't playing ball, possibly because they were moving in and out of other people's way.

We reached the glass skyscraper that was home to the Adventure Society and entered through the front door. Unsure what to do exactly, I approached the front desk.

Lucy, the blonde catonid was working behind it. She smiled at me as I approached and leant leisurely on the reception desk.

"Good morning, Mr Akabane. It's good to see you again. How did your class selection go yesterday?" She asked cheerfully.

"It went really well thanks. I was wondering what to do now. I know I'm supposed to complete some quests but Lucas said I needed a mentor or something."

As I spoke Panda wriggled his way onto the desk, kicking his hind legs as he went. When he reached the top he sat down cross legged, or as close to that as a panda can, and lit up his bamboo pipe.

I expected Lucy to say something as I was sure smoking wasn't allowed in here. But when she looked at him she blushed slightly and began petting his head instead.

"That's exactly right Mr Akabane. Your mentor is already waiting for you. She's over in meeting room B, it's just over there."

She pointed towards a small corridor leading out of the foyer.

"Thanks Lucy, you can call me Kaleb by the way. Mr Akabane is my father's name... though I've never actually met him..."

"Smooth," Panda said as he jumped down from the counter and began waddling towards the meeting room.

I felt my face go red as I awkwardly said my goodbyes and left as well. "So it is true that all humans are furries," Panda said as we walked,

"I was just being friendly. Besides, I think she's more interested in you...for some reason."

"What can I say, the ladies just can't get enough of my charming personality and dashing good looks," he replied smugly, taking another drag.

"Yeah, it's definitely got nothing to do with the fact that you're a walking, talking teddy bear."

We made it to the corridor and I quickly spotted meeting room B. It looked just like a non-descript meeting room from any office on earth. It had floor to ceiling, interior glass windows, blinds, a door and inside was a large, oval table with chairs scattered around it.

I knocked and then entered the room, Panda at my side. Sitting in a chair at the head of the table and smoking a cigar was a *WWE* wrestler cosplaying as a catonid – or at least that's what she looked like.

The catonid had long silver hair that reached her lower back, silver cat eats and a braided silver tail. Her eyes were dark blue and her thighs looked like they could crush me like an egg.

She leaned all the way back in the chair with her monstrous legs up on the table. She looked like a bodybuilder. If we weren't in a magical world I'd be thinking she was on steroids. Not that I'd say that to her face even if we were back on earth, I'm not that stupid.

"I've been waiting for you," she said menacingly in a medium pitched voice. She flashed me an evil grin showing off her sharp fangs. "Take a seat."

"Don't mind if I do," Panda said, jumping onto an office chair and trying, and failing, to put his stumpy little legs on the table like the catonid was.

"I think you're a bit too short buddy," I said, taking the seat next to him and patting him on the head. "Maybe stick to the cute and cuddly thing."

He gave me a deadpan stare before sitting back in his seat.

"So, you're the fresh meat I'm supposed to beef up?" She asked, taking a drag of her cigar.

The smoke she blew out was thick and it filled the room in mesmerising grey spirals. As I breathed in the second-hand lung cancer I detected a creamy after taste.

I used to smoke too, years ago, but I stopped after my grandma died of cancer. It felt like it'd tarnish her memory and somehow be disrespectful to continue smoking after that.

Though maybe I'd just been a pushover because my wife hated it and I'd grown sick of going out in the rain all the time for my daily nicotine hits. Either way, I had to stop when she got pregnant.

I felt a pang in my chest as the smoke brought back memories of her. I hoped she was ok. More than anything I hoped she wasn't here, in this world.

"That's me, Fresh Meat reporting for duty," I replied.

"Cute. I don't like cute," she replied giving me an assessing look before looking Panda up and down and curling her lip.

*We're in for a treat.* I thought, internally sighing.

"Right, here's how it's gonna go," she said, removing her feet from the table and leaning in towards us. "You've got me for one quest and one quest only, then you're on your own. So, I've taken the liberty of excepting a silver ranked quest which you're going to help me with.

"I don't expect you to do much considering how far above your level it is, but this quest is about teaching you how to be an adventurer and I can't do that if we take one of those pussy quests from the temp floor.

"Rescuing a cat from a tree might have its use in society, but it's no adventure now, is it? You're going to do what I say, when I say it, without complaint and if you do, you might just learn something that'll keep you alive in the future.

"I'm only doing this as a favour to Lucas so don't expect me to baby you. Also, just so you know, I'll add your name to quest completion form *if* you make it back. But I'll be taking the reward since it'll be me doing all of the work." She leant back in her chair as she finished and took a long drag of her cigar.

Ash dropped from it onto the floor, leaving a smouldering hole in the carpet. Not that she seemed to care.

"I appreciate you taking the time to help us and all, but I'm more of a learn by doing kind of guy. A silver rank quest is fine by me, but I'm not just going to stand back and let you do all the work. Naturally, if I'm pulling my weight I want in on the reward too," I replied, leaning forward and placing my elbows on the table.

Panda shot me a nervous glance from his seat. It struck me as a little odd that he hadn't said anything himself. He was usually such a loudmouth.

"You've got balls kid," she began, "speaking to a silver ranker like that. But your noob is showing. If you knew what it was really like to be an adventurer you'd put your dick away. This is a silver ranked quest and you're not even an iron.

"You can try to pull your own weight if you want to, but you won't be able to come crying to me when it gets you killed... you know cause you'll be dead."

"I guess we'll see," I replied, letting my bravado get the better of me.

Why was this woman treating me like a child. I was 28 years old; I had a kid on the way and a mortgage and all that adult crap.

She smiled evilly as she got up from her chair. It was then that I realised just how ripped she truly was. She had a ten pack; I didn't even know that was a real thing!

The way she dressed was a bit counter intuitive to me with her crop top and booty shorts, but far be it for me to question a mighty silver ranker.

She moved to the side of the room and opened a floor to ceiling locker. Reaching in she pulled out the biggest sword I had ever seen. The thing was almost as tall as she was, and she was a big lady. It was wider than me and it glinted in a malicious black steel which caught the light and blinded me.

"I guess it's time to go then Gonads," she smirked, hefting the sword onto her back like she was lifting paper.

"My name is Kaleb; I probably should have introduced myself earlier."

"Mine's Sally. Nice to be working with ya, Gonads."

# Chapter 22
## Sailing Is for Chumps

We followed Sally out of the Adventure Society building and I was honestly surprised that her footsteps didn't shake the ground.

I'd expected we'd head straight for the bridge but instead she began leading us further into town. Panda tugged on the hem of my trousers and I looked down.

"Be careful around her. I know you don't have magic sense, so trust me when I say she's dangerous. The magical pressure she emits is wild," he whispered, keeping an eye on our mentor as she strutted up the street.

I nodded to him in response. Perhaps that was why he was so uncharacteristically quiet in the meeting. I had wondered why he didn't speak up when Sally had said she'd be keeping the reward for herself.

I quickened my pace slightly until I was walking next to the silver rank bodybuilder.

"Is it ok if we make a quick detour?" I asked. "I need to buy some arrows."

"What kind of archer doesn't have arrows?" She replied scathingly. "Fine, there's a shop just round the corner. I'll take you there. You should stock up on some other supplies too, we might be gone a while.

"Lesson number one: an adventurer is always prepared. You never know how long a quest might take or where it's going to take you. So, you need a constant supply of food, water, and potions just in case. Especially at your level where you still need to eat semi-regularly."

I thanked her for her advice as she led us towards the supply shop. This quest could be useful after all if Sally was going to give me advice.

I'd played plenty of video games before, but having to think about things like supplies was alien to me. I was sure there was going to be more to adventuring than I realised and I was actually getting quite excited to see Sally in action.

It was obvious that there was a huge gap between us. I could tell just by looking at her, and Panda had said she gave off some kind of magic pressure as well.

I needed to see it. See the difference levels really made in combat.

Sally led us to an unassuming store called *Adventurer's Stockpile and Supplies*. That's right, the store's acronym would be ass. We were about to enter ass, a thought that wasn't lost on me.

Inside, the place reminded me of an Army and Navy store from back home. The kind of store that sold all kinds of gear and knick-knacks for soldiers to buy.

There was a myriad of battered armour in the corner, a few old swords, and bows. There was a selection of shelves on the wall entitled: *rations and potions*.

There were also bargain bins full of arrows and quivers in the corner. The thing I needed most was proper ammunition for my bow, so I headed there first.

The store really was a cluttered jumble sale and I had to scootch around so I didn't knock over any of the merchandise.

In the bargain bins there were lots of arrows and damaged quivers. They all had super low prices too which was a bonus. I didn't know how many arrows I'd need though, or why I'd want a quiver when I could just summon them from my inventory into my hand.

Hanging behind the bins was a black quiver that had been hung on the wall with a nail. I focused on it.

### Quiver of The Infinite (inferior)

**This quiver has an infinite supply of inferior arrows, meaning you can shoot as fast as you want without running out of ammo. Of course you'd know all about shooting fast.**

Ignoring the snarky remark from the system as I reached up and grabbed the quiver. It was perfect. Infinite arrows would be a huge boon to an archer, especially one who couldn't make every shot count yet.

I took it over to the counter and rang a little brass bell that was left on there.

I heard a rustling from in the back somewhere and a small racoon dog jumped up onto the counter, standing on its hind legs like a person.

I stared at it and it stared back at me. It had black fur around its eyes that looked like a burglar mask and the rest of its fur was greyish brown. It was wearing a little bowtie which made it look like a cartoon character. As I focused on it a notification appeared.

### Racoon Dog
**Similar in size and appearance to the racoon dogs of Japan, this little guy loves trash. That's probably why so many of them are low level merchants running pawn shops or any other cluttered store of crap you can think of.**

"Well, are you just gonna stare at me all day or do you need something? What? You never seen a racoon dog before?" he said with a 20's mobster accent.

"Actually, no I haven't," I replied. "Sorry for staring, I want to buy this," I said, holding out the quiver.

"Ah, you've got a good eye mister," he said, taking the quiver in his paws and looking it up and down. For all I knew he was appraising it, but I was sure it was just for show considering it was already in his shop. "It'll cost you one thousand five hundred gold pieces."

"1.5k for an inferior item?" Sally said, pounding her fist on the desk and making the entire counter shake. "Come on Tanuki, I know this guy is a noob but he'd have to be an idiot to fall for that line. He's with me, so treat him good yeah?"

*Tanuki?* I thought, *isn't that just the Japanese word for Racoon Dog?*

"Oh, Sally hi," Tanuki said backing up a few steps. "I didn't realise he was with you! Of course I'll treat him fairly. How about 1000 gold?" He asked cautiously.

Sally didn't even justify that with a response. She glared at Tanuki with the eyes of a predator and I saw her fangs glinting from within her mouth.

"Ok fine! 800 gold, but that's as low as I can go," he said, huffing as he gave Sally the stink eye.

She smiled back at him and I had to assume that it was good price. I had 989 gold so I could afford his asking price. I just hoped I could still get some potions and food as well.

This world's economy confused me. A single gold had gotten me a week at a bed and breakfast, yet a single inferior quiver cost *this* much. It didn't make sense. I could live at the inn for 16 years for the price of a single quiver.

"I'll take it." I said, nodding at Sally. "I also need some food and water supplies and potions if you've got any."

Tanuki's beady eyes lit up.

"I can give you a week's supply of food and water for two gold, the potions are gonna cost ya though. Those things ain't cheap. So, what kind do you want?"

I looked towards Sally, pleading for advice with my eyes. So far I'd only seen a health potion, I had five of them in my inventory from the divine loot box.

"You'll need some health, stamina and mana potions," she said, shaking her head as she looked at me. It was like she was speaking to a disappointing child.

"I don't have any mana," I said, leaning into her and whispering behind my hand.

I was certain that wasn't something I wanted most people to know. However, if she was going to be my mentor she'd find out eventually.

"Really?" She said in a calculating voice. "How interesting. Just get the other two kind for now then."

I ended up leaving the store with my new quiver, which I immediately equipped, a week's worth of rations, five inferior stamina potions and two inferior health potions.

Each potion was supposed to cost 30 gold, but Sally helped me work out a deal with Tanuki so I got them for about 26 gold each. Unfortunately, all of my money was now gone.

I'd spent everything I had in that little shop, but I was happy with my purchases. The quiver was a good find and as a clothing item I could wear it all the time.

Panda had begged me to buy him an enchanted cowboy hat that changed colour with your mood, but I didn't have enough gold left.

He'd been pretty reluctant to let go of it when it was time to leave. He even went as far as to demand Tanuki keep it behind the counter so he could buy it when he got back.

He lit up his bamboo pipe as soon as we left and Sally began leading us further into town. I had no idea where we were going since the exit bridge was the other way.

We mostly kept to the main street, walking in silence as I filtered around the people going about their business. I noticed that Sally didn't have to move for someone even once.

It was like they avoided her. She walked in a straight line and people parted around her like they were the sea to her Moses.

It was a little unnerving and I soon learnt to walk behind her, letting her shield me from the annoying amount of people.

We walked up the main street for a little while, eventually coming out at a huge port. It was all hustle and bustle there with sailors and traders carrying boxes of cargo from their ships.

Most of the ships looked like pirate ships. They were all wood and sails. It was awesome. There was also one that looked like a modern, luxury cruise liner.

It seemed out of place compared to the others and it was parked off to the side, taking up a lot more space than the rest of the ships in the port.

Sally led us to the end of a pier. There was a smaller wooden ship moored there. It had only a single mast and was tiny compared to the others.

She jumped down onto it, rocking the little boat and beckoned for me to do the same. I noticed a ladder and climbed down that instead. Panda clung onto my back, ripping my shirt with his claws because he held on so tightly.

It was a good job my new clothes came with self-repair. If even Panda could break them with ease I didn't want to know how bad they'd be after a fight.

"This is a cute little boat," Panda said as he walked around gingerly.

"It's a schooner, which is a ship, not a boat," she retorted. "Besides, you should be happy that a woman like me is content with a smaller one. You men always go around saying *size doesn't matter* after all don't you?"

Panda looked at me, he seemed at a loss for words. She'd done it. Someone had finally managed to shut him up. I laughed as Panda stared between me and Sally expectantly.

"So, I take it we're sailing to this mystery quest?" I asked, moving around the unsteady boat, and trying to get my sea legs.

"Sailing is for chumps," she replied as she moved around the ship, tying knots and fiddling with ropes and the sail.

I looked after her with a furrowed brow. Why were we on a boat if we weren't sailing?

My question was answered a few seconds later as Sally grabbed the wheel and the ship shot off into the air.

"We travel by air," Sally said, grinning maniacally.

# Chapter 23
# The Goblin King Coronation

I was caught off guard by the sudden propulsion of the schooner. For a small ship, it sure packed some g-force.

I was sent hurtling backwards as the little ship shot up towards the sky. At first, I slipped backwards on the slippery wooden deck, but then I began free falling.

More accurately, it felt like I was hovering in mid-air and the rear of the ship was rocketing towards me. That's just how fast it was.

I slammed helplessly into a wooden wall; the ship's wheel was directly above it. I could only assume it was the outer wall of the captain's quarters.

Sally cackled from above me as she spun the ship's circular wheel.

With a thud, Panda crashed into my stomach, knocking the wind out of me and the two of us were helplessly pinned to the side of the captain's cabin.

It all happened so fast.

After about thirty seconds of being crushed by the air pressure and Panda, the ship levelled out. The two of us fell to the deck of the ship in a tangled mess.

I picked myself up, groaning as I rubbed my sore head. I'd lost the feeling in my face because of the harsh, freezing wind.

"I can tell you two are flying novices," Sally said, vaulting the rail above us and landing with a thump on the deck. "You'll get used to it. The trick is to form a basic mana shield around yourself... oh wait, you don't have any mana do you?" She laughed evilly.

"You could have given us some warning," I retorted.

"What, and miss out on all the fun?"

Panda rolled onto his front and stood up gingerly. He wobbled towards the side of the ship, poked his head out over the side and began retching. Poor guy, he was quite possibly the first of his kind to fly in an open topped vessel.

I walked towards him and rubbed his back as he let it all out. Despite the cold from the wind, the view was magnificent.

We were sailing through the sky and it was simply amazing. Just above us floated a patch of fluffy looking clouds. They looked like sheep; I reached out towards them. I was so close I could almost touch them.

The sky itself was a Mediterranean blue and stretched out infinitely in all directions. It was an all-encompassing, beautiful reflection of the tropical waters below us.

We'd barely been flying for a few minutes but already the city of Havar was fading behind us. The skyscrapers that littered the town were almost as tall as we were, with the neon glow of the Adventure Society building standing above all the rest.

That building reminded me of the Tokyo skyscraper's I'd seen on TV. As a young boy I'd dreamed of travelling there and tracking down my father. My mother hadn't spoke of him much.

All I knew was that she met him whilst studying abroad and that she gave me his last name. With that name being Akabane, it was obvious he was Japanese. I didn't have many Asian features myself but I just knew that's where he was from.

Now I'd probably never get the chance to meet him. My own child would grow up never knowing their father either. It was almost like my family had a genetic disposition towards abandoning their children.

I knew that wasn't a fair sentiment. According to my mother my father never even knew she was pregnant. Still, it was a bit of a sore subject and one I was loath to repeat.

I didn't want to go home as much as I wanted to bring them here. At the same time the idea of my wife being alone in this world was terrifying.

I'd need to become much stronger if I was going to protect them in a place like this. That's *if* there was even a way to bring them to me.

"What are you sulking over?" Sally said, perching against the railing next to me.

"Nothing in particular," I replied, I couldn't tell her that I was an outworlder and I was worried for my family. It wasn't safe to admit that in a place where people skin outworlders for their ink. "When are you going to let us in on this quest?" I asked instead, attempting to change the subject.

"I'll need to be on your contacts list to share the details," she said, holding out her hand.

I had noticed that there was a contacts list in the options menu, I just hadn't given it much thought since I didn't really know anyone.

I looked at her hand in confusion.

"Don't tell me you've never done this before? Jeez, you're as helpless as a newborn sometimes. I really have my work cut out for me don't I?" She said, noticing my hesitation to take her hand. "You have to shake hands with someone to get their contact info. Once you do you'll be able to share notifications with them and call them through the interface."

"Interface? I've been calling it a HUD," I replied.

"I don't know what that means Gonads. You gonna shake my hand or not?"

Reluctantly I took Sally's enormous hand and shook. She squeezed mine so tightly I thought my fingers were going to break.

As we shook, a notification popped up on my HUD.

**You have received a new friend request from [Sally].**
**Accept request?**

**Y/N**

I mentally asserted yes and scrolled down my options screen. Like clockwork, the previously greyed out *contacts* sections was now clickable.

"Now I can share the quest with you, which means you'll get it too. You'll have to accept it though," Sally said as a new notification appeared.

**Sally has shared a quest with you.**
**Will you accept?**

**Y/N**

I accepted the quest and the notification appeared immediately. I could see Sally watching me with curious eyes as I read it.

**New Quest!**
**The Goblin King Coronation**
**Every century a new goblin king is chosen. He who is**
**destined to unite the clans and conquer the world – or**
**so ancient goblin lore says.**

**Crash the party, kill the king, and get to the *Winchester* for a nice cold pint whilst you wait for it all to blow over.**

**Objectives:**
*Stop the coronation 0/1*
*Kill throne candidates 0/4*

**Reward: *A New Active Skill***

I wasn't sure what shocked me more, the *Shawn of the Dead* quote or the amazing reward. I didn't have any active skills yet.

"Not bad as far as rewards go right?" Sally said, flashing me a fang-like grin.

"Definitely, I don't have any active skills yet."

"That's probably because of your lack of mana. Most active skills need mana to activate them," Sally replied, leaning back over the railing thoughtfully.

"She's right," Panda said, pulling himself back up and wiping his mouth. "The vast majority of active skills rely on mana for activation. That puts you at an advantage for this reward Kaleb. I can't think of any stamina activated skills that are below rare quality."

I had wondered about that. My class was unique but the system didn't assign rarity to my passive skills or my personal skills.

I had assumed that all the skills pertaining to my class were also unique but I could have been wrong. It seemed active classes came with an actual rarity.

If I was going to unlock a rare skill as my first ever active one then I needed to complete this quest. Traditionally in video games active skills were way more powerful than passive buffs. Of course, this place wasn't a game.

"That's good to know. Hopefully my passive skills will be enough to complete the quest," I said thoughtfully.

"Unless you have something super destructive like a bomb skill you won't make so much as a dent in the goblins at your level.

"You just need to back me up and you'll get your reward. If you're lucky I might train you up a bit too." She flashed me a devilish grin and suddenly I wasn't so sure that I wanted her training.

"I definitely do need to train," I said swallowing hard. "How long until we get to this coronation place?"

"The ship will get us to the island in a few hours, we'll have some walking to do from there though," she replied. "Which gives us plenty of time to do a little sparing."

I looked at her blankly as she moved to the middle of the ship, next to the mast. She opened both of her hands and suddenly the wind stopped.

I looked around bewildered as a large, blue bubble encircled the entire ship. It was semi-transparent and the sound of the wind disappeared with it as well.

Suddenly the ship felt eerily quiet.

"Well, come on then. Show me what you've got," Sally commanded, pointing at me with her other, muscled arm, bent and resting against her ripped obliques.

I stepped forward hesitantly. Something in the back of my head told me it wasn't a good idea to fight her, even if it *was* only sparing.

"What's the matter? I won't hurt you… much. Look I won't even use a weapon." Sally attempted to persuade me.

"This might be a good opportunity Kaleb. You haven't gotten to test out your new class yet," Panda said confidently as he backed up as far as he could and made himself small.

*Yeah, you look raring to go little buddy.* I thought.

With a deep sigh I summoned my bow and nocked an arrow.

"That's more like it!" Sally cheered, "gimme everything you've got."

172

I steeled myself for the attack. I didn't want to risk melting her with my acid but she seemed pretty confident. A part of me wanted nothing more than to wipe the grin from her face and I leaned into a primal urge: the urge, no, the desire to win at all costs.

I pulled back on the bowstring and took aim at her centre mass. There was no way I was going to risk a headshot, not after last time. I needed to play it smart and attack in a way that would definitely land hits.

I took a breath as I drew the bow and fired.

The arrow rocketed towards Sally much faster than the *Loconut's Hair* I'd been using before.

She opened her eyes wide, a feral grin on her face. Did she plan to take it head on?

*Bad move lady.*

It didn't matter how strong she was. Silver ranker or not, she was still made of flesh. She didn't have any armour on and my arrows were tipped with acid.

I had this in the bag.

The arrow struck her chest and she took it like a pro. It didn't even rip her crop top.

*What the hell!*

How was that even possible? She looked at me and tipped her head back as if to laugh. Then a hole started burning through the centre of her shirt and she looked down.

The skin in the middle of her chest had turned a deep red, but that was all. Even the acid had done little more than blemish her skin.

I wasn't done yet. There was no way I was going to lose so pathetically. I dismissed my bow and summoned the dagger. It was my strongest weapon skill.

Not only would it replenish my own health, but it also did acid damage and I was faster with it.

I rushed towards her and her dark blue eyes bored into me as if she was daring me to try it. I didn't back down.

I charged into her, holding the dagger out in front of me. With my bodyweight and speed adding to the pressure I would definitely pierce her skin. Then the acid would really shine.

Her skin might be super strong but were her organs?

She smiled and stood still once again, holding her arms out like a chav about to threaten to sic his older brother on you.

I made contact and pushed with all my might but it was like hitting steel. The dagger did less damage than the arrow and I looked down in disappointment.

Sally laughed and I looked up just in time to receive a back hand to the face.

Everything went black.

# Chapter 24
# You're Being Pathetic

"What happened to sparing? You almost killed him" Panda shouted.

"It was a simple backhand; I wasn't expecting him to be so weak. It's pathetic," Sally replied, indignantly.

"He's only level 9!" Panda screamed.

"Level 9? Most children are at least level 10. How could he be so weak at his age?"

My head felt like it had split open. My face felt swollen and everything was spinning even though I could only see an empty void.

I tried to open my eyes, everything hurt. The headache turned into a migraine as cracks of light shone into my vision. It was blinding.

My HUD flicked back on, blinking a red warning light. My HP was only at 1/101. I was dying.

Something had hit me; I remembered the brief contact but not how it happened. Had I been fighting someone? Sally! That's right I'd been sparring with Sally.

I heard heated voices close by but I couldn't make much sense of what they were saying. I wished they'd be quiet. My head hurt so much, I just wanted to sleep. I wanted it all to go away.

*Are you really going to allow yourself to die like this?*

A mysterious voice whispered in my mind. It felt familiar, comforting even.

*Get up Kaleb, you're being pathetic.*

I didn't want to get up. Everything hurt. My body was broken. Even the HUD was telling me to give in. The flashing red lights all around my blurred vision wanted me to surrender.

"Kaleb?" I heard a familiar voice. I think it was Panda. "Oh, thank God you're awake. Give me a potion!" He shouted, though I got the impression he wasn't shouting at me.

"No not a cheap one. A common one should do it. Look at his face, he needs a good one."

I felt myself fading away again. I wanted to sleep so badly, why were all these voices keeping me awake.

I felt something warm on my lips, then pressure as something soft rubbed my throat.

The warmth filled me as it sank deeper into my body. It began spreading everywhere and the pain started to fade. My HUD stopped flashing and I watched as my HP started filling up.

It was magical, serene.

I wished I could feel that way forever.

*** 

I woke up feeling refreshed. I wondered if I'd ever get used to the feeling of waking up like that. I didn't miss feeling like a zombie every morning but it was still strange to feel good after sleep.

Opening my eyes I sat up and stretched my arms. I looked around and found that I was in an unfamiliar cabin-style room.

I was laid on a single bed in a room with walls so close I could touch them from where I sat. There was a sliding door at the end of the bed.

How had I gotten here?

*That's right I nearly died.* I thought, rubbing my chin. Stubble had started to form. That was interesting, I'd always been clean shaven. Maybe it wouldn't be a bad idea to try growing it out. New world, new beard as they say. Well, I don't think anyone has ever actually said that, but it sounded like something people would say.

*Wait. I nearly died. Holy shit!* I realised in a sudden panic.

I pulled the covers off myself and started checking for injuries. I was still wearing my clothes and they seemed fine.

I seemed fine.

The door opened and Sally stood there, she had to duck to see under the door frame. She looked at me and her expression softened slightly.

She entered the room and sat on the edge of the bed, her weight tipped the mattress and I had to dig my feet in to stop myself from sliding towards her.

"So, you're awake. How are you feeling?" She asked with a kindness which was so uncharacteristic of her that it caught me off guard.

"I think I'm ok. Did I die?" I asked slowly.

"Not quite, but it was close," she replied, then she looked down at her hands. Her sudden bashfulness was off putting. "Listen, I'm sorry I nearly killed you. It's just that I didn't realise you were so weak. When Lucas asked me to look out for you he never told me you were an outworlder."

How did she know? I was supposed to be keeping that a secret. I swallowed a lump that had appeared in my throat all of a sudden. My mouth felt dry.

"I guess the cat's out of the bag huh?" I said, also looking away.

*Good going Kaleb. The cat's out of the bag? Seriously. You're talking to a damned cat lady.*

She didn't respond so I decided to keep talking. I felt awkward. This woman had just proved she could kill me with ease. If she wanted to skin me there was nothing I could do to stop it.

I got the feeling that wasn't the case though. Something about her seemed trustworthy. Despite the battle junkie trope she called a personality.

"How did you find out?"

"I saw the tattoos on your back when I carried you in here. Your shirt ripped. That self-repair option was a good choice. Panda filled me in on the rest."

It seemed self-repair really was useful. Without a spare shirt I'd have had to remain semi-naked for the whole quest. *Again.*

"Ah, I see," I replied, "where is Panda?"

"He's throwing up over the side again. He's not much of a flyer that one. He keeps coming back to sit with you though, that's been his routine for the past nine hours or so."

Nine hours? Had I really been out that long from a single hit? The director was right, I really was weak as shit. I needed to do some levelling.

"So, what now?" I asked hesitantly.

"Now, I train you up as much as I can in the short time I have you. It's the least I can do after nearly killing you." She smiled a fangy grin at me but there was no malice in her eyes this time.

"Thanks. I'm weak as shit, I need all the help I can get."

"Yup. Though don't beat yourself up too much. I am a level 90, the disparity between is no joke." She chuckled and placed her hand on my knee and I looked up at her. "For what it's worth, your attack did leave a mark on my skin. At your level that's quite impressive. It'll take work, the life of an adventurer is hard. But, if you're willing to put the effort in I think you have what it takes to make it in this world."

Before I could reply she stood up and ducked out of the door.

I took a moment to collect my thoughts. She was right, I'd been treating this assignment too lightly. How arrogant did I have to be to think I could pull my weight with someone like her?

I needed to get stronger and I needed to do it now. No more messing around. I took both my hands and slapped them into my cheeks.

In that moment, I resolved to do whatever it took to make it in this world.

Soon after, I got out of bed and left the room. It opened up into a cramped hallway that led into a dining area come kitchen.

It reminded me of a log cabin. There was fire burning in a metal fireplace on the back wall and Sally was cooking something on a small stove.

Panda sat at a table which took up most of the room and he was drinking a funny looking concoction. It looked like orange juice with bits of ketchup floating in it and from the look on his face as he drank it, it tasted like that too.

"Make sure you drink that all up. I won't have you throwing up on deck," Sally said as she cooked.

Her voice had returned to normal, no more of that maternal charm. I was glad. I was thankful for her words but I didn't want her like that all the time. I was starting to get used to her boorish personality anyway.

I walked into the room and Panda looked up at me. He still looked sickly but the colour was beginning to come back to his fur.

The concoction must have been some kind of travel sickness medicine.

"Ah, you're awake. Took you long enough," he said.

"Were you worried about me?" I teased. "I heard you didn't leave my side for a whole nine hours, apart from when you needed to throw up."

"Worried? Of course not. It's no skin off my back if you go and get yourself killed kid. I was just in there for the bed... yeah that's it, the bed was soft and I'm a creature of comfort," he retorted, refusing to meet my eyes.

"Sure," I replied lightly as I took a seat.

Panda took out his bamboo pipe and took a drag. Then he blew a few rings at me. For a sage, he was remarkably child-like at times.

Sally dashed over to him and slapped the pipe out of his mouth.

"No smoking at the dinner table Furball!" She yelled before returning to the stove.

"Furball? Look who's talking Steroid Test Kitten," he responded.

I wasn't sure what had happened between them in the time I'd been unconscious, but they seemed a lot less tense around each other, friendly even. Panda had barely spoken a word to her before.

Sally responded by brining three dinner plates over and slapping them down on the table. Each plate contained a pile of overcooked meat.

I was no culinary expert but I was sure it was a travesty to cook meat for this long. Steak was supposed to be rare or medium rare, that's where the flavour was.

This was more like ash than meat.

"Protein's all you need if you want to be strong like me," Sally said, taking a seat and flexing her enormous bicep at me.

"I eat bamboo and I'm plenty strong. Pandas don't eat meat," Panda said, pushing the plate away with both hands.

"Starve then," Sally said, taking the plate and scraping the copious amount of meat onto her own pile. "How about you Gonads. I made this to toughen you up so you better eat it." There was a slight threat in her eyes but it was marred slightly by the food in her mouth as she spoke.

I grabbed my plate and began eating with gusto. It lacked taste. It was chewy. Honestly, it looked like it was prepared and cooked by a toddler, and not one of those super smart ones that parents always brag about. A normal, bog-standard toddler.

Still, it was the best meal I'd had since arriving here.

"All this protein will feed your muscles and you're going to need it," Sally said, still eating as she spoke. "After dinner we're gonna train until you puke and then we're gonna train some more. We've still got half a day until we arrive and I need you in fighting shape for the quest."

I gulped. I'd never really been a *train till you puke* kind of guy. But I guessed I was going to have to be if I wanted to get stronger.

I was strangely excited to see how much I could grow in only half a day of training with a silver ranker.

# Chapter 25
# Train Till You Puke

"Come on, how is it possible to be this pathetic. I asked for a thousand push-ups, not two-hundred-and-seventy-one and a bit," Sally sighed as I laid sprawled on the deck of the ship unable to muster the strength for another one.

"We need to increase your strength stat," she continued. "Strength is vital for a melee fighter. You're gonna have your work cut out for you as both an archer and a light skirmisher."

Back on earth 271 push-ups would be quite the feat. It's not like I'd ever trained much back home. I was a driver for god's sake. I spent most of my day sat down.

I was impressed with 271, that was a good number. It really showed how much the strength stat affected me.

She was right though. In this world it was weak and I needed to push past my limits, both physically and mentally.

After I failed at the push-ups she had me attempt 1000 sit-ups. I managed 402. Then we moved onto 1000 squats. I got 364. Finally, she had me run laps of the ship.

I wasn't too bad at running. I'd played football in high school. Though it had been ten years since I'd graduated. But with my agility and strength stats combined I thought I did well.

This went on for hours. Every time my stamina got too low, she force-fed me a potion to bring it back. I learnt that there is a 60-minute cooldown on potions of the same type. So, I could take a health potion and a stamina potion at the same time, but not again for an hour.

It turned out that consuming two of the same potion type within the time limit had the opposite effect of what was intended. At least that's what Sally said.

She told me that she once took a second health potion ten minutes too early and it drained half of her HP. Luckily the HUD had a timer when I looked at the potions in the inventory.

That meant that I'd have to be careful in battle. Potions were a last resort because most fights didn't last anywhere near an hour so you'd only get to use one once.

After the running, the real combat training began.

"For now, in this quest, I want you on support duty. When we get to the island you'll be laying down cover fire with your bow and I'll do the close quarter fighting," Sally began.

"At your level it's too risky to have you close enough to take damage from the monsters we'll likely encounter. So, let's work on levelling your marksmanship."

Sally produced a number of disks from her inventory. The idea was that she'd throw them overboard and I'd have to hit them as they fell from the sky. Like clay pigeon shooting.

I took my position next to the railings and nocked my first arrow. I took a deep breath and breathed out halfway, a technique I'd discovered days before.

The *Novice Bowman* skill gave me some limited innate knowledge and muscle memory about all things bow related. It was useful as I'd only done archery once or twice before on a school trip when I was young.

Sally said that to level the *Novice Bowman* skill I'd have to practice shooting. The better I got on my own, the more likely the system would reward me with an upgrade which would solidify the skills I'd learnt.

I tried to clear my mind as I waited for Sally's throw.

She called out a countdown and then launched the first disk into the air. I waited for it to reach its apex and fired.

I missed and the disk hurled disappointingly towards the ground far below us.

I tried again and missed again. I kept trying for hours, taking stamina potions when I needed them. There was no way I was going to give up. Even if it was only once, I'd hit the target before we landed.

With a renewed energy I began to nock my arrow for what was probably the thousandth time. The infinite ammo quiver was a god send for training.

I took in a breath, breathed out halfway and Sally threw the disk. It careened lazily into the air and I traced it with my bow as it moved. I was so in the zone it was like time slowed down.

I wanted this so badly. I needed it.

I waited for the disk to reach the apex. I wanted to fire but held myself back. There was a moment between ascending and freefalling where the disk would appear weightless. Just before it fell and gravity took its hold the disk would appear to be perfectly still, floating in the sky.

That was when I took my shot. The arrow flew from the bow with unreal speed and smashed through the disk.

I pumped my first in the air and let out a cheer.

**Congratulations! You have upgraded a skill:**
***Novice Bowman → Apprentice Bowman***

"Sally my skill upgraded!" I shouted, reading the notification.

"Took you long enough. Apprentice anything is still on the lower rung of the ladder," she said dryly.

It had taken most of the day, the sun was already beginning to set and a serene orange glow washed over the deck of the ship.

Still, on earth it could take years to hone a skill like archery. Decades to master it. What was half a day compared to that.

"We're going to land soon. Give me 100 laps of the ship whilst I get dinner going," she commanded, walking back inside, and leaving me alone.

Panda had spent the first hour outside watching me train, but he quickly got bored. I'd revealed to him that I'd stollen the books from the library back at the cultist temple and he was ecstatic.

I'd given him a few random tomes from my inventory and he'd been happily laid in bed reading all day.

It turned out he was quite scholarly. I'd originally taken those books with the intention of reading them myself to learn more about this world.

But if I had to train like this every day, I doubted I'd have the time. It made sense to let Panda do the reading for me and give me the highlights of anything useful. At least for now.

As I ran endless laps around the small ship I was reminded of the bleep test I'd taken in high school. It was standard across English schools.

Basically, you'd run between two cones and you had to reach the next cone before the bleep sounded. It got progressively faster as the time went on.

That was pretty much what I was doing on the ship, since it was quite small. I already felt fast and more cardiovascular fit compared to when I'd ran earlier that day.

I wondered if the potions helped with that.

As I ran, I watch the sunset from the best view in the house. It took up most of the horizon as it began to sink beneath the vast ocean.

It was truly a sight to behold.

This was a world full of monsters and cultists who wanted my skin, but it was also a world full of beauty.

\*\*\*

Lucas sank wearily into his lush office chair on the top floor of the Adventure Society building in Havar.

Pouring himself a strong drink, he leaned back and swirled the amber liquid in his expensive, crystal glass. The new kid was becoming a headache already.

He thought his new task from his god would be easy. Keep a noob alive, how hard could that be right?

He'd nearly had a heart attack when his god had appeared suddenly in his mind and chewed him out.

*That stupid woman! Why did you choose a brute like that to watch over the boy? I thought I told you to keep him alive!* He'd screamed suddenly in Lucas's head.

*She spared with him and took his HP down to one point. One fucking point! He was on the verge of death. I had to speak directly into his mind to coax him into staying alive long enough for his daemon to pour a potion down his throat.*

*If he remembers that it could cause me some serious premature problems, you know? Honestly, you can't get the help anywhere these days you useless fuck.*

*If he dies before I can use him I'll kill you as well, and the stupid catonid with him.*

*Do you understand Lucas!*

"Yes, My Lord," he'd replied humbly.

The severity of the god's words and his outrage had shaken Lucas to the core.

He could feel the murderous intent coursing through his mind. The god's power was so far beyond his own it was barely comprehensible, and that was from realms away.

He shuddered at the thought of feeling that wrath in person. It was likely strong enough to kill him outright.

As he downed his drink and poured another he felt envy for the first time in years. He was envious of Kaleb and his lack of mana.

Without mana you couldn't sense the power and will of others. At least you couldn't until you surpassed the max level.

He would likely never have to feel the utterly unnerving feeling of an angry god inside his head. The pressure alone was extraordinary. It was terrifying.

He glanced out at the setting sun from his penthouse view. He had no thoughts about the beauty of the world around him only resentment for being the weakest in the main family.

Resentment for being forced to obey the whims of those more powerful than himself time after time.

He'd taken the position of director of the Havar branch because he was exiled. An idyllic location in a weak zone. It was supposed to be the easy life, practically retirement.

And it was, until Kaleb showed up.

His god hadn't spoken to him in ages. Then that outworlder came and he was reduced to the role of first bitch in the annoying tasks department.

He squeezed his glass as the anger welled up inside him and it shattered like it was made of Styrofoam. The amber liquid inside covered his hand and leaked onto the carpet.

He hadn't been this stressed in as long as he could remember. Well, that wasn't strictly true. A gold rank adventurer who had surpassed the level 100 cap had a very good memory after all, even if he had been stuck at jade soul for a century.

Still, it had been a long time.

As he began to settle down and pour another drink his god appeared again, calmer this time.

*The boy will arrive on the island before morning. He seems to have increased his bow skill. That better be enough to keep him alive.*

*A silver ranked quest is a bit much for a level 9 if you ask me. I hope you know what you're doing Lucas.*

He was calmer this time but he still felt agitated. A feeling that permeated through Lucas's mind as he felt his presence there.

"Sally will keep him alive My Lord. She is my most loyal adventurer and her talents are known across the islands," Lucas replied, his voice sounding tired.

*She better Lucas. The Goblin King Coronation is no joke. I remember when I took on that quest a few millennia ago.*

*It took an entire raid party of silver rankers led by a gold ranker – me. You must place a lot of faith in that catonid of yours if you think she can do it with a rookie and his panda.*

A few millennia? The calendar he knew only went back 20,000 years or so. He wondered what it was like living in the world before gods.

Lucas hadn't realised the quest was supposed to be so hard. It was a recurring quest; he knew that much. It popped up from time to time.

However, to his knowledge it hadn't activated in his lifetime. It was a silver rank quest; how hard could it be?

"She is very skilled My Lord."

*I hope you're right. For your own sake.*

# Chapter 26
# Squabbling Goblin Tribes

After a hearty dinner of badly cooked meat, the three of us tried to get a few hours of sleep. I tossed and turned for a while.

I was tired, or as tired as I got after barely a day in this world, but I just couldn't switch off. I was excited and nervous in equal amounts about arriving at the island.

The quest: *The Goblin King Coronation* was a silver ranked one. I hardly knew what that meant but considering my disastrous sparring session with my silver ranked mentor, it was certain to be a challenge.

I'd spent hours upon hours training my body and working on my bow skills. I'd even managed to level up my *Bow* skill and upgrade my marksmanship skill from *Novice* to *Apprentice Bowman*. Still, as I looked over my stats, I wasn't sure it would be enough.

**Status Sheet:**

**Name: Kaleb Akabane**
**Race: Outworlder**
**Class: Apex Predator (unique)**
**Adventurer Rank: Temp**
**Level: 9**
**Map Pieces 2/10,000**
**HP: 106/101 (106)**

Stamina: 139/139
Strength: 89
Agility: 39
Perception: 35
Vitality: 51 (56)
Intelligence: 16

Personal Skills: *Speak English Damnit!, Eat Anything*
Class Skills (Passive) Skills: *Bow (lvl 6), Apprentice
Bowman, Dagger (lvl 4), Acid Dhampir Dagger, Acid
Arrows, Environmental Hazzard*
Blessing: *Blessing of Wealth*
Familiars: *Panda (Daemon)*
Admission: *Pentagram [Right hand (Morningstar Hotel
and Spa)]*

Likely due to the guilt she felt over nearly killing me, Sally had given me free potions all day which meant I would be starting fresh on arrival.

I was oddly excited. The training had been hard but also kind of rewarding. I'd never really worked for anything back on earth.

Not because I lacked ambition, but because the world was a boring place to me. I loved my wife and had a great time with her and my friends and family. But work? No thanks, it was just a paycheck.

Eventually my brain ran out of things to think about and I managed to drift into a mostly peaceful sleep.

I woke up a few hours later to Sally's ham fist rapping on the door. It was finally time to disembark.

I hopped out of bed, full of adrenaline for the day ahead and walked out onto the deck of the ship.

We had already landed. Sally must have seen to that whilst I slept. She was stood at the bow of the ship, staring at the island ahead. Her long, silver hair billowed in the wind like a superhero's cape.

I joined her, leaning against the ship as I too, looked out over the island.

We had landed on an idyllic looking beach. A tropical paradise, seemingly untouched by man. From the shore I could see out into a dense jungle, thankfully not a palm tree one this time.

In the distance I could just about make out a huge mountain, possibly a volcano. Something told me that would be our destination.

After a few moments of serenity as Sally and I stared off at the island. We were brought back to earth by Panda's grumbling.

"I feel awful. Barely slept a wink last night," he moaned as he softly padded his way towards us.

"We both know that's not true. I could hear your snoring through the wall," I replied.

It wasn't a lie. He'd been sawing logs all night. How a cute little teddy bear could make a noise that unholy, I would never know.

"Listen up," Sally said loudly, turning towards us with a steely look in her eyes. "This place is known as the Forbidden Isle.

"It's home to countless squabbling goblin tribes. They're usually so busy fighting petty turf wars that they don't bother us, but that's about to change.

"Like the quest said, it's almost time for the goblin king coronation, an event that comes around once or twice a century. The last one happened before I was born so we only know what we know from the archives.

"The adventurers who have dealt with this in the past are either dead or so powerful they no longer give a shit. So it's up to us.

"We're going to fight our way through the jungle to reach our objective, that huge mountain in the distance." She pointed towards the silhouette of the mountain. It was huge, nearly reaching the clouds themselves.

"This isn't an easy task, even for me, so you need to be careful. Current marching orders and tactics are as follows.

"We engage only on my say so. I'll take the front with Kaleb bringing up the rear as archery support. Panda you... do whatever the fuck it is you do.

"Preliminary reports from our scouts back in Havar suggest that the enemy levels should be quite low this close to shore, goblins don't like water and their wars are usually over the land around the mountain.

"If I think you can handle it Kaleb, I'll let you try to get some solo experience. Either way you stand to gain some serious levels here. So, listen to me and I'll get you home safely and with a heap of experience to boot.

"Any questions?"

I was so shocked by her sudden change in demeanour I stood dumbstruck for longer than was socially acceptable. It was as if she'd transformed from a boorish battle junkie to a five-star general at the drop of a hat.

I guess being silver rank was more about just power.

Eventually I shook my head. I was sure she'd covered everything, more than I'd expected at least.

Panda raised his hand like a school child.

"What happens when we reach the mountain?"

"We do some recon, assess and devise a strategy," Sally replied confidently.

"So, in other words, you have no idea."

Sally ignored him and jumped off the side of the ship. Not wanting to risk breaking my legs, I climbed down the rigging on the side and joined her on the beach.

Without a word she marched off into the jungle and I stuck close behind her.

There weren't any trails as such, just a lot of foliage and tree cover. I hadn't seen a goblin in this world, but if they were what I thought they were then they'd have a natural camouflage amidst all the greenery.

It didn't take long before I got my first glimpse.

Sally put her hand in the air and I stopped, Panda bumped into the back of my leg.

She crouched down and beckoned me towards her with two fingers. She was in a bush and as I moved to join her the branches scratched at my skin.

She pointed two fingers to her eyes and then towards a small clearing in front of us.

A small green fellow in tattered brown rags was stood there. It was facing away from us and picking berries. Its head was bulbous with cauliflower ears like it had spent years in a boxing ring.

Its body was misshapen and out of proportion. The skin was hanging off in places, but tight around the joints and its bare feet were massively oversized with long, brown toenails.

I focused on it and a notification popped up.

### You have discovered a new monster:
#### Goblin Gatherer

**Goblins are one of the most well-known monsters in the known universe. It's probably because they fuck like bunnies and spread like the clap.**
**Seriously, these guys are some of the stupidest and ugliest guys you'll ever meet.**
**The Goblin Gatherer is one of the lowest in their convoluted hierarchy.**
**They do what it says on the tin, they gather. Fruits, discarded trash, dumpster babies. You name it, they'll take it.**

**Don't get too complacent though. All goblins are dangerous in their own right. They're like a Viking horde minus the sex appeal.**

I didn't feel like the notification was overly helpful, but it did tell me one thing. This goblin was likely to be my best chance at a solo fight.

"Do you wanna take this one?" Sally whispered directly into my ear. It made me tingle a little bit.

I nodded to her and she gestured with an empty palm towards it.

I already knew what I wanted to do. Despite being low on the food chain, it was probably a higher level than me which meant I had a slim chance of one shotting it.

With that in mind, I summoned my bow and nocked an arrow. After all the training I'd done with the disks, a stationary and significantly larger target should be child's play.

I aimed my shot and fired.

The arrow soared out of the bush and met its target with ease, embedding itself into the goblin's left leg.

With a child-like yelp, it dropped to the floor. I stood and exited the bush, already nocking the next arrow to hopefully go for the kill shot.

I walked forward confidently and saw the goblin's leg was bubbling. Its skin looked like the contents of a witch's cauldron as it bubbled and popped, spraying blood and pus everywhere.

It smelled revolting, like burning vomit roasting on an open fire. I had to resist the urge to gag as I aimed my next shot at its face.

The goblin looked at me with fearful eyes and opened its mouth in a silent scream. Then, after less than a second, an ear shattering scream.

It was so loud birds flew out of nearby trees and my eardrums felt like they were going to burst.

I fired my shot quickly and its head lolled back unnaturally.

I'd killed it! A monster from a silver rank quest and I'd eliminated it solo.

**You have defeated:**
*Goblin Gatherer (lvl 17)*
***Bonus experience awarded due to level disparity.***

Level 17? That was quite high. It almost felt too easy, not that I was complaining. The notifications rolled in and my level jumped a fair few times.

**Congratulations! You have advanced to lvl 10**
**Congratulations! You have advanced to lvl 11**
**Congratulations! You have advanced to lvl 14**

Five levels from a single kill? That was brilliant. My stats must have skyrocketed, I'd need to decide where to put my free points later.

These were the first levels I'd gotten since I'd chosen my class and I immediately noticed something different. It seemed I no longer got +5 to HP and Stamina, my classes stat upgrades had replaced that function.

Not that I was disappointed, it was a worthwhile trade off as I gained a lot more per level now than I had before.

I was, however, a little disappointed I hadn't gotten another skill. I was hoping I'd get one at level ten, but apparently not. I knew this wasn't a video game, but I'd hoped there would be some semblance of order to the acquisition of skills.

I felt Sally's hand on my shoulder as I congratulated myself.

"Good job Gonads, now get back in that bush. I'll take it from here, you cover me," she said hurriedly.

I was a little unsure what she thought was about to happen. Then I heard the horn blast sound through the forest.

I looked in the direction of the sound as a spear wielding goblin jumped out of the shrubbery.

He lifted his spear in the air and screamed.

I heard rustling as goblins came out of *all* the bushes around the clearing.

*So much for going back to my bush.*

We were surrounded.

# Chapter 27
# A Wild Gertrude Appears

Before I had time to react, Sally pounced on the first goblin. She moved so fast my eyes couldn't keep up and in less than a second she'd cleaved its head from its shoulders.

Her oversized sword looked difficult to handle in the jungle, but her overwhelming strength more than compensated as she destroyed the nearby bushes.

She killed three other goblins in the same strike who were hiding in the bushes that the first had appeared from.

The luscious greenery was splattered with blood and gore. It was like a nightmare.

I raised my bow and aimed at another goblin who had appeared on our left. It looked similar to the first one with a spear in hand and a bulbous, wart-covered nose.

I nocked and fired an arrow, aiming for its centre mass. It struck the goblin in the chest, the acid making short work of its brown rags and searing its chest.

It howled in pain as it looked down at bubbling, melting skin. Acid was a gross way to kill but it seemed to be effective.

Not waiting to see if it died, I moved onto the next threat. Another goblin had emerged from the side of the one I'd just shot and charged towards me.

I loosed another arrow which embedded itself in the goblin's stomach. The goblin fell to the floor, coughing blood and bile as a notification marker popped up in the corner of my HUD.

One of them had died. Good.

Getting in the zone, I shot a third and a fourth goblin, all coming from the same direction.

Meanwhile Sally was making short work of the rest of the clearing. She was like a woman possessed, a deadly efficient killing machine.

She cleaved entire groups of goblins in half, like cutting through butter, with a single swing. The foliage also took a hammering as she singlehandedly doubled the circumference of the clearing.

I absently thought that she'd be a good landscaper as I watched her strike a downwards swing of her gleaming black sword. The sword's edge cut easily though a goblin's head, splitting it in two.

The two sides of the head split apart in slow motion, falling away as if they'd been glued together, badly. Brain matter, blood and gore spilled out onto the ground with a nasty splosh.

I turned back to my side and continued to shoot. The goblins were endless, notifications kept popping up on my HUD as I dropped one after another.

I felt my shots become more powerful as stats and levels rained in, mid battle.

As I shot another goblin in the chest, the arrow pierced all the way through and embedded itself in a tree. How had that happened? I wondered what stat had made such a drastic change in my power.

I didn't have time to dwell on it though and I wasn't complaining as I fired off arrow after arrow.

The goblins were beginning to pile up in front of the bush which worked in my favour as I had even more time to aim and shoot as they scrambled over their fallen foes.

Seeing their brethren reduced to little more than bubbling husks seemed to enrage them. The attacking goblins screamed louder and scrambled with more vigour.

It wasn't going to help them though; I was in the zone. This was my Alamo but hopefully without my death marking the end.

We were surrounded by what must have been an entire tribe, but we weren't going down easily.

I learnt early into the fight that the acid damage stacked up. It wasn't an instant killer, but it seemed so potent and shocking to the goblins that they didn't have time to attack before it burned through their flesh.

Because of that I only needed one hit per goblin. It was far from an insta kill but I felt I understood my powers a little bit more because of this realisation.

Behind me, Sally continued to cover the other three sides of the clearing. If I was doing well covering my single bush, she was a genius at covering the rest.

She hacked and slashed and cleaved her way through more goblins than I could count. The ground was slick with the blood of our enemies and there was barely any green left on the blood-soaked foliage.

My world turned red. I was covered head to toe in the spray of goblin blood, mostly from Sally's vicious attacks.

As I continued to cover my section of the clearing I felt unsteady all of a sudden. The ground began to shake and the goblins before me seemed to get a new burst of energy.

I couldn't ignore it, but there wasn't much I could do about it either it. The shaking must have come from somewhere, but I didn't have time to dwell on it as I continued my onslaught of arrows.

"Kaleb look out!" Panda screamed.

I hadn't thought about him since the battle had started, I wondered where he had been.

I turned towards the shouting just in time for the world to turn upside down. Something gigantic and strong gripped my leg hard and in a flash I was viewing the goblins the wrong way up.

One goblin pointed at me and laughed and I shot him in the face with an arrow. I'd had a tight grip on my bow so I hadn't dropped it.

I pulled myself up with my abs just in time to see the snarling face of the biggest goblin I'd ever seen.

It was an off green colour and honestly looked more like a troll. It had tusk-like fangs and yellow, jaundice eyes.

It screamed at me and I felt like I'd been caught up in a hurricane from the power of its breath. I was hit with a nauseating wave of rotten eggs and perpetual morning breath as my hair blew backwards so hard I thought I was going to lose it.

**You have discovered a unique monster:**
***Gertrude The Giant Goblin***

**Once upon a time there was a goblin named Gertrude. She was born just a little bit different from all the other goblins in her tribe. You see boys and girls, Gertrude was a biiiiig goblin.**
**All the other goblins were scared of her and they teased her, saying things like *Gertrude Smash* when she got angry.**
**Unfortunately for them, one day Gertrude did smash. She smashed the skulls of all those who bullied her in her youth, she smashed their kids too and extinguished entire family lines going back generations.**
**Then she smashed the goblin she had a crush on. Though it is unconfirmed if he liked her back, her**

friend Tiffany told her that she'd heard from her friend
Jane that the boy goblin had a thing for bigger ladies.
The rest is history, Gertrude continued to smash the boy
goblin and they had lots of baby goblins and started
their own tribe.
Though not a contender for the *Goblin King Coronation*,
Gertrude is a recognised power in the Forbidden Isles
and is unique in that her clan is comprised solely of her
own flesh and blood.
The same flesh and blood that you've just slaughtered
and delivered excruciating, acidic death to.
I think she's pissed... just a hunch.

As soon as the identification notification popped up I knew exactly what it had said. It was like the information had been uploaded straight to my brain.

I wondered if this was a battle feature, because if I had taken the time to read the long-winded history of Gertrude, I'd probably already be dead.

Instead, though, less than a second passed and as Gertrude's horrendous breath stung my eyes, I pulled up my bow and shot an arrow at her.

She howled as the arrow pierced her eyeball and it exploded like a gore filled balloon.

It splattered my face and some even got in my mouth. I didn't even have time to react before she threw me away with her massive arms.

I soared through the air and crashed into a tree, uprooting it, and knocking the thing over. My HUD flashed red and I clicked down on a basic health potion just before my HP reached 0.

My bow flew out of my hand and broke in two.

I crashed and tumbled into the foliage, fighting for breath. My torso exploded with pain and I was pretty sure I'd cracked all of my rips.

My leg had come out of its socket and dangled limply as I tried to push myself up from the ground.

I felt some of the ribs fix themselves with a painful crack as the health potion went to work, but it wasn't enough.

I was alive, but I was in bad shape with a useless leg, cracked ribs and less than a quarter of my HP remaining.

I got the distinct impression that I'd be dead if it wasn't for my quick thinking in using a potion when I did.

I heard a terrible shriek from back in the clearing. It deafened me and I felt fluid leak out of my ears as my health dropped slightly lower.

Suddenly I was overrun.

Goblins from all around the clearing trampled over me as they scattered like a herd of cattle. They were frantic, desperately trying to escape the clearing.

Was the scream sounding their retreat?

I didn't know and I didn't have time to think about it. I was being trampled to death. I struggled for air as the light above me faded and goblins ran over my broken ribs. Each step caused a shooting pain, the likes of which I'd never felt before, to course through my body like lightning bolts.

My HP was dropping fast and I couldn't take another healing potion for at least an hour. I needed to do something fast or I was going to die.

Thinking quickly, I ejected all 500 books I'd stolen from the cultist library out of my body at the same time.

The books sprang from all over me, piling up and leaving me both surrounded and buried in thick tomes.

It seemed to work. There were so many books all occupying the same place that the goblins moved around them, rather than risk tripping over the tall hillock of books.

They moved like water, taking the easiest path. The path of least resistance, and in less than a few seconds it was over and the jungle was eerily quiet.

I wasn't sure what made me think to use the books. I just needed something to shield me from the goblins and they were the thing I had in abundance.

I was so glad it worked I even let out a half-hearted, painful cheer as I laid in the dirt.

I wasn't going to be moving for a little while. My body was completely broken. I hoped Panda was alright, I was going to have to ask him where he'd been hiding the whole time.

With nothing else to do whilst I waited for the others to find me, I began to check my notifications. Sally must have killed Gertrude and I bet she gave off some serious experience points.

Chances were if I hadn't levelled as I fought I'd have died from her throw. I was lucky, but I also felt that I did a good job for my first battle.

I'd definitely say that covering that bush and killing all those goblins counted as pulling my weight.

Even Sally couldn't have predicted an onslaught like that, it was insane.

If this was what we had to look forward to for the rest of the quest I'd be lucky to make it out alive. But I'd also probably be a respectable level by the time we were done.

It was high risk, high reward.

And speaking of rewards, it was time to check my post battle notifications.

# Chapter 28
# Perception of the Apex Predator

I didn't lay in the dirt long before Sally and Panda found me. I heard their voices and called to them in a hoarse whisper.

Sally ran to me, kicked the books out of the way and looked over at me from above. She was covered from head to toe in blood and gore. She looked more like a monster than the goblins.

"I thought you'd died," she said with a fang-like smirk.

"Not yet, though I can't move and it'll be an hour before I can take another potion," I replied feebly.

Without a word she knelt down and picked me as if I were a princess. She carried me back into the clearing which by now was a cesspit of blood, gore, and corpses.

She set me down against a tree and Panda walked over to me, looking utterly disgusted at his blood-stained paws as he trapsed through the carnage.

"I'll loot the goblins whilst you heal, it should help with the smell," she said grimly.

She moved away and began the looting process. The goblins exploded into confetti this time, rather than silver bits.

In the middle of the clearing laid the eyeless corpse of Gertrude. Now I got a better look at her, she definitely did look more like a troll than a goblin.

Her lifeless husk was gigantic, standing at least 20 feet tall. It was no wonder she threw me away so easily, and so powerfully.

She wore nothing but a loincloth and her saggy green breasts were sliced open savagely. Her corpse was covered with deep cuts, meaning Sally had to slash her a few times to finish her off.

Panda finally reached me after treading as carefully as he could across the battlefield.

"You look like shit," he said with a smirk as he sat next to me.

"When did you become a red panda?" I asked.

He gave me a poignant look.

"Are you going to check your notifications or what? I bet you've levelled like crazy after that," he said.

I had been about to check them when Sally found me and since I needed to rest before I could take another potion I figured I may as well sort through the notifications.

It definitely had nothing to do with my child-like excitement for the coming levels.

**You have defeated Goblin Spearman:**
**(lvl 12) x13**
**(lvl 17) x9**
**(lvl 24) x2**
**(lvl 31) x1**

*Bonus experience awarded due to level disparity.*

Wow, that was a lot of goblins. I was surprised I'd killed so many. I hadn't stopped shooting for the whole fight and their corpses were piling up but that was still a lot of bodies.

"This is why I told you to pick the *Apex Predator* class," Panda said, "unique classes are always super powerful. You wouldn't have had a chance of killing that many without the bonus acid damage.

"They were also quite weak, or at least most were so that probably helped."

"Most of them were above my level so I'll take it," I replied back
cheerily. Honestly, I was just happy to have survived. "I wonder if I
got anything for helping to beat big Gertrude over there."

**You have assisted in the defeat of a unique monster:**
***Gertrude The Giant Goblin (lvl 35)***

***Bonus experience awarded due to level disparity.***

***Experience decreased due to lack of damage inflicted.***

"She was that tough?" I asked breathlessly.

"You should have seen Sally fight her. It was insane. She didn't
take a single hit, scoring slash after slash. That big goblin didn't
know what hit her," Panda replied animatedly.

I was happy to have done any damage at all to a monster that far
above my own level. If I'd have been alone I would have died for
sure.

It was time for the good part, I wanted to check my new level.

**Congratulations! You have advanced to lvl 15**
**Congratulations! You have advanced to lvl 16**
**Congratulations! You have advanced to lvl 27**

Holy crap! I'd gone up 13 levels in that fight. That was insane.
Though considering the sheer number of goblins I'd killed I could
see that the levels were starting to come slower.

Still, I was super happy. I now had 90 free points to allocate
including the 25 I'd got from killing the first goblin solo. I'd also
gained 247 stat points from my class. That was a huge boost.

Even with that huge boon the notifications weren't done.

*Bow* has advanced to lvl 7
*Bow* had advanced to lvl 8
*Bow* has advanced to lvl 10

**Due to *Bow* advancing to lvl 10 you can now choose a new combat skill.
Pick 1/2**

Perfect, I needed a new bow skill. Well, at the very least I really wanted one.

I noticed that my bow skill seemed to level a lot slower than my actual level. I wondered if it gained experience based on different parameters. Maybe it was linked more heavily to how I used the bow rather than the experience I got from defeating monsters. I couldn't be sure though.

There was still so much about levelling up and the system that I didn't understand.

Putting that aside for now, I greedily asserted yes and the notifications popped up.

I only got two choices this time though, but one of them did come with a rarity marker.

**New Skill:**
*Power Shot*

**Charge up an arrow before releasing to increase damage. Charging heavily consumes stamina.**

That one seemed like a standard gamer bow skill. It didn't come with a rarity but I was certain it would be pretty powerful.

Stamina was my highest stat so it would be a good choice.

"If you choose that one, you'll finally have an active skill," Panda observed.

It was tempting, an active skill would be useful in combat. Panda had said before that they were usually more powerful than passive skills.

But as I read the second notification, my decision became clear.

### New Skill:
### *Perception of the Apex Predator (rare)*

**Slow down time for a period determined by the amount of stamina you use on the skill. Cooldown is determined by the amount of stamina used on the skill.**

That was the one. There was no competition. Slowing down time seemed super OP. It also had my class name in the title so it had to be good right?

"What do you think?" I asked Panda.

"Get the rare one. Always get the rare one," he replied, imparting his sagely wisdom.

I agreed, so I mentally asserted yes.

I felt dizzy for a moment as an innate knowledge of how to use the skill flooded my mind. It wasn't like knowledge I'd actually learnt; I couldn't explain how to use it or the details.

But like muscle memory, I felt that I could tap into it and call on it without a struggle.

Despite my injuries I wanted to try it out. The notification said nothing about exclusive combat use and I had the feeling I could use it whenever.

I decided to tread lightly for the first time so I poured 10 stamina into the skill.

I looked towards Sally who was only a stone's throw away and as she took her next step her footfall paused. Then it hit the ground less than a fraction of a second later.

I could have blinked and missed the time change. This was going to take some practice and probably an insane amount of stamina to be useful.

I wondered how much I'd need to pour into it to get a full second. Judging from my test I was betting a lot. Possibly more than I currently had.

Still, it was a useful skill that would grow as I did. By the time I was Sally's rank I'd probably be able to get a few seconds out of it and that was nothing to sneeze at in a battle.

The battle in the clearing had only lasted about three minutes and I'd killed countless monsters and been thrown into a tree by Gertrude. So, a few seconds had the potential to seriously affect the outcome of a fight.

"Where do you think I should allocate my free points?" I asked Panda.

"Well, you've got like 90 of them, right? I'd probably put it all into vitality. You're an ok fighter but being taken out by one hit is a quick way to die.

"You don't want to be a glass cannon in this job. I know you probably want to throw it all at stamina, but your stamina levels up faster than your health anyway. Also, if you add all the free points to your health you'll gain 90 HP right now.

"That'll save us some time since your basic health potions won't put you back to full health. And, you know, it'll be almost an hour until you can even take one."

Considering his words I decided to trust his wisdom. He was my daemon after all, I had to take his advice at least some of the time, otherwise what was the point in summoning him?

I threw all my free points into vitality and immediately felt warmth flooding through my body. It was similar to the feeling I got when I took potions.

With a painful click that made me gasp, my dislocated leg clicked back into place. A few equally painful cracks and my ribs healed too.

My health was still low and I was covered in deep purple bruises on my chest. But nothing was broken anymore and the residual pain went away almost immediately.

My torn shirt was starting to thread itself back together as well thanks to self-repair. It was like watching a scab growing on your skin.

It was oddly therapeutic, if a little odd.

Before I got back to work, I decided to check my stats screen.

**Status Sheet:**

**Name: Kaleb Akabane**
**Race: Outworlder**
**Class: Apex Predator (unique)**
**Adventurer Rank: Temp**
**Level: 27**
**Map Pieces 2/10,000**
**HP: 97/271 (293)**
**Stamina: 73/255**

**Strength: 215**
**Agility: 103**
**Perception: 99**
**Vitality: 221 (243)**
**Intelligence: 34**

**Personal Skills:** *Speak English Damnit!, Eat Anything*
**Class Skills (Passive) Skills:** *Bow (lvl 10), Apprentice Bowman, Dagger (lvl 4), Acid Dhampir Dagger, Acid Arrows, Environmental Hazzard*
**Active Skills:** *Perception of the Apex Predator (rare)*
**Blessing:** *Blessing of Wealth*

## Familiars: *Panda (Daemon)*
## Admission: *Pentagram [Right hand (Morningstar Hotel and Spa)]*

The improvement was immediately apparent. HP was now my highest stat but my stamina was nothing to scoff at either.

I'd used quite a lot of it in the battle so ideally I'd need to take a few potions or rest up before we got into another one.

The 10% vitality buff I got from my *Boots of Resit Environment* were really starting to show their worth now. They gave me an extra 23 HP, that was quite literally the difference between life and death in the last battle.

I'd been at a measly 7 HP before I allocated my free points. If it wasn't for the boots I'd be dead right now.

I also noticed that I'd gained a new section down near the bottom of the stats. The active skills section had finally unlocked with my new, rare, time slowing skill added into the mix.

All in all, I felt like I was starting to become useful. Hopefully I'd be an even higher level by the time we finished the quest.

Sally had told me that most noob adventurers were around the level 30 mark, give or take. So, I was hoping to hit that by the end of this quest. And Panda, when I'd said my progress was amazing had poured scorn on me. Apparently, there were ranks to work on and something called a jade soul once you hit your level cap.

All temp adventurers had to undertake three quests before they qualified to take the exam. If the other newbies were all thirty when they started, then I'd have some catching up to do.

Assuming they each gained a level or two in each of their three mandatory quests, I'd need to be at least level 33 before the exam.

Ideally I'd be closing in on level 40.

After checking my stats I heaved myself up using the tree I'd been leaning on for support. Sally had just finished turning the last goblin into confetti and she walked towards me.

"You seem better, free points?" She asked.

I nodded. She was a seasoned, silver rank adventurer. Of course, she knew exactly how I'd healed so fast.

"Good, then let's get moving. I expect to be at the summit of the mountain by night fall. If we don't get there in time then we'll be spending the night in the jungle and this jungle gets scary dangerous at night."

"Ok, let's move," I replied.

"Also, I have some loot for you. You need a new bow since your other got smashed by the tree don't you?" she said with a fangy smile and a wink.

# Chapter 29
# Longbow of the Giant Goblin

Sally offered her hand out to me and produced a black bow with a sickly green tinge emanating from it.

I took it gladly and focused on it, causing the notification to pop up.

**You have received a new item:**
*Longbow of the Giant Goblin*

**This bow was carved from the forearm bone of a unique monster: *Gertrude the Giant Goblin*.**
**Just as she smashed her old clan into oblivion, you smashed her. You dirty bugger.**
**I mean, whatever tickles your pickle am I right?**
**I'm still judging you though.**

*Longbows can fire accurately over longer distances.*
*+5% strength*
*Grants use of the skill: Sniper*

**\*Sniper can only be used whilst this item is equipped\***

I desperately needed a new bow after my old one snapped in two from the impact with the tree. This one seemed far superior to my old one too.

+5% strength was a decent bonus and it came with a new skill. I wondered what the skill did.

I accepted the bow into my inventory and focused on it in there. The notification for the bow appeared, along with a further notification explaining the new skill.

### New Skill:
#### Sniper

**Not to be confused with sniping, the skill; *sniper* allows the user to see further distances. Like a telescope built into your eyes.**
**Don't go using it to creep on catonids whilst they're changing. I know you're a furry, but at least don't be a creep.**

"I am not a furry!" I said forcefully, looking up into the air.

Panda howled with laugher as I lamented the dickish system and its insulting notifications.

That aside, the skill was quite useful. It'd definitely help me take shots from further away, which I guess was the point.

I had no idea what sniping was, though I assumed it was dirty. It didn't matter, I'd received a new bow and it came with an attached skill.

I quickly checked my stamina and saw that it had increased by 10. It wasn't as good as the 10% vitality boon my boots gave me, but it was still 10 extra points for free.

"This is great! Thank you," I said to Sally who ignored me and continued walking.

As I followed her she said: "That's the only loot you're getting from that fight. Everything else was worthless, but a bow has no use for me. I'll have to sell the crap I looted when we get back."

"That's another thing about adventuring. Reward money is alright, but selling loot is the best way to make a living. You don't need much for general provisions but if you want to get better equipment you'll need more than most nobles.

"Good equipment is rare and therefore it costs a bomb. You probably noticed, but that quiver of yours was an inferior item and it still cost its weight in gold."

I had noticed the odd discrepancy between cost of living and adventurer equipment. It was like the difference between buying a loaf of bread or buying a car back home.

As she brought up gold I winced as I remembered my blessing of the god of wealth. I'd probably missed out on a small fortune by letting Sally loot everything.

I dropped back slightly to walk next to Panda.

"Should I tell Sally about my wealth blessing? We just missed out on a truck load of gold back there," I asked in a hushed whisper.

"I wouldn't. It's a great blessing but you got it from Chrysus. He's not well liked among the adventuring community, or anyone with a shred of morality really."

I nodded and picked up my pace to catch back up with Sally as she cleaved her way through dense shrubbery with her massive sword.

I wondered if she'd understand if I explained how I got the blessing. It wasn't like I'd asked for it, I didn't like the guy either.

It was kinda forced on me, and it was a good bargain. Who didn't like gold?

In the end I decided to keep it to myself for now. There would be other opportunities for me to loot things, if not on this quest, then on the other two.

We continued walk for a long time, mostly in silence. Slowly but surely the looming mountain came closer into view. It was a natural behemoth, towering above us and stretching out as far as the eye could see.

It still reminded me of a volcano, but I couldn't be certain of that. I'd never even seen one in real life, only on TV. Besides, for all I knew, volcanos didn't even exist in this world.

After a few hours of walking, I'd consumed both of the inferior potions I'd purchased, and two of the basic potions I'd been given in a loot box and my health was finally full.

I noticed that my HP increased slowly over time, at my best guess it refilled by about one point every ten minutes. That was painfully slow. I wondered if there was a skill that would make it go faster.

My stamina increased too, even though I was walking. It seemed to increase by roughly one point per minute so after a few hours it was past halfway.

There was so much to learn about the way my new body worked. The stats had the ability to give me superhuman strength. Potions healed broken bones like it was nothing.

Yet I could still break them, I could easily die. Stats were still taking some getting used to. I'd played video games before, who hadn't right? But I wasn't an avid gamer. I spent too much time at work.

Though I understood the concept of stats and had the common sense to guess what they did, I still wasn't overly confident with some of them.

"I can't believe you murdered all of those innocent books," Panda said suddenly, it was the first time any of us had spoken in a few hours. "All this walking is boring the shit out of me. You couldn't have even kept just a couple of them so I could do something whilst we walk?"

"Honestly, at the time I was seconds away from being crushed to death so the thought didn't really occur to me," I replied. "Next time I'm being crushed by a goblin horde I'll make sure to make your potential boredom my top priority."

"That's all I ask...I tried to save some of them you know?" He replied quietly. "But they were all tarnished, ripped, unsalvageable".

"I'll buy you some more when we get back." I relented. "At least I got a huge boost to my levels."

"Don't be too self-congratulatory, you still have a long way to go," Sally said, dropping back to walk at my side.

I looked at her and nodded. I knew she was right, but wasn't I allowed to be happy for myself, even just a little?

"Most people of this world hit the level 30 plateau by the time they're 18. Everything below that is still considered to be kid's levels," she smirked teasingly.

"Maybe so, but I'm not that far off and I've only been in this world a few days."

"True, but you have been fighting monsters which is the easiest way to level up. It's a phase two technique. Usually those below level 30 have never even seen a monster and gain their levels through apprenticeships and education," she replied.

As I watched her, I noticed her eyes scanned everything around us. She reminded me of a beast stalking its prey.

"What is phase two?" I asked, suddenly very confused.

"Oh yeah, I keep forgetting that you don't know anything. The levelling system is split into phases. Phase one encompasses levels 1 to 30. In this phase it's very easy to level up and you don't even need to fight monsters to gain the required experience.

"Phase two, levels 30 to 50, is harder and you either have to kill things or become very good as a professional. Phase three is levels 50 to 90. Most people on the island will never even reach this phase and those who do will usually be stuck in it unless they go to the continent.

"Phase three, for an adventurer at least, is all about killing high level monsters. You gain experience from the skill and difficulty it takes to slay them. You *can* grind through it like in phase two, but it'd take decades.

"Phase four is where I'm at now and I've been stuck at it for about a year. I haven't gone up a single level yet, though that could be because I haven't left the island since I was in phase three.

"Phase four is 90 – 100 and it's the wall that most never cross. Even on the continent it's rare for people outside of the Adventure Society to hit the level cap.

"There's also something called phase five that's apparently about beating the level cap but I don't know much about it yet. The director is supposed to be a phase five but I've never asked him about it."

That was a serious amount of information to take in all at once. I'd store it away for later. For now, the important thing to focus on was that it would get harder at level 30.

So, right now level 30 was my goal. I would reach it before the exam at the least. Maybe if I was lucky, I'd reach it by the end of this quest.

We didn't see a single other goblin for the rest of the day. It was eerily quiet in the jungle and Sally was certain there were more around.

The lack of contact put us all on edge. I got a feeling they were watching us, waiting to attack. But Sally said goblins aren't smart enough for that and I needed to get out of my own head.

Eventually, after about five hours of walking in mostly silence. We reached the foot of the mountain. It was so big that I couldn't see the top or the sides from where I stood.

It was a bit of an odd mountain in that it started very suddenly. One moment you were stood on soil in a jungle and then bam, a mountain like a brick wall was there.

It looked as if it had been ripped from a different place entirely and was dropped on the Forbidden Isle.

Sally grabbed me and threw me over her shoulder. She picked up Panda by the scruff of the neck to his vulgarly phrased protests.

"What are you doing?" I asked, much less calmly that I would have liked.

In lieu of answering she squatted down, and I felt a circulating and pulsing power through her skin. I couldn't put my finger on what it was exactly, but it felt strong, feral even.

"Don't you dare!" Panda shouted.

I looked at his panicked face just in time for her jump. And when I say jump, it was more like a rocket taking off.

"Fuck!" Panda screamed.

We were above the trees in seconds and I saw a platform on the mountain which was now below us. We landed with a crash and then Sally let me down.

I felt dizzy and disoriented, but the whole ordeal was over quick which was… something.

As my head finally stopped spinning, I had a quick look around the area. Embedded into the mountain before us was a huge, iron door.

"I'm guessing we have to go in there?" I asked.

"We certainly do," Sally replied with a devilish smile and battle drunk eyes. "There are still a few hours of light left. We'll scout out the interior then retreat and make camp here for the night."

Before giving us a chance to reply, Sally stepped up to the huge iron doors. They were intricately carved, depicting a goblin sitting on a throne with a crown of light hovering above its head.

I was getting some serious dungeon vibes.

Sally pushed on the doors and they swung open inwardly.

Nervously, I followed her inside.

# Chapter 30
# The Gob Gob Tribe

You are now entering a safe zone.

*WARNING*
All combat is prohibited inside this safe zone. No
damage will be inflicted. Any breach of these rules will
result in punishment.

We entered through the large iron doors and I was immediately hit with a notification. This area was a safe zone.

That was weird, I was expecting a dungeon. The ominous warning about receiving punishment for attacking worried me.

Immediately inside the doors was a narrow cave tunnel lit by floating balls of light that littered the walls. It looked a bit like the runway at an airport and I got the feeling the light was guiding us somewhere.

"A safe room," Sally mused. "This is unusual. Stay on your guard and let's go deeper in."

I nodded and stuck close behind her with Panda hot on my heels. He didn't say anything but I could practically feel the unease reverberating inside of him.

We walked down the narrow cave tunnel for a short while. I had my new bow summoned into my hand and my inventory ready to summon my dagger at a moment's notice.

If we were attacked in here, I was unlikely to get a good shot off before they reached us. The tunnel was simply too narrow for effective ranged attacks.

However, it didn't take long before the cave opened up and we arrived in a carved-out chunk of it. It was a small, stone room with high, flat walls.

It was definitely manmade or, goblin made? As we stepped further in the dim light of the glowing balls faded and bright, ceiling orbs came to life all around us.

With the room well-lit we could see to the end of it, where a small archway was carved into the stone, leading deeper in.

Just before the archway and to the side of it was a wooden desk. A goblin sat there, fiddling with a dagger, and looking bored.

She was dark green and her face was less bulbous than the goblins we'd fought earlier. She looked up as Sally drew her weapon and approached.

"You can't fight in here. The punishment will activate dumbass. Didn't you read the safe zone notification." The goblin spoke like she thought she was a gangster.

She rested her head in her slim hands and glared up at us with a bored expression.

Something about her demeanour seemed different from the other goblins I'd encountered. She spoke surprisingly well and she looked less... gross.

I focused on her and a notification appeared.

**You have discovered a new monster:**
*Higher Goblin*

Now, I know it says higher in the title but don't go thinking these guys deserve rights or anything. A higher goblin is the evolved form of the various other types of goblin.
Through diligent training and level hunting they've acquired intelligence due to their stats.
And when I say intelligence, I mean they're less likely to scream and grunt – but only slightly.
Goblins are like that stereotypical southern trailer trash guy you went to high school with: just because he *can* speak doesn't mean he won't fuck his cousin.
As part of the evolution process, *Higher Goblins* start to look a little less gross and a little more human.
That doesn't mean you should sleep with them though.
Goblin AIDS are no joke!

I wished I could say that the notification cleared everything up, but it was mostly just bad jokes about incest and AIDS. Reading it felt like watching an episode of *South Park* but without the hilarity.

I did learn some information though. She was likely a high level, which meant she was dangerous. The system had basically said that goblins evolved when they reached a high enough level.

Considering the boss monster we fought in the woods; I wondered if this higher goblin was an even higher level.

*Thank God it's a safe zone.* I thought.

"We're here for the coronation," Sally said without dropping her sword.

"Well duh," the higher goblin replied as she moved onto trimming her nails like a bored receptionist. "You're cutting it a bit late though; it's being held tomorrow night. Most of the other clans have been here for a week already.

"Which clan are you with?"

"We're not with a-" Sally began, but before she could finish Panda stepped out front and spoke over her.

"We're a delegation from the Gob Gob Tribe," he said confidently.

Sally opened her mouth, staring dumbstruck at the Panda. I placed a calming hand on her shoulder and shook my head slightly when she looked at me.

It was worth seeing what he was trying to do. I didn't know if safe zones could be revoked for certain guests and I was starting to wonder if this was like a *DnD* campaign where there were lots of ways to complete it.

Panda had obviously opted for the charisma check approach and I figured it was worth seeing it play out.

"The Gob Gob? Oh yeah… you don't look much like goblins," she said sceptically, eyeing the three of us up suspiciously.

"We're from the eastern continent, it's just a racial difference. I assure you that we are all from the tribe. We've travelled a long way and we're tired from our journey," he replied instantly.

*He's pretty good at this.* I thought, not taking my eyes off the *Higher Goblin.*

"Fine whatever, I'll add you to the guest list then I guess. Go on through, there's a spare room you can use on the third floor. Party starts tomorrow morning so you probably want to rest up.

"I don't know how they do it where you're from, but we go hard down here. Dusk till dawn, you get me?"

Panda thanked her and we wearily walked through the archway. Sally gave her the stink eye the entire time, refusing to sheath her sword. But the goblin didn't seem to pay any attention to her.

The archway led into a short, cobbled corridor with a spiral staircase at the end. It went both up and down. We'd been told we had a room on the third floor though so it made sense to head up for now, which we did.

"The Gob Gob Tribe?" I snickered at Panda as we climbed the stairs.

Sally still had her sword drawn and was carefully watching around every corner. My bow, however, hung loosely in my hand for now.

"What?" he replied incredulously. "It's a real goblin tribe from the eastern continent. Try reading a book some time, it might cure that stupidity you've got going on."

"That was some quick thinking back there Furball," Sally said quietly. "Now, if we're careful, we might be able to get right up to the king candidates before we get attacked. Assassination isn't really my style but with you two here I'm willing to take whatever advantages we can get."

It was the most she'd spoken since she'd lectured me about ranks back in the woods. She was a quiet and professional adventurer when we were working. A stark contrast to her out of work persona.

After a short climb we reached the end of the line. We hadn't seen any other floors on the way up, but I had to assume that this was the third floor.

That must have meant we entered on the second and the first was below us.

The spiral staircase opened out into a well-lit foyer with a balcony at the back and a few rooms on either side. I had no idea which room was ours.

Once again there was a little desk with a strange goblin manning it. This one dressed in a scarlet bellhop's uniform with golden trimming. He was quite concerning to look at with oversized ears and an oval head.

He quite literally looked like someone had shoved a green American football on top of a headless Halloween decoration.

Panda approached him, that charismatic swagger he displayed downstairs coming back to him.

"Good evening, we were told that a room was ready for us on the third floor, could you show us which one it is?" He asked, putting on a snooty, gentleman's accent.

It was quite a change from his usual drawl which reminded me of a South Jersey accent.

The goblin looked at us with a gormless face. Then, without a word, it turned towards the furthest door on our left and pointed.

He moved a bit like a zombie, it was weird. I quickly focused on him and found out that he was a regular goblin. Apparently, they didn't do much in safe zones.

Due to their aggressive and unintelligent nature the system had to make them practically catatonic to prevent them from attacking guests and facing the mysterious punishment.

Before heading to the room, Sally wanted to look over the balcony. She said it could be useful for scouting the place out.

She was right.

The three of us peered over the edge of the stone rail that hemmed the opera-like balcony. It looked directly over what appeared to be a ballroom.

I'm not joking.

A full on, aristocratic, classic manga trope ballroom. Except it was filled with goblins.

They stood around drinking wine and chatting like socialites. At the far end of the ballroom was a large, golden throne that reminded me of the throne in the cultist temple.

I really hoped we weren't going to face a god. That was the last thing I needed. To be smited by some arrogant asshole who thought he was all that was not how I wanted to go out.

"What the hell is going on here," Sally said, finally lowering her sword and staring with an open mouth at the scene below us.

"I think it's a ball Sal," Panda said. "That's what posh people go to cause they're too snooty to drink in bars like you and me."

*Since when had he called her Sal? They seemed awfully chummy.*

"Call me Sal again and I'll throw you over the side," she replied threateningly.

*Never mind.*

"I guess that's why it's a safe zone," I said. "We're probably going to have to attend the party and talk to them to find out who the candidates are. Then we'll have to kill them."

"Don't forget about the punishment. There must be more to it. Something we're not seeing," Sally replied. "Anyway, for now let's check out this room and try and get some rest."

She left and we followed her through the door the goblin bellhop had pointed out to us. To my surprise, he was still pointing at it, immobile.

The system must have made him absolutely catatonic.

Inside, the room looked much the same as the one I'd rented at the inn back in Havar.

It pretty much contained two single beds and a toilet room. Not that we really needed anything else.

Sally claimed the bed closest to the door, something I was happy to let her have. Safe zone or not, if something did attack us in our sleep, I'd rather she was the one dealing with it.

Besides, she was probably stronger than anything in this place so it wouldn't even be a threat to her.

Sally sat on the bed and pulled out, what seemed to be, a magic camping stove from her inventory.

She touched it and a faint blue light flowed from her hand causing a little flame to appear on the top.

"Shame you have no mana, mana stoves are like the first thing I'd recommend a new adventurer buy," she said absently as she pulled some meat out of her inventory and began cooking it on the stove.

It seemed that meat didn't go off inside her inventory. If that was the same for me it would be useful, though I couldn't rule out the possibility of it being a skill.

With her carnivorous tendencies it wouldn't surprise me at all if she'd purposely acquired a skill specifically to stop meat spoiling.

Just as the outside of the meat was turning brown and my mouth was watering from the smell, there was a knock at the door.

# Chapter 31
# The Goblin King Ball

Sally immediately summoned her weapon. She usually kept it on her back and drew it the old-fashioned way, I had no idea why but it certainly looked threatening.

This was the first time I'd seen her summon it instead.

She jumped from the bed, like it was a springboard, and I followed her lead, summoning my bow.

"You guys are too jumpy. It's a god damned safe zone, what do you think is gonna happen?" Panda laughed sauntering towards the door.

To Sally's horror he opened the door casually and stood in front of our visitor. It was a skinny and tall goblin wearing priest-like robes and a pair of glasses that were too narrow for its large head.

"Pardon the intrusion," the goblin began, holding both hands together in front of its chest like a grovelling peasant. "But I thought it would be prudent of me to introduce myself. My name is Gobtta and I belong to the order of priests in service to the goblin king coronation ball committee.

"I just wanted to welcome you to the celebration. If you need anything during your time here please don't hesitate to ask."

Sally and I both stared dumbfoundedly at Gobtta, she lowered her sword and I my bow. This goblin seemed about as threatening as a kitten – if that kitten had no fur and wore ill-fitting spectacles.

I focused on him and saw that he was a higher goblin, so perhaps he was more dangerous than his demeanour would suggest.

"Thanks for that Gobtta, nice to meet you," Panda said, offering out his paw to shake.

Gobtta jumped back in fright as he looked down at Panda, standing by the doorway. He hadn't seemed to realise that the daemon was standing there.

*A goblin with a nervous disposition? He must get bullied.* I thought as I felt my lips twitch as I stifled laughter.

"Do you have an itinerary for tomorrow?" I asked suddenly.

It had occurred to me that this was a great opportunity to get some much-needed information out of him. We were currently stumbling around in the dark with this quest and gaining some insight into how this whole coronation worked could be useful.

"Of course, sir, it's a verbal itinerary though if that pleases you. Most of our guests can't read," he said, bowing slightly.

I told him that would be fine and he began reciting the day's events. Starting with morning socialising and ending with the crowning ceremony. We talked late into the night until we'd squeezed every droplet of information out of Gobtta.

Then a few hours after he'd arrived Panda filled out a form, passed it back to the nervous goblin and we bade him goodnight.

I fell asleep the moment my head hit the pillow in the safe zone bedroom. I wasn't too physically tired but it turned out that mentally I was exhausted.

It had been a long day. I'd levelled up a bunch, killed some goblins, nearly been trampled to death by said goblins, been thrown through a tree by a giant goblin and received a new bow and skills

– not necessarily in that order. If things continued it wouldn't be long before I could say that it was *just another Tuesday.*

That night I had an oddly lucid dream.

***

I was back in my hometown, walking home after a few beers with the boys. It wasn't late, barely half past ten in the evening.

We tended to have a lads meet every month or two. We saw each other all the time because our wives were friends too, but sometimes it was good to have a catch up without them.

I walked up my street in the typical English drizzle and shakily put the key in the lock to my front door. I lived with my wife in a small semi-detached house in some no name town on the outskirts of the city.

It was peaceful there most of the time and managing to get on the property ladder by the age of 28 was quite a feat these days. Not that I hadn't worked my ass off for it.

When I opened the door all the lights were out. Layla must have gone to bed already. That was odd, she was usually a bit of a night owl.

I walked inside and stepped in something that splashed up my legs.

*What in the…*

Had there been a water leak or something? I reached for the light switch and as the hallway light flickered into illumination, I found myself ankle deep in blood. The entire downstairs seemed to be flooded.

I let out a gasp and dashed into the living room. What on earth had happened? Was she ok? Was the baby ok? I reached the living room door, which was barely a few steps away, and burst in.

There she was, laying on the ground with a spear through her stomach.

I felt my eyes begin to tear up, but not as fast as an infernal rage coursed through me.

A cultist stood over her with a malicious grin on his face and a piece of tattooed skin in his hand. He grinned maliciously and his eyes twinkled with an evil satisfaction.

I pulled my dagger out of my inventory and before I even knew what I was doing, charged like a snarling boar. I tackled him to the ground, driving my knees into his chest as I stabbed the dagger into his face over and over until it was nothing more than bloody pulp and crushed bone.

After a while of stabbing, my arms began to feel weak and the tears caught up to the rage. I began sobbing uncontrollably and breathing heavily.

I looked back towards my wife as she lay half submerged in the blood. Her face was so pale, she looked…peaceful.

Eventually I dragged myself off the cultist's corpse and moved towards her. Her eyes were still open. The spark of life that once illuminated them, extinguished like a candle flame in the wind.

I went to close them. It was respectful. She was at rest now and most people don't sleep with their eyes open.

"Layla," I whispered as my fingers brushed over her eyelids. "I'm so sorry."

I sat like that for a while. Staring down at her face and crying. Until something out of the corner of my eye caught my attention.

Her stomach moved; the skin looked like it was alive as something poked at it from the inside.

*Oh no. Please don't.*

Two tiny, clawed hands poked out through the spear wound and began tearing at her skin. I was horrified as I watched it happen, like a deer in headlights.

A blood covered; monstrosity began to climb out of her. It had an umbilical cord wrapped around its neck, its face was purple and bruised and its lips were peeled back revealing pointed, shark-like teeth.

Eventually, to my horror, it made its way out and stood up on stumpy legs with too much skin for the size of its bones. It picked up the spear, wrenching it out of Layla's gut and stared at me with venom in its sunken eyes.

It lifted the spear and I was frozen. I sat there, tears dripping down my face as I let the monstrosity stab me through the heart.

"I'm so sorry," I whispered.

*If you want to save them you need power.* A familiar voice said as I laid dying next to my wife. *I can help you.*

\*\*\*

I woke up with a start, gasping as I sat up straight like a man possessed. I must have looked like something from a horror movie.

I was drenched in sweat and shaking. *What was that? That dream... it was so vivid. Whose voice was that at the end?*

My face felt wet and I lifted my hand to my cheek and realised I had been crying. Sleep crying, now that was a new experience.

For the first time since I'd arrived in Celestia I didn't feel refreshed after waking up. I felt awful, just like I used to do on a morning back on Earth but without caffeine to perk me up.

I looked around the room and saw Sally fast asleep in her bed next to mine. Panda was laid at my side, sprawled out on his back with his arms and legs splayed as he snored like a chainsaw.

I focused on my breathing and began to calm down. It was just a nightmare. Probably the result of refusing to think about Layla and the baby for so long.

*In through the nose, out through the mouth.* I chanted to myself in my head. If I just focused on my breathing, I'd be ok.

I knew it had been gnawing at the back of my mind but I was so busy trying to survive that I'd pushed it away.

Still, I felt guilty. I could explain it away as much as I liked, this world was hard, dangerous and every day was a fight to survive. But at the same time, I felt more alive here than I ever did back home.

I was enjoying it and I felt so terribly guilty about that.

I hunkered down under the covers and laid awake for the rest of night. I didn't want to risk sleeping. What if it happened again?

I stayed like that for a few hours, hugging myself under the duvet, until morning finally came and I pretended to wake up with the others.

I needed to put my game face on. Today was the day we finished this quest and I needed to be at my best. So, I forced a smile, said good morning and the three of us headed out with Sally and Panda none the wiser.

Still, I wondered whose voice that was. Just before I woke up, I heard it like someone was talking into my mind. It felt so familiar to me but I just couldn't place it.

I tried to push the thought away as we got dressed and left our room.

"Right guys, is everyone clear on the plan?" Sally asked as we exited.

Panda and I both nodded and we walked past the goblin bellhop who was still stood pointing at our door. He must have been like that all night.

It was kind of creepy. If he wasn't a vicious, unintelligent monster I'd have felt sorry for him. As it was, it was kind of funny. Like we had our own, living signpost just in case we forgot where our beds were.

"You look awful," Panda said quietly to me. "Did you sleep ok?"

"Just worried about the quest," I replied. I couldn't allow the nightmare to distract me, not today.

He grumbled quietly to himself. I wasn't sure he believed me, but at least he was smart enough to leave it alone.

We began walking back down the spiral staircase. Sally had her sword on her back. I didn't summon my bow this time, there was no point.

After our conversation with Gobtta, we were certain that no one would attack us until after the king was crowned.

We walked past the entrance on the second floor we'd used the day before and continued heading down.

"I wonder if the food will be any good," Panda mused. "I'm starving."

"The hosts are goblins, just chew on some bamboo like you normally do," I replied.

"I'd love to but I ran out."

At that both Sally and I stopped and stared at him.

"How? It's only been a day since we left the ship!" I said and Sally said something almost identical at the same time.

"The only thing to eat on the ship was meat and I'm a Panda. I've been using my own supplies since we left Havar," he replied indignantly.

"That's still only two days," I replied in disbelief. "You packed enough of the stuff to last a week; we all did."

"Well, I got hungry…and I ate it all already."

"What are you gonna do if the goblins only serve meat?" Sally asked.

"Then I'll have to do as the goblins do I guess, well it's that or starve."

"I thought you said you were a vegetarian?" Sally asked in a suspicious tone.

"And I thought Pandas were herbivores," I added.

"I am and we are. But we're also a very hungry people and desperate times call for desperate measures. Hopefully they'll serve salad though, it is a ball."

"A goblin ball," I pointed out.

We continued walking in silence and eventually made it to the bottom of the spiral staircase.

It led to a short hallway with a grand archway at the end. I walked towards it and entered the ball.

*The final boss battle awaits.*

# Chapter 32
# You Can't Sit with Us

We walked through the grand archway into a place that reminded me of a Viking Hall. There were long, wooden tables that stretched the length of the room.

Fires lit the sides, emitting a smoky atmosphere which reminded me of going to the pub with my mum before the smoking laws changed back home.

At the far end sat a large golden throne and a small group of well-dressed goblins stood near it chatting. Most of the goblins were on, or around, the long tables.

They drank a red coloured liquid which could either have been wine or blood. It was hard to tell, them being goblins and all.

The tables were filled with large loafs of steaming bread, something resembling chicken wings, and towering piles of red meat. There wasn't a vegetable in sight.

"Sorry mate, looks like they're carnivores." I said to Panda as we entered the room.

"Well, I guess it's to be expected. Goblins aren't exactly cultured and only animals are uncultured enough to live on meat alone," he sighed.

"Watch it!" Sally hissed at him, throwing him a dirty look with her predatorial eyes.

"You're literally a half cat. Where's the insult?" He retorted.

"I'll have you know I'm a civilised and complicated lady."

We both cracked up at that and her eyes shot daggers at us as I clutched my stomach.

We walked along the side of the longest table and Sally grabbed a few chicken wings to go. The goblins mostly ignored us. Though some of them did glance in our direction, speaking in whispers as we passed by.

It reminded me of high school.

Panda squeezed in between two goblins at the table, grabbing a chunk of bread and tearing into it. He wasn't really needed for this part of the plan but I didn't want him to sit alone with the enemy.

Luckily for me, a small goblin with a high-pitched voice sorted that issue for me almost immediately.

"You can't sit with us!" She said as a few of her goblin pals stared at him.

Rolling his eyes he got up and left, but not before taking the entire loaf of bread with him, much to their dismay.

The thick smoke from the fires all around us stung my eyes as we headed for the throne. There were log fires, scattered around the hall, and the smoke they emitted smelled particularly strong, blinding my sense of smell to anything else.

I couldn't quite place the smell, but it was almost herbal. Definitely not the smell one expected from a log fire.

Though, considering the company we were in, that probably wasn't a bad thing. Goblins weren't exactly known for their hygiene and herbal smoke was a damn sight better than goblin stank.

As we reached the throne the four well-dressed goblins stood before it turned to greet us.

"Ah, do we have another contender?" the first one asked.

He was a short goblin with a body shape more reminiscent of a dwarf: stout and muscular with a beer belly. He had a huge double headed axe on his back that was taller than he was.

*I wonder if there are dwarves in this world?* I thought absently as I looked him up and down.

He wore a nobleman's jerkin in a ruby red colour, and black pants. He didn't wear shoes though; I don't think goblins used them. Their feet *were* rather large.

"Don't make me laugh Gerald!" Another goblin said in a very deep voice. "They're not goblins, how could they be contenders for the throne?" He snorted and chuckled to himself.

This goblin was much taller, coming up to my upper chest. He was dressed the same as Gerald but he wore all black and his jerkin was embellished with convoluted embroidery.

He had a bow on his back which I guess made sense considering his stature. I found myself feeling a little competitive when I looked at him.

"Poppycock Giles," Gerald began, "Of course they're goblins! They couldn't have even gotten in here if they weren't."

"We're actually from the Gob Gob tribe," I interrupted, stealing Panda's lie from the previous day. "It's on the eastern continent so we look a little different to you westerners."

"See Giles, they're foreigners, that's all," Gerald said, as if my bullshit explanation explained away the fact that we were clearly not goblins.

"Well foreigners can't compete either," Giles moaned. "It's against tradition. We've held this contest amongst ourselves for eons, why would we break tradition for them now?"

"Now, now settle down Giles you old prude," a fat goblin said from behind them.

He was short and very fat. He was almost as wide as he was tall, a chode of a goblin if I ever saw one. He wore a green jerkin and had a mace hanging at his side. The spiked metal thing on the top was covered with dripping blood.

"Oh of course you'd take his side!" Giles complained. "You've got your head so far up his ass you can see through his mouth."

"That's enough!" The final goblin said. "You can sort out your petty squabbles in the arena. Besides, your bickering is making my ears bleed."

The final goblin was muscular. He barely even looked like a goblin; He looked more like a male counterpart for Sally if anything. Except he was green and he had a bushy white beard.

I got a bad feeling from him which doubled when I saw that he wielded a giant sword, just like Sally did. He looked oddly human apart from the skin colour. Perhaps that was why Panda's lie was working, either that or goblin intelligence was unusually low.

"Sally look, he's just like you!" Panda cried. "Maybe you should go on a date or something. You could talk about steroid abuse and the obviously compensatory weapons you like so much," Panda snickered, he seemed to have made the same connection I did, but I wasn't suicidal enough to say it out loud.

Sally, however, didn't say a word. Her fist moved so fast that neither Panda nor I saw it until it made contact with the top of his skull. If this was a cartoon a line of ducks would have circled his head.

He swayed for a moment but stayed on his feet, he looked dazed and then he abruptly apologised. It must have hurt.

"Listen boys," Sally began, walking forward and towering over all but the big guy. "I'm entering this competition. I spoke with Gobtta last night and he said it was perfectly within the rules. Any problems with that?" She added in a menacing tone as she eyed each of them in turn, flashing her fangs as her predatorial eyes bored into them.

"No," the first three squeaked in unison.

The big guy didn't respond at all, which I took to mean he approved.

The first part of the plan was completed.

The previous night when Gobtta knocked on our door he told us about the competition. It was a tournament to find the strongest among the clans.

It was a tradition among the goblins. Each clan would put forward their strongest warrior in a battle royale to see who was the toughest.

We'd planned to have Sally enter the tournament under the guise of being sent by the Gob Gob Tribe for that very purpose.

It was the only way we could think of to circumvent the safe zone rules, as the competitors were allowed to attack each other as long as they did so in the arena.

I wouldn't be able to help her without incurring punishment myself, not that she'd need my help. She was strong enough to take down Gertrude the Giant Goblin in just a few hits so I doubt I would have helped much anyway.

It was a shame though. Just looking at Giles filled me with bloodlust. He was an archer and I wanted to pit my skills against his. Also, he was an asshole.

"Great," Sally continued after no one objected. "In that case, where's this arena so we can get started?"

"It's over there," Gerald began, pointing to a small hallway just off the side of the main hall. "But the competition doesn't start until tonight."

"Oh, I get it," Sally began in a taunting voice. "You cowards need till nightfall so you can get drunk enough to think you stand a chance against me, is that it?"

"How dare you!" Giles said, and I couldn't help but join in myself. The sight of him made my blood boil for some reason.

"Shut up, you lanky green fuck," I said, crossing my arms and standing next to Sally. "I can tell you're a coward just by looking at you. I bet you couldn't hit the side of a barn with that bow."

"How... how dare you sir! I demand satisfaction."

And I swear to God, he actually pulled out a white glove and threw it at the ground in front of me. That really happened.

"I'll take you on any time, any place beanpole," I retorted.

I didn't know what was wrong with me, but the mere sight of the guy made my blood boil for some reason. I wanted nothing more than to pound him into the ground in front of all his friends.

The raucous chatter from the room abruptly stopped. The entire hall of goblins turned to look at us in complete and utter silence.

Then a notification flashed up on my HUD and I grinned.

*Ask and the system shall provide.*

**You have accepted a dual whilst inside a safe zone.
The safety features will be turned off for you and
[Goblin Giles] in 30 seconds. You may only attack each
other during this time. Any attempt to harm others
within the safe zone will result in punishment.**

"If you saw that notification then I'm sure you now understand what a grievous mistake you've made by challenging me," Giles said, placing his hands on his hips. "However, I am a gracious goblin and if you get down on your knees and beg me for mercy I might just grant it."

"I had your mum down on her knees and begging last night, but it wasn't for mercy," I replied and both Panda and Sally snorted in unison.

"What's come over you all of a sudden?" Panda asked, nudging my leg as he stifled his giggling. "This isn't like you at all."

"I don't know but I can't help myself. Looking at this guy just makes my blood boil," I replied, clenching my fist as the mere thought of him pissed me off.

"I think it's the fire smoke," Sally answered ponderously, stroking her chin as she thought. "It smells like it's infused with wild takka berries, probably to keep the smell mild. In high doses they're known to send people berserk.

"Assassins used to use them in blowpipes to make their enemies attack each other. It doesn't seem to be affecting anyone else though, it might have something to do with your race."

Well, that was unfortunate. I had been drugged and I didn't even know it. Not that knowing it made me want to back down in the slightest.

"Alright then pipsqueaks," the big goblin began. "I want this nice and clean. You'll stand at opposite ends of the room and when I say so, you each get to take one shot at the other, and I mean *one* shot." He eyed us both in turn.

Giles drew his bow and stepped down off the platform by the throne and I walked to the opposite end near the entrance, drawing my own.

The big guy moved into the middle and we each drew and nocked an arrow.

This was going to be interesting. I wondered how good of a shot he was. The big guy didn't say we had to stand still and take it either, this wasn't a cowboy shootout after all.

With that in mind I cleared my thoughts of everything apart from hitting my target.

"Ready?" the big goblin asked.

I nodded and took a deep breath as I drew the string. I started letting it out slightly as I aimed for Giles.

"Go!" He shouted and stepped back out of the way.

I immediately activated my new skill: *Perception of the Apex Predator,* using most of my stamina. I knew I'd have merely a fraction of a second before time sped back up but it should be the edge I'd need to make sure I fired first.

I loosed my arrow, aiming straight for his chest. I didn't need a headshot to kill him when I had acid powers. I just needed to land a good hit on the centre mass and my class would do the rest... hopefully.

My arrow rocketed from my bow and soared across the room. Every goblin in the room had turned to watch and it was completely silent.

My arrow hit its mark, tearing through Giles' jerkin as he screamed in a high-pitched voice and fell backwards onto the ground before being able to fire off his own shot. Some of the crowd members laughed at him and I grinned.

My victory was assured. I was the better archer and now everyone in the whole room knew it.

Giles went down before even firing a shot. I started to walk back towards the throne and my friends.

"Oi, what do you think you're doing. You don't get to move from that spot until someone dies or you've both taken a shot!" The big goblin shouted, a large vein pulsing on the side of his forehead.

I looked at him, stunned for a moment and then pain exploded in my neck as Gile's arrow tore through my throat.

# Chapter 33
# It's Not Joking If Nothing You Say Is Funny

I gagged and gasped for breath that wouldn't come as my windpipe was torn by the surprise arrow. I'd been careless. Turning away from my opponent before the kill notification came was a rookie error.

My health had taken a nosedive from the single hit, I had less than a quarter of my HP remaining. The fact that I was even alive after taking a hit like that was remarkable and was a testament to the power of stat points.

My HP was dwindling, lowering more and more by the second as the arrow stuck out of both sides of my throat. I bet I looked like Frankenstein's monster.

I found my health potions in my inventory and clicked on one.

**\*WARNING\***
***You cannot use potions during a duel, don't be a bad sport.***

"Shit!" I shouted, or at least I tried to shout it. What came out of my mouth was more akin to angry gargling.

Beginning to panic I looked towards Giles. He was laid on his back and looking worse for wear. His breathing was laboured and far louder than normal. It sounded like bubbling water as he fought for breath through the acid which ravaged his chest cavity.

From the looks of things, he'd literally pulled himself into a sit-up to fire off the shot and then fallen straight back down.

If my line of thinking was right, I'd have to outlast him in order to win the duel and survive. Once he died I could take a potion. So, our little duel had become a life-or-death battle of wills.

I looked him over, seeing the pained expression on his face as the skin on his chest bubbled. It was disgusting and it looked like his skin was sinking, caving his chest in as the acid melted the bone.

It truly was a horrible way to die. I was glad it was my power and not his.

The pain in my neck was excruciating. I couldn't breathe and if I swallowed I'd tear my flesh even more. I don't know if you've ever noticed this, but as soon as you realise you can't swallow, you really, really want to.

It's like having a staring competition. People don't realise how hard it is to not blink until they're focusing on it.

That's exactly what was happening to me, but with swallowing. I knew that if I allowed myself to swallow, my Adam's apple would move up my neck, bringing the lodged arrow with it and tearing into even more of my throat.

I continued staring at Giles as I struggled with my base urge to swallow. Perhaps I could use psychological warfare to make him die faster.

The idea was simple: he was on the ground suffering whilst I stood up, straight faced.

I stared at him, putting on my best bored look, as I folded my arms. He'd never know the excruciating pain and internal struggle I was going through. Not if I kept a straight face.

He, on the' other hand, looked dreadful. He could barely keep his eyes open as the acid melting his chest cavity began spreading to other areas.

Soon he'd be a pile of goo, staining the floor of the banquet hall. I just needed to hold out long enough for him to die in the process.

My health continued to drop, but it was much slower than I'd expected. The power of stats was really something. Back on earth I doubted anyone could survive an arrow to the gullet.

We stared at each other for a while, the entire hallway was deathly silent. I wondered if they understood the intensity of the battle of wills we were having.

My HP eventually dropped down to 3/271 and I struggled to stay on my feet. I stared at Giles the entire time with a bored expression and crossed arms, but internally, I knew I was dying.

I didn't have long left.

But he looked worse. After what felt like the world's longest staring match, Giles finally lost the ability to keep his head up and dropped to the floor. A few seconds later a notification popped up and I immediately hammered down on a health potion.

My HP shot up and the arrow got pushed out the side of my throat. It was an awful experience as it slowly moved through my gullet and dropped away. Choking me both literally, and because of the excruciating pain it caused, the entire time.

Sally and Panda rushed towards me as I gasped for breath and put my hands to my neck, feeling around the wounded area. It was like I had a phantom arrow lodged in my throat. It was gone, but I could still feel it like it was really there.

"You're a reckless fool, I should have never allowed you to duel that guy!" Sally shouted, slapping me on the back of the head like I was a badly trained dog.

"I knew you'd win," Panda said cooly, patting me on the lower back.

Sally shook her head and turned away, obviously concerned for me. I felt bad, but I also felt great. I'd really shown that Giles prick who was boss.

I took a breath and wondered if I even needed to breathe anymore. I'd been unable to for most of the duel, though my perception of time was likely distorted because of the pain. For all I knew the whole ordeal could have only taken a minute.

It felt like a lot longer than that to me though.

Another notification popped up and I decided to read through them.

**Opponent: [Goblin Giles] has been defeated. You have won the duel, congratulations!**

**Duel rules have now ended and HUD functions will return to normal.**

**You have defeated Goblin Giles (lvl 30)**
**Bonus experience awarded due to rank disparity.**

It seemed that Giles had only been a few ranks higher than me. Despite killing him solo, I didn't gain a single level.

Either he was so weak I barely got any experience, or the experience threshold was getting higher. I voted for the latter. Giles wasn't exactly a strong opponent, but he was a good shot and he lasted a while against my acid.

*Tenacious little fucker.*

**New Achievement!**
**Shot to the Heart**

**...Yes, you're to blame, you gave his shirt...a blood stain.**

**You won a duel with a single shot to the heart. Shame
you're too weak to have pierced it, but I guess melting a
guy's skin with acid is also an acceptable way to win.**

**Reward:** *Duellist's Loot box*

I was sure the system didn't have the legal rights to that song,
but I doubted it cared about getting sued. It was seemingly all powerful after all.

The promise of a new loot box was exciting, I hoped it'd be
something good.

I still had two more notifications to read through so I continued
opening them.

**You have unlocked a new personal skill:**
*Minor Poison Resistance*

**After being affected by the fumes of wild takka berries,
you did something reckless and survived.**

*Minor resistance against poisons.*

After reading the notification I felt my head start to clear. Like
there had been a fog inside my skull and I'd only just realised it was
there.

It was a bit like sobering up on the way home from a night out,
but a little more surreal and a lot less vomit inducing.

As the fog cleared, I couldn't remember why I'd wanted to fight
Giles in the first place. I remembered that something about him had
rubbed me the wrong way, but I couldn't remember what that
something was.

It was a strange feeling, akin to memory loss, but not quite.

Regardless, I never wanted to lose control of myself like that again. It'd worked out this time, but even a cat only had nine lives.

## Quest Updated!
### *The Goblin King Coronation*

**Every century a new goblin king is chosen. He who is destined to unite the clans and conquer the world – or so ancient goblin lore says.**
**Crash the party, kill the king, and get to the *Winchester* for a nice cold pint whilst you wait for it all to blow over.**

**After making your way to the mountain on the Forbidden Isles, you managed to gain admission into the Goblin King Ball.**
**Whilst there, you goaded Giles, a goblin king candidate, into challenging you to a duel where you killed him in full view of his clan and the other attendees.**

### Objectives:
*Stop the coronation 0/1*
*Kill throne candidates 1/4*
**Reward: *A New Active Skill***

*A quest update?* It was the first time I'd seen one of those. It seemed that Giles was a candidate, so taking him out could only have been considered a good thing.

The quest description had also updated to include my duel, that was certainly new.

As I opened it, I exchanged a look with Panda.

"Who'd have thought *he* was one of them," he said quietly. The noise and chatter from the goblins had sprung back up the moment Giles had died. "I guess Sally will have to give you a piece of the reward now, you've done a quarter of the quest by yourself."

"I don't reward reckless behaviour, even if you were under the influence," Sally said indignantly, turning back towards us.

I chuckled and apologised and she grunted.

There was still one thing left to do before the duel could truly be over. It was looting time!

I walked towards the mostly melted corpse of Giles; the other three goblins were stood around him.

"Well, that's one less contender. I wonder if I can convince the kid to kill the rest of you for me." Gerald chuckled.

"Giles would have died first anyway, look at him. He's all gristle and bone," the fat goblin added.

They looked up at me as I walked towards them.

"You sure you don't want to enter the competition yourself?" The fat goblin asked, a slight smirk on his lips.

"Be quiet Gerad, you know as well as I do that only the strongest in each tribe can participate. The big one is clearly stronger than he is," Gerald said, shaking his head.

"Oh, will you stop being such a fucking stick in the mud. I was just having a little joke with the boy."

"Why are you always like this Gerad. It's not joking if nothing you say is funny!"

The two continued bickering back and forth like an old married couple and I had to raise my voice a few times to get them to stop.

"Oi!" I shouted, louder than I'd meant to, and the two stopped and turned towards me with stunned expressions. "I'm just here to get my loot, so if you'd kindly move out of the way I'll take it and be on my way. Then you can go back to bickering or flirting or whatever that was just now."

"Loot? You mean to desecrate Gile's remains?" Gerald asked with a shocked expression on his face.

"Loot?" A deep voice rang out from behind me. "Goblins can't loot bodies, everybody knows that. Looting abilities are a perk of adventurers and the higher races," it said and I turned on my heels panickily.

The big, muscular goblin who had officiated the duel stood in front of me with a predatory grin plastered onto his face.

# Chapter 34
# Spidey Senses

The huge goblin stared at me with predatory eyes and a vicious smile plastered on his lips.

"So then, *adventurer*, what made you think you could get away with attending the goblin king coronation?" He asked.

I'd have to think quickly if I wanted to avoid their ire. I was certain that the safe zone rules would still be in effect, but our plan would be ruined if we were ousted as adventurers.

The entire quest hinged on our being able to field Sally in the competition. If we couldn't do that then we had no way to attack them without the punishment affecting us. A punishment that we still didn't understand.

"I want his bow. That is what I meant by looting. The spoils should rightfully belong to the victor after all," I replied with faux confidence. "To be perfectly clear, I plan to take it by hand. As you said, goblins don't have looting abilities. Everyone knows that." I folded my arms and raised my eyebrows at the big goblin, pretending to be offended.

"Ah...I see," the muscular goblin replied slowly, furrowing his brow.

My gambit was a long shot. Hell, the entire ruse of pretending to be goblins in the first place was completely absurd. I was sure it had only worked so far because of Panda's charisma and their innate stupidity.

He'd told us that he had a high affinity for charisma and he even had a special skill that allowed him to convince others of pretty much anything, providing they were stupid enough.

It worked by pitting his charisma against theirs, if his was higher he'd win. It seemed overpowered to me but it had worked in our favour so far.

I, however, didn't even have a charisma stat, so perhaps it was included with intelligence, which I also had very little points in.

"Very well then," he replied. "However, I have a request. *You* will participate in the tournament instead of your friend," he smiled evilly as he looked me up and down.

"Out of the question!" Sally roared as she came marching over. "I will be your opponent in the tournament and that is final!"

The huge goblin turned to her and the two squared off. I didn't have mana, but I could still sense their postulating as their auras battled against each other.

It was a faint and intangible presence. I barely registered its existence. Still, it was there.

The two locked eyes for an uneasy moment before the huge goblin let out a deep, rumbling laugh.

"Fine," was all he said before walking away.

*That was close.* I thought, wiping the back of my hand over my sweaty forehead.

Sally gave me a subtle nod that said she wanted to talk to me in private. I followed her.

"Wait, I thought you wanted Gile's bow?" Gerald called after me.

"You keep. All this pointless chatter has soured it for me," I replied, lazily waving a hand over my shoulder.

There was no point in taking it. His bow was a common piece of shit bow like the one I'd been using before. I'd recognised it when he pulled it out during the duel.

I did want to loot him, for the gold if nothing else. But after that interaction I decided it wasn't worth the risk, as frustrating as that was.

I followed Sally into a dark corner, away from prying ears.

"We need to be careful around him," she said in a hushed tone, clearly meaning the muscular goblin. "He's much more powerful than the other two."

"Yeah, he seems more cunning too," I replied. "Something about him really sets off my Spidey senses."

"What does that mean?"

"It's the sixth sense one gets after being bitten by a radioactive spider," I replied nonchalantly.

"Is this a skill you have? I haven't heard about it before," she asked, a look of confusion on her face.

"Yes, but from before my time here. You see I was on a school science trip to this big corporation that researched DNA and genetics.

"To cut a long story short, a spider bit me and I got all these awesome powers like shooting web and the ability to kiss girls whilst hanging upside down in the rain." I smirked and she gave me a deadpan glare.

"You're speaking nonsense aren't you. This really isn't the time for idiocy." She folded her huge arms. "Gobtta has informed me that we have a few hours before the tournament starts. I think we should return to the room for now.

"That last encounter and your duel were too reckless. We can't be found out before I enter the tournament. Besides, you're low on health and stamina and we're low on potions."

"I don't heal very much without potions; my regeneration is really slow," I replied.

"It will improve as your level increases. In the meantime, I'll teach you meditation. That should get you back to full HP before we need to come back down. If you can pick it up quickly that is."

With that she marched out of the hall and I followed her, grabbing Panda from a table by the scruff of the neck as I went.

He was stuffing his face with bread, earning some nasty looks from the goblins. They cheered as I carried him away.

*So much for charisma.*

We retired to our room and Sally sat down, cross legged on the bed with her palms resting on her knees and facing upwards.

Her middle finger and thumb were connected, making a circle on each hand.

"Sit on the other bed like I am," she commanded.

I sat on my bed and crossed my legs, placing my palms face up over my knees and connecting my middle finger and thumb.

"Good, now straighten your back," Sally said and I complied. "Meditation is about delving into your inner soul. Being completely at one with yourself. You need to feel the connection between your soul and the natural auras that surround you."

That was easier said than done, how was I supposed to delve into my soul? I wasn't even sure if souls were a real thing!

"How exactly do I do that?" I asked, "I don't even know what a soul really is. It was always a bit of an arbitrary term back on earth."

"The soul is the vital energy that makes up your very being. It is everything you truly are, not necessarily the mask you show to the world.

"To delve into your soul, you have to be honest about who you are. You can't lie to your own soul as most people do to themselves and others," she said, closing her eyes as she spoke to me.

I still wasn't sure what she was getting at. Had I been lying to myself? If so, what had I lied about? It was all a bit confusing and spiritual to me.

"Listen kid, there are some breathing exercises to help with sensing your soul," Panda said from the side of me. "First off close your eyes and imagine your body. As you breathe in, visualise the air being taken in through your mouth.

"Then visualise it as it circulates throughout your entire body. That's the first step. After that I want you to visualise that flow changing into energy. Try seeing it as vitality first, so maybe think of it as being red like blood?"

I nodded and took his advice. As I closed my eyes, took in a deep breath, and visualised the energy. I began to feel a strange tingling in my hands.

It wasn't much, but I could feel it. It was like I could see the energy circulating around my body. It was like there was a single piece of intangible red rope that spread throughout my limbs, my organs and even my brain.

The rope was cut though, it was shredded in certain places. As I breathed in, small amounts of red, vital energy entered my body and I visualised them filling in the shredded gaps.

It was quite therapeutic and I felt calmer than I had in days. There was something beautiful in the simplicity of fixing the small tears on the rope.

As I did this, the tingling in my hands became more pronounced and spread to other parts of my body. It was a strange sensation. I wondered what it meant. As I continued to work on fixing the rope by bringing in new energy from my breathing and twisting it together in the gaps of the rope, I started to sense something else.

It was like there was a ball of circulating energy deep within my core. I couldn't quite see it, but I had this slight feeling that it was there, lying dormant.

It was frustratingly out of reach. I could almost see it, but if I reached out with my mind to grab it, my metaphorical hands seemed to slip right through it.

Deciding to leave it for now, I continued fixing the rope until it was completely mended and then, with a smile, I opened my eyes.

Sally sat watching me, her sword laid across her lap as she cleaned and polished it with weird cotton balls on a stick.

Panda was laid next to me and he looked up as my eyes opened. He smiled and nodded his head slightly.

"Well done kid, looks like you worked out how to heal yourself without much help. You must be a natural, just look at your HP."

I did and it was full. It'd been just below the quarter mark when we'd started.

I grinned in satisfaction as it dawned on me that the broken red rope in my mind was my hit points. I'd replenished them myself and it had only been a few minutes!

"You finished just in time; I was about to grab you. It's almost time for the tournament," Sally said distractedly as she continued concentrating on her sword.

Almost time for the tournament? That wasn't for another four hours. There was no way I'd been meditating for that long.

"Time flies when you're in a deep trance kid," Panda said, sitting up and patting me on the arm with his soft paw. "Some people have been known to meditate for weeks at a time. Some of the strongest in the world have meditated for years, even decades at a time," he continued.

"Time distorts when you're in there. That's why you've got to do it in a safe place, ideally with someone to watch over you. There are some people who make a living out of killing people during meditation and looting their stuff.

"It's actually quite a lucrative trade or so I'm told…not that you should do that."

Well, at least I'd spent that time productively. I felt like I'd barely even scratched the surface of meditation. I wanted to know what that weird core energy was. I wanted to touch it.

That would have to wait for now though. With my HP full, I chugged a stamina potion, filling it up to halfway.

Sally added a small coat of liquid to her sword then stowed it on her back.

"What does that do?" I asked, standing up and stretching both my arms out.

"You'll see," she replied with a playful, yet deadly, grin.

We returned to the hall and saw the last of the goblins piling through the arena door in single file. We moved to join them just as Gobtta appeared.

"Miss Sally, if you'll come with me, I'll show you to the arena. Your party is welcome to watch from the stands through there." He pointed towards the door that goblins were queuing to get through.

"Good luck," I said to Sally as he turned to leave. "Not that you'll need it."

# Chapter 35
# The Wandering Ronin

"Remember to stab that muscle-fuck with your *steel* sword, don't let him stab you with his flesh one. We can all feel the sexual tension between you two but this is a fight!" Panda called after Sally as she turned to leave with Gobtta.

"Fuck you, Panda," she shouted back, showing him her middle finger over her shoulder.

I smirked and Panda and I followed the line of goblins through the cramped hallway.

There was excited murmuring through the passage as we walked slowly behind a group of small female goblins. The atmosphere reminded me of queuing up to get into a gig venue back home.

"Have you seen Geralt?" A small goblin girl with saggy breasts said excitedly.

"Oh yeah, he's so dreamy. I wonder if I'll get that beautiful if I ever evolve?" Her friend replied.

"What are the chances of your evolving? I'm the one who's going to sit on his face and make him love me!" The first retorted.

The two shared a glance and then turned away from each other, each in a huff. They folded their arms and continued to walk down the hallway in silence.

I got the impression they'd have fought if it wasn't for the safe zone been in place.

It was a shame though, if one of them had attacked the other I might have got to see what the punishment was.

We continued walking through the passage for a short while until it opened out into a huge underground arena.

It was like an old coliseum, but underground. The roof was covered in jagged stalactites, growing down menacingly. It was a high roof that you could only see because of all the glowing balls on the walls.

The whole place was lit up like a *WWE* showdown. I wouldn't even have been surprised to see a few cameras dotted about. Though I knew that this fight wasn't scripted – unless there was something Sally wasn't telling me.

The audience layout was a high rise of tiered seating, reaching far above where the passage came out. It was already filled to the brim with goblins muttering excitedly and causing a general ruckus.

We'd have had no chance without the safe zone being in effect, there were thousands of them.

I pushed through the crowed and elbowed my way to the pole position looking over the lowest barrier – which was basically just a small stone wall that came up to my naval.

The nearby goblins gave Panda and me a wide berth as they shot scathing glances at us and whispered to each other.

In all honestly, I was glad they were weary of us. It gave us more room and meant that I didn't have to be in close proximity to a bunch of gross goblins.

Though it was more than likely Panda they didn't like, after he ate all their bread.

"I don't think they like you," Panda said as he clambered onto the wall and sat down idly.

"Me?" I replied incredulously. "You're the one who ate all their bread."

"You killed one of their leaders," he replied blankly. "Technically that means someone in that clan should try to avenge him, but they can't because of the safe zone rules. I also think they're scared of you considering you melted the guy and then stood there glaring at him with an arrow sticking out of your neck."

Now he mentioned it, that probably was terrifying for them. Good, let them be scared. It might make them hesitate before attacking me.

I hadn't considered how badass I probably looked in that dual, I was just doing everything I could to survive.

A few minutes after we entered, the tournament finally began with an audible notification which popped up on my HUD. It was read by a voice akin to a boxing announcer.

*Welcome to tonight's main event!*
*The tournament to decide who's the top gob. The fight that proves might is right. The battle that separates goblins from cattle.*
*That's right folks, it's the one you've all been waiting for.*
*The Goblin King Coronation!*

The crowd went wild. Cheers and banging circulated the arena. It was so loud I could barely hear myself think. I'd been to concerts before but this was the loudest crowd I'd ever heard.

As the deafening cheers continued, the competitors began entering the arena. The arena itself was a large, empty square with a sandy floor and literally nothing else.

In the middle was an altar, which I thought was pretty ominous, but there was nothing on it so it was probably just part of the aesthetic.

The announcement continued.

*Alright, let's meet our first contestant.*
*He's the leader of the Northern Mountain Tribe that*
*makes its home just above your heads.*
*With a whopping record of having bed the most goblin*
*women on the island and spreading more clap than*
*Charlie Sheen, it's the one, the only Gerald Gobings!*

The crowd cheered fervently. He made quite the spectacle out of it too. Lifting his axe off his back, he swung it around his head and blew a few kisses to the audience.

They loved it. The shrieking hoard of female goblins simply ate up his showmanship.

*What was that about Charlie Sheen?* I thought, furrowing my brow. How would the goblins even know who that was? It didn't even make sense to use an earth reference in this context.

*Our second contestant is the ruler of the Seashore Tribe,*
*famous across the Forbidden Isle as the inventor of the*
*bomb fishing technique. But can he fight as good as he*
*fishes?*
*It's Gerad Grey!*

This time it was the fat goblin's turn to prance around in the sand. He seemed less of a showman than Gerald as he simply lifted his mace in the air and looked up. Still, he got a fair amount of cheering and applause.

Neither him, nor Gerald impressed me too much. I got the impression they were a similar strength to Giles, the one I'd beaten in a duel.

That placed them at around level 30, which was respectable compared to my 27, but didn't hold a candle to Sally's level 90.

The next contestant was the only one that worried me.

*Our third contestant needs no introduction.
He's the crowd favourite to win for obvious reasons
and he steals the ladies' hearts without even trying. A
famed warrior and living legend among the tribes of the
Forbidden Isles, though he doesn't have a tribe of his
own currently.
It's The Wandering Ronin himself, Geralt the Great!*

The entire arena shook with the stamping, clapping and screams from the goblins. I'd never heard anything so loud.

If there were any nearby boats sailing past the island they'd likely think the mountain was about to burst. It was beyond deafening.

Geralt, the muscle-bound goblin strode forward a few steps and unsheathed his sword, taking it in a two-handed grip.

Unlike Gerald, he made no show and dance. He simply readied himself and nodded slightly. The sign of a true professional.

He didn't need to show off, his fighting would do the talking for him. A monster with that kind of calm, collected confidence was one to watch out for.

I remembered earlier, when we queued in the passageway, a female goblin had said he'd evolved. Wondering what that meant, I focused on him and a notification popped up.

**You have discovered a unique monster:**
*Geralt the Great*

**Geralt is no mere goblin. His story is long and full of hardship, love, and loss. But you don't give a flying fuck about that do you? I thought not you heartless bastard. Have you never heard of good storytelling? Backstories are the corner stone of a pre-fight episode.**

**Well, anyway.**
**He killed a metric fuck tonne of other goblins and humans and basically anything he came across whilst**

**wandering around the forbidden isle. He did that for decades.**

**Until one day he evolved into a *Hobgoblin* shedding his scrawny green skin for one hell of an upgrade. *Arine*, eat your heart out, am I right?**

Interesting. So, Geralt was a hobgoblin. I recognised the name, but back on earth I was sure they were associated with throwing bombs shaped like pumpkins and riding around on hoverboards whilst a certain spider-like individual tried to beat them up.

Sadly, the system didn't deign to tell me any useful information about hobgoblins in general. It just made more passive aggressive passes at me and name-dropped *Arnie*.

The system seemed to have a real thing for cultural references. I wondered if that was why it chose outworlders from earth? Or maybe it only learnt about our culture through us. Who knew? It wasn't important right now.

Not when the announcer was about to introduce Sally.

**Our final contestant has come a long, long way folks. She's travelled all the way from the eastern continent to take part in our illustrious event. The more the merrier I say!**
**Not much is known about her except she likes talking smack and she's copied Geralt with her massive sword.**
**A copy is never as good as the original, but in the interest of good sportsmanship, I'm sure she'll do alright.**
**It's Sally... she wouldn't give us her last name.**

The arena was silent, you could have heard a cricket chirping and in my overactive imagination, I did. Panda and I began cheering at the tops of our voices, earning us some mucky looks from the goblins.

Who cared, fuck them. I wanted to cheer on my mentor. Sally looked up at me and nodded but made no further attempt at showmanship or fanfare. That was probably for the best.

She didn't need to show off, she was strong enough to let her actions speak for her. I was a bit pissed that the announcement had done her dirty like that though.

It played up all the other contestants making them sound like god's chosen, and then gave a lacklustre and frankly rude introduction for Sally.

Speaking of the announcer, it piped up again.

**With our contestants introduced it's time to explain the rules.**
**It's pretty simple, this will be a battle royale. The last one standing takes the crown, simple.**
**Oh, and speaking of the crown, let's bring it out!**

A shaft of light appeared from the ceiling as a large, golden crown floated down and landed on top of the alter in the middle of the arena.

It turned out it *was* there for a reason.

The crown was hemmed with deep purple, satin-looking fabric and it had colourful jewels embedded into it. There was no denying that it was a proper crown.

With it being made for a goblin king I'd half expected some twisted brambles or something. But it seemed that they knew their jewellery.

**Alright, with that done let's get on with the show!**
**Kill! Kill! Kill!**

The crowd began screaming and cheering once again as the action kicked off. I had to admit I was excited to see what Sally could do for myself, if a little nervous.

I clutched the wall in front of me so hard my knuckles turned white as I glued my eyes to the action. Using my new *Sniper* skill to zoom in and out at will. I'd summoned my bow onto my back to activate it.

Sally drew her sword calmly and widened her feet in a readying stance. At the same time Geralt leapt across the arena and swung down with his giant sword, slicing straight through Gerald's axe to his head, splitting him in two like cracking an egg.

Which, coincidentally, was exactly what it looked like as his brains leaked out onto the floor and the two halves of his body slid apart.

Meanwhile, Gerad charged at Sally with his mace raised above his head. He screamed in a comically high-pitched voice as he closed in on her. She hadn't moved since taking up her fighting stance.

He pulled his disproportionate arm back and just as he went to swing his weapon Sally struck. She reminded me of a coiled snake, her body was overflowing with kinetic energy and she unleashed it in one impossibly fast movement.

Her sword neatly decapitated Gerad, who, from the look in his eyes, didn't even realise it had happened.

His head rolled harmlessly across the floor as his fat body went limp and fell in a lifeless pile next to Sally.

Geralt watched her do this and smiled as his eyes locked with hers.

It was like lightning leapt between their gazes as the two power-house locked eyes.

The real fight was about to start.

# Chapter 36
# Sally of the Gob Gob Tribe

The ground shattered at their feet as both Geralt and Sally launched themselves at each other. The entire arena shook and the audience fell silent.

You could hear a pin drop whilst I watched anxiously from my perch behind the low wall at the front of the tiered seating area.

Sally slashed down a blow so fierce that the wind force created from it blew my hair back. Geralt intercepted, blocking the lightning-fast attack like it was child's play.

As the two swords clashed together the arena shook once more. So, this was what a silver rank battle looked like. I was impressed and more than anything, I wanted to possess that kind of power myself.

If I could one day be that strong, I'd have no problem protecting myself against cultists and monsters and pretty much anyone else who wanted to harm me.

More importantly, it would be the first step to one day bringing my wife and unborn child here. Not that I knew for sure if that was even possible.

The crown glinted ominously on the alter in the centre of the arena. Despite the fierce battle brewing right next to it, it didn't budge an inch.

As the two swords clashed together, a stalemate of seemingly inseparable talent ensued. Sally smiled and took one hand off her hilt, moving it to the top of her blade.

With movements that flowed like water she leant into the blade, forcing Geralt's sword back towards him. Then she pushed down on the top of her blade, using her entire bodyweight, and cut before spinning away and creating distance. All in one flowing movement.

Geralt grunted as his shoulder was sliced open and blood began leaking out of the wound. Back on earth a wound like that would be a finisher. It'd likely kill a person. At the very least they'd need immediate medical treatment and surgery.

But to Geralt, it was a mere flesh wound as he grimaced slightly and pressed on. He launched himself at Sally as she spun to create distance from her last attack.

She jumped back at the last second, narrowly avoiding a powerful strike, then dashed back into the fray with a myriad of slashes which ripped multiple minor wounds into Geralt's toned stomach.

It was a close fight, but she was winning. I watched in awe as it all played out in front of my unblinking eyes.

"Ha! Not bad Sally of the Gob Gob Tribe," Geralt pronounced. The arena was so quite that we could hear every word. "I didn't expect much from a catonid but you've put on quite a show."

Murmurs began emanating from around the arena as the crowd took in what had been said.

"How did he see through our ruse?" Panda exclaimed in a shocked tone.

"To be fair mate, it was a ridiculous charade. We don't look anything like goblins," I replied.

Still, Panda's charisma skill had worked on the others, as proven by the shocked voices whispering all around us. For Geralt the

Wandering Ronin to be able to see through it must have meant his stats were high.

"If he fights on par with Sally then there was no way my charisma skill was going to work on him," Panda said, still enthralled with the battle below. "My stats scale with yours and you're way weaker than he is."

"How do your stats and skill work?" I asked, it occurred to me that I knew very little about how my familiar operated.

"I'm a non-combatant daemon familiar. So, in place of the strength stat, I have a charisma stat. My intelligence and charisma are both my highest stats and the others are…adequate, I guess.

"In this current incarnation I only have two skills. One of them allows me to quickly research and retain knowledge. You know, cause I'm a sage and all.

"The other allows me to attempt to convince other people of things by pitting my charisma stat against theirs. Of course, most people and monsters don't have a charisma stat. It tends be included as part of their intelligence.

"Which is why you believe everything I tell you, you dimwit." He chuckled. "Joking aside, I can't actually use my manipulation skill on you. It doesn't work since you're technically my master," he added, still keeping his eyes glued to the arena floor.

It was useful to know more about how his skills worked. That meant that as I got more powerful, so did he. I wondered if he'd unlock more skills as I grew.

It could be useful if he could develop something to help me in combat, even if it wasn't directly related to fighting.

"What was that about *this incarnation?*" I asked.

"As you know I've been alive a long time and served other masters. I incarnate each time, starting at the level they summon me at and growing alongside them."

"So does that mean you know what other skills you'll develop?"

"Nope, sorry kid. It doesn't work like that. I get different ones every time and it's related to how your powers grow and work too. The only constant is the sage skill because, as I may have mentioned, I'm a sage."

That was a shame. Though it was worth a try just in case. I guess I'd have to wait and see what else he could do.

I turned my gaze back towards the arena where Sally and Geralt found themselves in a sword-locked stalemate once more.

"If you knew I wasn't a goblin then why did you allow me to enter this tournament," Sally asked through gritted teeth as the two tried to force each other back.

"I wanted to fight you," Geralt replied with a lecherous smile playing on his lips.

As Sally opened her mouth to reply, Geralt took the opportunity to kick her in the stomach. She doubled over and was launched across the arena, slamming hard into the stone wall which crumbled around her.

As she peeled herself off, I could see a Sally-shaped hole where she'd landed. She'd completely annihilated that part of the wall. I could see through the hole to the stairs which presumably led back to the hall.

She wiped some blood from her lips and glowered at the hob-goblin in front of her.

Using the wall to launch herself this time, she flew at Geralt like a missile and stabbed her sword straight into him. He dodged at the last second, but her sword went straight through his shoulder all the way to the hilt.

He grunted and slammed his elbow repeatedly into Sally's back as he tried to throw her off. He lifted his sword with his free arm above her head.

I found myself shouting, "Sally, watch out!" but she didn't need my assistance as she jumped back, leaving her sword skewered through her opponent's shoulder, just a few inches from his heart.

Geralt used the space created to wrench Sally's sword from his shoulder with a deep growl of pain. It must have cost him a lot of HPS as he was looking worse for wear now.

However, he now held both of their massive swords and wielded them together. His own sword was held in his good hand and Sally's drooped, held by the injured side.

Still, she had no weapon and he had two. He grinned maliciously at her.

Sally quickly began looking around for something and then her eyes stopped on a single spot in the arena. She dived towards it and rolled, grabbing Gerald's axe.

The dwarf shaped dead goblin lay nearby. Geralt had finished him almost the second the battle royale had started.

"This isn't my preferred weapon, but it'll do" she said smugly as she took a few test swings. Her entire body was enveloped in a glowing red aura.

Geralt smiled and his body glowed as well as he watched her. "Very well, then I guess it's about time for me to wrap this up."

"What are they doing?" I asked Panda hurriedly.

"It's a warrior skill called *Berserker* it seems they both have it. Basically, it makes them stronger and feel less pain. It can also make them angry and reckless. It doesn't run out until their mana and stamina are empty. It's a powerful skill that drains both of those stats very quickly."

I watched on as I felt a powerful pressure surround the arena. The two were glowing intensely and it was hard to watch them. They were blinding.

Then they both leaped at each other and I lost track of what was happening.

They moved so fast it was a complete blur to me. I could barely keep up with any of it as they clashed all around the arena at the speed of sound.

I had no way of knowing who was winning, until suddenly the glowing stopped and the two of them stood panting and facing each other in the middle of the arena.

Geralt was doubled over, unable to lift either arm, he panted like a dog as blood dripped from a myriad of wounds which covered his entire body.

Sally, on the other hand, barely had a scratch on her. Though she panted all the same. Had she won? It was hard to tell.

They stood there for an agonisingly slow second. Then Sally's chest burst as blood splattered from a deep gash which appeared to form from her left breast to her right hip.

She fell to her knees and then face planted the floor. She'd been defeated.

**And the winner is...**

"No!" I found myself screaming before I knew what I was doing.

I had my bow in my hands and an arrow nocked. I aimed at the swaying half dead hobgoblin who seemed like he might keel over any second. I pulled back the drawstring and shot, anger coursing through me.

It exploded from the bow string with more power than I'd ever used before, draining half my stamina in a single go. I didn't have time to think about that though.

It penetrated the back of Geralt's head and exploded out the front of his face.

His body dropped to its knees and fell to the floor as gore leaked out all over the sandy arena floor. I heard the notification and knew he was dead. It was followed by a few others that I didn't have time to check.

I vaulted over the wall and rushed towards Sally as she bled out. She was unconscious and in bad shape. She wasn't breathing but I couldn't tell if that was normal at her level.

Pulling out a basic health potion, I tipped her head back and poured the entire thing down her throat. The wound closed slightly but refused to heal fully.

I didn't know what to do, was she dead? Was there nothing I could do to help?

Panda moved to join me as I heard the jeers from the crowd above. The goblins began throwing stones and rotten fruit they'd somehow gotten hold of.

I didn't care, I had more important things to deal with, like keeping Sally alive. I wouldn't allow her to die.

"Kid, we need to go now!" Panda shouted as he half climbed, half fell from the balcony.

I ignored him and started tapping Sally's shoulder's begging her to wake up. I was dead without her. But more than that, she was my mentor and I didn't want her to die.

"Kid we need to go now!" Panda said, running towards me.

"What do I do, she won't wake up?" I screamed at him.

"I don't know, carry her or something. We can deal with that later. Right now we need to get out of here before we get killed."

"They won't kill us, we're in a safe zone."

"That didn't stop you, did it?"

"That only worked because the safety feature was disabled for the combatants in the arena."

Gobtta had told us as much when he'd visited our room the previous night. My initial plan had been to provide ranged support whilst Sally fought. She said no. She told me it was too dangerous and I wouldn't do much harm anyway.

The way the system managed to enable combatants to fight in a safe zone was to revoke their safety temporarily. It was the same when I duelled Giles.

"Read your notification. You're being punished!" Panda shouted.

*The punishment!* In my haste I'd completely forgotten about it. I opened my notifications and there it was.

### *WARNING*
*You have broken the safe zone rules.*
*It's punishment time bitches!*

# Chapter 37
# Punishment Time

APPROXIMATELY 18 HOURS EARLIER...

"Well, Gobtta, why don't you come in for a minute and you can tell us all about this tournament," I said, inviting him into our room.

I felt especially devious as I coaxed our new friend into being an information source, something we were sorely lacking.

"Um... yes of course, don't mind if I do," he stuttered nervously as he entered our room. He played with his hands which he kept in front of his chest and he looked around like a meerkat on sentry duty.

"So, how does this work?" I asked. "Can we field as many people as we like or does each clan only get one?"

"Each clan can nominate one warrior to fight in the tournament. Usually, they go with their strongest since they want to win.

"The winner gets the crown and will become the next goblin king. Naturally, the clan who takes victory gets pride of place in the new regime. So it's quite a big deal," Gobtta responded.

"I'll do it," Sally said immediately.

It did make sense to send her. If we could only choose one person then she was the natural choice. I didn't like the idea of being sat on the side lines for it though. It was my first proper, Adventure Society sanctioned quest and I wanted to be the one to complete it.

"How does this arena place actually work?" Panda asked, lighting up his pipe. Just as he pulled it to his lips Sally slapped it out his hand and gave him a stern look. "Obviously, I know what an arena is, but this is a safe zone."

"The system has ways around combat in safe zones. In this case, you'd be signing your name on a sanctioned contract which basically says that whilst in the arena, your safety is temporarily revoked," Gobtta answered, looking between the three of us nervously.

"Revoked?" I asked. "As in, completely gone, so hypothetically an audience member could harm one of the fighters?"

"There's nothing hypothetical about it. Anyone can harm someone who's safety has been revoked, though they'll then be subjected to the punishment."

We talked for a bit longer after that but eventually settled on Sally soloing the arena and taking the crown. Much to my dismay.

\*\*\*

Time seemed to stop as I crouched over Sally. I could look around, but I couldn't move a muscle.

Rocks were frozen mid throw, the goblins seemed to be frozen too. The entire arena was silent.

It had happened as soon as I'd checked my notifications as Panda had demanded. I was being punished, but why was the world frozen?

**\*WARNING\***
*You have broken the safe zone rules.*
*It's punishment time bitches!*

*Oh shit.* I thought, still frozen in time.

This was really bad. I could take damage but I couldn't fight back. That was a worst-case scenario if ever I'd heard one. I was trapped in the middle of an arena, surrounded by thousands of angry goblins who hated me because I'd just killed their soon-to-be king.

I looked around the room urgently, I had no idea when time would unfreeze, but I'd use every spare second I had to formulate a plan.

I would not die here and I wouldn't lose Sally either.

*Loot the corpse and take the crown.* That same familiar voice from my dream said, startling me as it appeared randomly in my mind.

"Who are you?" I asked out loud.

There was no reply. I looked towards the corpse of Geralt. He was right in front of me, if I could move my arms I could touch him.

I focused on him for a moment and the loot notification popped up.

**Do you want to loot *Geralt the Great*?
Y/N**

I mentally asserted yes, then looked towards the crown. I was just out of reach, but I could probably grab it as soon as the world unfroze.

*Good, now get the crown.* The eery voice whispered into my mind.

Time unfroze and a lot of things happened all at once. I span on my heels and reached out to grab the crown. The second my fingertips brushed it's golden, shiny surface, I pulled it into my inventory.

"For fuck's sake Kaleb let's go!" Panda screamed as he sprint-waddled towards us.

I span back just in time to see the goblins around us start throwing dynamite. Hissing fuses spat sparks that lit up the air like bonfire night as the red cylinders of death rained all around us.

I grabbed Sally under the arms and pulled her onto my back. She was surprisingly easy to lift with my upgraded strength stat. Still, she was a lot bigger than me, so it wasn't *that* easy.

The dynamite began landing at our feet. It fizzed and sizzled as the already short fuses got shorter. By my best estimate we had less than a second to get clear of the blast.

There were hundreds of sticks of dynamite being thrown though, so where exactly were we supposed to go to escape it?

Then it clicked and I dived forward, pushing the ground away with all the strength my legs could muster, just as the first stick of dynamite exploded.

We flew through the Sally shaped hole in the wall that had been created when Geralt kicked her into it during the fight.

Behind us, dynamite sticks exploded one after the other like firecrackers. Panda stumbled through the minefield of explosions, completely unscathed.

"I feel like some kind of super panda, I'm impervious to bombs!" He shouted with the gusto and innocence of a child.

Of course he was ok though, *his* safety hadn't been revoked. It was also likely that Sally's had been turned back on now we'd left the arena, since it was only disabled temporarily.

I turned towards the stairs, with the unconscious catonid still on my back. I needed to get out of this place. I couldn't win if I couldn't do damage so there was no point in trying to kill the goblins.

The only thing to do would be to run like hell and try to get back to the ship. Hopefully, Sally would wake up in time to fly the thing, but we'd deal with that later.

For now, I needed to get back outside.

I began sprinting up the stairs with Sally on my back and Panda following at his own pace. I noticed my stamina drain, annoyingly fast as I moved with Sally.

She weighed a lot more than me so I guess that was why it was so taxing. Still, I could barely feel the difficulty. Something I was sure to regret later. The DOMS would be mad.

I reached the top of the stairs and found myself back in the hall. I began moving towards the exit when an unassuming goblin in priest robes jumped out in front of me.

"You used me!" Gobtta shouted in a squeaky, sad voice. "You weren't even goblins. You should never have been allowed in the tournament!" He shouted as tears began forming in the corner of his eyes.

He was shaking, obviously terrified. I respected that, but I didn't have time to waste on him.

"I don't have time for this Gobtta, sorry," I said, moving around him and continuing to head for the exit.

"F-f-f-fuck you, human scum!" He stuttered. Then he took a horn out from beneath his robes and pressed it to his lips. Flipping me off with his free hand as he blew into it.

A loud, deep sound reverberated around the hall and as it stopped, I felt a rumbling. The floor began to shake and shouts of anger and profanity started coming from the passageway leading to the arena.

*Oh shit. They're coming. Gobtta you wanker!*

I didn't stay long enough to see them pour out of the passage like a burst water pipe. I simply turned and ran as fast and as hard I could towards the exit.

Before I'd even gotten halfway across the hall I knew they'd entered it. Partly because of the very audible insults being thrown my way, and partly because of the very tangible spears being thrown my way.

In a nutshell, things were thrown.

I continued running, opting for a zig zag rather than a straight line in a desperate attempt to avoid the thrown objects.

I was sure that Sally was immune to their attacks now that we'd left the arena, which should have made her the perfect human shield. But I didn't want to risk it, so I tried to protect *her* from incoming fire as much as I did myself.

Panda waddled a few meters behind us, right in front of the goblins who were gaining ground. I wasn't worried about him though; he was definitely immune to damage.

Most of the goblins ignored him anyway, it was me they were after.

I reached the large door at the end of the hall and threw myself up the spiral staircase. I was starting to feel the exhaustion of carrying Sally whilst I ran for my life.

My breathing was laboured and my muscles screamed at me to stop. On my HUD I could see that my stamina was running dangerously low.

I only had a single inferior potion left though and I needed to save it for the optimum moment. I had no doubt that I'd need it.

I burst onto the second floor with the goblins hot on my heels and ran towards the exit. As I ran through the archway, the receptionist goblin barely looked up from her nails as she preened them.

*How much cuticle care could one person need?* I thought as she boredly said: "Thank you for your patronage."

She didn't even realise what had happened. Though her attitude quickly changed as an entire goblin hoard charged after me.

Panda was lost in the fray; I had no idea where he was. The goblins had longer legs and had likely overtaken him. I knew he was immune to damage currently, but I still hoped he was ok.

I reached the cave quickly and sprinted through the jagged tunnels which led back outside. I dug deep as my legs protested. I didn't need to get much further, I was nearly there.

I pushed and pushed with the goblins barely a meter behind me and screaming bloody murder. Then I saw it, the massive doors that marked the entrance to the mountain and my exit to the jungle.

I ran straight towards the still open doors and practically dived outside. I'd made it! Now I just had a jungle to cross.

**You are now leaving the safe zone.**

I took my stamina potion and carried Sally towards the edge of the cliff.

*The edge of the cliff? Fuck.*

It was then that I remembered how we'd originally reached the plateau by Sally jumping an impossible distance into the air.

We were trapped between a sheer drop and a hoard of goblins. Some rescue this turned out to be.

# Chapter 38
# Me Against the Horde

I heard the rumbling of thousands of goblin footsteps behind me as I peered over the cliffside.

I was trapped between the horde and a drop that would likely kill me. Without Sally's incredible power I had no way to quickly descend the mountain.

I needed to act quickly and with purpose.

I gently laid Sally down and stepped in front of her, facing the entrance to the mountain's interior. I pulled out my bow and nocked an arrow. I would have to fight.

Me against an entire horde of goblins. This would be no easy feat. I had no clue how long I could hold out. My stamina was already quite low, the inferior stamina potion I'd taken had only provided a slight boost.

The footsteps and screaming grew louder and I began my attack. I pulled the drawstring back and loosed an arrow, just as the first goblin appeared.

It pierced his chest and he screamed out in pain as his skin began bubbling. He dropped to the ground and was immediately trampled by his frenzied cohorts.

I took another arrow and fired, then another and another. I didn't even stop to check my accuracy. I fired as quickly as possible and with my stats being upgraded the way they were, that turned out to be fast.

Goblins started to drop in the entrance but there was no time for reprieve. There were so many of them, like a swarm of locusts. They flowed through the entrance incessantly and I continued firing as fast as I could.

My stamina drained slowly. Luckily, my usual bow attacks didn't use up too much of it. The attack I'd launched earlier, however, had taken half of my stamina in one go.

How did I do that? It was so powerful. A shot like that now could be a game changer. Though more than likely it'd be less effective here since I'd run out of stamina far before being able to kill them all.

Fortunately, the entrance to the cave provided a bottle neck of sorts. I couldn't damage them until they stepped outside the safe zone, but the number of corpses kept piling up.

Soon the goblins were climbing over their dead brethren to try and get to me. It made my work slightly easier, though it didn't slow them down much.

I had angered them immensely. It was easy to forget that these were simple monsters when I'd just attended a ball with them.

Though they could speak and reason, at their core they were still feral beasts. And they were out for my blood. The blood of the man who had just killed their uncrowned king.

Speaking of the crown, it was currently stored in my inventory. I didn't have time to examine it but I wondered if it could be useful here. If I wore it, would I become the goblin king?

It was worth a chance so, as I continued firing arrow after arrow into the bottleneck, I equipped the crown.

I felt its weight, heavy on my head as it appeared out of my inventory.

"Stop in the name of your new king!" I shouted, hoping the crown would add some form of magic authority to my words.

It had the opposite effect.

"Usurper!"

"King Slayer!"

"Kill the furry!"

The goblin's attacked with even more fervour, some of them continuing to charge even after being hit by one of my arrows.

Using the crown was obviously a mistake.

*Shit.*

I unequipped it and continued firing, though they were gaining ground. Notification after notification appeared on my HUD and I willed them all away to be looked at later.

The corpses piled up, there must have been hundreds of them laying in front of the door. They helped slow down the other goblins a bit, but unless I could get that pile tall enough to completely block the entrance the distraction would be negligible.

As more and more goblins came swarming out from the cave, I found it harder and harder to deal with them.

The corpse mountain had an adverse effect on me too. Whereas at the start of the showdown the goblins all ran in a straight line, they now had to avoid the corpses and manoeuvre around the pile.

This slowed my attack speed immeasurably as I had to aim at each one individually before firing, rather than simply keep launching arrows into the same area.

Soon my attack broke down as the first goblin reached me. Cursing under my breath I pulled the bow back into my inventory and equipped my dagger.

I wasn't as proficient with the dagger, but a bow was no good for close quarters and I had nowhere to run. There was nowhere for me to retreat to either, so creating more space and continuing the volley was out of the question.

As the first goblin reached me I saw a burning, feral hatred in his eyes before I slashed at his neck and he dropped to the floor, a fizzing mess, and I felt a faint warmth as my skill *Acid Dhampir Dagger* refilled my health slightly.

They seemed to be fighting on pure instinct. Charging at me with no plan or skill, just overwhelming numerical superiority.

It was like one of those zombie survival games I'd played online. Alone, they were relatively weak and easy to deal with, it was the numbers that got you.

Whilst you killed one, another would attack from the side, then another from behind and soon you were surrounded by an entire horde.

As the second goblin reached me, less than a second after the first dropped, I stabbed out and pushed the dagger through its face.

The next reached me and I slashed its stomach open, guts cascading onto the floor like a broken bin liner. They just kept coming and I found myself in a meditative state as I slashed and stabbed and did my best to dodge incoming attacks.

It was almost tranquil. Like every fibre of my being, every muscle in my body was working as one single entity with the sole purpose of fighting.

I danced around them, slashing and stabbing, though trying as hard as I might to avoid it, I was taking some serious hits. It wouldn't be enough though. My stamina was dangerously low and my health was taking hits as well.

I was no seasoned warrior and though I fought in a trance, I wasn't going to last much longer. Still, I had to protect Sally, I refused to leave her, and I had another reason to survive.

I couldn't leave my unborn child without a father. I knew how it felt growing up without one. I wouldn't do that to my own flesh and blood. No way.

I fought on, slicing, and stabbing and dancing my way around my attackers as corpses soon started to pile up around me.

It was almost euphoric. The trance of battle. The feeling of my entire body working as one towards a singular purpose, mind, body, and soul acting as one entity.

I could easily see how it could become addictive, though perhaps not in this particular scenario. The bodies piled up as I slaughtered the goblins. I barely noticed my HUD as it began flashing red.

Then I felt something tug at my ankle and I fell to the ground hard, it woke me from my trance and to my horror I saw that I was down to barely a single HP.

My body had felt numb during the trance. I couldn't feel anything accept the euphoria of battle. Now, however, I felt every wound, every slash, every bruise, and it was utter agony.

I quickly slammed down on a healing potion, luckily, I hadn't used one yet, and felt a bit of release. The pain, however, was almost debilitating. I saw a half dead goblin gripping my ankle and I kicked him hard in the face and scurried backwards.

It was too late. Being brought to the floor was enough. I was surrounded by the horde of charging, frenzied goblins. As I tried to get to my feet I was knocked back down and stomped on.

Within seconds an impenetrable wall of goblins surrounded me and began kicking and stomping. Their screeching was so loud I could barely hear myself think. I felt wetness dripping from my ears as they bled from the harsh, high-pitched wailing.

I wondered if this was a type of goblin skill attack. It was certainly draining my HP and I didn't have much left to spare.

Thinking quickly, I began crawling through their legs, slashing at the ankles of each creature I passed by. They began dropping, but the ones at the centre kept attacking the corpses that had been beneath me.

They seemed to be too frenzied to notice that I'd already left. Finally seeing a hint of light, I clawed my way out of the horde and managed to shakily get to my feet.

They looked like full on zombies now. Piled in together in a mosh pit of fury. They hadn't noticed me, but it wouldn't be long. Luckily, Sally still laid untouched at the edge of the cliff.

I hadn't seen Panda in a while either. I hoped he'd just stayed inside where he couldn't take damage. That would be the smartest approach for a non-combatant like him.

I had no idea what to do, but I needed some kind of exit strategy. Just as I had that thought I heard more screaming and turned back towards the huge iron doors.

Even more goblins were climbing over the corpse pile. They were endless. One thousand goblins don't sound like that much, especially when you consider the mega cities on earth that are home to millions of people.

But have you ever looked at one thousand people all at once? More than that, have you tried to fight that many? It's a lot more than you'd think. Especially when they're all charging at you, and you alone.

The new goblins headed towards me and I carved up a few. My arms were struggling to move and I found my breath to be laboured.

As I began fighting the new goblins, the mosh pit started noticing me and moved to join in. I was trapped between them and the mountain wall. I had nowhere to go. My health was low, my stamina had almost run out and I could barely lift my arms.

It was futile. I was going to die here having achieved nothing and protected no one. My child was going to grow up without a father and worse, without ever knowing what happened to its dad.

I kept fighting and taking hits but the sheer number of goblins was overwhelming. If I was going to die though, I was going to die fighting.

I didn't want anyone to say that I gave up. I was going to fight them to my last breath.

Then everything seemed to stop, just for a moment. As a large crash sounded out behind the horde and both the goblin horde and I turned to look.

A man in golden armour stood before us. His impossibly white cloak billowing out behind him.

He raised a single hand and opened his mouth, uttering words I couldn't hear over the goblin's screams. Suddenly, it was like they'd forgotten about me. The entire horde turned its bloodlust on the newcomer as he flashed me a smile.

He hovered above the ground. That's right, he freaking hovered! And he moved backwards gently, playing the Pied Piper to the horde of vicious goblins.

He moved backwards until he was floating off the side of the cliff. He was hovering, high above the trees, as if the cliffside stretched out a few more meters.

The goblins continued to follow him as if entranced. It must have been the spell he'd cast – at least I thought it was a spell.

As they followed him, they plummeted off the side of the cliff. He made it look so easy. In less than a minute the entire hoard that had harassed and nearly killed me, simply walked off the edge of the cliff.

I stared at him in awe for a solid five minutes or so. I stood rooted to the spot as the new goblins which arrived from inside the cave joined the queue. Waiting their turn to walk straight to their deaths in an obsessive attempt to reach and attack the man.

Once the final goblin fell, the man began floating towards me.

# Chapter 39
# Soul Shot

"Looks like I got here just in the nick of time," a deep and friendly voice said.

*Wait, I know that voice.* I thought as he landed in front of me and unequipped his armour.

Standing tall in a familiar, embroidered suit, was Director Lucas. I just stood there, staring at him with an open mouth. I probably looked less intelligent than the goblins.

"Kaleb, are you ok?" He asked, cocking his head slightly as I stared at him.

"Th-thank you," I stammered, struggling to say even that.

"No worries. Sally is an old friend of mine and I sensed that she was in danger. You did well to defend her for so long. I'm honestly quite impressed."

He looked around at the carnage I'd caused. A huge sizzling mass of flesh blocked the doorway. It was so revolting. The bodies were so badly damaged by my acid attacks that you couldn't tell where one started and another ended.

A similar, but more sporadic pile, was near the unconscious Sally.

"Your powers are no joke. This is definitely… something," he said, pulling a handkerchief from his pocket and using it to cover his nose.

I barely noticed the smell anymore. My clothes, skin and hair were covered in goblin blood and gore. I'd become numb to it. Though it would be nice to have a quick shower.

"I bet you've advanced through quite a few levels from this battle. From the sense of your aura, you've advanced to phase two.

"That's good progress, I wouldn't have been able to allow you to take the exam at phase one. It was part of the reason why I asked Sally to take you with her on this quest.

"Though from the looks of things, in doing so, you might have just saved her life." He chuckled and glanced sympathetically at Sally.

"Will she be ok?" I asked.

"I think so, she might be unconscious for a few days though. We should leave as soon as possible and put her to bed on her boat so she can heal."

"She'll get upset if she hears you calling it a boat."

"Oh, I know," he grinned. "Why do you think I call it that."

Director Lucas moved towards Sally and gave her a quick check over with his powerful mana sense ability. He explained that it was a common but extremely useful skill that allowed him to sense life force and power in others.

Whilst he did that, I walked past the goblins, looting their corpses as I went. The notifications were a lot simpler when the goblins were piled up. Though the notification for the biggest pile, near the door, made me do a double take.

**Do you want to loot *goblin* [various] x213
Y/N**

213 goblins, just in that single pile. I knew I'd killed a lot of them, but I was more than just a little impressed with that number.

I asserted yes and received 2130 gold coins. So, each goblin was worth 10 gold. That was useful to know. The weird blessing I'd received from the god was pretty damn useful if I did say so myself.

I looted the rest and received another 1620 gold from the 162 goblins I'd killed with my dagger whilst in a trance, along with a plethora of low quality, rusted weapons Overall I'd killed 375 goblins.

As incredible as it was that I'd taken out that many solo, it was still a far cry from the 1000 that had chased me. I wouldn't have had a chance of survival if it wasn't for Lucas. I quite literally owed the man my life.

Around about the time I finished up the looting, which thanks to the grouping feature didn't take long, Panda came out of the woodwork.

"Is it over?" he said, stepping gingerly among the dissipating corpses towards us.

The bodies didn't evaporate into silver dust or confetti this time. They simply began to evaporate as if they were liquid. They decomposed slowly and just disappeared.

"Yeah, the director saved us," I replied.

"Well, that's good, though judging by all these melting corpses it looks like you did your fair share as well."

Lucas walked towards us, holding Sally in a princess carry. He walked as if she was as light as feather as her long silver hair dangled down.

"Are we ready to go?"

"Fuck yes!" me and Panda both replied in unison. I looked towards him as it happened and we laughed.

"Well, alrighty then. Grab onto my leg please," he said as his body lifted off the ground.

I shared a look with Panda, but I was too exhausted to question it. I grabbed onto his ankle and he began flying towards the ship.

Holding my own bodyweight with my arms was super easy with the stats I had, despite my drained stamina. I was fatigued after the battle, but I still had just enough energy to do something as simple as that. The affect stats had on my body was truly incredible.

We flew over the tops of the trees, the warm, tropical air blowing in my face as we went. It was actually kind of pleasant.

It only took a few minutes to reach the ship where Lucas lowered himself down and I stepped off with Panda clinging to my back.

"I'm going to put Sally to bed. You two should get some rest too," he said as he disappeared into the interior of the ship.

"Well?" Panda said after a long moment.

I was stood still, staring after Lucas, and my mind was blank. I was so exhausted I didn't know what to do with myself.

"Well, what?" I asked.

"Well, are you going to check your notifications? That was a major battle for you. You'll probably have levels and new skills to choose from and all sorts."

Honestly, I was so tired from the fight that the thought hadn't even crossed my mind. I found myself getting a second wind once he mentioned levels though and I eagerly dived in.

I had gained levels, achievements and hopefully a new skill. In fact, I had so many notifications that they appeared in organised tabs under that section of the HUD.

I opened the tab for levels and kills first.

**You have defeated a unique monster:**
***Geralt the Great (lvl 97)***

*Bonus experience awarded due to level disparity.*
*Bonus experience negated due to low health of monster.*
*Experience decreased due to lack of damage inflicted.*

I'd never seen anything like that before. It must have been because he was practically dead already when I shot him.

Still, it felt a little rude. Though I was glad Sally would get most of the experience for the kill. She deserved it.

*Congratulations! You have advanced to lvl 28*
*You have defeated Goblin Washer Maid (lvl 24)*
*You have defeated Goblin Fuck Boy (lvl 19)*

It went on like that for quite a while. It took more than ten minutes to click through the literal hundreds of goblins I'd killed.

They were all lower level than me but the sheer amount of them must have added up.

*Congratulations! You have advanced to lvl 29*
*Congratulations! You have advanced to lvl 32*

*New skills are available.*
*Choose a new skill?*
*Y/N*

I grinned like a child as I read the notification. I'd hit level 32. I was officially stronger than the average child!

I'd had to kill a serious number of goblins to get so few levels though. I guessed Sally was right about levels taking more work in phase two. No more random experience bumps for me, probably.

I mentally exerted yes on the skills list and, like last time, I read through them all.

*Soul Shot (ancient)*

Due to a complete lack of mana, you've realised the potential of the soul earlier than most. You have gained a deeper understanding of the soul through meditation. As demonstrated already, you have unlocked the potential to infuse the power of your soul into certain attacks.
Who'd have ever thought meditation would be so useful. Next you'll be unlocking a skill for virtue signalling monsters to death.

*The amount of power used is directly proportional to the amount of stamina you've chosen to assign to the shot.*

*Soul Shot,* that sounded epic! Or, well…ancient. I thought back to when I shot Geralt in the back of the head.

That arrow had flown from the bow with immense power behind it. It had also drained my stamina. I must have worked out how to do it accidentally.

It was an emotionally charged situation. I guess it was like those stories of mothers lifting cars off their children. I'd activated it because of the situation and my deep-seated need to save Sally.

I did wonder if that meant I'd be able to do it again without the skill though. I probably would but I bet it would be much harder.

### Battle Trance of the Apex Predator (rare)

Due to your experience in hard battles you now have the ability to become one with the very life essence of the battlefield.
Enter a trance as you carve your way through monsters, you battle junkie you.
This skill consumes stamina.

*When this skill is in use, pain nullification activates.*

*Battle Trance of the Apex Predator* could be a useful skill. It was pretty much what I'd already done during the fight with the goblin horde.

I'd lost all sense of self and a euphoric feeling enveloped me as I danced around the cliff, killing monsters.

The only issue was that it cut off my senses. I would have kept going until I died, without even realising it, if it wasn't for that goblin tripping me up.

It was a good skill, but I was a little scared of it.

Those two were the only skills I had to choose from this time. For me it was a no brainer.

"Do you even need to ask?" Panda said as I looked towards him.

I didn't. It was glaringly obvious to me that I needed a good power attack and the system was offering me a brilliant one on a silver platter.

I quickly accepted *Soul Shot* as my new skill and I felt my brain fuzz as knowledge seemed to download directly into it.

It was like I knew exactly how to activate and use the new skill, but not necessarily anything more concrete than that.

After I'd accepted the skill, the notifications continued.

> **Bow has advanced to lvl 11**
> **Bow has advanced to lvl 12**
> **Bow has advanced to lvl 25**

> **You have reached the maximum level for the Bow skill.**
> **Bow has infused with the skill; Apprentice Bowman,**
> **causing it to evolve.**
> **Apprentice Bowman has evolved into:**
> **Newly Qualified Bowman (0%)**

> **The Newly Qualified Bowman has learnt the basics and**
> **is ready to begin the long road to mastery. He has**

grown into his weapon through constant fighting and shooting things to death.

From now on, the bowman will need to complete greater feats to further refine his craft.

Upon reaching 100% proficiency with the bow as the *Newly Qualified Bowman* level, this skill will advance.

*Proficiency improved.*

*A minor bonus to the effect of agility will be added when a bow is equipped.*

This time I didn't feel new knowledge enter my brain; it was more like the skill I'd built up by shooting the goblins had solidified inside me.

It felt like a boost to my muscle memory when using a bow and was sure to be useful. It was odd that my new skill was governed by a percentage though.

I needed to ask Panda about that, but before I could, another notification appeared on my HUD.

# Chapter 40
# Genocidal Maniac's Apprentice

*Dagger* has advanced to lvl 5
*Dagger* has advanced to lvl 6
*Dagger* has advanced to lvl 9

*Dagger* advancing was a nice boost to my melee proficiency. I hadn't used it much on this quest, but it had been invaluable during the later stages of the fight.

I would have died long before Lucas had arrived without it. I really needed to invest some time into training with the dagger. I wondered if I could unlock a proper proficiency skill for it like with the bow.

More immediately, would I get a new skill at level ten? I had done with the bow skill.

I'd have to train up my dagger skill a little more to find out.

Having sifted through all of the skill, level and kill notifications, there was just one category left: achievements.

*Here comes the passive aggression.*

**New Achievement:**
**Experience Thief**

And there it is.

I was beginning to think that the system only awarded me these
farcical achievements to insult me. It's not like I was trying to steal
experience, I was trying to save Sally's life.

I wouldn't even open them if it wasn't for the promise of loot
boxes. My last few had given me some good stuff. I guess it was
worth the insults…kinda.

### New Achievement:
*Genocidal Maniac's Apprentice*

You singlehandedly wiped out over 35% of an entire
population on the Forbidden Isle.
Following in the footsteps of Hafez Al-Assad, Vladimir
Putin, and Joseph Kony, you're well on the way to
being a real piece of work.
Keep it up!
There's nothing like a good slaughter to really beat back
that crippling ED you obviously have.

Reward: *Genocide Loot Box*

I was at a loss for words. Not only had the system compared me to a bunch of war criminals, but it also thought I had ED!

I'd literally just gotten my wife pregnant not that long ago. I worked perfectly fine down there. Was I sexiest man of the year? Definitely not, but it didn't have to call my manhood into question.

Panda burst out laughing after reading the achievement with me. I probably shouldn't take it to heart. I knew the system was a dick.

After that battle though, I wasn't thinking clearly. I really needed some sleep.

With all my notifications squared away, it was time to finally go to bed.

"I'd tell you to keep the hanky-panky with *Palm*-ala *Hand*-erson to a minimum, but it doesn't sound like you've got what it takes to please her anyway," Panda said as I walked towards the cabin.

He laughed so hard at his own terrible joke that when I looked back to give him an admonishing gaze, he was literally rolling on the deck of the ship clutching his stomach.

"I hope you get fleas," I said as I entered the interior of the ship, causing Panda to laugh even harder.

I still had the quest notification to open, but it could wait until the morning. It had promised a new active skill and on the off chance I got any say in what that was I wanted to be clear headed for it.

***

Lucas laid Sally down gently in her captain's cabin. It was a far cry from the tiny, single bedrooms he'd passed on his way through the ship's interior.

It was surprisingly indulgent for a woman of her tastes. There was a double bed, a porthole window and even a dressing table.

He was most surprised by the last part considering she hardly wore clothes at all. As a *Barbarian* she gained defence bonuses for wearing less.

She was the walking personification of the proverb: less is more.

Her wound was quite deep, it was obvious she'd taken a serious slash from her opponent.

*How did Kaleb manage to get her out of there?* Lucas wondered as he examined the wound and applied a healing salve from his inventory.

Sally was no slouch, so if she'd taken this level of damage then the monster who did it must have been fearsome. How had a phase one outworlder managed to save her.

He felt the familiar presence of his god's aura seep into his mind and, finishing up applying the salve, he reported in.

"The boy is safe. He did remarkably well, though I think he'd have been killed if I hadn't arrived in time," he said aloud, taking care to keep his voice low.

*Good. I warned you that the Goblin King Coronation required more than a single silver ranker.*

"You did, yet they did remarkably well. How did a phase one manage to save Sally, My Lord? She's the strongest person in these parts... apart from me."

*I cannot provide a clear answer. I can only see glimmers of his soul. Without him holding my blessing, I can't watch him omnipotently. I only managed to speak to him briefly this time in a dire moment.*

*However, a powerful enemy laid dead at his feet when I did.*

"Of course, My Lord, I shouldn't have brought it up. He currently holds the blessing of the wealth god from what I understand."

*That is correct. That buffoon Chrysus beat me to the punch.*

Lucas felt a surge of incalculable rage in his mind that wasn't his own. He made a mistake in mentioning Chrysus. He knew full well the sordid history between the wealth god and his lord.

He regretted it as the immense power from his god's aura coursed through his brain. It was like a migraine, apart from the nasty side effect of making his eyes bleed.

He pulled a handkerchief from his inventory and dabbed the blood from his face and eyes.

*Keep an eye on the boy until he's back in Havar. I have a quest you should give him before the exam.*

"Yes, My Lord," Lucas replied and he felt the aura of his god leave his mortal body.

*I need a drink.* He thought, pulling a glass and bottle from his inventory. He poured the amber liquid carefully before downing the beverage in a single gulp.

"You should really just drink from the bottle if you're gonna down it anyway. It saves on the washing up," Sally groaned from her bed.

"You're awake then?" He asked suspiciously.

"I've been awake since that insidious presence entered you. I'm quite attune to powerful auras you know."

Lucas let the silence hang as he poured and downed another glass. He sighed heavily and sat down on the edge of Sally's bed.

"For what it's worth, I like the kid," Sally said, lifting herself up on her elbows. "I don't get along too well with the almighty kind, but your god certainly picked an interesting guy."

"Will you continue to watch over him for me?" Lucas asked, but he already knew the answer.

"I'll do my part, but he needs to experience things on his own if you want him to develop."

He'd expected as much. Sally was the hands-off kind of teacher. Still, if she liked Kaleb, then perhaps his task was worth all the stress that came with it.

***

I woke up feeling myself again after, what could only be described as, the best nap I'd ever had.

The fog in my head had cleared and I was ready to see my new skill. Thankfully, I hadn't dreamed at all this time. I had to admit, I was a little weary of sleep after the nightmare I'd had in the mountain.

I shuddered at the thought of it. It felt so real, and that voice. Where had I heard it before?

Pushing those thoughts aside I decided to finally check my quest notification.

**Quest Complete!**
*The Goblin King Coronation*

**Every century a new goblin king is chosen. He who is destined to unite the clans and conquer the world – or so ancient goblin lore says.**
**Crash the party, kill the king, and get to the *Winchester* for a nice cold pint whilst you wait for it all to blow over.**
**After making your way to the mountain on the Forbidden Isles, you managed to gain admission into the Goblin King Ball.**
**Whilst there, you goaded Giles, a goblin king candidate, into challenging you to a duel where you killed him in full view of his clan and the other attendees.**

Your party member infiltrated the tournament of the goblin king where she successfully defeated candidate *Gerad*.
Goblin king candidate *Geralt* killed candidate *Gerald* so you didn't have to.
After a gruelling fight, you successfully eliminated *Geralt* with a sneak attack to the head.
You claimed the crown for yourself.

Objectives:
*Stop the coronation 1/1*
*Kill throne candidates 4/4*

Hidden Objective:
*Steal the crown 1/1*

Reward: *A New Passive Skill*

*WARNING*
*Due to the completion of a hidden objective. The reward has changed to a unique passive skill.*

As I read through the updated quest, I realised the system had added an abridged, blow by blow account of our activity.

When I reached the end, I wasn't sure what to think. I really needed more active skills, but surely a hidden objective would yield a better reward?

I nudged Panda before opening the new skill. He'd been asleep at the foot of the bed and didn't seem to want to wake up.

"Panda, I need your help," I said, shaking him firmly.

"Let me sleep!" He groaned.

"But I need some sagely wisdom and you're the only one I can turn to," I replied in a playful tone which got his attention.

He sat up and rubbed his eyes with his paws. It would have been cute if I didn't know his lacking personality. I used to think Pandas were adorable, but this one…not so much.

With Panda awake and ready, I opened the reward skill.

**You have unlocked a new passive skill:**
***Usurper (unique)***

**Due to your needless refusal to bow to kings, your soul has been forever changed.**
**The bane of gods and royalty alike, you're not only defiant and disrespectful to authority. You've gone as far as to usurp the throne of the Goblin King from its rightful heir.**

***Your soul has gained strength.***

***You are immune to monarch-based soul manipulation skills.***

I had no idea what that meant, but it sounded good. I didn't think I had a problem with authority myself though.

I'd always done my job back on earth and followed the rules laid out by the various driving companies. Would someone who had a problem with authority do that? I think not.

"That's a great skill," Panda said, still rubbing sleep from his eyes. "I'm glad you woke me up for it. I've only ever seen that skill be handed out once before and it came in handy a few times."

"What does it mean?" I asked.

"Some of the more powerful adventurers, gods and kings have skills called *Monarch* skills. They differ slightly from person to person but for the most part they subjugate people.

"Sometimes it's a charisma thing and the victims don't realise it's a skill. Sometimes it's through mind control or other nefarious means.

"Being immune to it will be a huge boon if you ever meet some-one with a skill like that. Assuming they don't decide to outright kill you for having it that is."

"Oh great. More powerful people trying to kill me. Isn't being hunted for your skin bad enough?"

"You're preaching to the choir there, kid."

# Chapter 41
# One Pump Chump

After finishing the quest and acquiring my newest skill there was only one thing left to do. Assign my free stat points. Considering both of my active skills relied heavily on stamina, I decided to, once again, put all 25 points into the strength stat.

Extra health would have been a good choice too. But I was itching to try out my new *Soul Shot* technique. I wanted to be able to use *Perception of the Apex Predator* to greater effect too.

As it currently stood, I could barely get half a second of time dilation out of it by using almost all of the stamina I had. I was going to need a huge well of stamina to draw from if I ever wanted to use it mid fight.

With that decided I went ahead and placed all of my free points into strength and checked my stats.

**Name: Kaleb Akabane**
**Race: Outworlder**
**Class: Apex Predator (unique)**
**Adventurer Rank: Temp**
**Level: 32**
**Map Pieces 2/10,000**
**HP: 331/306 (331)**
**Stamina: 318/305 (318)**

Strength: 275 (288)
Agility: 118
Perception: 114
Vitality: 246 (270)
Intelligence: 39

Personal Skills: *Speak English Damnit! Eat Anything,*
*Minor Poison Resistance, Usurper (unique)*
Class Skills (Passive): *Newly Qualified Bowman (0%),*
*Dagger (lvl 9), Acid Dhampir Dagger, Acid Arrows,*
*Environmental Hazzard*
Active Skills: *Perception of the Apex Predator (rare),*
*Soul Shot (ancient)*
Blessing: *Blessing of Wealth*
Familiars: *Panda (Daemon)*
Admission: Pentagram [Right hand (Morningstar Hotel
and Spa)]

I'd grown quite a bit over the course of the quest. I enjoyed being able to see my stat increases and changes in real time. It helped keep me motivated in my goal of getting stronger.

I sat back for a moment and smiled to myself as I read through them. Then I slid off the bed and left the cabin.

The moment I opened the door I could smell the enticing aroma of a home cooked meal. It didn't smell like copious amounts of overcooked meat though.

I headed into the kitchen-come-dining room with Panda hot on my heels.

"Sally!" he exclaimed, waddle running towards her like an over-zealous toddler.

She sat at the table, wearing a fresh bandage over her wound. I was surprised it hadn't healed yet. Usually sleep and a potion did the trick for me.

"Morning Furball," she replied with a fangy smile.

"You seem to be doing better," I said, pulling a chair out and joining her.

"Thanks to you. It seems you saved my life Gonads." She laughed. "What did I tell you about not doing anything reckless and stupid?" She asked, her tone changing all of a sudden as she leant forward and hit the top of my head.

It felt like my head was a church bell that had been unceremoniously rung. I was dazed for a good moment before I could see properly again.

It seemed that even wounded, she was a powerhouse.

"Yeah, sorry not sorry. Someone had to complete the quest didn't they," I replied.

"From what Lucas here tells me, you killed a few hundred goblins on your way out too. No small feat for such a puny weakling."

"Coming from the woman wearing a bandage in a world with healing potions."

She laughed and so did I. It was nice to know that she was doing ok. I was curious about the bandage though. However, she seemed to have no intention of explaining it.

So far in my time in Celestia, I'd healed up completely every time. Scars didn't last long and I had no lingering wounds. A health potion or a good night's rest would cure just about anything.

I was beginning to wonder if I could even grow limbs back. Though it was more likely that healing would just close up the stump.

"I see you've reached phase two," Sally said idly.

"Yeah, not too shabby for my first week in this world, eh?" I grinned.

"It's passable," Director Lucas said. I searched to find where his voice had come from and realised he was the one cooking the food.

He stood in the kitchen wearing his signature embroidered suit and white apron that was branded with a facsimile of the Adventure Society slogan.

*Adventure Society: Frying The Monsters Under Your Bed.*

I thought it was a bit tacky, but I still found it amusing.

It was an odd sight though, to see the gold ranked adventurer who'd saved me by Pied Pipering an entire horde of goblins off a cliff in an apron.

"What can I expect now that I'm a phase two?" I asked the room.

Panda was the first to reply, jumping onto the table. He placed his paws behind his back and began pacing.

"Well kid, phase two is a good starting point for a rookie adventurer. Now you've hit it, the levels are going to come slower. You should gain a new skill every ten levels from now on as well."

"I've been getting them randomly so far," I cut in.

"That's how the system operates with outworlders. You arrive here with the strength of a newborn. Whilst children in this world are expected to take about eighteen years to reach phase two, you don't have that long.

"You're dropped into this world, usually as an adult, and expected to fit in and make it work. The system compensates for this by granting outworlders a few boons.

"One of those is the random acquisition of skills. Kids in Celestia have their entire childhoods to decide what kind of path they want to follow and the skills that come with that path are often granted to them at later phase one levels.

"You don't get that luxury, so the system grants you skills at random, allowing you to choose some of them and basing the skills it gives you off what you accomplish and how you fight."

I had wondered about that. The system had seemed to give me skills based off things I'd done. My *Apex Predator* class was given to me because I pushed that cultist guy into a vat of acid.

Thinking about it, I'd also been offered other classes based on how I'd fought. Like the *Trucker* class that was entirely based on how Panda and I escaped from the cultist hideout.

"What other perks do I get?" I asked enthusiastically.

"Achievements," Panda replied poignantly. "No one else gets them. Only you outworlders. They're a good thing to have as well, those loot boxes are no joke."

"He's forgetting the most important thing about phase two though," Sally interrupted. "It's a much harder path to walk for an adventurer than it is for professionals. You'll have to face harder monsters and put yourself in more and more danger if you want to advance.

"Grinding weaker foes isn't an option for adventurers in this world. You can kill them too, don't get me wrong, but at a certain point you won't gain any experience from them.

"The system is fair, but it has a sadistic personality that thrives on violence and high stakes. Never forget that."

Her words rang true from what I knew of the system so far. It had given me some great skills, though it was rather passive aggressive and rude. But it also seemed to take pleasure in my suffering.

It rewarded me for killing and gave me quests that kept putting me in more and more danger. Not to mention it tattooed me with a map piece that some creepy cultist dudes wanted.

Speaking of the cultists, I hadn't seen any since we'd escaped their temple. That was only a few days ago but it felt like much longer.

A lot had happened in that time.

"That's enough work talk for now," Lucas said, walking towards us with plates in his arms. "You'll overload the poor boy."

He placed the plates down on the table in front of us and my mouth began watering. It was a full English breakfast, or close to it.

I was sure there weren't any pigs in this place, but something on my plate certainly looked like bacon.

In fact, the entire plate looked just like a full English: bacon, sausage, eggs, baked beans, hash brown, tomatoes, mushrooms, you name it.

I slyly gave the mushrooms to Panda when Lucas turned back around. Mushrooms were not my thing. Not only did they taste awful, but they also *felt* awful in your mouth and they held no real nutritional value.

Why would any self-respecting person eat them? Mushrooms were a big bag of nope.

Luckily, my familiar was the herbivore equivalent of a waste disposal unit and he sucked them down like a vacuum cleaner.

His breakfast was quite different to mine and Sally's. He had a bowl full of greens and some bamboo. Lucas must have stocked up before he came. No way the dude carried bamboo in his inventory normally.

After breakfast I rushed to the deck of the ship. My hunger had gotten the better of me, but I had an active skill I could actually use and I just had to try it out.

When I'd picked the skill an innate knowledge of how to use it had downloaded into my brain. It gave me quite the headache.

I pulled out my bow and nocked an arrow.

Sally had followed me outside. Despite her bandage she didn't seem overly injured. Without a word she produced a plate from her inventory and I nodded to her.

She counted down from three and launched the plate into the air.

As I pulled back the bowstring I could feel my soul's energy coursing through my entire body. Like the red rope I'd visualised during meditation, except this energy was acid green and more ethereal.

The rope seemed tangible, almost like I could pick it up and use it. But the green energy felt more like mist, like something I could manipulate, but never touch.

That was energy that my instincts and skill knowledge wanted me to tap into. I visualised it seeping through my fingers and into the arrow.

I could practically see it warping around the arrow itself until it was glowing with an acid green energy. This all happened in a fraction of a second. Then I fired it.

It blasted out of my bow, like a rocket taking off. When it hit its target, the plate vanished. It had been completely vapourised and the arrow just kept going.

I really hoped it wouldn't accidentally kill someone. I wasn't expecting it to be that powerful.

"Nice!" Sally exclaimed giving me an approving nod. "Though you might want to use less power next time, at your level, that probably took up all of your stamina. You don't want to be a one pump chump."

I checked the stats on my HUD and she was right. From that single shot I'd dropped from 318 to 23 stamina. I was going to need to practice a lot more if I wanted to reliably use *Soul Shot* in combat without passing out.

Still, I was happy with the power I had at my disposal. Every adventurer needs a powerful attack, that one hit kill attack that they pull out for the big boss.

Now I had one, I felt more like I belonged at Adventure Society.

And speaking of the society, looking over the side of the ship I could see their skyscraper lighting up the Havar skyline.

We'd be back in an hour or so by my best guess, and I had a lot of stuff to do.

# Chapter 42
# Not The Religious Type

We arrived back in Havar less than an hour after I spotted the Adventure Society building. Landing with a splash, Sally docked the ship and we departed at last.

It felt like ages since I'd left Havar for the *Goblin King Coronation* quest.

Sally left with the director to hand in the completed quest. She promised to give me a fair share of the reward as payment for dragging her out of the arena.

Then, almost as soon as we'd stepped off the dock, I found myself alone in the big city. Well, apart from Panda.

"What's the plan kid?" Panda asked, lighting up his bamboo pipe as we walked leisurely away from the port district.

I had a few things I wanted to do. With loot money burning a hole in my inventory I figured it was about time to buy some armour, assuming I could afford any.

I'd also promised to replace some of the books I'd ruined in my makeshift defence against Gertrude's goblin tribe.

Panda had bugged me about it incessantly on the journey home. He complained that he was bored and a lack of mental nourishment would somehow make him less sagely...or something like that.

I also had a few loot boxes to open and I needed to return to the inn to open them.

"I'm thinking, loot boxes, armourer and then we'll try and get you some books," I replied casually as we left the port.

As we wandered onto the main street, I found myself smiling at the quirky city with its modern skyscrapers, medieval taverns, and races of all kinds.

It really was something straight out of an isekai manga.

"You know you could have opened one of them inside the mountain," he muttered as we walked.

"Oh yeah, it's any safe area, isn't it?" I chuckled. The truth was, we'd been so preoccupied with the quest that I'd completely forgotten I had a loot box to open.

I'd also been a bit busy meditating. I'd earned a *Duellist's Loot Box* after I defeated Giles in single combat. I was low on stamina and HP after that though so I was taught how to meditate.

Everything had happened so fast after that; the thought had honestly never crossed my mind.

After about ten minutes of walking down the busy main street, I made a turn down an alleyway that Panda assured me was a shortcut to the *Sleeping Giant Inn* where I still had a room for three nights.

The alleyway was a tight, cobbled back alley and it was deserted. It ran between some shops and cut through to the next street over which was where the inn was located.

We weren't exactly rushed for time, but I was keen to open my loot boxes before I went armour shopping. The last thing I wanted to do was waste my money on something only to find out the loot box had given me something better.

At the head of the alley a robed man turned off the street and headed towards us. I didn't pay much attention; the alley was a cut through to the high street after all.

Still, something about his robe caught my attention. It was familiar.

He had his head down as he walked and honestly, he was unassuming.

"Watch out!" Panda yelled, as we were about to meet him in the middle.

I jumped back, as the tip of a blade slashed through the air where my throat had been less than a second earlier.

I summoned my dagger and took a few steps back. Who was this guy and why was he attacking me?

Acting on instinct I dashed forward, aiming my blade at his stomach. With lightning-fast reactions, he blocked me and with a second, hidden dagger from under his cloak, he struck.

I managed to avoid it, barely, and kicked out at him. He grunted as I knocked him back and I pressed the advantage.

Moving forward I took a swing at his face. He bent himself backwards at an unnatural angle and avoided it. A proper *Matrix* dodge if I'd ever seen one.

I took a step forward and thrusted the dagger at his exposed chest, but he brought up one of the two daggers he was holding and parried me.

Whoever this robed fighter was, he was very skilled.

I jumped back to reassess.

I seemed to be no match for him in close quarter melee, but I had another trick up my sleeve.

I started walking backwards quickly as I dismissed my dagger and summoned my bow. Nocking an arrow I activated my new skill: *Soul Shot*. I began building up power into the bow, my internal energy flowing out of my hand and wrapping the arrow with an acid green glow.

The man dashed forward, both daggers in his hands and I loosed the arrow.

In the cramped alleyway the backdraft from my own shot knocked me off balance and I stumbled. The man couldn't dodge an attack like this.

There was only room to move forwards or backwards and the arrow's speed was insane.

It passed right through him and I cheered internally. No notification came though.

My arrow crashed out of the alleyway and flew into the front door of a shop a street over, blowing the door off its hinges as civilians gasped and cried out.

*Oh crap, now I'm gonna have to convince them I'm not a terrorist.*

I looked up and down the alleyway but the robed man was nowhere to be seen. Where had he gone? I couldn't have killed him, there was no notification.

"Well met," a crackly voice said from behind me.

I spun on my heels, resummoning my dagger. The man was a few meters away from me. I couldn't make out any of his features. His blood red robes covered him completely and his hood draped over his face.

"Chrysus sends his regards," he said, before disappearing in a cloud of smoke leaving nothing but a piece of paper that drifted side to side as it fell to the floor.

"What was that all about? Panda asked curiously.

Chrysus, the god of wealth was the man who'd forced me to take his rather useful blessing. He was also the leader of the cult that had captured me.

His goal was to piece together the Celestial Map by skinning the outworlders to get their tattoos.

He'd asked me to join him and I'd refused. Though he did succeed in getting me to take his blessing. It was either that or die, and the blessing was the only reason I could loot gold from monsters.

I stepped forward tentatively, still on guard from a possible surprise attack, and picked up the paper.

> **You have been granted the honour of being allowed to compete in the high priest's tournament.**
> **The winner will be granted riches of Chrysus, God of Wealth.**
> **The tournament will take place in six months' time.**
> **Do you accept?**
> **Y/N**

"He wants me to compete in some high priest tournament thingy," I said aloud so Panda could hear me.

"Attacking you in the street's not a very polite invitation," Panda replied.

"Agreed. It worries me a bit though. He seemed to find me without any trouble. I wonder if the blessing allows Chrysus to track me?" I said, thinking aloud more than I was talking to Panda.

"Blessings allow Gods to know where you are and talk to you directly. Though they rarely use them for that," Panda said, taking the paper from me and skimming the text. "This is a big deal. Being the right hand of a god is no joke, it's instant access to a metric fuck tonne of power kid."

"Fuck no. I'm not the religious type."

"Well either way, you should keep the invitation. It's enchanted so it could be valuable."

I had to admit, it did pique my interest, but I had no intention of ever serving a god. Especially not a deranged cult leader who wanted to murder 10,000 outworlders to complete a silly map.

The guy was a lunatic and I wanted no part of it.

I touched the paper and added it to my inventory and then walked back onto the main street we'd originally come from.

"Let's go the long way around, I'm pretty sure I blew up a shopfront with my arrow on the other street."

"Good idea," Panda replied. "It'll be fixed quickly, magic is useful like that, but it's better to avoid unnecessary confrontation at your level... and the owner will be pissed."

"Maybe we should stop by the Adventure Society on the way back to the inn. I probably have reward money to collect anyway," I mused.

Panda nodded and we began walking in that direction. Despite the commotion on the adjacent street, the high street was quiet.

People moved quickly, manoeuvring around each other as they went about their busy lives. They were seemingly oblivious to the fight that had just happened down the alley, or maybe they were just used to it.

The Adventure Society was up ahead and we arrived a few minutes later. I walked through the large double doors into the foyer. A group of temp adventurers were looking over the quests on the noticeboard.

I'd need to pick my second mandatory quest soon, but we'd just gotten back so it could wait a day or two.

Instead, I walked over to the desk to the beaming, friendly smile of Lucy. She was the blonde catonid receptionist who had a thing for Panda.

"Hello Mr Akabane, good to see you've returned safely from your quest. How did it go?" She asked politely.

I distinctly remembered asking her to call me Kaleb last time we'd spoken, but I had been a bit awkward about it so I couldn't fault her for remaining professional.

"Oh, you know, the usual. Killed a lot of monsters, nearly died a few times, got some levels, saved a silver ranker from a horde of goblins. Just a regular Tuesday really," I replied cheekily.

She chuckled at my response as Panda began climbing onto the desk. She helped him the rest of the way up and began fondling his ears.

"It sounds exciting. You'll be glad to know that Sally handed in the return forms about ten minutes ago. She stipulated that the reward was to be split evenly between the two of you. You must have made quite the impression for a silver ranker to do that. Though I don't know what a Tuesday is."

Panda sat quietly as she stroked him, he looked to be thoroughly enjoying himself.

"She's a good friend," I replied thoughtfully, ignoring the invitation to explain earthen days of the week.

"Friend? That's quite the bold statement Mr Akabane, but far be it for me to question you." She smiled but looked confused.

Was it really that strange for a silver ranked adventurer and a new recruit to be friends?

"So, what's the reward?" I asked. "Sally never told me."

"Let me just grab it for you," she said, ducking under the desk for a moment. I heard the distinct sound of jingling.

She appeared back a moment later with a large pouch in her hand.

"Most quest rewards are paid in gold; this one was no exception. Every now and then the guild offers rare items as rewards, but they're usually reserved for gold ranked quests or higher.

"Anyway, here's your reward: 1000 gold coins," she said, holding the coin pouch out towards me with both hands.

I accepted it gratefully, adding it to my inventory. Interestingly enough, I'd earned more than that from my looting power.

Still, a grand in gold isn't anything to scoff at. Hopefully it'd help me buy something cool before my next quest.

I thanked her and left the building with Panda, I still had loot boxes to open.

"You know, flirting with the receptionist is a bit cliché kid," Panda said as we left.

"Then what were you doing purring as she fondled your ears?" I shot back.

"Me and her are both animals with evolved intellect. Call it animal magnetism,"

"Aren't you old enough to be her great, great grandfather?"

"Shut it kid. At least I'm not a furry."

# Chapter 43
# Stalin's Stylish Socks

After leaving the Adventure Society with an extra 1000 gold in my inventory, we went the long way around to the *Sleeping Giant Inn*.

It seemed that no matter what time of day it was, the city was always a hive of activity. Bustling with life as lycanids, catonids, humans, and other races I didn't recognise rushed around the various districts.

I made a mental note to go exploring when I had some free time. So far, I'd only been to the docks, the society district, and the high street.

That only covered a small part of the huge city. I wondered if there was anything interesting to find on the other side of town.

We reached the inn and went inside. I greeted the lycanid landlady who blushed slightly as I spoke to her and retired to my room.

**You are now entering a safe zone.**

I sat down on the bed in the small room and eagerly dived into my rewards section on the HUD. Panda sat next to me, watching what I was doing.

He could see the major actions on my HUD due to his nature as a daemon familiar.

I found the loot boxes and began the opening procedure. Loot boxes opened one after the other once you clicked to open one. Luckily, I didn't really have any time constraints.

*You are in a safe area. Open all loot boxes?*
*Y/N*

### Duellist's Loot Box

**You've won your first duel! How very old fashioned of you. From knights to cowboys to immoral plantation owners, duels were the pinnacle of minor dispute resolution.**
**Is your neighbour mowing the grass too early? Is your grandma doing that thing where she licks a handkerchief and uses it to clean your face? Is your significant other's snoring keeping you up all night? There's only one solution.**
**Pistols at dawn!**

**Reward: *Dueling Glove***

The box popped open like a shot being fired from a gun and firecrackers exploded all around it as a single white glove floated out of it and disappeared into my inventory.

### Little Bitch Loot Box

**As the name implies, this box has been rewarded due to your bitch move of stealing someone's kill by getting in the last hit right as they were about to die.**
**We've already covered this. Take your damn reward.**

**Reward: *Personal Skill: Health Sense (common)***

A new personal skill? That was unexpected. I didn't even know you could get skills through boxes.

"You've done well there, kid," Panda said, nodding to himself.

As the box opened, there were no flashing lights, no fireworks, or confetti. Just the resonating sound of a someone saying the word "bitch."

Followed by a small, almost tangible light that flew into my chest and disappeared into me.

*Classy.*

### Genocide Loot Box

**Since you love mass murder, it stands to reason that you'd also love the king of the gulags, *Joseph Stalin*. As such, I hope you enjoy this one-of-a-kind reward. Remember the only clothing you brought with you to this world? Because I do. Don't say I never give you anything thoughtful.**
**I'm sure you're *Russian* through this notification to get to your fabulous reward, so I'll stop *Stalin* and tell you what it is.**

### Reward: *Stalin's Stylish Socks*

I wasn't quite sure what to think about that. I was a little taken aback by the reward in all honesty.

"Who's *Joseph Stalin*?" Panda asked with childlike curiosity.

"Use that sage skill of yours and *google* it," I replied monotonously.

I waited a moment as the golden box played tense orchestral music whilst the lid opened slowly. A pair of bright red socks appeared with a golden embroidery that depicted a hammer and sickle.

*These socks better be good. I feel disgusted just having them in my inventory.* I sighed inwardly as they disappeared in a bright red light.

I'd studied Russian history in school and it was equal parts interesting and horrifying. Those guys sure had it rough after *Lenin* died.

"Oh my God, I just looked him up. Kaleb you absolutely cannot wear that item," Panda said loudly.

Shaking my head slightly, I dived into my inventory to check out what my rewards actually did.

### Duelling Glove

**I demand satisfaction! Wearing these gloves increases your accuracy with all ranged weapons.**

***+10% agility.***

That wasn't bad. A boost in stats was always welcome and you could never have too much accuracy.

I equipped the glove and immediately felt a small sense of power course through me.

I wasn't too keen on the look of it though. Wearing a single white glove reminded me too much of *Michael Jackson.*

I wasn't going to let a little thing like fashion get in the way of a powerful item though. It fit snuggly on my right hand, the hand I used to draw the bowstring. It coincidentally covered my pentagram tattoo as well.

I wasn't actively trying to hide it or anything, but since it signalled that I was a player killer, accidentally or not, it was probably good that I wouldn't be showcasing it anymore.

Oddly, the glove seemed to shape itself entirely to my hand. It didn't feel like I was wearing a glove at all.

I touched the bed sheets and could feel them just fine. It was like the glove was a part of me.

Moving on I decided to check out the other item I'd received.

## Stalin's Stylish Socks

**These socks let everyone know that you're in charge.
With their bright red colouring and their golden
hammer and sickle, you'll be the talk of the town.**

Was that it? An item that did nothing at all. No stat bonus, no skill, no…nothing. That made the choice of resigning them to the depths of my inventory, never to be seen again, that much easier.

"What was the point of even getting a reward like that?" I asked Panda incredulously. "It doesn't even do anything."

"Not all rewards are useful." He shrugged like it was normal to get duds in boxes. "I was summoned by an outworlder a few centuries ago who got crappy rewards all the time.

"This one time, the system gave him a loot box that took up the entire room and when it opened all he got was a t-shirt that said: *I went to another world and all I got was vast cosmic power.* Utter let down."

Oddly, it was kind of comforting to know that I wasn't the only one the system was a dick to.

Putting my crappy socks aside, I went into my skills and focused on the new one.

### Health Sense (common)

**Sense the health of those around you.
Usually reserved for healer classes, Health Sense allows
you to sense the HP level of those around you.**

That was interesting. As I read the new skill, I felt a small amount of knowledge enter my brain allowing me to use the skill.

It was simple. I looked towards Panda and focused very slightly and his health appeared floating above his head.

It didn't tell in numbers how much he had; it was more of a health bar. It was currently green and full to the brim.

*Just like every video game I've ever played.* I thought with satisfaction.

I wasn't sure how useful this skill would be but it was definitely novel. I liked it.

Standing up decisively. I decided it was time to go buy some armour. I wasn't sure exactly what I wanted, but spending money on something that would help keep me alive seemed like a good idea.

"Panda, can you take me to an armourer?" I asked.

"Certainly, there's one a short walk from here."

He led me out of the inn and down the street a short way. We passed by the shop I'd accidentally shot an arrow into and an angry looking lycanid stood in front of it, lifting a patchwork door up and attaching hinges to it.

*So much for magic.* I thought, feeling a tang of guilt.

"Hey, is there anything I can do to help you with that?" I asked, approaching the man.

I wasn't the most moral of people but I had been the one to destroy it. I had no intention of telling him that, but it was only right that I at least offer to help him fix it.

"Not unless you've got one hundred gold coins spare so I can hire a mage," he replied in a deflated tone.

"No problem," I said, pulling 100 gold from my inventory and handing it to him.

He dropped the door and looked at me with an open mouth. He seemed shocked so I opened his hand for him and deposited the money into it, most of it spilled onto the ground with a myriad of clinks.

I began walking away before he called out to me.

"I don't understand, why would you...thank you! Come back any time, my treat!"

He sounded grateful and I felt good at having done a good deed. Besides, 100 gold wasn't that much considering how much I'd earnt from looting monsters and collecting the quest reward.

It was only right that I pay to fix the thing I broke. Not that I would be admitting that it was my fault to the owner any time soon.

He seemed to run a small restaurant, maybe I would pop in some time for a meal. I hadn't tried much of Celestia's cuisine so far after all.

"Well, that was a waste of money. Just think of all the books you could have bought me with that," Panda grumbled as we walked.

"How much do books cost in this world?" I asked.

"Depends on the book. The magic printing press doesn't mass produce too many of them. Only the really popular ones. You can get those cheap but for a rare one it can be expensive."

"Well then let's hope I have enough left over, after I buy some armour, to get you one."

Panda led me to a large shop a little further down from the restaurant. It was the only building on the street that was fully detached, though it was also only a single story.

A neon sign glowed above it in purple writing that said: *Andy's Armour Emporium.*

It struck me as a bit odd for an armour shop to have a neon sign, but I guessed it was probably a wealth thing. There were a lot of adventurers in town and from what I'd heard, gear was insanely expensive.

I walked inside and heard the sound of clanging metal coming form the back somewhere.

In the front there were mannequins galore, covered in all sorts of armour. One looked like a medieval knight, there was one

330

wearing a golden cloak and another dressed like robin hood with a green jerkin and feathered hat.

One set in particular caught my eyes though.

It was jet black and the torso piece was covered in intricate embroidery. It had black pants with knee pads and a cool, hooded cloak that covered half of the face with eye slits to look out of.

I wasn't certain if that would block my vision or not, but it looked awesome.

I walked up to the counter and read a small sign that had been left there.

*In back.*

It seemed the armourer was a man of few words. Walking around the desk I went into the back room where the source of the clanging was coming from.

A tall, well-muscled man with broad shoulders and unkempt brunet hair was working.

He stood over an anvil and seemed to be hammering a helmet with vigour. He didn't even notice me come in. It was mesmerizing to watch and I found myself staring for a solid few minutes.

He was wearing armoured black pants, boots, and a dirty, brown leather apron over his front.

His body glistened with sweat. He was obviously the hard-working type.

"Excuse me," I said, attempting to raise my voice over the loud clanking of his hammer.

He didn't seem to hear me. I looked at Panda and he shrugged. I guess I'd have to shout louder.

"Excuse me!" I shouted, cupping my hands around my mouth.

Still nothing. I could barely hear my own voice over the noise so it made sense that he wouldn't hear me either.

I walked towards him and tapped him on the shoulder to get his attention instead.

Without warning a large hammer swung at my face.

# Chapter 44
# Up Shit's Creek

I ducked down instinctually and, as the hammer swung over my head, jumped back up with an uppercut.

The man batted my hand away with his own as if he was swatting a fly and I jumped backwards, summoning my dagger.

He stood opposite me, holding his hammer limply in his right hand. He looked me up and down with calculating eyes.

"You shouldn't make a guy jump like that you know?" He said in a gruff voice, scratching the back of his head with his free hand. "I nearly broke your face." He laughed loudly.

"Yeah...maybe next time try looking at the person trying to get your attention instead of trying to kill them," I replied, placing my dagger back into my inventory.

"Well in my defence, if you tried using your words instead of tapping me this wouldn't have happened."

"I did, but your hammering was too damn loud for you to hear me," I replied irritably.

"Is that so?" He said, rubbing his hairless chin. "Then in that case, allow me to offer my apologies. So, anyway, what can I do you for?"

I took a deep breath. The man was irritatingly carefree. He could have taken my head off and yet there he was laughing about it as if it was a happy accident.

"I'm in the market for some armour and my familiar recommended your shop."

Panda stepped out from behind me and blew out a puff of smoke from his bamboo pipe.

"Long time no see Andy," he said, giving a slight wave with his free paw.

"Panda? I guess some unfortunate soul summoned you again, and so soon," Andy replied, grinning at the daemon. "After what happened with—"

"I don't want to talk about that," Panda cut in swiftly. "This is Kaleb, he needs armour. Think you can help him out."

Andy looked a little hesitant at Panda's sudden interruption. He looked at him with an odd gleam in his eyes, I think it was pity.

"Yeah, sure thing," he said, placing the hammer down on the anvil. "Let's talk in the front and I'll see what I can do."

He walked past us and I turned to follow him. I gazed at Panda who seemed normal, but something bugged me. I hoped he was alright. He'd never really talked about his last master but it was obviously a painful memory for him.

Back in the front of the shop Andy jumped up onto the countertop and sat cross legged. He turned to face me as I moved back to the customer side of the counter.

"So, what are you in the market for Kaleb?" He asked with a smile.

"I don't know exactly. I'm new in town and I don't really know how expensive armour is here, or what's on offer. I do like the look of that though," I said, pointing at the black armour that had caught my eye earlier.

"Good eye. That's one of my finest works. The whole set will set you back 50,000 gold pieces. "

"50,000?" I spluttered.

I knew armour was supposed to be expensive in Celestia but that seemed like an awful lot.

"I've got just shy of 5000," I countered. "What can I get with that?" I asked nervously.

Andy looked at me thoughtfully and rubbed his non-existent beard again.

"That set comes with a bracer. I could give you that for 5000, but then I'd be breaking up the set and no one wants to buy an uncompleted set of armour," he mused thoughtfully; it sounded more like he was thinking out loud than conversing with me.

"I've got some boots that'd cost something similar but they're designed for heavy fighters and you look more like an officer worker than a knight.

I opened my mouth to say something back but thought better of it. I was still wearing a shirt and suit pants after all, so he had a point.

"I might still have a basic leather breast plate in the back," he continued. "Though honestly, I'd suggest you save your money and come back when you can afford the 50,000 gold.

"And believe me, I'm *only* saying that because you're Panda's new human. Normally I'd take the money and run." He chuckled, tapping his fingers on the table in an oddly syncopated rhythm.

I was disappointed. I thought the 4700 gold I had would at least get me something. I really wanted that black armour though. Something in the back of my mind told me it would be worth the wait. Then I had an idea.

"Can I put a deposit down so you won't sell it to someone else whilst I make more money?" I asked hopefully.

There was no point in waiting to buy the armour if it was gone the next time I came in.

Besides, looking around the shop it was the only thing that would suit me. Most of the armour Andy was selling was full plate and looked like it was made for a tank style class. Accept, of course, for the Robin Hood cosplay, but even I had enough fashion sense to know wearing that would be committing social suicide.

"I think I can make that work. For 2000 gold I promise not to sell that set for a month. You'll have to pay more to keep it off the shelf for longer though, I've still got to make a living." He winked and simultaneously clicked his tongue.

"Ok, and what happens if I'm away on a quest when the month is up and you sell it, do I get my money back?"

"I'll give you half back if you fail to meet the deadline. However, the money you give me now as a down payment will go towards the overall cost of the set. So, you need to come back here with 48,000 in a month if you want it.

"Or you need to come back with at least another 2000 to buy yourself more time."

It seemed reasonable enough. I had no idea if I could make that much in only a month though.

I looked towards Panda for advice.

"Don't look at me, I'm a sage not a financial adviser," he said, taking another drag and blowing it towards me.

"Ok fine, it's a deal," I said, offering Andy my hand.

He shook it vigorously and grinned at me as I handed him the money.

"Nice doing business with you Kaleb. I guess I'll see you in a month."

With that he hopped off the counter and disappeared into the back of the shop.

"Was that really a good idea kid?" Panda asked as we left the shop. "Andy's good and all, but you don't even know what that armour does. It could be a pile of hot garbage."

"My instincts say it'll be worth it. Besides, what's the point of killing monsters if you don't look good whilst you're doing it?" I flashed him a toothy grin and he face palmed... or face pawed.

Now I just needed a good quest to earn some more money. Ideally a farming style quest where I could kill a lot of monsters.

With my wealth blessing that should be the fastest way to get a lot of coin, as fast as possible.

I started walking towards the adventurer guild to find out.

"Hey kid!" Panda shouted from behind.

I was so used to him following me all the time that I was surprised to turn around and see him still standing in front of the shop. "Book store's that way," he said, pointing over his shoulder.

I honestly had no interest in going to the bookstore right now, but I had promised to get him something.

"Here," I said, tossing him a coin purse with 700 gold in it. "Go get whatever you want and meet me back at the inn. I need to go to the Adventure Society before it closes."

Panda jumped up and caught the bag. He opened it and grinned.

"No problem kid, I'll see you later," he said, practically sprinting away before I could change my mind.

I got the sinking feeling that I'd given him way more gold than he needed.

*Good going Kaleb. You just keep throwing gold away when you need to save 48,000 in a month. This attitude is why you were always in credit card debt back home.*

With a light shake of my head I went to the Adventure Society. The sun was starting to set when I arrived, I wouldn't have long to choose my quest before they kicked me out.

On the upside though, the notice board was deserted. It seemed most temporary adventurers didn't come by this late in the day.

I walked towards the board and scanned it quickly. As expected, they were mostly simple fetch quests.

**Temp Quest: Find my cat.**
**Temp Quest: Collect 30 mushrooms from the wetlands.**
**Temp Quest: Bring me 40 Loconut's hairs.**

They were the standard beginner quests from an RPG game. They paid next to nothing and way too boring for a protagonist like me to deal with.

I couldn't have hit the *nope* button faster.

Then I saw a slightly different quest. Its parchment looked old and worn, like it had been pinned to the notice board for a long-ass time.

As I read it, I began to understand why no one had taken it. I grimaced just looking at it, but it would definitely help me to pay for my armour and I might even get a few levels in the process.

It was perfect.

I pulled it off the board and took it over to Lucy who took one look at it and also grimaced.

"Mr Akabane, this quest has been here for over a year. No one has ever shown interest in taking it before. Are you sure you want it?" She asked tentatively.

"Yes please Lucy," I replied happily. "It's perfect for what I need. Besides, the poor sod who posted it can't be very happy that no one has sorted it out."

"It was posted by the local government and you're right; they aren't very happy. The director was considering using it as a punishment quest." She looked worriedly at me.

"Oh really? If it's so bad you could pay me more to complete it," I replied cheekily.

The quest did only pay 500 gold. That was quite a lot in this world, but it was barely worth more than the fetch quests and would be much more work. No wonder no one wanted it.

"The quest giver sets the payment on temp contracts. Believe it or not that's quite a big reward from the government. They're quite stingy."

*I guess some things are universal no matter what world you're in.* I thought.

"If you're sure then I'll assign it to you," she eventually said with a sigh. "Just make sure you clean yourself up before handing it in."

She added my name to a register behind the reception desk and I walked out of the society building happily.

A new notification appeared on my HUD, making it official.

### New Quest!
*Up Shit's Creek*

There have been reports of a slime infestation in the sewers under Havar. Investigate the matter and exterminate them.

### Objectives:
Exterminate all the sewer slimes 0/1
Find the source of the slimes and deal with it 0/1

Reward: *500 gold.*

*\*Speak to the Adventure Society to claim your reward. Reward payable upon the successful completion of the above objectives\**

It was the perfect quest to raise money. Slimes were low level monsters in most video games, so it should be the same in Celestia.

More importantly, there were usually loads of them. So my looting power, combined with a large number of low-level monsters should equal a lot of gold coins in a short amount of time.

I was a genius. That armour would be mine in no time!

With a spring in my step, I headed back to the inn for a good night's rest. In the morning I'd start my quest of hunting slimes and making bank.

I had never been so glad I'd accepted a blessing from that annoying, self-proclaimed god. It almost made it worth nearly being skinned alive by a crazy cult.

Almost...but not quite.

I returned to the inn just as the sun fell beneath the sky. As I walked through the door I heard a familiar voice and the sound of cheers and laughter.

What had Panda gotten himself into?

# Chapter 45
# That Bitch Athena

"Next round is on me!" Panda squealed with joy as he lifted a wooden tankard in the air.

The crowd cheered and chairs scraped across the floor as they rushed to the bar to place their orders. Panda flipped the lycanid landlady a gold coin and whooped as he downed his drink and gestured for her to refill his tankard.

"What the hell are you doing!" I shouted as I entered the inn, causing the entire place to go silent.

"Kaleb! There's my guy. Come drink with us!" He slurred, pointing his tankard at me, and sloshing a thick amber liquid all over the floor.

"What happened to buying books?" I asked sternly as I crossed the room and the patrons moved aside for me.

"I got a whole bunch!" he slurred happily. "They're in our room. Oh, speaking of the room I paid for the rest of the month with the change I got and now I'm celebrating."

"Celebrating with *my* money," I said darkly.

I wasn't a cheapskate or anything, but I was saving up to buy armour. I was about to go wade through a dirty sewer, killing slimes to meet that goal, and my familiar of all creatures was throwing my money about like he was *Kanye West* on an egotistical presidential election campaign.

"Well...yeah," he said and swayed on the counter slightly. He'd obviously drank quite a bit already.

I'd only been gone a short while. Where had he found the time to buy books, pay rent *and* get sloshed.

"How much have you had?" I asked exasperatedly.

"He's only had a single drink," the lycanid landlady replied. "The one in his hand is his second."

"Only one?" I replied, flabbergasted. "Jesus, I really didn't take you for that much of a lightweight. Give me the coins you have left."

Panda reached beneath his fur and handed me a coin pouch, it felt significantly lighter than the one I'd given him before.

*He must have pulled that from his inventory. There's no way he kept that pouch inside his fur.* I thought.

I placed it into my inventory and saw that there were 53 gold coins left. He'd spent a lot, though from the sounds of it he mostly bought books and paid rent so I couldn't be too mad.

"How much to buy a round for the bar and keep him in drinks for the evening?" I asked the land lady.

"A few gold should do the trick," she smiled lecherously. It sent a shiver down my spine.

I placed three gold coins on the bar and kept the rest. It could go towards my armour fund.

"Have fun, but don't wake me up when you come to bed. I've got a busy day tomorrow," I said, petting Panda on the head.

"You're the bestest kid," he slurred. "You hear that guys? Kaleb's buying us all a round!"

The people in the bar cheered and lively chatter and drink orders ensued.

I guessed he did deserve to blow off some steam, especially after the goblin king coronation. I, however, had a new quest to start in the morning so I'd be retiring early.

***

Chrysus sat lazily on the golden throne in his domain. He leant his head onto his hand, his chiselled jaw line felt like an artistic masterpiece.

It was a perk of reaching godhood. The ability to choose and shape one's own appearance was a privilege of the truly powerful.

He wasn't one of the major gods. Those guys had churches in most major cities. He, however, had a vast network of worshippers, they just mostly did their worshipping in private.

Naturally, as the god of wealth, many of his merchant followers wore pendants made from gold coins. This was the universal symbol of his flock.

Of course, he also had his cult. They, however, were mostly hidden throughout Celestia. Their work was a bit taboo for the more narrow-minded mortals of the world.

It didn't help that bitch Athena had condemned his actions publicly. He'd get even with her one day though, once he got his hands on the treasure at the end of the Celestial Map.

The scar across his chest ached as he thought about Athena. It was a difficult task to permanently scar the body of a god. It was a slight he would not soon forget.

"My Lord, I have returned," a hooded man said, entering the huge chamber and dropping to one knee with his head bowed.

He wore a blood red cloak which completely covered both his body and face.

"Ah, Antonius. Have you delivered the invitations?" Chrysus asked, not bothering to raise his head from his hand.

"Yes, My Lord."

"And how did my newest blessing recipient do?"

"He fought well for someone of such low level. Though I could have killed him easily if you'd ordered me to my Lord."

Chrysus tipped his head back, finally removing it from his hand and laughed in a way that was more like a deep roar.

Antonius shivered as a wave of pure magic power washed over the room. It was malevolent even though his laugh was joyful. Thus was the nature of his god and master.

"I've been watching him a bit lately. Did you know he managed to survive against an entire goblin hoard at only phase one?"

"That is quite impressive My Lord. I would expect nothing less of a person you deemed worthy of your blessing," Antonius replied, still keeping his head bowed. He didn't dare to look the god in the eyes. His entire body quivered merely from being so close to such overwhelming power.

Not to mention the god's appearance. His muscularity was fierce and the slight scaling on his face made for a frightening visage.

"Quite so, it's the old merchant's intuition in me. I know a good product when I see one. He's going to be very useful to me in the later stages of the fight for the map.

"Providing he lives that long. Tell me Antonius, how did he react when you gave him his invitation?"

Antonius squirmed uneasily. He had feared being asked this question. His Lord was not known for his well-balanced emotional temperament.

"I think his exact words were...*fuck no*, My Lord," he said awkwardly, squeezing his eyes shut and expecting the worst.

"I expected as much." Chrysus sighed, returning his head to his hand. "No matter, I will have to think of another way to entice him. Tell me, is Diako's puppet still running the Adventure Society in Havar?"

"Yes, My Lord," Antonius replied, feeling slightly more at ease now the bad news had been delivered.

"Perfect," Chrysus replied with a twisted smile plastered on his lips.

***

I awoke the next morning feeling refreshed and raring to go. My new quest awaited me and I was eager to get a good start.

Panda was passed out on his back nearby. He was fully starfished with his limbs outstretched. I'd already decided to do this quest without him.

It was going to be a simple grind and he wouldn't be that helpful. Besides, if he knew it was in a sewer he'd moan the entire time.

I left him a note on the bed saying I was going out for a while and that he should stay in the room and read his books. I didn't know how long the quest was going to take, but I didn't want him getting into trouble without me around to help.

Despite being a daemon familiar and self-entitled sage, he acted so often like a child. That made him a bit unpredictable.

I also left him two gold coins for food and warned him that if he spent it all before I got back he'd have to go hungry. Basic necessities like food and drink were extremely cheap in this world.

I didn't understand how, but it was quite idyllic. If only it was that easy to solve world hunger back on earth. Though a large part of me, having seen how *this* world operated, was starting to believe the hunger crisis was more about greed than a lack of produce.

I could have been wrong though. It's not like I was that up on current affairs and the big issues. I was a truck driver not an economist.

Leaving the room, I headed downstairs and quickly ate my prepaid breakfast of stew and hard bread before leaving the inn.

I made a quick stop at *Adventurer's Stockpile and Supplies* and bought a few healing potions, some more stamina potions and two weeks' worth of rations.

There was no way I was going to be gone that long but it was always good to be prepared, as Sally would say.

Though I was loath to depart with the money. As the old saying went, you have to spend money to make money and potions were lifesaving supplements.

The previous day, Lucy had told me that I'd need to report to the sanitation building to enter the sewers and start the quest.

It was only a few streets away from the Adventure Society building so I found it with ease.

It was a small, unassumingly square building with a tall, wire fence around it. The only thing about it that stood out was that it seemed to be made from concrete, at least it looked like it was.

The walls were solid and grey without a hint of bricks and mortar in them. It certainly looked dreary enough to be a government building.

In contrast, all the other buildings in Havar were glass skyscrapers or medieval taverns and stores – at least the ones *I'd* seen were.

I walked up to the front door, which was made of solid wood, and knocked loudly. After a few moments of pacing in front of the door in my impatience, it opened.

A small, old man stood in front of me wearing a mucky grey overall.

"Can I help you?" He asked in that typical old man voice. It sounded feeble, but from his muscled frame I doubted it was a true reflection of his physical ability.

"Sorry to bother you. I'm here from the Adventure Society. I've accepted the quest you posted," I replied as politely as I could. Gotta respect your elders and all that crap.

"Ah, yes! Come on in young man." His tone lightened up at my introduction and he held the door for me as I entered the concrete-looking building.

Inside it looked like a storage closet. There were mops and buckets and tools lying around. Large pipes were bolted onto the ceiling and a constant churning noise echoed around the place.

"Please excuse the mess. My work here keeps me so busy I don't always have the time to tidy up," the old man said as he led me through the room.

"Nah, don't worry about it. You should have seen my house back home. It was always a right shit tip," I replied.

"Oh, where are you from?" He asked inquisitively.

*Shit, I'm not supposed to act like an outworlder. Maybe I should temper my accent a bit too.*

"I'm from a small island in the north, you won't have heard of it. It doesn't even have an Adventure Society. I came here to join up," I said, thinking quickly.

"Well, you've come to the right place. There's plenty of Adventure Society work to be done in and around Havar."

"So I've noticed."

He led me through the dreary building to a small room with a circular hatch built into the floor. He bent down and lifted it and I immediately got hit with the stench of a city's worth of excrement and waste. It was revolting.

"Here, put this on."

He said, passing me a paper mask that gave me flashbacks to the covid 19 pandemic. I wasn't certain it was going to do much until a notification appeared on my HUD.

**New item:**
*Mask of Purification (inferior)*

**A simple mask that purifies the air around the wearer's mouth and nose, eliminating 99.9% of bacteria and odours.**
**The unfortunate side effect is how wet the inside of the mask gets when you breath. It can be pretty gross after a while. Make sure you brush your teeth before wearing it or you'll smell your own bad breath all day.**

I slipped the mask on over my face and felt relief immediately as the smell disappeared. It wasn't completely gone, but in place of the overwhelming smell of excrement was the smell of a mild, lingering fart instead.

That was much more manageable.

"Thanks," I muttered, my voice sounding muffled due to speaking through the mask.

"No problem young man, just be careful down there." He said, gesturing towards the open hatch.

I looked at him and he smiled back. He wasn't wearing a mask but he was probably used to the stench since he worked there.

Taking a deep breath, and instantly regretting it, I turned around and descended the ladder into the sewer.

# Chapter 46
# Slave To the Grind

The ladder bottomed out into a wide sewer tunnel. It had a walkway on either side and was surprisingly spacious.

I looked up as the hatch closed with a grating clank from above me.

*I hope it opens from this side too.* I thought, sighing into the stifling face mask.

The sewer was lit by glowing red spheres of light which seemed to float near the tunnel's ceiling. They must have been made with magic.

To my knowledge, Celestia hadn't discovered electricity yet. I guessed there wasn't much need for earth-style modern technology when you could fix most problems with magic.

Looking around I could see that the tunnel led in both directions. I opened the map that Director Lucas had given me on my HUD.

It was mostly greyed out, but I had an option to click on local map and I saw myself as a small dot inside the tunnel.

I wasn't sure how the sewer system was laid out, but hopefully I could use the map to find my way back if it turned out to be a maze.

I probably should have asked for a sewer map before I climbed down the ladder.

*Oh well, too late now.*

For no reason at all, I decided to go left and set off in that direction.

I stuck to the path at the side of the sewer tunnel, the mid-section was covered in foul looking, brown water. I hoped I wouldn't have to go into it, it was so gross.

After less than a few minutes of walking I came across a little blue blob sitting on the path in front of me.

*This must be a slime.* I thought, focusing on it.

**You have discovered a new monster:**
**Slime**

**As a hallmark of low-level monsters, the Slime is a common and weak foe. Usually where there's one there's an entire colony.**
**Unless you come across Rimuru, they're unlikely to cause much trouble to an intrepid adventurer such as yourself.**

Did the system just make an anime reference? I wondered as I finished reading the notification. I guess I should see how easy these things are to kill.

Summoning my bow, I nocked an arrow and fired it at the blue, gelatinous blob. It exploded as the arrow passed through it and chipped the concrete flooring.

**You have defeated: Slime (lvl 11)**

"Level 11, seriously?" I muttered to myself.

If they were all going to be this weak then this quest was going to be boring. So much for all the experience I was hoping to get.

With a sigh, I mentally asserted that I wanted to loot the slime and received ten gold coins and a vial of concentrated slime.

That confirmed my theory that all monster's paid the same amount. Though maybe some higher levelled ones would give a bit more bang for their buck. I had no idea what concentrated slime could be used for, but it was interesting that it came in a vial.

I put that odd fact down to system fuckery and continued onwards. Maybe I'd be able to sell it somewhere when I got back above ground.

As I continued my trip down the rancid sewer tunnel I came across a few more lone slimes, killed them and looted them. Every time, they evaporated into dim blue light particles.

The quest had said there was an infestation, but honestly there didn't seem to be that many of them so far. I wondered what the *source* it mentioned was.

Where did slimes even come from? The system notification didn't say and I couldn't think of any game I'd played that offered an explanation.

Their weakness was a little frustrating. I'd have to kill them by the thousands to have any chance of gaining a level, but at least they were good for farming coins.

I just hoped there were enough of them down here to pay for my armour. I'd need to kill more than 4000 of them to make the amount I needed.

As I rounded a corner, my wish came true.

The sewer tunnel widened and to my left I saw another ladder leading to the surface. Surrounding the ladder, the floor, and stuck to the ceiling was a gaggle of the little blue bastards.

There were so many of them I couldn't tell where one started and another ended. It was like looking at the inside of a beehive.

*I guess payday has come early.* I thought with a little smirk as I began shooting them.

My first arrow hit one of the ceiling slimes which exploded like a water balloon, covering me in sticky, blue goop.

I wiped it from my eyes, grimacing with disgust and took a few steps back.

"I'm not making that mistake again," I muttered as I began picking them off, away from the splash zone.

After about 30 minutes of extermination, my stamina was beginning to drop into the red. The slimes showed no sign of attacking me or moving at all really.

So, I decided to meditate rather than waste a potion. I sat down on the damp ground in a cross-legged position and placed my hands on my knees, forming a circle with my thumb and ring finger.

Closing my eyes, I breathed in deeply and imagined the air turning into energy as it entered my body. I immediately saw the thick, red rope which I had visualised as my health the first time I'd meditated. It looked stronger than before, thicker, as it stretched out around my body and into my limbs.

I needed to get my stamina back so I'd have to decide how to visualise that. At first, I thought of it as a green light, but my *Soul Shot* skill caused a green glow when it empowered my arrows.

In my case, I was pretty sure that green represented my soul energy. Likely because of my class being so heavily linked with acidic powers.

In that case I'd need to choose a different colour. I'd seen stamina represented as a yellow bar in some of the games I'd played, so that was the logical choice for me.

As I recalled the colour, I began to see a thin yellow coil that swirled around my arms and legs, ending in my stomach.

It was all connected, as if the stamina itself originated in my core and reached out to all of my limbs and extremities from there. It was a faded yellow and part of the coil was bent out of shape.

I focused on sending the energy I'd breathed in towards it as I sank deeper into my own mind and subtly manipulated the blank energy, turning it yellow and sending it into my core.

Whilst it was there, I visualised it wrapping around my core and strengthening the coiled stamina. It slowly began to glow with a more vibrant, almost golden sheen.

My core pulsed with a magnificent glow as it sent the vibrant colour of energy outwards.

It travelled along the coil towards my limbs, looking like a curly straw, as energy ran through the centre and slowly brightened up my entire body.

It took a lot of concentration to manipulate the energy this way. It was quite mentally draining, and I had no sense of the outside world. I wondered if I could feel pain in this deep of a meditative state.

Surely, my body would alert me if I was under attack? As I meditated, I felt more at one with my inner self than I ever had before. It was like the ultimate self-reflection.

Deep in my core, buried beneath the stamina coil, I could still see the faint blue ball I'd seen the last time.

It had changed slightly from before.

The previous time I'd meditated it was like an ethereal blue ball of mist that I couldn't touch no matter how hard I tried.

This time, however, it seemed to be more of a bluish green and it was ever so slightly more tangible. The transparent quality had filled in slightly from before.

I wondered if that was because of the *Soul Shot* skill I'd unlocked. The skill used my soul energy to coat my arrows and fire them with much more power. Perhaps that was why my soul had a greenish tint to it. It stood to reason that the more I developed and the more I unlocked skills relating to the soul, the more it would change.

Hopefully that wasn't a bad thing.

The more I tried to reach out to it, the further away It seemed to be, like one of those dreams where you walk down a hallway with a door at the end of it but every time you get close it zooms off into the distance.

It was frustrating but I was sure that with practice I'd reach it eventually. The mystery of it all called out to me.

I longed to touch it, to mould it, to unleash its potential.

After what felt like only a short amount of time, my stamina coil was beaming like a sun and I awoke from my meditation.

A small, blue slime sat on my lap. Peacefully jiggling in front of me. It was actually kind of cute. I almost felt bad as I stabbed it with my dagger and it deflated like a popped football and died... *almost*.

I stood back up, resummoned my bow and started shooting the next wave of arrows. I had the feeling I would have to meditate and recover stamina a fair few times before I could kill them all.

*Well, you asked for a metric shit tonne of slimes to farm and now you've got it.* I thought with a slight smile as the ceiling slimes exploded one by one.

This was what *I* called grinding. It was almost like early on in an MMO. Except I'd killed a few hundred of them by now and still hadn't gained a single level.

Actually, I take that back, this was *exactly* what grinding in an MMO felt like.

After a short while I dropped back into my seated position and meditated some more. It was oddly satisfying directing energy into my stamina coil.

It was similar to that feeling you get when you wipe down a surface with a wet wipe and it sparkles afterwards. It was a bit of a chore, but there was a certain amount of satisfaction to be gained in the monotony.

After my core was full once more, I stood up and fired off more arrows.

Slowly but surely, as I mixed between meditation and firing arrows, the slimes on the ceiling were exterminated and I was given the option to mass-loot them, which I did.

### Loot: *Slime (lvl \*various\*) x896*
### Y/N

I mentally asserted yes and gained 8960 gold coins and the same amount of concentrated slime vials. This quest was going to be lucrative.

I'd barely even started too. If there were gaggles of these things all over the sewer then I'd be rich as fuck by the end of it.

I'd stumbled onto a veritable gold mine!

Before I could move on, I'd have to take out the slimes on the ladder and in the area surrounding it. This was going to be a tedious quest, but it was the easiest money I'd ever made.

I dropped back down into a meditative pose, grinning from ear to ear.

What can I say? I guess I'm just a slave to the grind.

# Chapter 47
# Intermission: The Desert Samurai

The Samurai marched across the barren wasteland known as the Kalhatchi Desert.

Despite the excruciating heat, The Samurai showed no sign of a lack of comfort. Dressed head to toe in red and black samurai armour, she certainly looked the part – if a little out of place.

She wore a black Oni mask with white tusks under a tiered helmet of red metal. Her body was strapped up with red and black armour, metal shoulder plates gave her the image of one much broader than she.

She wore a single katana-like blade at her hip. There was no need for this of course, she could just as easily hold it in her inventory – but where's the fun in that?

It had been almost a month since she'd first arrived in Celestia, confused and afraid. Now it felt more like home to her than her real home ever had.

She'd been introduced to various sword-style martial arts from a young age and had taken to them immediately. Praised as a prodigy, The Samurai had won numerous tournaments and cemented her name firmly in the local history books as the youngest kenjutsu master in a generation.

The thing is, back on earth that's all she would ever be. A marital artist. Not that there was any shame in that, but training in the sword purely for the sport seemed like such a waste to her.

She often felt like she'd been born a few centuries too late. If only modern warfare was fought with the honour of old. She was certain she would thrive on a battlefield. A place where she could truly take her passion for the sword to the next level.

Could you even call yourself a practitioner of the sword if you'd never used one with the intent to kill?

Of course, she could never voice that opinion back on earth. It was barbaric and spat in the face of her discipline. However, she couldn't help how she felt.

Being spirited away to Celestia had finally given her the chance to truly prove herself. To hone her technique on a quest for power the likes of which her home world would likely never know.

She had been afraid at first. The system had announced that she was been hunted, her body marred with a tattoo of a map fragment.

One minute she was riding the train, the next she was here, in a desert.

She'd been attacked by low level monsters almost immediately and after the first few kills, she found herself smiling at her good fortune.

Upon finding a strange box, the system had offered her a choice of three weapons. Naturally she had chosen the sword.

Her first sword was a straight edged western style blade. It was quite different from the type she was used to, a far cry from the wooden bokken she had used for over a decade in her tournaments and training.

Still, it was that basic sword that led her to realising the potential she had to rise in power and become a true force to be reckoned with.

She wandered the Kalhatchi Desert, searching out stronger and stronger opponents and by the time she finally found a piece of civilisation, she had already reached phase two.

At least that's what the locals had called it. According to them, anything below level 30 was known as phase one and was most commonly associated with the children of this world.

In a city named Kal, she found her way to the Adventure Society, a tall glass building resembling the Burj Kalifa from her world.

Kal was a metropolis in the middle of a wasteland. Surrounded by water, the only water for miles around, it was like a futuristic facsimile of Venice with waterways in place of streets and tall glass buildings rubbing shoulders with their medieval clay counterparts.

She had decided to hide her new race of outworlder, instead telling the Adventure Society receptionist that she hailed from the far east.

It wasn't a complete lie, more an omission of truth. Fortunately, they had accepted her at her word and offered to give her a class in exchange for her joining their society and accepting quests.

It sounded like a win-win situation to The Samurai whose only goal was to find stronger enemies and improve her level.

The warrior's journey was a battle after all.

She had been given a myriad of classes to pick from after being forced to sit through a few videos of corporate propaganda.

However, she didn't need to read further than the first class offered to her: *Samurai.*

### Samurai (unique)

**The samurai were famous warriors from earth known for their fierce attacks, impeccable swordsmanship, and code of honour.**
**Sadly though, honour doesn't pay the bills in this world. Perhaps you should start an Oni-fans. Get it?**

You have demonstrated your skill with the sword already, seeking out tough foes and besting them with ease.
Speaking of, have you heard about the samurai who committed seppuku? He had no guts.

Selecting the Samurai class unlocks the following skills:

*Summon Armour.*
*Summon Familiar.*
*Way of the Sword*

*Selecting the Samurai class will award the following stat points per level:*

*+6 strength / +5 agility / +2 stamina / +1 vitality / +5 intelligence*

The Samurai didn't even finish reading about the class before she gleefully accepted it. When you know you know.

It turned out to be the perfect fit for her. Though the vitality she gained per level was negligible. However, if she didn't get hit, it wouldn't matter. She also had +5 free points per level which evened the playing field a little.

The skills it offered her were exactly what she'd wanted. *Summon Armour* was self-explanatory, though it had a hefty upfront mana cost. She soon realised that if she simply never took it off, it stayed with her.

It cost no mana to keep it on, but she imagined it would take mana to repair it if she took damage.

*Way of the Sword* gave her a significant boost to all sword skills and increased her chances of being offered more as she levelled up.

She didn't try her *Summon Familiar* skill until after she'd left the Adventure Society. Like with her armour skill, the upfront mana cost was pricey, but the familiar stayed with her after that.

She'd named him Pocco and he was a large white wolf with red eyes. He was such a cutie! Though his fur had a tendency to get stained when he ripped monsters apart.

She took to questing like a pig takes to muck. Accepting all three of her mandatory quests the very next day.

They had mostly been minor clearance quests where she was sent to locate a den of low-level monsters and defeat them.

She'd only gained a few measly levels from them despite slaughtering monsters in the thousands with the help of Pocco.

However, as she approached the third and final quest location, her gut told her that this one would be different.

**New Quest:**
**Red Robe, Brown Pants**

**The Adventure Society has received reports of cultist sightings in the nearby southern oasis.**
**Traverse the Kalhatchi Desert and investigate.**
**P.S. Investigate is code for mass murder.**

**Objectives:**
*Locate the cultist lair 0/1*
*Eliminate all cultists 0/1*
*Defeat the cultist leader 0/1*

*Reward: Honour is the only reward a samurai needs*

*Only joking, it's really a weapon rarity upgrade token.*

As she read through the quest one more time, she couldn't help but tingle with anticipation.

The cultist leader was sure to be strong and she greedily coveted the generous reward.

She had finally gained her current sword in a loot box she'd gotten for scaling her sword skill five levels in a single day. It had come in the guise of an achievement called *overachiever* which came with an unnecessarily rude, and slightly racist, notification that likened her to a Korean mathlete.

She could hardly complain though after receiving a weapon similar to the one she had trained with back home.

It had been three and a half weeks since she'd left Kal to carry out her three quests. She was looking forward to bathing when she finally returned.

The desert heat was no joke, but a true samurai never complained. Especially with Pocco around, trapped in his fur coat. The poor wolf panted non-stop and she'd even had to carry him at one point after he passed out from heat stroke.

As they crested a sand dune, she finally caught sight of her target.

The southern oasis looked like a mirage, shrouded in a heat haze. For a moment she doubted it was really there.

The Aztec style temple sitting in the middle of the luscious palm trees confirmed the reality of it though.

She could tell from a single look that it was the cultist's lair. This would be her first time killing non-monsters, a true test of her warrior's resolve.

Gritting her teeth and clenching her fists she marched onwards towards the lair that would soon become a battlefield.

The journey took longer than she'd expected. It turned out that when you see something that looks close by in a desert, it's probably not.

It was almost dark by the time she arrived and the scorching heat had given way to subzero temperatures. Pocco perked up with the change in climate, he lived for the cold and raced on ahead as they spotted a frosted pool of water.

The Samurai ran behind him, she was just as parched as he was. Removing her mask, she dropped to all fours next to the wolf.

As Pocco lapped happily at the water, she fully submerged her head and sucked in as much as she could manage.

It was refreshing, but icy cold. It stung her throat and eyes and her face went numb in seconds. But it was the best tasting water she'd ever had.

*I should really buy provisions next time.* She thought to herself.

She'd spent an unnecessary amount of time cooking and eating the monster's she'd killed. In future, if she had rations, she could eat on the go.

Finding water was especially hard and if it wasn't for her stats giving her an inhuman resistance to starvation and dehydration she would have died over a week ago.

She pulled her head out of the water and felt her face freeze up as the freezing air brushed against it. Replacing her mask should do the trick, it had built in magic climate control. Possibly the single best perk to have in a desert.

Though it could only do so much against the extreme elements found in the Kalhatchi.

Pocco's fur was also frozen. He didn't seem to mind, however. He was built for the cold after all.

After a few moments basking in the watery goodness, the two of them rose once again and continued onto their target.

A nighttime attack seemed more to be a ninja's speciality than a samurai's, but she *was* facing down nearly one hundred foes by herself.

Giving herself the element of surprise was simply good tactics. Besides, it's not like anyone could blame her for choosing the smart attack.

The samurai of the past might have been brazen enough to wait until morning and simply waltz into the lion's den and announce themselves.

But she was alone in this world. She wasn't a feudal lord beholden to some outdated sense of honour. Her honour code was entirely her own to shape.

For all she knew she was the only samurai in all of Celestia, so defining the archetype was her prerogative.

Besides, she fully intended to challenge the leader to single combat, once she'd dealt with his men that is.

Looking towards her faithful familiar and offering a simple nod. She marched in the direction of the temple with anticipation and adrenaline coursing through her veins.

# Chapter 48
# The Desert Samurai's First Blood

The Samurai and the wolf crouched low. Hiding in the shadows on a narrow ledge overlooking the Aztec-looking temple that was most likely the cultist's hideaway.

She scouted out the area, creating a rough layout in her mind. The temple was enclosed on all sides with only a single entrance that she could see.

The main gate led into a courtyard which was currently deserted apart from a few guards who roamed the area. They would be easy pickings. The only challenge would be killing them all before they could alert the others.

Despite it being late at night in the Kalhatchi, the unblemished sky cast a midnight glow, allowing the moon free reign to light up her foes and the surrounding area.

She chose to see this as a good omen, even though it would make it harder for her to sneak in.

The layout of the temple seemed rather simple from the outside. The courtyard led to a single building at the back which was tall and tiered.

Perhaps she would face more challenging opponents as she climbed the floors. That would certainly be interesting.

She nodded to Pocco and began climbing down from her vantage point. It was time.

The bottom of the cliff she'd used as a lookout tower was directly adjacent to the right-side wall of the courtyard. Hugging it, she crept slowly towards the gate.

She held a masterful control over her body. Her steps were silent and even her breathing deliberate.

As she rounded the corner she caught sight of the glow of a lit torch: the first guard who had been positioned at the gate.

Though only one carried a torch, she knew there was a second standing a few meters to the side of him. Gesturing with her hands, she ordered Pocco to take out the second guard.

The torch wielder belonged to her.

She unsheathed her blade slowly, making sure not to scrape the metal edge on the sheath. She didn't need to do this. She could just as easily have summoned it to her hands, avoiding any chance of making sound.

But the risk was what made it fun.

Her heart pounded and adrenaline rushed through her as she steadied her two-handed weapon and crept further forward.

She could practically smell the guard's sweat as she pounced like a jaguar and dissected the man from shoulder to hip.

He didn't even have time to yelp as her decisive blow cut his body in two.

She marvelled at her new power as his torso slid away from the rest of his body with a muffled thump and the sloshing of blood and guts.

Back on earth, no amount of training and skill would allow someone to cut a person in two like that. Let alone with such ease.

Slicing through the guard was as simple as slicing butter. The feeling was exhilarating.

Less than a second after she'd landed her hit a second muffled thud hit the ground as Pocco tore the jugular from the other guard.

For a moment she wondered if the cultists chose to adorn red robes to hide the blood stains of their enemies. She dismissed this thought upon feeling how weak their auras were.

She seemed to have a natural talent for gauging an opponent's strength. From what she had gathered it was due to her naturally high mana.

Her bonus to the intelligence stat helped with that. She had discovered early on that the number of intelligence points one possessed directly correlated to the amount of mana they had.

When she looked at a person she saw their mana. It glowed around their skin like a semi-transparent, living aura.

These men were weak. The mana did not love them like it loved her.

Their auras were barely visible, a completely intangible reddish hue that barely even constituted as a glow.

She felt nothing but disgust for her dead foes.

Their deaths had offered her nothing but the satisfaction of soaking her blade in human blood for the first time.

Back on earth it was common in literature and media for people to feel something after killing a human for the first time. Some vomited, others cried or had night terrors.

She, however, felt nothing.

She wondered why people made such a fuss out of killing. It was easy, simple.

Human history was built on the billions of lives lost on the battlefield. Did it make people feel better about themselves to pretend it affected them? If killing was such a heinous crime, then why was her race so hell bent on war?

They must have been lying about the emotional impact. Perhaps it was a clever ruse to make the wolves seem less dangerous to the hens.

All of these thoughts raced through her mind in a mere second or two as Pocco dragged his victim's body into the shrubbery.

She left hers where it fell. She needn't stain her hands by touching it. If the cultists were all this weak, then she'd vastly overestimated them.

There was no need to hide anymore.

Besides, there were only two more guards, sitting idly on the stone steps which led to the temple doors.

Stepping out from behind the wall, she brazenly waltzed towards them. Pocco panted as he proudly trotted next to her. His muzzle was dyed crimson.

*Now this makes me feel like a real samurai.* She thought gleefully as the two men did a collective double take.

"How did you get past the—"

Her blade swept effortlessly through his neck before he could finish his question. His head flew through the air, mouth still agape, mid-sentence.

Before the second man even had time to widen his eyes in surprise, his head also left its neck.

"Pathetic," she muttered to herself as she ascended the steps to the temple doors.

The doors themselves were rather large. At three times her height and twice her width. They seemed to be made of gold that glinted in the pale moonlight.

There were intricate carvings on them depicting a kingly figure sitting on a large throne. A sparkling crown sat atop his head with golden light shining out of it.

*How tacky.*

367

Placing a hand on each door, she pushed hard and an ear-splitting creak sounded through the night as the doors swung inwards.

She gripped her katana with both hands, adopting a readied stance so she would not be caught off guard by any attackers.

However, as she entered the interior, there wasn't a soul to be found.

The ground floor was a huge, open throne room. A large golden throne took up most of the back wall. It was grandiose, to say the least.

*Come closer warrior, I wish to speak with you.*

A strange voice spoke directly into her mind. She could feel its mana, just a sliver of it, running through her head. It felt powerful, more powerful than anything she'd faced so far.

She felt her lips curl upwards. This was the fight she'd been waiting for. A worthy opponent, at last.

"Who are you? Come out and face me?" She announced loudly to the room, looking around for the source of the voice.

*That's no way to speak to a god. My minion's will hear you.* He teased in her mind.

"Your minion's will all die by my blade and then so will you."

*Ha! I love your confidence. Very well, let's see shall we.*

All around the room robed cultists appeared as if out of thin air. There must have been at least 80 of them, which, according to the quest, would be all of them.

The Samurai wasted no time. She wasn't going to let them gain the advantage. She turned to her right and leapt towards the closest group: a cluster of around 12 cultists.

They had an array of different weapons from axes to basic swords, to polearms and spears. It mattered not. The Samurai cleaved through them before they'd even readied their weapons.

She didn't even need to use a sword skill to do it. They were simply too weak to pose a threat to her.

On the opposite side of the room Pocco had also begun his assault. He pounced at the chest of a burly, club wielding neanderthal and ripped happily at his face as the man screamed. Pocco's tail wagged wildly.

The Samurai was almost distracted at how cute he was. He really was the best familiar she could have asked for. She adored animals.

People... not so much.

She continued her advance cutting down attacker after attacker. Not a single one managed to land a hit on her. They were slow and weak. Hardly worth the effort of killing.

She moved her head slightly to the side as an arrow whizzed past. She whistled and Pocco was upon the archer, tearing at his throat.

The familiar was a natural born killer and loyal to a fault. They were a match made in deepest depths of hell, at least that's what she hoped her enemies thought.

Not that many of them had time to think before she sliced into them.

They fell one after the other as she danced upon their corpses, a laughing reaper of chaos. Perhaps that would be a better monicker for her than The Samurai.

Reaper had a nice ring to it. Though she was rather fond of the name the locals at the Adventure Society had given her after she told them the class she was given.

In no time at all the temple floor was slick with the blood of the cultists. Anyone would think a ritual sacrifice had taken place. The sheer amount of blood stored in the human body amazed her.

How could so much liquid be held inside such a small skin bag. It was as if people were bigger on the inside. She had read once at school that the intestines alone could stretch 15 feet long.

A fact that seemed to ring true as she disembowelled the scream-ing man in front of her. His intestines clung to the edge of her blade and as she pulled it back like a fishing rod the organ just kept com-ing – like a clown pulling handkerchiefs from his sleeve.

It was mildly amusing, but not as amusing as his pleading whim-pers as he looked on in horror at the scene before him. It must have been horrifying to see one's own intestines pulled from inside them.

That was what he got for daring to face her at such a pathetically low level.

From the notifications that kept popping up on her interface, the cultist's she'd killed were all barely at phase two.

How weak did they have to be to barely scratch the second phase after decades of living in this world, when she was well on her way to phase three after barely a month?

As she dealt with the penultimate cultist and sheathed her sword, the leader showed his face.

His robe was topped with a crimson wrapping that covered all but his deep black eyes. It certainly looked more fitting for a desert scene.

He laughed and stepped into the middle of the room, in front of the throne, spinning a khopesh in each hand.

The khopesh was an ancient Arabic weapon she'd learnt about during her martial arts training back home. It had a distinct and vicious look to it.

The blade itself was shaped like a sickle with a flat edge rather than a point. It was a slashing weapon rather than a stabbing one and if her memory served it was popular amongst the soldiers of ancient Egypt.

The leader tossed one khopesh into the air and caught the spin-ning blade as it fell back down. His posturing did not impress The Samurai.

"Let's dance," he said in a hoarse whisper of a voice.

She simply nodded and activated one of her sword skills.

### Midnight Slash (common)

**Unsheathe your blade in an instant 10-foot leap to slash through foes. This skill imbues the wielder's blade with dark mana.**

*Activating this skill has a medium mana cost.*

The Samurai drew her blade and disappeared from the cult leader's vision. He looked to both sides but saw no sign of her, then he heard the unmistakable sound of a blade being sheathed once more.

Turning towards the noise would be the last act of his pitiful life as he fell to the ground, staring up at his severed legs which were standing up on their own.

"Your turn," The Samurai said, looking up at the golden throne.

# Chapter 49
# Kaleb one, USSR zero

I finished off the last of yet another mass gathering of slimes. It felt like I'd spent weeks wandering around the sewers exterminating the little buggers.

Annoyingly, my HUD didn't display the time or day so I had no real way of measuring how long I'd been down there. However, the wispy stubble on my face was begging to form an actual beard, so it had probably been a while.

Time rolled into the same monotonous cycle of killing slimes, meditating, and then killing more slimes. It was a lesson in tedium, that was for sure.

I did learn a few things about how my body worked in this world though. It turned out that by meditating often, I completely negated the need for sleep.

I hadn't slept a wink the whole time I'd been down here. I'd also gotten adept at meditation. I couldn't know for sure, but it felt like I recovered much faster now and the act of meditating required a lot less concentration.

Of course, there was the monetary benefits too. I'd killed over 10,000 slimes as I worked my way through the sewers.

Not only could I afford to buy my armour, but I could buy a spare set of it too if I wanted. I just hoped I'd be able to complete the quest before my deal with Andy ran out and he sold it off.

I also learnt that through diligent meditation, my food and water requirements dropped significantly. I'd brought two weeks' worth of rations, yet I'd only eaten five days' worth.

Of course, for all I knew I'd only been in the sewer for five days, but I was sure it'd been far longer than that. It was hard to tell, but my intuition told me it'd been longer.

After the first few swarms I'd started mixing up my extermination technique. I still used my bow to deal with the ceiling slimes, but I'd started using my dagger for the ones on the floor and walls.

It'd worked too, as after a few thousand stabs I'd gained a level in my passive *Dagger* skill, upgrading it to level 10.

More excitingly, just like with the old *Bow* skill which had since merged with my *Bowman* skill, I got a new skill upon reaching level 10.

**You have unlocked a new skill!**

*Novice Apex Skirmisher*
**The *Novice Apex Skirmisher* is a wizard when it comes to wielding small blades – or at least he has the potential to be. Oh, I'm sorry. I forgot that you don't have any mana, calling you a wizard was probably a bit of a low blow huh?**
**But like seriously, what kind of adventurer doesn't have any mana? You are so lame.**

**Anyway, back on topic:**
*Proficiency improved.*
*Unlocks dual wielding proficiency.*
*An inferior bonus to the effect of agility will be added when a small blade is equipped.*

I was really beginning to despise the system's idea of busting balls. I got that it had some weird personality trope going on, but did it have to be a dick every time?

I had spent some time wondering if it was this over the top with everyone. If nothing else, the thought kept me occupied as I wandered through the sewer system.

The new skill seemed to be the melee version of my Bowman skill. So, it was likely that once I reached level 25 in Dagger the two would merge and become a percentage leveller instead.

Interestingly, the Skirmisher skill had apex in the title, which was part of my class. I wondered if that meant it was more powerful than a normal skirmisher skill.

Speaking of percentages, I'd gained slightly in my Newly Qualified Bowman skill. After painstakingly executing thousands upon thousands of slimes I'd managed to gain a whopping… 0.2%.

In all honestly, I think seeing that number be so low was worse than if it had just stayed at 0. I knew the shooting wasn't difficult, or far, or against an opponent that even fought back or moved.

Still though, you'd think 10,000 slime murders would have given me more than 0.2% and a single level in a passive melee skill.

I hadn't gained a single overall level either.

It was disheartening to say the least, but I could buy my armour when I was done. That was something to look forward to and money was an easy motivator.

I also felt like I'd gained a much deeper understanding of meditation. That might not constitute to direct stats and level gain, but it had to be useful in the long run.

Occasionally I'd open the map feature on my HUD as I cleared an area of slimes. I'd explored a lot of the sewers. I expected the sewer system to be a maze but it was more like a simple circle that would eventually meet back at the ladder I'd used to enter the place.

There were small pipes running through the walls which I had to assume connected to bathrooms around the city.

I was just starting to close in on the halfway point of the main circle though, so I was going to be stuck down here for a while longer yet. Frustratingly, I'd yet to find a single sign of the source of the infestation, which was one of the quest objectives.

The sewer system itself was only the size of the city, which was big, but nothing you couldn't walk in a few hours on the surface.

The issue was how long it took to dispatch the slimes and more importantly, how often I had to meditate during each bout of extermination. If nothing else I'd learnt that I seriously needed more stamina if I wanted to quicken my killing speed or win drawn out battles.

I had a feeling it was going to be my most useful stat for the immediate future.

I also made a mental note to ask Panda if there was a way to increase stat point gain. Nineteen fixed points and five free points a level seemed pretty good at first, but if levels were going to take weeks to get now that'd reached phase two then I needed to find a faster way of getting more points.

As I approached the halfway point of the sewer tunnel on my map, something odd appeared.

A large oval cistern appeared on the map, just off the side of the tunnel. Minimising it on my HUD I looked around but saw no sign of it.

I wondered what it was. Maybe a treasure room? That would be cool. Who doesn't love hard-to-find loot drops?

Still, the immediate area looked no different from the rest of the tunnel. There was nothing but walls and a river of faeces as far as I could see.

Speaking of faeces, my purification mask was looking worse for wear and the inside stank to high heaven. The moisture from my breath had started to form little bits of mould on the inside of the mask and I'd had to use some of my ration water to wash it.

I'd honestly considered just taking it off, but I quickly brushed off that idea when the sewer stench hit me as I washed it.

As I stared blankly at the sewer walls and re-checked my map, a brilliant idea came to me.

Pulling out my bow I began charging a Soul Shot.

*I hope damage to public property won't cause the quest to fail.* I thought as my arrow began to glow with a green aura-like light. *I guess we'll find out. Here goes nothing.*

I fired the arrow into the nearby wall. On my map, that spot was where the cistern supposedly was. The wall exploded inwards as my arrow passed through it, causing concrete to shatter and fall all around me.

The damage kicked up a cloud of dust and I was once again glad for my mask, even though the dust stung my eyes.

I waited a moment for the dust to clear and to my delight the wall was covering a hidden area.

"It's looting time!" I sang to myself as I crossed the threshold into the mysterious cistern.

**You have entered a hidden boss room.**

The notification popped up on my HUD and I tensed up in anticipation. It was like something from a dungeon crawl.

*Maybe they'll call me Dungeon Crawler Kaleb.* I thought as I re-summoned my bow and nocked an arrow in anticipation. *Nah, too many syllables.*

The cistern was dark and surprisingly spacious. I couldn't see all the way to the back. The glowing red balls of light that lit the sewer didn't extend this far.

I stepped back out of the cistern for a moment. It was a long shot, but if this boss room really did work like a game then I'd probably be safe as long as I was outside.

Thinking quickly, I delved into my inventory. I needed a light source. Luckily, I had just the items.

I summoned *Stalin's Stylish Socks,* a *Rusted Golbin Sword* and the *Pervert's Lighter* I'd looted from the stag party all that time ago.

I wrapped the socks around the tip of the sword, skewering them in place and making a ball out of the material which I tied off.

I then set them on fire.

*Good riddance. Kaleb one, USSR zero.*

I had no idea what the socks were made of but they lit up like the fourth of July. The blaze nearly burnt my eyebrows off as I held the makeshift torch at an arm's length.

A new notification popped up on my HUD.

**You have created a new item:**
**The Eternal Torch of Communist Supremacy.**

**I gave you a thoughtful gift and this is what you decided to do with it? Well fine then, fuck you! You wanna go? Let's go.**
**The Eternal Torch of Communist Supremacy is a fire that will never go out. Lit by Lennin who got his spark from Karl Marx (and perverted it), communism is the prefect ideology for wannabe dictators and genocidal maniacs alike.**
**Though the flame of communism has been handed down for generations, you are its latest recipient.**
**Glory to the motherland comrade.**

**\*WARNING\***
*This is a bonded item and cannot be lost, sold, destroyed,
or given away.*

**\*WARNING\***
*Possession of The Eternal Torch of Communist
Supremacy has marked you as an enemy of various
powerful economic groups throughout Celestia.*

"Uh oh, I think I hurt its feelings," I said aloud as I read the worrying notification.

What exactly did it mean by *powerful economic groups?* It sounded like the magical illuminati or something. Knowing this crazy place that's probably exactly what it meant.

I'd have to ask Panda about it when I got back.

For now though, I had more immediate concerns. I threw the torch as far as I could into the cistern.

The light danced across the walls as it flew in an arch into the circular room. Then it hit something, or more accurately; bounced off something.

As the room was lit up, I saw the biggest slime I'd ever seen. It took up most of the large room on its own and it was a mixture of blue and brown gelatine.

More noticeably, it had a kind of...face. A black outline of a frown and eyes with straight, black eyebrows pointing towards where its nose would be.

"Looks like I've pissed off two things that can kill me in less time than it takes for a kettle to boil," I sighed, nocking my bow. "On the upside, it looks like I've found the source of the infestation."

# Chapter 50
# Are You Still Mad About That?

I nocked and arrow and fired at the slime monster from my position in the sewer tunnel. If my theory was correct, it'd help me in the long run.

**All damage negated.**

I thought that might be the case.

I nocked another arrow and stepped over the threshold before firing again.

This time there was no notification. The arrow pierced the slime's gelatinous body and broke into tiny particles almost instantly. Was the slime adsorbing my arrow?

Thanks to my Health Sense skill I could see a floating bar above the boss slime's head. It barely seemed to move as the arrow penetrated it.

However, I was still firmly in the testing phase. So I stepped back outside the boss room.

**Boss health has been fully restored.**

After completing the simple test, I had a rough idea of how this new boss room feature worked. It seemed that I couldn't cause it damage unless I was inside the boss room. If I left it would go back to full health so there was no loophole to exploit.

That was a shame. My original plan had been to step in, shoot and step back out. I could have done that on repeat for as long as it took and meditated when I needed to refill my stamina.

However, it seemed like that plan wasn't going to work.

I'd have to kill it in a single fight. I could, in theory, leave the room if I lost too much health. But then the fight would start over from scratch.

It was a useful failsafe but one I'd be loathed to take.

I didn't know for sure, but it stood to reason that the boss slime couldn't damage me if I was outside the room either.

At least that would put us on an almost equal playing field.

My biggest concern now was how to do enough damage to kill it. My arrow barely left a dent, figuratively speaking since I pierced all the way through and got adsorbed.

Hopefully my *Soul Shot* skill would even the playing field a lot. Either way though, this was going to be a royal pain in the ass.

I had one last preparation to make before entering the chamber. I focused on the slime and a notification popped up on my HUD.

**You have discovered a new monster:**
*Slime Queen*

**Have you ever wondered where slimes come from?**
**They come from the *Slime Queen*, obviously.**
**Like a queen bee, her life's purpose it to pump out**
**babies. Don't feel bad for her though, she's asexual so**
**there's no vaginal chaffing involved. Then again, her**
**entire body is kinda like lube anyway...**
**Oh, one last thing. The *Slime Queen* is impervious to**
**acid. Ha! That's what you get for destroying my present.**

"Are you still mad about that? It was a pair of socks!" I shouted at the ceiling like a crazy person.

Despite the system's nonsensical jokes and aggression, it did give me some useful information for once.

Firstly, if this *Slime Queen* was creating the little slimes then she was likely to be the source of the infestation mentioned in the quest.

Secondly, she was impervious to acid damage. Making my class completely useless in this fight.

*I guess it's gonna be an old-fashioned slog.*

With my preparation done, it was time to kill this thing.

I raised my bow and nocked an arrow before stepping into the boss room once more. This time, as I drew the bowstring back, I focused as much stamina into the arrow as I could.

*Soul Shot* leaked a green glow from my fingers and onto the arrow. Usually, I fired them at this strength, but this time I wanted more.

I continued channelling stamina into the arrow. The green glow got brighter, casting an eerie glow on me and the walls nearby.

I felt an immense tension in my arm and the bowstring. It felt like if I forced any more stamina into the shot I'd break my arm – or the bowstring, or both.

*So, this is my limit.* I thought, noticing that my stamina had dropped below halfway just from this single attack.

Grinning maliciously, I fired the arrow. It literally blasted from the bow, forcing me to stagger backwards slightly.

It was like a missile being fired from a bazooka. I was so shocked I didn't even nock another arrow as the first flew through the air so quickly my eyes couldn't even register it as it seemed to instantly impact with the slime.

It flew straight through the slime's gelatinous body and exploded in acid green light. I cheered involuntarily as the slime's health dropped by half.

"Holy shit that's so OP!" I said to myself.

At this rate all I needed was another shot like that and I could kill the behemoth in two hits.

The slime's face changed.

It's drawn on appearance shifted from a frown to an O shaped mouth and its eyebrows dropped in an angry line.

*I think it noticed me.*

It seemed to breath in as the air around me shifted and I was dragged towards it. It was like being in one of those indoor skydiving places, except it was a horizontal pull.

I tried to ground myself but it was no use. Panickily, I raised my bow and fired three arrows in quick succession.

They seemed to do no damage at all as they entered the gaping mouth hole and burst into particles inside its body.

*Is that going to happen to me?*

There was no way. I was not going to become slime food. Fuck that noise.

I nocked another arrow and began channelling stamina through my *Soul Shot* attack. If I could get off one more good shot before I was sucked in it'd die and I'd be safe.

I pushed my stamina to its limits once more feeling as if my arm was going to break. Then I released the string and fired.

It was a straight shot. I was mere inches from entering its mouth. This had to work.

The arrow blasted with such force I lost the grip on my bow. It left my hand and got sucked into the slime, but not before the arrow entered its mouth.

Once again, a green aura exploded out of the arrow upon impact and the slime... cried out?

I didn't even know slimes could make noise.

This one made a deep, growling sound like a demonic rottweiler.

Focusing on my *Health Sense* passive skill, I looked up once more at the slime's health bar. It hadn't worked.

It had taken some damage, good damage even. Its health was now clearly in the red. But it wasn't dead.

That was the last thought I had before I was swallowed by the gelatinous beast.

My entire body went numb as I was surrounded by slime. I couldn't breathe, though I wasn't exactly going to try to breathe inside this disgusting mess.

I felt my clothes and mask disintegrate around me. My bow was hovering just in front of me and it looked worse for wear.

For some reason it hadn't completely disintegrated yet. I reached out and brushed it with my fingertips and pulled it back into my inventory.

It was too late for my clothes, but the bow might be salvageable. A myriad of notifications blinked onto my HUD.

**You have been poisoned.**
**Poison negated by Skill: Minor Poison Resistance.**

**You have been poisoned.**
**Minor Poison Resistance has failed to negate the poison effect.**

**You have been subjected to stamina drain.**

**You have been subjected to HP drain.**
**Item: purification mask has been destroyed.**
**Item: black shirt has been destroyed.**

*Item: white belt has been destroyed.*
*Item: black pants has been destroyed.*
*Item: black shoes has been destroyed.*

It continued like that in a constant stream of incoming stat buffs and item destruction.

It was irritating, but not as concerning as what it all meant.

Checking my HUD I could see my HP and stamina draining rapidly. I entered my inventory and clicked on a stamina potion.

It barely did anything as my stamina continued plummeting.

I had no idea how the poison was going to affect me but I could deal with that later. From the look of the notifications my *Minor Poison Resistance* skill had put up a valiant fight but had been quickly overwhelmed by this toxic environment.

I summoned my dagger.

If I was going to die in the pit of the slime queen's stomach, I was going to at least give it some bad indigestion.

I began slashing at the space in front of me. Moving through the slime wasn't easy, but there wasn't that much resistance either. Though with the slime having immunity to acid I had no idea if I was even causing any damage.

I tried to look around but everything was blurred and my eyes stung with an intense, overpowering heat.

I wondered if that was being caused by the poison.

Floating ahead of me was a tangible looking orb. I wandered what it was? Was it the slime's brain? Do slimes even have brains?

I didn't have time to work out the answers.

My dagger was looking worse for wear as the slime's body dissolved it bit by bit.

Slicing at it from the inside didn't seem to be doing anything and my HP was almost in the red. I slammed down on a healing potion but it'd only buy me a few more seconds.

After that I'd be digested.

Gross.

Doing the only thing I could think of, I pulled the dagger back into my inventory and began swimming towards the glowing orb.

I was betting my life on the hunch that it was part of the slime, an important part.

It looked more tangible than the rest of its gelatinous body and I had no idea what else to do.

I didn't want to die here.

I wasn't going to leave my unborn child without a father. I had to beat this thing. I had to beat it so I could get stronger and bring them here and protect them.

I swam forward in a haggard front crawl. I felt like I was moving in slow motion. The slime's body was hard to move through.

Still, I cut through it with my arms and legs and propelled myself forward.

The slime was bigger than me by a fair bit, but it wasn't even the width of the local swimming pool back home.

I didn't have far to go.

My lungs burned and I breathed in on reflex, swallowing a huge chunk of goop. I began retching as the burning got so much worse.

*You idiot! Slime isn't oxygen.*

I felt the tips of my fingers brush against the orb. It was tangible, it felt solid, hard even. If it was hard then I could smash it. That was the crux of my last-minute master plan,

I summoned my dagger and as my arm rotated around in the front crawl style, I slammed the tip of the blade into orb with all of my failing strength.

Nothing happened.

*Shit, have I backed the wrong horse here? Am I really going to die? No. I won't lose.*

Instinctually, I thought of the feeling I got when I used the *Soul Shot* skill and I channelled all of my remaining stamina into my dagger.

The dagger glowed with a faint green aura, I could feel the strain on the weapon even though I had barely any stamina left to use,

I brought the dagger down with my last ounce of strength just as my stamina reached zero.

The dagger and the orb both smashed simultaneously and a bright, blue light emanated from it, blinding me.

# Chapter 51
# A Giant Newborn Baby

My dagger smashed like a pane of glass and the orb simultaneously broke into larger fragments.

As the orb broke apart it emitted a bright blue light which blinded me. It was like staring at the sun.

My eyes burned but I couldn't look away as the amazing and dazzling light enveloped the entire room.

Then, for a moment, I felt weightless as the slime around me seemed to vaporise.

The weightlessness lasted for less than a second before I fell to the floor on my back. My HUD flashed red as the bit of health I had left dropped into the deep red zone.

The slime queen exploded outwards at the same time, like a viscous water balloon. It literally seemed to pop and gooey slime innards painted the wall bluish brown.

They also painted me from head to toe. I must have looked like the latest recipient of a *Nickelodeon Kid's Choice Award*.

*I'm alive.* I thought dazedly as my victory finally sank in.

"Fuck yeah!" I screamed.

I started cackling hysterically like an evil witch as joy and relief flooded through me. I'd pulled it off, if only by the skin of my teeth.

I'd have to work on not getting so close to death next time though. It was becoming a bit of a habit and one that I'd rather not repeat.

I tried to punch my arm into the air but it wouldn't respond. My entire body was paralysed. A worrying thought occurred to me: maybe the slime's gelatine had a paralysing effect as well.

Also, the poison was still coursing through me. I wasn't out of the woods yet.

I'd have to work on regaining my strength later. Right now, I needed to get my health back up and I needed to do it fast.

I only had a few HP remaining and the poison was still inside me. Though I didn't know how effective it was, I wasn't going to risk it.

How tragic would it be to beat the slime queen boss monster only to succumb to poison a minute later?

I couldn't take anymore potions so I dived into meditation.

It was a little odd doing it without my usual pose, but I'd gotten so used to the feeling that being flat on my back didn't stop me.

As I focused on breathing deeply and visualised my inner circuitry, I saw the problem.

My health was tinged.

The vibrant and thick crimson rope that usually represented health had a purple tinge to it.

*This must be the poison.*

The rope was broken and frayed all throughout my core and limbs. I'd have to focus on fixing that up first.

I began channelling energy into the rope. Visualising the oxygen, I breathed as vital energy which I could mould into health or stamina at will.

It was like dough: pliable and ready to be shaped.

I breathed deeply, almost in a trance as I concentrated on sending the raw energy to my rope of health.

It worked, but much slower than usual. Parts of the rope began twining together, fixing the parts where they were severed.

However, the colouring was still wrong and the rope continued to fray even as I directed energy to it.

It was like something was fighting me.

Like the poison was destroying my rope at the same time as I fixed it.

I was slightly faster though, so as long as I kept it up I wouldn't die. But I *would* be stuck in a relative stalemate.

I needed to focus on the poison itself. If I could destroy that then I could heal myself unimpeded.

I began to visualise what it would look like to get rid of the poison. At first it seemed simple. The rope needed to be red, I needed to purge the purple tinge.

That was easier said than done though. As I focused on channelling energy for that purpose, nothing seemed to happen.

Maybe I was visualising it wrong.

If I thought of the rope as an actual piece of material rather than a metaphor for my health, maybe that would help.

If a real rope was off colour, you'd need to wash it. So perhaps if I imagined the energy washing over the rope rather than pulsing inside of it, that would do the trick.

It didn't.

Back to the drawing board I tried to think of another way to purge the poison. Perhaps it was inside the rope, fraying it from there.

If that was the case I'd first need to expel the poison. With that in mind I visualised the raw energy flushing through my rope like a pipe.

I wanted it to force out anything inside it, purifying it internally.

After a while of trying to focus on that, it seemed to work.

My rope started looking redder as little drops of purple were expelled from it and seemed to float in my blood.

After a while of focusing on that, the rope shone a vibrant crimson once more and the fraying began to fix itself.

Still, the purple blobs remained.

I'd need to purge them completely if I wanted it gone. Otherwise, they'd probably just bind to the rope again eventually.

I imagined the energy flooding through my entire body this time, not just the rope.

I felt it, like the cold, intrusive feeling when you get a vaccination.

The energy flooded through me and as it's bright, white light touched the purple blobs they evaporated.

*Booyah!*

I was now poison free and back to full health. Next, I needed to recharge my stamina coil.

With the hardest part done though, the next bit should have been a sinch.

I switched views and looked at my body through the metaphorical eyes of stamina. My coil was dark.

I could see it sitting there, but there wasn't even the slightest tinge of yellow. I'd need to fix that. It shouldn't be difficult but it might take a while.

I'd never fully drained myself before. I had no idea what kind of adverse effects it might have on my body.

I began visualising the raw energy flowing through my mouth and into the core of my stamina coil.

It worked, but it was a slow process. It was like lighting a campfire on a windy day.

Sparks came and died before they took flame. I concentrated and repeated the process over and over but the most I could manage was a slight yellowish hue in the very centre of my core.

I needed to try a different approach. Maybe something more powerful, like a jolt, would work.

I visualised the energy flowing into my mouth and stopping in my throat. I kept it there, drawing more and more raw energy in.

Then I pushed the energy together, compressing it into a tight ball. I rotated the ball, making it spin faster and faster until it glowed with a magnificent white.

Then, and only then, I mentally catapulted it into my core.

It hit me with a start.

I gasped and felt my heart pound faster. My core lit up with a magnificent yellow light like the glowing, golden sun.

It had worked, though I felt a bit sick from doing it.

I felt myself cough blood and ended my meditation for a moment to role onto my side.

Outside of meditation my whole body ached like I'd just been at the gym for hours on end.

I dropped back into mediation and could see why. The yellow light rushed through my stamina coil and within moments it was lit up brighter than ever before.

It seemed full.

How had I done that? It'd had an almost immediate effect. I'd never experienced it before, apart from when taking a potion.

I switched back into health view and understood why I'd coughed blood.

The rope has completely split apart in multiple places in my core. Somehow, forcing the restart on my stamina had damaged my health badly.

I took a few calming breaths and did what I always did. I gently focused on moving the energy into my core to fix the rope up again.

It took some time but before long it was fixed and I exited meditation again.

I opened my eyes to see the boss room pained almost entirely with blue and brown goop.

My HUD was abuzz with notifications and a loot marker hovered in front of me.

I guessed it was as good a place to start as any.

### Loot: *Slime Queen*
### Y/N

I mentally asserted yes, of course. Why wouldn't I? I received two things. Firstly, a whopping 1000 gold coins.

It seemed that the 10 coin a kill rule didn't apply to boss monsters. 1000 was a drop in the ocean after all the slimes I'd massacred. Still, I wasn't going to say no to more money.

Secondly, I received something called a slime core.

I delved into my inventory and focused on it.

### You have received a new item:
### *Slime Core*
**The core of a slime is akin to its brain and heart. It is the only weak point on a slime and for more powerful variants, the only way to truly finish one off.**

That was all it said. I was thankful that there weren't any snarky remarks, but it still didn't tell me what I could do with it.

What it did do was confirm my suspicions about the glowing orb I'd broken my dagger on. That must have been the slime's core.

I wasn't sure if it was luck or instinct that made me swim towards it. Either way, I was just thankful it had worked.

I sat up, feeling oddly good.

The mediation really had worked wonders. I felt physically refreshed.

Though I was sure I'd spent a long time meditating this time around. I looked around the room and saw that my creepy, clingy torch was still burning bright.

I picked it up and threw it out of the boss room into the sewer water. I blinked and it appeared back in front of me, still burning.

*I guess there really is no way of getting rid of it.*

I pulled it back into my inventory. There was nothing I could do about it now.

The boss room was cast into darkness. It was merely an empty cistern now though.

I got to my feet and left the room, walking out into the sewer tunnel. Then it hit me.

The stench was inescapable.

It had been mild in the boss room, like a hidden force field kept the odour away. Out here though, the stench was everywhere.

It hung thick in the air, almost tangible as it made my nose crinkle and gut wrench. The rest of this quest was gonna suck balls.

I placed my hands over my eyes, wiping them as they watered from the smell. I brushed them through my hair as I groaned and felt the soft touch of skin.

*Skin, wait… where's my hair?*

I began rubbing my bald head like a man possessed. My hair was nowhere to be found. Had it dissolved along with my clothes inside the slime.

I jolted as I realised…my beard.

My hands jumped to my chin, patting, and hoping to feel the coarse new beard I'd been cultivating. My new look for this world.

It was gone.

Hesitantly, I looked down.

*Yup, thought so. I look like a porn star down there.*

It seemed all of my hair was gone. My leg hair, my arm hair all the way to the hair on my head.

I was completely bald. Like one of those expensive cats that old aristocratic widows liked to buy.

I slumped my shoulders and sighed. I looked like a giant new-born baby.

# Chapter 52
# Something Much More Sinister

After a few moments of lamenting my loss of hair, I moved on. Hair grows back, and for all I knew I'd have a full head of it before the end of the quest.

I summoned the only other clothing I had. The spare cultist robe I'd looted from the second cultist I killed, and the cock sock.

So, in a matter of minutes I'd gone from a well-dressed adventurer to one who looked like an eccentric pervert...*again*.

At least I'd be able to buy some more clothes when I returned to the surface. I was at the halfway point of the sewer. The hard part was over.

I still had one thing to do before I finished the circuit though. The most exciting part of any hard battle.

The notifications.

**You have defeated *Slime Queen* (lvl 40)**
***Bonus experience awarded due to level disparity.***

***Congratulations! You have reached level 33.***

The slime was a fair few levels above me. It wasn't as high levelled as Geralt but then again, he would have butchered me with ease.

Gaining a level was awesome. I wondered if I was already close after the 10,000 slime's I'd killed. I guess it didn't matter, a level was a level after all no matter how I came by it.

I continued reading the notifications.

*WARNING*
*Highly condensed natural energy has formed inside you.*
*This could result in death.*

*Notification ignored.*

*WARNING*
*You have forcefully overfilled your stamina. If you do not cease this action you may die.*

*Notification ignored.*

*WARNING*
*Overloading your stamina has caused your HP to rapidly decline. Ignoring this notification may result in immediate death.*

*Notification ignored.*

*WARNING*
*Despite my constant warnings, you are still overloading your stamina.*
*Death is imminent.*

*The strength of your soul has cured the symptom: imminent death.*
*Your stamina has been expanded.*
*Your soul has strengthened.*

"Fuck," I practically whispered as I read the warning messages.

It seemed that when I condensed the energy during meditation to kickstart my stamina core, I'd nearly died. How strong must my soul be to break the system like that?

Was it a fluke, or did I have some kind of weird soul power? Also, what did it mean by expanding my stamina.

**You have gained a new title:**
***Audacious Soul Expander***

**Few who walk the path of forceful expansion survive. Even fewer have the audacity to do it at such a low level.**
**You forcefully expanded your stamina and lived to tell the tale. You know that's quite literally spitting in my metaphorical system face.**
**I'll let it go this one time, but if you try it again you will die. Let this title serve as a reminder and warning not to fuck with the system.**

*+10% overall stamina*

**\*This bonus is calculated after percentages gained through items\***

I was at a loss for words. I'd gained my first title and I got it through meditation. I didn't even realise I could use my soul to expand my stamina.

The whole situation was mind boggling. By all rights, I should have died. Yet somehow I survived *and* got rewarded for it.

A further 10% was huge *and* it was calculated last. That meant it stacked with the 5% I already had from my *Longbow of the Giant Goblin.* I needed to make sure I got it repaired as soon as I got back to the surface.

I quickly checked my stats and saw the huge leap in stamina. Maths wasn't my strongest suit, but from what I could tell the 10% was calculated after the 5% from the bow was added. It was like compounding interest but for stats.

One day, that was going to be huge.

I wondered if my passive *Usurper* skill was the reason I was still alive. It said that it increased the strength of my soul.

Was that why I was still alive? I couldn't know for sure. Maybe I was just naturally gifted in that department.

*The man with the well-endowed soul. Sounds like a movie, though not a very good one.* I thought, quietly grinning at my good fortune.

Still, I would have to be an idiot to try it again. The system made it clear that it would kill me if I did.

Or at least, I couldn't try it again for a while. Who knew how powerful I'd get if I broke through the level cap.

From all accounts those guys were like gods. Maybe then I could give it another go. For now though, that was a distant dream for the future.

I was happy to take the money and run, proverbially speaking. Speaking of the system, I probably needed to let it know I wasn't trying to fuck with it.

It might be an asshole, but it was obviously the supreme power in these parts and I didn't wanna get on its bad side. Including the incident with *Stalin's Stylish Socks,* I'd already pissed it off twice in one day.

"Message received. Sorry about that, won't happen again," I said, facing the ceiling.

I was glad there wasn't anyone around. With my cock sock and robe coupled with my tendency to talk to the sky, I was basically screaming *this guy is a lunatic* to anyone nearby.

That was the last notification. Overall, I was over the moon with the outcome, if a little terrified that I might accidentally get myself killed by meditating.

Who would have thought it. Meditation: the silent killer.

After giving myself a moment to calm down and taking stock of my inventory. I set out once more to clear the sewers and get back to the ladder.

However, I had no weapons.

My bow was broken, my dagger had disintegrated. I guess I'd have to fight like a *DnD* monk…or improvise something.

Speaking of my dagger. I was surprised the system didn't give me some kind of notification for the attack I'd used.

I'd basically used *Power Shot* on a dagger.

It was a super weak version of it, but it was still the same principle. I wondered why it let that slide. Was it normal for people to do weird things without a skill for it?

Then again the green glow was faint. Perhaps I'd imagined it. Maybe I simply charged up the attack and used a lot more strength than normal.

Who knew. I'd definitely need to experiment with it if I wanted to find out. Though for that I'd need a new dagger.

I walked for quite a while before I came across the next gaggle of slimes. There didn't seem to be as many this time as there had been before.

Had taking out the queen dwindled their numbers?

Maybe I'd just taken the path of most resistance to get to her. Either way, I needed to take them all out if I wanted to complete the quest.

The closest one to me was on the floor, so I stepped on it. It smushed into the ground with a nasty squelch and covered my foot in blue goop.

It died easily, like they all did. Though I wasn't keen on being covered in slime goop for every kill.

Also, how exactly was I supposed to step on the ceiling slimes?

I had a mini-lightbulb moment and pulled an arrow from my *Quiver of the Infinite*. As I thought, I didn't need a bow to stab something with it.

It likely wouldn't be very effective against a well levelled foe. But these slimes were all weak as shit. So, I walked under the ceiling slimes and stabbed them one by one as I went.

I quickly got covered from head to toe in slimy gelatine goop but I stopped caring after a while and even began stepping on the floor slimes again.

I quickly fell back into the monotonous loop of killing slimes, meditating to recover, and repeating.

It felt like it took less time to reach the original ladder, but it was likely still days. It was definitely a slog to reach the end.

As my HUD map of the sewer finally filled in fully. I reached my original ladder. One, final slime was sat gently wobbling in front of it.

I stood on it, it smushed and I let out a loud cheer as the quest notification appeared on my HUD.

*Finally.*

### Quest Complete!
### *Up Shit's Creek*

**There has been reports of a slime infestation in the sewers under Havar. Investigate the matter and exterminate them.**
**You have entered the sewer system and come across some slimes. Extermination time me thinks.**
**You have discovered the lair of the *Slime Queen*, is she the source of the infestation?**

**You have defeated the *Slime Queen* and stopped the infestation.**
**You have eliminated the final slime.**

**Objectives:**
**Exterminate all the sewer slimes 1/1**
**Find the source of the slimes and deal with it 1/1**

**Reward: *500 gold*.**

***Speak to the Adventure Society to claim your reward.***
***Reward payable upon the successful completion of the***
***above objectives****

I almost jumped for joy as I read through the quest notification. It had updated as I completed various parts of the quest just like last time.

It was like a quest log from a game. Maybe that was in case I started a quest and then got side tracked. Were side quests a thing in this place?

I'd have to go to the Adventure Society to claim my 500-gold reward. Though that didn't seem like much compared to the gold I'd earned from my blessing.

I'd have to thank Chrysus next time I saw him.

Actually, on second thought. That guy was an asshole so maybe not.

***

Frank wandered around the old maintenance building, just like he did every day.

He was old enough to retire, but he honestly didn't know what he'd do with himself if he didn't work. Working for the Department of Sanitation and Maintenance wasn't a bad gig anyway.

He'd spent his twilight years working for them and he wouldn't have it any other way.

Mostly he just maintained the pipes which led to the sewer system. Every now and then he'd have to traverse the sewers himself to fix a leak, but it was no trouble.

Today wasn't one of those days.

Today was an average, steal a wage kind of day where he'd do very little and spend most of his time pottering around the old building.

Or at least, it was supposed to be one of those days.

Frank heard a loud banging sound coming from the next room over.

*What could that be? Has one of those damned pipes broken again?* He thought with an internal sigh as he shuffled his way into the room.

BANG, BANG, BANG.

He heard as he entered the room. It seemed to be coming from the sewer hatch.

Had those damned slimes mutated? He wasn't sure what he'd do if that was the case. Of course, there was always the chance it was that adventurer he'd let in.

No, it couldn't be. He was long dead. He'd been in there an entire month, to the day. It was obvious he'd been killed.

No one could survive in that stench for that long with only a disposable purification mask. The smell was poisonous.

It was only a minor poison sure, but a whole month? No way.

BANG, BANG, BANG.

"Hold your horses I'm coming!" Frank yelled. "Damned slimes making an old man rush around," he muttered to himself, because a mutated slime was the only explanation, he was sure of it.

He hesitated as he bent down to open the hatch. Should he really let this mutated slime lose on the city?

BANG, BANG, BANG.

If letting it loose got it to shut the hell up, it'd be worth it. Besides, it was his job to deal with this kind of stuff. If he left it there before seeing it, it'd be dereliction of duty. He opened the hatch and took a few steps back.

The stench was particularly bad today. He could smell it even through his government issued odour eliminator.

He readied himself for the mutated slime that would no doubt climb out. However, it was no slime.

He had released something much more sinister. A thing more heinous than his small mind could have ever thought possible: a hairless pervert.

The bald man crawled out of the sewer covered in slime and shit. Worse, he was wearing a dirty sock over his penis and a tattered red cape.

"Good to see you again old man," the pervert said.

Frank fainted.

# Chapter 53
# Rich Orphan Turned Vigilante

I rushed forward to catch the old sanitation worker before he hit the floor. I knew the sewer smell was bad but I hadn't expected it to affect him like that.

I caught him and gently lowered him to the floor. He had fainted. The slime that covered my body dripped to the floor where I knelt next to the man, causing a puddle to form at my feet.

He wasn't going to be happy when he realised he was the one who'd have to clean it up.

*Oh well. At least he didn't have to fight the Slime Queen.* I thought to myself as the man stirred.

I was crouched next to his head where I had caught him before he fell. His eyes opened slowly and I smiled at him. A friendly face would be comforting in this situation.

"Ah! Get that thing away from me!" He yelled hysterically as he shuffled backwards with the speed of a man half his age.

He pushed himself into a corner stared at me in horror.

"Don't you recognise me?" I asked, bewildered as the man shook. "I'm Kaleb, the adventurer who came to complete your quest…it's completed now by the way, you shouldn't have any more slime trouble."

The man stared back at me for a minute. He blinked a few times as if struggling to comprehend what I'd said.

"*You're* that adventurer kid?" he finally replied.

"Yup, that's me."

"How? You were in there an entire month. The poison from the smell should have killed you," he began slowly as the implications of his words dawned on me. "Why are you wearing a sock on your penis?"

"Did you just say I was in there an entire month?" I asked quickly.

"Well yes. I let you in there exactly a month today. I thought you were dead."

Without reply, I stood up and rushed out of the building. I didn't want to be rude but I had somewhere I needed to be.

I threw the door open as I ran into the street. The busy people of Havar stopped their business to stare at me but I barely noticed as I set off running towards my destination.

*Andy better not have sold that armour.* I thought as I sprinted away from the sanitation building. *If it's gone and I've just wasted an entire month in the sewer for nothing, I don't know what I'll do.*

I ran so fast that I almost skidded around the corner onto the high street. People cried out, gasped, and muttered to their friends as I ran past. Mostly though, they just held their noses.

"What is that awful stench?" a catonid said.

"What is he running from?" a human said.

"Why is he wearing a dirty sock on his penis?" a lycanid said.

I ignored them all as I raced towards my goal.

My upgraded stats almost seemed designed for running. My legs moved faster than I thought possible and I could turn on a dime. It must have been due to my agility and strength stats.

How fast would I be able to move at the level cap?

The feeling was awesome, but I didn't have time to appreciate it as I closed in on my destination: *Andy's Armour Emporium.*

I burst through the front door to the familiar sound of clanging coming from the back. I looked around but the armour wasn't on the stand anymore. Was I too late?

"Andy I'm back!" I shouted as loudly as I could as I jogged up to the counter.

The clanging stopped and the broad human in the brown leather apron came out from the back of the shop.

"You actually heard me?" I asked, placing both hands impatiently on the counter and leaning towards him.

"Heard you? No, I smelt something awful and came to investigate. Who are you and what are you doing in my shop dressed like...*that?*" he asked aggressively as he gestured to my attire.

"It's me, Kaleb," I replied, taken aback. Why did no one recognise me? Surely my lack of hair wasn't enough to make me look that different? "Panda's summoner," I quickly added.

"Oh Kaleb, cutting it a little close aren't you?" He laughed, his demeanour changing instantly. "You smell like a sewer, kid, and why is there a dirty sock on your penis?"

"I took a quest in the sewer and a slime queen burnt off all my clothes and hair. This was all I had to change into in my inventory," I explained, I felt in less of a hurry now he knew who I was but I still needed to know if he still had the armour I'd worked so hard for.

"Ah I see," he replied, folding his arms, and stroking his chin and nodding. "You do realise that you look like an eccentric pervert like that right? It would probably be more dignified to just stay commando."

"I'll grab some new clothes soon. Do you still have the armour?" I asked hurriedly.

"Of course I do. A deal is a deal. Besides, that set had been on display for three weeks before you came in. The chances of my selling it the same day our deal ran out were always low." He chuckled. "I'll fetch it for you, but first do me a favour and take a shower, there's one in the back."

He motioned into his smithing room with his thumb and I nodded. My whole body relaxed as he spoke. I could finally get my armour and I would happily take a shower.

Holding his nose, Andy led me through his workshop to a small shower cubicle hidden off to the side.

"I keep this here for when I work up too much of a sweat. Don't want to scare of the customers, you know?" He chuckled as I walked into the shower room. "I'll bring you some clothes, so why don't you go ahead and incinerate what you're wearing," he said, as he walked off I did exactly that.

I removed the cloak and the cock sock, both of which were tattered and covered in slime and sewer muck, and I threw them into the fire.

It was a mistake. The smell got worse.

My nose was pretty desensitised though so I ignored it as I entered the shower cubicle and pulled the chord. Glorious water rained down on me. It was the best feeling ever.

Blue gunk, brown dirt and, what was likely human, excrement flowed from me into the drain. It was disgusting. I knew I was dirty but this was a whole other level.

The water at my feet turned black instantly before draining away. I must have been in the shower for like half an hour before the water finally ran clean.

When I walked out of the shower, I found a pair worn brown pants and a tattered shirt wating for me. I slipped them on and walked back out into the main store.

"What happened to the sewer monster?" Andy asked.

"What happened to these pants?" I returned gesturing to the brown monstrosity he'd left for me.

"Touché," he replied with a chuckle. "So, to business. Are you ready for your armour?"

He had no idea how ready I was. It was all I'd thought about for the last month in the sewer.

"Yup." Was all I managed to reply with.

"…And, do you have the forty-eight thousand gold we discussed?" he asked.

"I do," I replied, delving into my inventory to check.

"Perfect, I'll send you the request," Andy said.

*What request?* I thought, and then a notification appeared.

**You have received an inventory transfer request from (Andy) for 48,000 gold coins. Would you like to accept? Y/N**

That was weird, I didn't even know you could request inventory from people. I guess it made sense though. If I ejected 48,000 gold coins onto the floor it would fill the shop.

I mentally asserted yes and another notification appeared.

**Please enter your pin code.**

Pin code? What the fuck. I didn't have a pin code. I didn't even know that inventory transfers existed until a few moments ago.

A number pad appeared on my HUD and I took a breath. Maybe it was just one of those default pins like they did back home sometimes. I focused the number pad and tried entering 1,2,3,4.

*You have entered the wrong pin. You have been locked out of inventory transfer for one week. Thank you for using system banking. Have a nice day.*

Locked out, after just one attempt? What kind of bureaucratic bullshit was this? Well, I guess I didn't have a choice. I'd have to flood the store coins after all if I wanted to pay him.

I looked up at the ceiling and growled, "fuck you." Then I pulled the money from my inventory and it scattered across his countertop, spilling onto the floor, and practically burying Andy in gold. It's not like looted gold came in neat little bags, so I made it rain all over his shop.

His eyes lit up like a dragon adding to its horde.

"That was a little rude. Have you never heard of manners? Also, how did you get this so fast?" He asked first in a pissed off tone and then in a shocked whisper as he picked up a coin and bit it, like he thought it might have been made of chocolate.

"That's a trade secret," I replied with a wink.

In truth I didn't want to tell him I was blessed by Chrysus. As a merchant he probably wouldn't be offended by it, but why take the risk?

I didn't understand the religion here yet. There seemed to be lots of gods and they all had different reputations and connotations attached to them. Honestly, I didn't want anything to do with any of them.

"Fair enough," he replied. "Well, as promised, here's your armour," he said, pulling it from his inventory. "It's all yours kid."

It was just as awesome as I remembered. Fitted black pants with padding in the knees, an embroidered black torso piece and a cloak as black as the void with a hood that covered the top half of your face with slits for your eyes.

It was badass.

I quickly pulled it into my inventory and a new notification popped up.

You have received multiple new items:
*Shadow Armour (epic)*

The *Shadow Armour* set is an epic rarity ensemble of black armour that appeals to emo kids and fans of rich orphans turned vigilante.
Here's a tip, try speaking in an unnecessary hoarse voice to really add to the effect.

*Full set:*
*Shadow Cloak:* a cloak that blends into the shadows increasing stealth. With the hood up you can shield your aura from others.

*Shadow Light Armour:* +10% vitality.
*Shadow Pants:* +10% vitality.
*Shadow Boots:* +15% agility.
*Shadow Bracer:* +5% strength.

*Full Set Bonus:* When all pieces of the set are equipped, turn invisible once a day for an amount of time dictated by your intelligence stat.

I equipped the set and immediately felt the surge of power to my stats. There was a lot to unpack here. I bet I looked like a certain orphan turned vigilante in my all-black gear.

Firstly, most of the armour gave me stat boosts which were definitely welcome, especially considering they stacked.

Though the boosts themselves weren't huge, they would be one day. I wondered if there was a cap for what percentage boosts you could have. Theoretically I could just keep adding to them until my stats were insane.

The cloak had an interesting effect. I'd have to experiment with the whole blending into shadows thing.

The hood was self-explanatory. From what I understood from what Panda had told me, people with mana – AKA everyone who wasn't named Kaleb Akabane – could sense auras.

It was a way for them to distinguish the powerful from their peers. I didn't have this ability. However, I probably did have an aura of my own. The hood would hide it, probably.

I was a little sad that there weren't any gloves but at least my agility boost was good. I'd lost both my white glove and my *boots of resist environment* in the fight with the slime queen. So I was over the moon to see how good the stat boosts were which replaced them. Also, the set bonus was freaking awesome!

I would have to practice with it. Turning invisible was like a superpower. Something like that could really turn the tide of a battle, especially when mixed with the aura hiding hood.

I'd be invisible both to the eyes and the senses.

The only problem was that it worked using my intelligence stat. The lowest stat I had by quite a bit.

From what I understood, intelligence was all about mana, so I had never put anything into it because, well… I didn't have any mana.

I'd have to change that going forward. I still had five free points from my level up, so I threw them all into intelligence.

As I read through the item specs and lost myself in thought, the door to the shop slammed open.

"Andy! Get out here right fucking now."

# Chapter 54
# I'm A Sage, It's What We Do

I looked at myself in a large freestanding mirror as I equipped my new armour. I grinned from ear to ear. It was definitely worth the money, even if I did look a bit like an edge lord assassin.

It had been a while since I'd checked my stats. I knew they'd grown a lot since the last time and with the addition of the new percentage boosts I'd gained from my armour I was excited to see what they looked like.

**Status Sheet:**

**Name: Kaleb Akabane**
**Race: Outworlder**
**Class: Apex Predator (unique)**
**Adventurer Rank: Temp**
**Level: 33**
**Map Pieces 2/10,000**
**HP: 381/331 (381)**
**Stamina: 388/325 (388)**

**Strength: 282 (310)**
**Agility: 121 (139)**
**Perception: 117**
**Vitality: 251 (301)**
**Intelligence: 50**

**Personal Skills:** *Speak English Damnit!, Eat Anything, Minor Poison Resistance, Usurper (unique), Health Sense (common)*
**Class Skills (Passive) Skills:** *Newly Qualified Bowman (0.2%), Dagger (lvl 10), Novice Apex Skirmisher, Acid Dhampir Dagger, Acid Arrows, Environmental Hazzard*
**Active Skills:** *Perception of the Apex Predator (rare), Soul Shot (ancient)*
**Blessing:** *Blessing of Wealth*
**Familiars:** *Panda (Daemon)*
**Titles:** *Audacious Soul Expander*
**Admission:** Pentagram [Right hand (Morningstar Hotel and Spa)]

I blinked a few times as I read through it all. My stat sheet was getting long. Most noticeably, my stamina had overtaken my health.

My intelligence was pathetically low though compared to my other stats. I'd need to work on that if I wanted to use the *Shadow Armour's* full set bonus. It was a skill that let me turn invisible once a day.

As I admired my new armour, the bell above the door to the shop rang violently.

"Andy! Get out here right fucking now." A muscular lycanid shouted.

As he spoke, spittle and froth flew from his mouth. He sounded angry, but more noticeably he had to duck to get through the door.

He must have been eight foot tall. What a giant.

I turned towards the commotion and looked on as Andy came trotting out from behind the counter. He looked like an entirely different man as he bowed and ringed his hands together.

"What can I do for you?" He asked feebly, not looking the lycanid in the eyes.

"It's pay day," he replied with a growl.

"Of course. Please send my regards to your master," he said, offering out a large coin purse.

The lycanid snatched it from his hands and left in a huff, slamming the door behind him.

Andy sighed and lifted his head. He turned to me, casting out his usual presence of strength and mercantile cunning as if nothing had happened.

It was as if the feeble man who stood before the lycanid was a completely different person.

"I'm sorry you had to see that Kaleb. How's the armour?" He asked, striding towards me with the confidence of a powerful man.

"It's great," I replied, slightly distracted. "What was that?"

"He works for the Morningstar Collective; I owed them protection money," he sighed, scratching the back of his head awkwardly with his hand.

*Morningstar…where have I heard that name before?*

"Who are they?" I asked flatly.

"They're a crime syndicate. They do all the crimes. In this case it was racketeering but honestly that barely even scratches the surface," he said, moving towards the counter and leaning against it. He looked exhausted.

Then it hit me; I had an active quest that mentioned *Morningstar* though it was a bit different from what Andy seemed to be talking about.

### A Good Time, Not A Long Time

**You've been marked as a guest of *The Morningstar Hotel and Spa*. I wonder what mayhem and fun awaits behind its doors.**

It was the quest that had appeared after I'd opened the loot box I got for accidentally killing Brad, the other outworlder, in the cultist hideaway.

I'd completely forgotten about it. Though maybe I should consider trying to complete it sooner rather than later. The reward was awesome.

"Is this collective related to the Morningstar Hotel and Spa?" I asked.

"Yes, that's one of their many business ventures. There's one here in Havar, though they have them all over Celestia," Andy replied.

"Do you know where it is?"

"No. Rumour has it you can only see it if you've been invited. I wouldn't go poking into their affairs though. Yaldabaoth is unhinged and crazy strong, it's better to stay off their radar if you can."

"What's a Yala-bread loaf?" I asked.

"He's known as the malevolent god of debauchery and he's scary as shit. He's the current chairman of the Collective. Just... don't go poking around there," he said, sounding exasperated towards the end.

"Sure," I replied slowly. "Well, thanks for the armour mate. I'm sure I'll see you around," I said, raising my hand as I left the store.

*Maybe I should level up a bit before entering this hotel place.* I thought. That was my original plan anyway and Andy seemed to be terrified of them.

Besides, I still needed to complete my third quest so I could take the adventurer exam. For now, though, I needed to hand the sewer quest in and replace my weapons.

First though, I needed to collect Panda. He was probably worried about me.

I headed back to the *Sleeping Giant Inn.* No one muttered about me as I walked past this time. The street was still busy, as usual, but I seemed to blend in much easier this time.

I entered the inn and headed upstairs as the lycanid landlady smiled lecherously at me and waved with her fingers.

A shiver went down my spine as I half smiled, half grimaced back at her. I opened the door to my room to find Panda laid on the bed with a book in hand.

He was on his front, kicking his feet behind him. The room was full of dirty plates and bottles and there was a stack of books covering over half of the room.

"Ay up ma-" I began but Panda lifted his paw in the air to shush me. A little taken aback, I obliged.

A few moments later he turned his page and then put the book down. He sat up, stretched, and turned towards me.

*He hasn't seen me in a month and he shushed me to finish his page?*

"Hey kid," he said, yawning as he spoke. "Back so soon?"

"It's been a month," I replied incredulously.

"Has it really?" he replied. "I lost track of time reading. It happens sometimes. So, I see you got that armour you wanted."

"I did yeah…have you really been reading this entire time?" I asked, though from the stack of dishes and the smell of unwashed panda I already knew the answer.

"I'm a sage, it's what we do," he shrugged. "These books are great by the way; I've learned so much. I'm gonna need some more though." He looked up at me with big eyes, it would have been adorable if he wasn't surrounded by squalor.

"Sure, we'll get to it. First though, I need new weapons and hoped you might know a guy."

"There's a quaint little store not too far from here. I'll take you; I could do with some fresh air anyway."

"You're telling me," I replied, shaking my head lightly as he unstuck himself from the bed.

We left the room as he groggily rubbed his eyes and yawned again. As we passed the landlady, I tossed her a gold coin and asked her to clean the room and extend our stay.

"Gods it's bright out here!" Panda exclaimed as we exited the inn. It was around midday and the sun was high.

"I guess your eyes go a bit funny when you spend a month locked in a room," I chuckled.

"You spent a month locked in a sewer," he grumbled.

"Yet somehow the room smelled worse," I sighed.

He led me back in the direction of the armourer and I was beginning to get the impression that the only shops he knew were the ones on this street.

Still, he hadn't steered me wrong so far so I followed him. I really needed to get my bow repaired and I needed new daggers.

Currently I was a weapon-less adventurer and that couldn't mean anything but trouble. I felt naked without them. It's funny how quickly you get used to a new situation.

Not too long ago I went about my daily life without fighting or carrying weapons at all, yet now the idea of not having any felt alien to me.

*Human adaptability at its finest.*

As we walked I took the opportunity to grill Panda on some of the questions I had from my time in the sewers. One of which was potentially more life threatening than the rest.

I told him about the *Eternal Torch of Communist Supremacy* and how it came into my possession. He listened quietly as I explained and then I asked him what *powerful economic groups* were.

"Well shit kid, you broke the first rule: never piss off the system," he responded after patiently listening to my explanation. "When the system creates weird items like this it's hard to know exactly what the effect means.

"I haven't heard of this particular one before. Though I know what the economic groups are. They're powerful organisations who rule the various countries around the world.

"Like shadow rulers really. No one knows who controls them, but they're steeped in ideology and you can tell which country supports which group by how that country is run.

"For example, Havar is obviously part of the socialist group. Though I wouldn't exactly call them powerful, they're one of the smaller ones from what I've heard."

"Havar is a socialist state?" I asked. I hadn't really considered how countries were run so far; I'd been a little busy trying to survive.

"Well yeah," he said poignantly. "Basic necessities like food, shelter and water are practically free. However, luxury item costs are insane. Just look at that armour you're wearing. Fifty-thousand gold coins for some glorified clothing when a bed and food cost you a single gold a week.

"You do the math kid, but I'm sure that armour is worth multiple lifetimes of food and board at the inn. That's not normal."

I guessed he was right. The local economy was out of whack here, though I wasn't sure that alone constituted as socialism as I understood it. I'd figured it was a quirk of this world that adventurer gear was expensive but apparently not.

"Speaking of gold coins, are they the only currency in this world?" I asked. It had struck me as odd that I hadn't seen any other denominations of coins yet.

"Why would we need other coins?" Panda asked, scratching his chin.

"Because giving someone fifty-thousand gold coins at once is a bit extreme?" I replied, furrowing my brow, and thinking back to how I'd flooded Andy's store with coins.

"But we all have access to an inventory space and transfers."

He clearly didn't understand what I was getting at. I guess it wasn't seen as an issue so I dropped it, mostly.

"Speaking of transfers, how do I find out what my pin code is?" I asked.

"You can set it up at one of the societies. We can do it later," he replied.

I'd have to make a mental note to do that. Though I'd probably have to wait a week since I'd been locked out. *Stupid system.* I thought.

My mind wandered back to the economic factions and my weird new torch. If Havar constituted as poor in this world, then I wondered what the richer nations looked like.

"If this item makes everyone who's not a communist hate me, then does that mean the Havar government are going to end up as my enemy?" I asked suddenly, the last thing I wanted was to be labelled an enemy of the state or something just because of some stupid item the system wouldn't let me throw away.

"I doubt it," he shrugged, offering no further explanation. "Anyway, we're here. Let's shelf this for another time."

We stood in front of a large, multistorey store with polished red wood on the frame and a hand painted sign above the door.

It said: *Wendy's Wonderful Weapons.*

*These store owners sure love their alliteration. This was the third store I'd been to that had a name straight out of a fucked-up Dr Seus book.*

Through the large windows I could already see racks upon racks of weapons. I wondered what kind of person Wendy was, and more importantly, how she knew Panda.

For a familiar he seemed to know everyone in these parts. The little guy definitely got around in his last life.

"I thought you said this place was quaint?" I said to panda monotonously.

# Chapter 55
# Never Trust a Furry

I pushed open the door to *Wendy's Wonderful Weapons* to the sound of light jingling.

The interior was full of wall-mounted racks and locked cases. From a quick glance I saw a lot of axes, swords, and maces. Sadly, there were precious few daggers and bows.

As with the other stores, there was a typical counter sitting at the far side. A beautiful and small... *woman* stood behind it. She smiled at me from across the room.

Her skin was the colour of midnight purple and she had pointed ears, covered slightly by thick and long black hair.

*Is that an elf?* I wondered, as I approached.

Elves were the pinnacle of other world races in fantasy shows back home, though I'd never seen a small one with purple skin before.

More oddly, her eyes were black with red pupils. She'd almost look demonic if it wasn't for her polite and intoxicating smile.

I focused on her and a notification popped up.

**You have discovered a new race!**
*Svartalf*

**Hailing from the small subterranean kingdom of
*Svartalfheim*, the *Svartalf* are a kind of dark elf, dwarf
hybrid race.
Known for their impressive alcohol tolerance and love
of metal working, the *Svartalf* are a proud race with a
sordid history.
There is a legendary mystery surrounding their
creation which many have pondered, but none have
been able to answer:
How did a dwarf manage to pull an elf?**

That was surprisingly informative for the system. I thought as I read through the notification.

"Welcome to Wendy's," she said with a surprisingly girly voice. "How may I help you today."

"Hi, I'm Kaleb," I responded, feeling my face flush as I spoke to her. She was mesmerising and had I not been a married man I might have even plucked up the nerve to ask her out – though probably not, she was way out of my league.

"I'm looking for someone who can repair my bow and hopefully sell me some new daggers," I continued.

"Ah, that won't be a problem. I have a workshop upstairs where I do repairs. Can I see it?" she asked cheerfully.

I summoned the Bow of the Giant Goblin from my inventory and placed it on the table. The dark black bow looked worse for wear with its bowstring cut and the wood cracked in multiple places.

The Slime Queen's body had really done a number on it. Though I guess I was fortunate it didn't dissipate completely like my hair and clothes. Not that I was bitter or anything.

"Wow, this has sure seen better days, hasn't it?" The Svartalf mused as she picked up the bow and thumbed it over. "Repairs won't be cheap. I'd quote it to be at least 500 gold, maybe more."

"That won't be a problem," I said, producing the money and scattering it on the table. Her eyes lit up as she saw it.

I'd replace it as soon as I turned in the quest anyway, though 500 wasn't all that much with my full coffers. The blessing of the god of wealth really was OP.

"Thank you for your patronage, sir. I should have this ready for you by tomorrow afternoon. Since you've paid up front I'll push you to the front of the queue." She smiled at me again as she scooped up the coins and placed them into her own inventory.

"Seem's you're as one dimensional as ever Wendy." Panda said snidely as he clumsily attempted to climb onto the counter.

For the first time since I'd arrived in town, an acquaintance of Panda, didn't reach over to help him up onto the countertop. I felt a certain tension in the air as they locked eyes. It was a far cry from his usual relationship with the merchants we'd met previously.

"Panda. So, you're back, are you?" she said harshly, looking him over and curling her lip.

"Yup, the kid here summoned me. That's what happens when someone actually wants you around, not that you'd know what that's like."

What on earth is going on here? I thought, taken aback at the open hostility between the two.

Wendy completely ignored him, put back on her smile and turned to me politely.

"I'm sorry sir but we don't allow pets in the store. They tend to climb all over the furniture and clutter up the place." She gestured to Panda who was still trying to get on top of the counter. "I'll have to ask you to leave him outside please. I can lend you some rope to tie him up though, so he doesn't wander off."

Her smile and polite customer service voice was chilling. I gulped before answering.

"Panda, go wait outside…I won't be long," I said, trying not to stammer.

"But Kaleb!" he protested, looking up at me with his big anime eyes.

We locked eyes for a moment and I refused to back down even though I felt bad about it, then he sighed and departed.

What was all that about.

"Thank you for your cooperation, sir," Wendy said, before grinning sinisterly at Panda. "Now then, shall we see to your other needs."

"Please, I'm looking for some daggers," I said.

Since my Dagger skill had levelled up and given me the Novice Apex Skirmisher skill, I'd been itching to try out a dual wield.

The skill specifically said that I'd gained proficiency with dual wielding but I hadn't had the chance to try it out yet.

"Of course sir," Wendy replied, returning completely to the previously polite and respectful Svartalf that had first greeted me. "As Havar is mostly populated by lycanids I mostly sell larger weapons. However, I think I have a few daggers in the back that I can bring out for your perusal."

"Sounds good," I replied and she excused herself leaving through the small door behind her.

I breathed out. That was intense. I was getting used to fighting monsters but tense social situations were still alien to me.

As a truck driver, I'd spent most of my life on earth away from people. Office politics, weird social cues, and stuff like that perplexed me.

In my personal life I was fortunate in that my wife navigated those areas within our friend group. I just followed her lead.

Wendy and Panda obviously had bad blood and I wanted absolutely nothing to do with that. I really hoped she wouldn't start charging me more now that she knew I was his new summoner.

Wendy returned quickly, carrying a dusty display case with two daggers in it.

"Thank you for waiting," she said as she plonked the case down onto the countertop and wiped it with her hand.

Dust flew everywhere, catching in the light that shone through the window. It looked like a mini cyclone of dust particles was flying off the case.

"I'm afraid these are all I have in stock currently. They're quite simple, steel daggers. They don't have any enchantments on them but I'm sure they'll do quite well in your capable hands."

Was she flattering me on purpose? From where I was standing they just looked like normal daggers. Barely an upgrade from my original one.

"How much?" I asked candidly.

"Since they're the last we have in stock I couldn't let them go for less than twenty-thousand gold," she said brightly.

"And they're just normal, unenchanted daggers?" I asked incredulously.

"I assure you sir, despite their lack of enchantments, these daggers are of the highest quality."

I know a hard sell when I hear one. She's trying to rip me off. I thought critically.

"I'll give you five thousand for them," I said, even that was probably too much but I didn't have much to base it off.

"Five thousand?" she asked. "Forgive my rudeness sir but that price is an insult."

"Trying to sell me unenchanted daggers for twenty thousand is what's insulting. Do I look like I was born yesterday?" I asked.

Though, from a certain point of view, I pretty much was born yesterday as far as this world was concerned. I didn't even know what an enchantment truly was, but if I had to guess it was the thing that gave weapons special skills and stat increases.

If these daggers didn't have any of that then they were hardly worth what she was asking for. They couldn't be.

"I could probably drop to ten thousand, since you seem so well informed," she said, still talking in that sickly sweet customer service voice.

"Fine, it's a deal," I relented. I had no idea if I'd just been ripped off, but I had plenty of money left and I needed the daggers, so I didn't really have much of a choice.

I'd still managed to knock her down to half price so that had to be something.

"Perfect!" She chimed brightly, her ears twitching slightly as she smiled up at me.

I had a feeling deep in the pit of my stomach that told me I'd just become a victim of daylight robbery. At least from her reaction to the sale.

No matter. I really did need the daggers so it wasn't like I had much of a choice.

I summoned the 10,000 coins and dropped them unceremoniously onto the countertop. A literal mountain of coins formed from my hand and her eyes lit up like a Christmas tree.

She didn't even complain that I hadn't requested an inventory transfer as she handed me the daggers and began scooping up the coins.

I added them to my inventory and a notification popped up.

**You have acquired a new item:**
*Steel Dagger x2*
**Slightly better than an iron dagger.**

That was the only description. I'd definitely been ripped off. My previous dagger was just called a…dagger. So, they were probably better than it was. At least that was something.

*I guess an upgrade is still and upgrade even if you have to pay through the nose for it.* I told myself. Besides I still had plenty of money left. I'd gained over 100,000 gold from my slime slaying.

Even after buying the armour, the daggers, and paying for my bow to be fixed, I still had over 50,000 left. I'd gained 1000 just from killing the slime queen, not to mention the slimes I'd exterminated on the way out.

"Thank you so much for your patronage sir!" Wendy said, bowing slightly. "Your bow will be ready for you tomorrow afternoon."

"Yeah, see you then," I said, exiting the store with a little wave.

I walked outside and stopped for a moment as the door closed behind me with a little jingle. I sighed and looked towards the sky.

"She ripped you off didn't she?" Panda said. He was leaning against the storefront with his arms crossed.

"Yeah," I said solemnly. "Is that why she kicked you out?"

"No, she kicked me out because I told my last summoner to break up with her after I saw her on the arm of a busty catonid girl.

"I knew she'd rip you off because you don't understand how money works here and a good merchant can smell that kind of weakness a mile away."

I knew Panda's previous summoner was a woman who'd been dear to him. He barely spoke of her but from what I'd pieced together she'd died not all that long ago.

When I'd summoned him it had barely been a minute since she passed, at least to a few thousand-year-old daemon like him. I think it had been closer to a decade.

I wondered if he'd open up to me about her someday. I wasn't going to pry but it could be useful to know what happened to her.

For now, though, I needed to visit the Adventure Society and hand in my completed quest. I'd probably put it off for too long already.

I wondered what new quest I'd end up taking. I only had one left to complete before I'd be eligible to take the exam and become a fully-fledged adventurer.

I couldn't wait.

"Don't even think about sleeping with her," Panda said warningly.

"I'm married Panda," I replied with a sigh.

"That didn't stop you from hitting on Lucy at the society."

"I never hit on her. You're the one who cuddles up to her every time we go there."

"My mother always said; never trust a furry," he said as we set off in the direction of the Adventure Society building. It was going to be a long walk.

# Chapter 56
# Always Expect the Unexpected

We arrived at the Adventure Society's gigantic glass building and entered, approaching the front desk.

Lucy, the blonde catonid receptionist greeted me with her usual charm.

"Mr Akabane, it's been a while. Your new armour is lovely." She smiled as she walked around the side of the reception desk and picked Panda up under the arms, placing him on the desk where he sat and began puffing smoke from his bamboo pipe.

"Thanks," I replied. "I came to hand in the quest I took. It's been completed."

"That's brilliant news. If you could just fill out this report I'll arrange for your reward," she said, reaching under the desk and passing me some paper and a pen. She then leant on the counter and fondly scratched Panda behind the ears.

I took the form from her. It was basically a field report. It asked me to explain what had happened during the quest.

It was a simple matter; except I only knew how to write in English.

My personal skill *Speak English Damnit!* Allowed me to understand other languages and somehow it translated my speech, or maybe everyone else had a similar skill that translated speech for them, but it didn't say anything about writing.

Panda looked towards me and nodded.

I guessed it was worth a shot so I began writing my report in English. I explained about the 10,000+ slimes I'd exterminated, the slime queen, and described the circular layout of the sewers.

I also included the weakness of the slime queen being the core, her level and the affects her body had on me when I was swallowed.

That was a little embarrassing to admit, but the only use of these reports that I could think of was to gather information. If my embarrassment could save another adventurer later down the line then it was a small price to pay.

It didn't take long to fill out the report and I quickly returned it to Lucy, looking on nervously as she examined it.

"Wow, you defeated a slime queen by yourself? That's quite impressive Mr Akabane. I think it also warrants a better reward.

"This was supposed to be a temp level quest but it seems it should have been posted for iron rank adventurers instead."

I sighed in relief as I realised that she could read my writing. I had no idea how the skill had translated it, but I put it down to system fuckery and was just glad it worked.

"If you'll follow me Mr Akabane, we'll go report this to Administrator Gonzo right away."

I had no idea who that was but I nodded anyway and followed her behind the reception area.

There was a door at the back which led into an office-style hallway. The walls were adorned with corporate propaganda posters. There was even the famous one I'd seen on TV with a cat hanging onto a washing line.

I still found it strange how similar the backroom work environments in Havar were to the ones back home. Outside of the offices the world was a pure fantasy land, yet bureaucracy still prevailed inside office buildings.

Perhaps bureaucracy was universal, that was a chilling thought.

We passed through an area of cubicle spaces which were mostly dominated by bored looking humans who were clock watching.

At the back of that room was a small office. Lucy knocked on the door and it opened on its own.

She entered and we followed.

The office itself wasn't anything to write home about. It was small and windowless with a desk piled with paperwork shoved in the corner and a few seats on our side of it.

Sitting at the desk, looking rather stressed, was a catonid man with grey whiskers.

"Administrator," Lucy began. "This is Mr Akabane, he is a temp adventurer who joined us recently. He has just returned from the slime extermination quest and his report was quite unusual."

"Let's have a look," Gonzo replied without looking up from his paperwork. He held out a slender hand and snatched the paper from Lucy.

He scanned over it for a moment and I watched as his facial expression went from bored, to intrigued, to outright shocked.

"A slime queen, living in the sewers? It seems you've done us quite the service Mr..."

"Akabane sir," Lucy advised.

"Yes, yes, Mr Akabane. Good job, I'll have your reward upgraded."

"Thank you, sir," Lucy said, bowing slightly to the distracted administrator before gesturing for us to leave.

We walked in silence back through the cubicle area and to the reception desk.

"So, what will I get from this upgraded reward?" I asked as we returned to the reception area.

"More gold probably and it'll be added as a feat to your record with us. We look at those when it comes time to promote people.

"It doesn't apply to you yet, but once you pass the exam and become iron rank you can be promoted within that rank.

"The maximum is a three-star promotion which qualifies you for more complicated quests. These are usually less about fighting and need more of a delicate touch. There can be more to adventuring than fighting monsters."

A three-star ranking system within each actual rank? Yup, this place was the epitome of corporate bureaucracy.

"Oh, cool," I said sceptically.

"For now, I believe the director wished to speak with you. I'll have your reward ready when you're done."

She smiled and I took that as my cue to leave. I walked towards the magic elevator with Panda in tow.

I pressed the button in the centre of the magic circle on the wall but nothing seemed to happen. I tried again, still nothing. I pushed it a few more times before I registered Panda snickering behind me.

"What?" I asked irritably.

"You need mana to use a *magic* elevator," he replied, giggling as he spoke.

"Well then it's a good job I've got a familiar to do that for me," I replied.

He huffed and began trying to reach the button which was just too high on the wall for him.

"Oh, can't you reach?" I asked teasingly.

He glowered and I picked him up so he could press the button for me. The elevator arrived and we took it to the top floor.

It opened into the familiar and large office of Director Lucas. The man himself was stood straight backed and facing out of the window that took up the entire back wall.

I approached, but he didn't turn around. I moved to stand next to him and took in the glorious view of the city of Havar.

It was truly a sight to behold from this high up. No wonder CEO's felt so powerful if they got to see views like this every day.

It felt like the entire city was beneath us as I took it in with all its glory. The busy people rushing through the streets below looked like ants from this high up.

"Beautiful, isn't it?" Lucas asked absently as he took a sip from a fancy crystal glass.

"It's certainly something," I replied.

"You know Kaleb when I first moved here I was disappointed with the transfer. I was supposed to be an influential figure on the continent, but alas my power topped out and I had no more potential to show my tyrannical father.

"He sent me out here as punishment. Over the years though, I've come to enjoy the laid-back island lifestyle. It truly is a paradise," he sighed. "Take a seat."

I complied and sat next to Panda in front of his large desk.

"I heard you fought a slime queen on your most recent quest."

"Word sure travels fast around here," I replied.

"I'd like to offer my apologies. Had we known, we never would have posted that quest on the temp board. Of course, the issue with adventuring is that quests are submitted by non-adventurers.

"They often can't tell the difference between different types of monsters. They rarely get the numbers right and they have no idea which ones are powerful and which are insignificant.

"We do our best to grade each request correctly, but we don't always get it right. Information is often lacking when quests are submitted. That is a lesson you'd do well to take heed of," he said, refilling his glass with amber liquid from a finely cut decanter.

I understood what he was trying to say but I honestly didn't see what all the fuss was about. The slime queen wasn't easy to defeat, sure, but the rest of the quest was about as safe as I could imagine.

The slimes didn't even fight back. It was a slaughter.

"Anyway, you did a fine job defeating the queen and lasting down in the sewer for such a long time. I guess you must have a poison resistance skill," he continued.

"That's right, how did you know?" I asked slowly.

"Because the sewer's fumes are poisonous. Something else that wasn't included in the quest proposal."

"Oh great, and no one thought to tell me that before I went down there?" I snapped.

"So it seems," Lucas continued calmly. "Adventuring is a dangerous game as I'm sure you know."

He didn't even apologise that time. I'm sure he thought it a moot point due to my *Minor Poison Resistance* skill, but not everyone had that. Hell, he didn't even know I had it before I came back.

I got the distinct impression that these corporate assholes would have happily let me die down there from a stupid oversight. I'd be lying if I said it didn't piss me off.

"Anyway, that's not what I called you up here to discuss," Lucas continued, brushing past my anger at the fucked-up situation. "I wanted to talk to you about your final trial quest."

"An interesting one has come across my desk recently and I'd like you to take it."

"And what kind of oversights should I expect on this one," I asked bitterly, folding my arms, and sitting back in my seat.

"Adventurers should always expect the unexpected so naturally you should proceed with caution on every quest. However, this one should be straight forward," he replied calmly.

"We've received word that a fortress wall has appeared on one of the smaller islands just off the coast of Havar. We believe that it belongs to a small sect of cultists. We usually leave them alone as long as they tend to keep to themselves, but this group is a little too close to the city to just leave them be.

"The quest is to go there and investigate. Use of lethal force is permitted. Though, of course, if you deem it unnecessary then that is also acceptable as long as you gather enough information to justify your choice.

"It is also acceptable to return and advise we send a full adventuring team if you deem them to be too numerous or strong for a single adventurer to handle.

"The choice is yours."

"Is this a test?" I replied bitterly.

"Everything in life is a test young Kaleb," he smiled secretively.

It seemed simple enough. Having multiple ways to complete the quest would be a first. Hell, I could just go have a nosey and then come back and I'd qualify to take the exam.

Overall, it seemed like a pretty good deal. Still, something about it didn't sit well with me. The director had just shown me his callousness in how he spoke about the *oversights* on my last quest.

"Fine," I said after a few moments of silence.

"Perfect. I'll have Lucy assign it to you on your way out."

That was obviously my cue to leave but I needed to ask something first that had been tickling the back of my mind.

"Is it normal for the director to meet with temp adventurers?" I asked as I stood up from my seat.

"Define normal Mr Akabane. Your entire existence is extremely abnormal. There are over four billion people of various races that inhabit Celestia. Do you know how many outworlders we have?"

"I'm guessing not many," I replied.

"Less than three thousand that we know of, though I'm sure there are more. Outworlders are known of only by the powerful and those in the know. Most citizens think of you as a fairy tale. That is how rare you are.

"So, whilst I don't make it a habit of meeting with low ranked adventurers often, you are an exception. So, naturally, if you ever need anything please don't hesitate to come see me." His tone moved from dark to friendly in a single sentence.

I couldn't sense mana, but my intuition told me there was more than meets the eye with this one. I learnt something valuable though: the Adventure Society only knew about 3000 of the 10,000 outworlders in Celestia.

The system had transported 10,000 of us here, but Lucas didn't seem to know that.

*I'd better keep that to myself for now.* I thought.

# Chapter 57
# Intermission: Jack the Reaper

Jack laid on top of a flat roofed building located on the top of an unassuming hill. The rain poured down, but he barely noticed. It didn't even obscure his vision thanks to his unique skillset.

He looked through the scope of his sniper rifle: a weapon that was seemingly alien in this medieval facsimile of Earth that called itself Celestia.

He had been in the middle of a job when it happened. Back on earth he'd lived a relatively interesting life. He'd joined his country's armed forces at a young age and was selected for sniper training.

He'd later qualified for the special forces and partaken in wet work all over the world. He'd been taught how to survive in the harshest of climates. How to fight with guns, how to create explosives, how to kill effectively.

He'd partaken in work so extreme and politically sensitive that he'd have been disavowed by his country if he was caught.

He was on one such mission when he'd suddenly found himself transported to this strange new world. The system called it Celestia and it had warned Jack that he was being hunted. That was nothing new, he'd been hunted in multiple countries across four continents. It had never worked out well for the hunters.

He found himself on the outskirts of a large city on an island found roughly where the United Kingdom would be back on Earth.

Interestingly this city was called Britania. It was too close to the reality he knew to be a mere coincidence. The city itself resembled Victorian England with its old-fashioned architecture, aristocratic factions and a King sat on the throne of a grand palace.

The only place in the city that seemed out of place was the Adventure Society building. In contrast, it was a large skyscraper which mildly resembled the shape of a gherkin.

It was made almost entirely out of glass and was way too modern to fit into the nineteenth century look of the rest of the place.

Naturally he'd avoided it.

Even the name of the place pissed him off. *Adventure Society,* it sounded like a group of kids playing fantasy and cosplaying as heroes. *No thanks.* He was a professional killer. He didn't have time for kid's games.

Luckily for Jack, he had a certain skill set which proved to work even in this strange world. He had been trained by the best in the world and stood among the elite warriors of Earth.

He'd entered the city of Britania under the cover of darkness less than a few hours after arriving in this new world. He hadn't even seen one of these so-called monsters.

In his experience, humanity was the most frightening monster of all anyway. A strong beast might kill you, but it wouldn't torture you, abuse you and slaughter your family just to send a message.

No, humanity was far more fearsome than any semi-intelligent beast could ever hope to be. He'd learnt that lesson over and over throughout his career. Most recently, destabilising drug cartels on the South American continent.

That propensity for sadistic violence was what made his job so interesting. He was under no illusions of grandeur. His job was a dirty one, he wasn't a good guy. But if you want to protect people from the bad guys, you need an even worse guy to take them out. That was Jack.

He snuck into the city and quickly found a target. A nobleman, walking home drunk in the closed off part of town.

He probably thought his gated community provided him protection, but he'd soon learn that there wasn't a security system good enough to keep Jack out.

He'd grabbed the man by the throat, dragged him down a shadowed back alley and squeezed the life from him. It was nothing he hadn't done before.

Things were the same as they always were. It was a universal truth that no matter the world you're in, death is death.

Right now he was trapped behind enemy lines and survival was his only priority.

After killing the noble he stole his clothes and quickly deposited his military uniform, along with the corpse, in a dumpster. He then set it on fire using the matches he'd looted from the man.

That was sure to cause quite the stir among the citizens, but there was no way they'd be able to identify the body with their meagre technology.

After that he had blended into local society. He'd rented a small loft space in the centre of town and soon started getting quests from the system.

They were simple and they all fell under the same umbrella term: assassination.

From what he could tell, the system was omnipotent and it seemed to reward action with power.

He'd raised his level quickly and soon his activities had gleaned him the monicker *The Reaper*. Within a few short weeks he'd become infamous all across Britania. The unidentifiable reaper. A serial killer of ill repute, stalking the streets of Britania.

Wanted posters had appeared everywhere, of course they didn't show his likeness. How could they? He'd left no witnesses to his endeavours.

Early on he'd been offered the choice of three weapons. He'd chosen a magical one. A wand that allowed him to channel his high mana into casting spells.

He didn't have any offensive spells at the time, but he soon found another use for the wand.

After a few successful quests he'd gained a plethora of precious metals, magic stones, and items that most people would consider to be junk.

What's the saying; one man's trash is another man's treasure?

After a lot of experimentation he'd managed to create a weapon much more familiar to him, a sniper rifle. He'd even created a rudimentary silencer from a tin can.

It wasn't the most elegant looking weapon, but it did the trick.

Which brings us back to the roof overlooking the palace.

Jack laid in the rain, looking down the sights of his crafted weapon. He'd gained a few skills which increased his vision's capabilities far beyond what a normal human could do.

He gazed down the scope, looking straight into the ball room. Tonight was the night of the royal ball and he had a new quest to complete.

**You have received a new quest:**
*Regicide*

**The annual Britannian ball is about to take place. The stuffy upper crust of the city state of Britania will all be in attendance.**

Your mission, should you choose to accept it, is to assassinate King Edmund VII and end his wretched line for good.

The fool is the product of incest and as such has the libido of a rabbit but the sperm count of a Chernobyl survivor.

Killing him at the ball will surely sow chaos.

Objective:
*Kill the king during the ball 0/1*

Reward: *The satisfaction of destabilising a corrupt country. Also, a permanent 10% increase to the intelligence stat.*

*WARNING*
*This is a timed quest. Failure to complete it before the ball ends will result in a punishment.*

Jack didn't take kindly to being threatened. This punishment threat was the first of its kind he'd seen in this world.

Most quests didn't come with strings attached. Still, he relished a challenge and the 10% increase to his intelligence was a good reward.

Intelligence seemed to govern the amount of mana he had and that was his most important stat. Especially since he'd created his sniper rifle.

Besides, it wasn't going to be a difficult quest. He had the perfect vantage point, the perfect weapon and a perfect view through the poorly designed windows which looked straight into the ballroom.

He'd laid atop the roof for hours. His whole body was numb from the cold, rainy weather. It didn't bother him much though. He'd endured far worse back on Earth.

He'd watched the snooty nobles lounge around laughing pompously, drinking their expensive drinks, and wearing their expensive clothes. All whilst their citizens slaved away to make them money whilst starving and living in squalor.

It was a truly detestable country. Not that he cared much about the suffering of others, or about politics. Still, he would have no remorse for the victim he was about to kill.

It was almost time. As if right on schedule, the king made his grand entrance.

*Only four hours late to his own party. What a prick.* Jack thought critically as he moved his scope over the chest of his target.

The man was the personification of inbreeding. His jaw jutted out oddly, his forehead was too big and he wore a long fur cloak, dyed red, which trailed behind him.

The impracticality alone was enough to send Jack into one of his famous rages. Though he was a professional and wouldn't allow his own emotions to impact his ability to complete a task.

He took a deep breath, steadied his heartbeat, breathed out slightly. He'd already taken the wind and bullet drop into account so he aimed slightly to the left and above his target.

He called it bullet drop, but that wasn't really an accurate description. His rifle shot pure magic power.

He used a skill to infuse his mana into the rifle and when the target finally stood still to address the crowd, he fired.

The magic shot zoomed out of the rifle, almost silently, then it broke the sound barrier with a crack that echoed across the quiet noble district.

It shattered the window and in less than a second he saw red mist in his scope as the king dropped to the ground, a gaping hole through his chest.

*I can hear the screams from here.* He chuckled to himself as he pulled the sniper back into his inventory. It was time to go.

Just as he was about to jump off the roof though, he found himself in a dark hall. Had he seriously been teleported again?

He looked around, summoning his weapon once more. It wasn't designed for close quarters but a gun was still a gun.

The hall had roman columns on either side and there seemed to be the shadow of a throne or maybe it was an altar.

"Put that away, I have no interest in harming you." A powerful voice boomed through the hall.

Jack squeezed the trigger but before he could fire off a shot the rifle disappeared.

"Fast reactions. I like it." The voice chuckled.

Suddenly the room lit up as braziers burst into flame on each column and Jack could finally see who was talking.

Or more, what was talking.

Sitting on a throne of bones was a hooded shadowy figure. It had no face, but its outline seemed humanoid. Looking into the space between its hood, Jack saw only the void.

He trembled with fear, but also with a strange excitement. It had been years since he'd felt emotion this powerful. It was a truly foreign feeling at this point.

"Who are you?" He demanded, curbing his emotions as he'd been taught to do.

"I am the god Diako and I want you to join my organisation," the shadow said in a terribly powerful and deep voice.

"And why exactly should I do that?" Jack responded brazenly.

"Because I can set you on a path to power beyond your wildest dreams. If you don't believe me, then perhaps let me show you what I mean."

A notification popped up on Jack's interface.

**Diako, The God of Shadows has offered you the following class:**
*The Reaper (unique)*

**Having made a name for yourself in the city state of Britania through murder most foul, the unique class** *The Reaper* **is open to you, and you alone.**

*Selecting The Reaper class unlocks the following skills:*
*Faceless man*
*Silent shooting*
*Basic weapon maintenance*

*Selecting The Reaper class will award the following stat points per level:*
*+10 perception / +10 intelligence*

Jack read through the class offered to him with bated breath. It seemed so powerful. He didn't know the specifics of the skills, but a unique class offered only to him. One that offered 20 stat points per level on top of the five free points he automatically knew he'd gain.

"What is this?" he whispered.

"This, my child, is just the beginning."

# Chapter 58
# Pandas Are Not Aquatic Mammals

"If there are luxury yachts in this world then why does Sally fly around in a pirate ship?" I asked Panda as we sailed out from Havar harbour.

He shrugged as he took another drag from his bamboo pipe. We leaned on the modern, metal railings gazing out at the beautiful turquoise ocean.

Director Lucas had chartered a yacht for us to use in our scouting mission and it was awesome. It was a sleek, white vessel with its own bar and crew.

I felt like a celebrity or an *Instagram* influencer or something. The comfort was a far cry from Sally's flying ship.

Though to the best of my knowledge this yacht couldn't fly.

It had barely been a day since my chat with Lucas. After leaving his office I'd accepted the new quest and received my upgraded reward.

Lucy had given me a little bag with 1500 gold coins in it. The reward had been tripled due to the slime queen's presence.

Not that I was complaining.

After another night at the inn we'd packed up Panda's books, gotten him some more and picked up my bow from Wendy's. It was as good as new and I felt like I had a limb reattached upon receiving it.

It was odd how fond of the weapon I'd become. It was a bit like a safety blanket at this point, we had been through a lot together.

I'd picked up some more rations and potions whilst I was in the neighbourhood. A good adventurer is always prepared after all.

As we sailed out to sea on the fancy yacht, it was hard to imagine all the blood and death that had surrounded me over the past month and a half.

Havar was just so idyllic. I mean, the sea was turquoise for god's sake. It was beautiful.

It also dawned on me that I'd been in this world for well over a month now. I wondered how my wife Layla was doing as my heart ached at the thought.

Our child had probably been born by now. It was due a few weeks ago, assuming time moved at the same pace here as it did back home.

I'd missed it. One of the biggest moments in a person's life and I'd been busy fighting slimes in a sewer instead.

I didn't even know what gender it was. We'd decided to wait and let it be a surprise. Layla could be old fashioned like that.

I smiled sadly to myself as I thought of her. I wondered if she knew I'd been taken somewhere against my will. Mostly, I just hoped that she didn't think I'd run away.

"Downtime sucks," I moaned, "when are we gonna get to this island?"

"We'll get there when we get there, chill out kid," Panda said from behind me.

I realised that he wasn't standing next to me anymore. How long had I been lost in thought? I turned towards the sound of his voice.

He was laying on a sun lounger with his pipe in one hand and a drink topped with one of those little umbrellas in the other.

*Where did he get sunglasses from?*

"You don't waste any time," I chuckled, strolling towards him, and pulling up a deck chair.

I must have looked out of place in my full body armour set. I'd need to invest in some more casual clothes for my days off once we got back. Maybe I could get Taylor to make me a Hawaiian shirt.

"Well, you were staring off into space for like thirty minutes. What's a panda to do but have a drink and a smoke and enjoy the life of luxury?"

"Just don't get used to it. I'm still pretty sure Lucas is just buttering me up for something," I said darkly.

I kind of liked the man and he had saved my life during the goblin king coronation quest. Still though, something about him didn't sit right with me. Especially after our meeting the previous day.

I sat forward in my chair, pulling up the quest I'd been given for the third time today.

### New Quest:
### *I've Been Expecting You, Mr Akabane*

**A mysterious new structure has appeared on an uninhabited island just off the coast of Havar. I'm getting some serious evil villain's lair vibes from this one.**
**If there's a mountain shaped like a skull, you know what to do.**

### Objectives:
*Kill all the inhabitants on the island 0/1*
*Or*
*Spare them and report your reasoning 0/1*

*Or*
*Investigate the island and report back 0/1*

**Reward: 500 gold coins and admittance to the next Adventurer exam.**

***Speak to the Adventure Society to claim your reward. Reward payable upon the successful completion of the above objectives***

It was the first time I'd seen a quest that had multiple choice objectives. The easiest one would surely be to poke around a little and head back.

Though I had a feeling it wouldn't be that simple. I had no problem with killing the cultists, if that's what they actually were, and farming the experience. Of course, that was dependant on their levels and how many of them there were.

The objective that seemed the most peculiar to me though, was the option to spare them. Lucas had specifically told me that they were cultists.

However, the quest itself made no mention of them. It was definitely weird.

Either way, I had a feeling that this quest wasn't going to be as simple as the director had made it out to be. I felt like he was testing me. But what was he testing me on? It could be my judgement skills.

Lucy had mentioned the star ratings and the increasing complexity of quests as one progressed through them. I guess they already knew how I fought from the first quest. I showed them I could work independently from the second.

This third quest could be a judgemental test. Thinking about it so much was beginning to make my brain hurt.

"Hey, can I get one of those please?" I asked the bartender whilst pointing at Panda's drink.

"That's more like it kid!" Panda said, raising his glass. "And get me another whilst you're at it my good man."

The bartender was a quiet man. He was dressed in a clean, white uniform that looked very official.

His name tag said *Mark* and he was a male catonid. His fur was also white and I'd wondered if that was part of the reason he'd got the job - so he matched the uniform.

There was also a chef and the guy sailing the yacht on board. We hadn't met either of them yet and I wasn't even sure if we'd have time for food before we reached the island.

"How much do you think Lucas spent chartering this ship for us?" I asked Panda whilst Mark began shaking drinks and throwing bottles around like the silent showman he was.

"Dunno, it's a luxury though so it probably wasn't cheap. My advice: don't look a gift yacht in the mouth kid. You can take that as my sagely wisdom for the day." He chuckled as he put his empty glass down and moved his paw behind his head.

He seemed to have no trouble playing the spoilt rich kid. I felt a tad uneasy though. I hadn't been on many holidays before. Luxury was practically an unknown quantity to my family.

We'd always been workers, drinkers and occasionally caravaners. I remembered driving up to the coast with my mum as a kid.

We'd rented a caravan for the weekend and I thought it was cool. It was nothing compared to this though.

Mark brought the drinks over and I thanked him. They were a rainbow of colours. Mine had a blue layer, a purple layer and was topped off with a red layer.

It tasted amazing. I couldn't even begin to describe the flavours considering they were mostly new to me. But it was delightful.

A few hours passed as we lounged around on the boat before the island finally came into view.

It looked small and was covered with tall trees. There was a beach at the front that looked deserted. Not far back from the treeline was a large wall that seemed to extend around the entire island.

It was made of stone and had battlements dotted every few hundred meters or so.

It reminded me of one of those old Spanish sea forts you'd see in historic TV programmes. It looked disused, but maybe that was because of how old it looked.

"Hey Mark, have you ever sailed out here before?" I asked the bartender who offered a single nod in reply. "Has that fort always been there?" He shook his head.

That was odd. Why would someone erect an old looking fort on a small island.

I guess it was my job to find out exactly that. I watched the fort as we edged closer to the island. I couldn't see any sign of movement at all.

It looked abandoned, which was a tad unsettling in my opinion.

"Hey kid, I was thinking. You can just leave me here whilst you do your thing. I'm not really cut out for spooky fort exploration if you catch my drift," Panda said, sitting up slightly in his chair and eying the island suspiciously.

"Oh no, not this time. I left you behind when I went into the sewer but this is different," I replied. "Two pairs of eyes are better than one and who knows what we'll find out there."

He opened his mouth as if to protest but thought better of it as he sighed and grumbled slightly. I knew he was no good in a fight but I might need him for something non-combat related.

Besides, why should he get to stay on the boat whilst I did all the work?

The yacht began slowing down and pulled up close to the island.

"Is it safe to leave the ship here?" I asked Mark. "Isn't it a little obvious?" He shrugged.

"Thanks for your help Mark, it's always a pleasure chatting with you," I said as I rose from my deck chair and moved to the railings.

"Mr Akabane?" A new voice shouted from the top deck. I looked up to see a human in a similar uniform to the bar tender, except he was wearing a white captain's hat with golden inlays and a black peak.

"I assume you're our mysterious captain?" I asked.

"That's right. Captain Ronnald at your service. I just wanted to inform you that I've engaged the cloaking device so you don't need to worry about us being detected.

"Just try to remember where we're moored when you're heading back."

*A cloaking device, of course. Why didn't I think of that.*

"Thanks for the heads up. I guess we'll be off then."

"Good luck," he replied cheerily before disappearing.

"How would a cloaking device even work," I muttered to myself.

"It'll be a magic circle that's been permanently etched into the deck somewhere," Panda replied absently.

"Makes sense I guess, about as much as anything does in Celestia. This is why I wanted to bring you along." I smiled evilly at him.

"Yeah...so how are we getting to the island? I don't see any dinghies," he asked anxiously, shooting me a fearful look.

"Oh, I have an idea," I replied, continuing to flash him my evil smile as I moved towards him.

"What are you doing kid, you're being weird."

I bent down quickly and scooped him up as he wriggled to get free.

"Kaleb don't you dare! Pandas are not aquatic mammals!"

451

I jumped over the edge of the yacht as Panda screamed in a high-pitched voice.

# Chapter 59
# Athenile 347-35

With Panda clinging to my neck for dear life, I swam to shore. We weren't very far away and with my increased strength stat it turned out that I could swim damned fast.

We reached the shore in only a minute or two and I walked out of the water and resummoned my armour. Naturally I'd unequipped it as I dived off the boat.

Panda fell from my back as we reached dry land and started hacking up water. His fur was a mess, all puffed out and standing erect in flurry tufts.

It was quite the sight.

"I...hate...you," he said between spluttering.

I chuckled and surveyed our landing zone. We were on a golden, sandy beach. The kind that lacked seaweed or pebbles or...well anything other than sand.

I was sure that back on Earth people had to clean beaches to get them to look this nice. I wondered if it was just a natural phenomenon of this world.

Barely a few dozen feet away, the beach gave way to clusters of tall trees. The trees themselves were fairly barren.

They didn't seem to have any leaves or branches apart from right at the top. I hadn't seen trees like this before back home.

They looked a little out of place compared to the rest of the scenery.

Behind them was the fortress wall. A stone behemoth that completely blocked my view and stretched as far as I could see.

"I need a better view," I murmured to myself thoughtfully. Panda was still puking up sea water on all fours.

I wondered if I could climb one of the trees somehow. They seemed to be taller than the wall. I'd climbed some of the smaller trees that grew near our house when I was a kid.

With my new super strength I was certain I could climb these ones too.

I walked towards the closest tree and tried to wrap my arms and legs around it. The idea being to shimmy up it. However, the trees had a rather large circumference and they felt kinda slippery.

That's when I had a lightbulb moment. I equipped my two new daggers, reached up, and stabbed the first one to the bark.

It held and when I put my weight onto it, it barely budged. That should do the trick. I got the idea from an artic survival show I'd watched once where they used pickaxes to climb ice cliffs.

Using a similar method I began climbing the tree. The ascent was effortless and I soon found myself near the top.

At the top of the tree there were still only a few branches, but they were quite thick. I swung my leg up and over one and hoisted myself onto it. I was sure my agility stat had come in handy for that manoeuvre.

I shimmied along the edge a bit until I cleared the foliage that was blocking my vision. From there I got a relatively unobstructed view beyond the wall.

From my vantage point I could see most of the island. The large stone wall seemed to be built in a circle the entire way around.

The area near the wall itself was barren, but there seemed to be some kind of village in the middle.

I used the *Sniper* skill that came with my bow to zoom in. It was powerful, essentially giving my eyes the ability of high-powered binoculars.

I saw a slew of small buildings surrounding a large stone castle.

The buildings were made of wood and some of them had smoke coming out of their stone chimneys. There was definitely something living there.

It was a little harder to tell with the castle. The strangest thing about it was the perpetual black cloud that sat above it. The rest of the sky was cloudless with a lovely summer heat beating down.

However, a dark black cloud hung over the small castle structure.

It was like something from a fairy tale.

I watched for a little while but couldn't see any people or creatures. There were definite signs of life though. I'd have to get closer to find out more.

I climbed back down the tree using the same method I'd used to climb up. Panda was sat near the bottom, wringing out clumps of wet fur and grumbling to himself.

"We're making a boat for the return trip," he muttered as I approached him. "Well, what did you find out?"

"The wall covers the island like we thought and there's a small village in the middle. It's got a weird castle with a cloud over it in the centre."

"That's strange. Sounds like a curse or magic of some kind. Did you see any cultists?" He asked.

"No. I didn't see anyone actually, but there were signs of life," I replied.

"I take it this means we have to go there then?" He sighed, pulling out his bamboo pipe and taking a few drags in quick succession.

"I guess so," I said in a much chirpier tone.

I was quite enjoying this quest so far. Now we'd arrived I felt like a real adventurer. You know, the kind that actually goes on adventures and explores the unknown instead of just exterminating monsters all the time.

I was like *Indian Jones* and Panda was my *Short Round*.

I scooped Panda up and had him hold onto my back whilst I used my daggers to scale the stone wall. It was a lot more effort to force my dagger through the stone than it was with the wood.

Though thanks to my strength stat I still managed it. It didn't take long to climb up and over it.

We stood in a barren wasteland of ploughed mud. It could have been farmland, but I honestly wasn't too sure what could grow here. Potatoes maybe? Does Celestia even have potatoes?

The village was a straight walk from the wall and it didn't look too far away. It wasn't very large but had enough buildings to warrant a population of a few hundred people.

Which made it even stranger that I couldn't see anyone, even now. I walked with my *Sniper* skill active, just in case.

I was hoping to gain some kind of idea of who lived there before we arrived. But alas, after about forty minutes of walking, we reached the village without spotting a single person.

"Are you sure this place isn't abandoned?" Panda said as we passed by the first building.

It didn't look abandoned to me. None of the wooden buildings were in disrepair and there was smoke coming from a few of them.

It was almost like everyone had just disappeared, and not so long ago.

"It looks lived in," I replied thoughtfully. "Maybe we should look inside a house?"

I knew it was rude to just let yourself into someone's home, but I needed to gather information for part of the quest.

I turned towards the closest house. It was a small single-story hovel really. It had a smoking stone chimney, but the rest of the house was made from wooden logs.

It had a rustic, log cabin-in-the-woods vibe. I actually kind of liked it.

I knocked on the thick oval door. We waited about a minute but no one answered so I pushed and the door swung open.

"Leaving your door unlocked is a bit of a safety concern," Panda pointed out as we entered.

The house consisted of a single room. It had a few tattered beds on the back wall, an old looking carpet, and a blackened pot simmering on the fireplace.

*That would explain the smoke.* I thought as I moved towards the cooking pot.

There was something bubbling in it. It smelled good too.

"This is weird," I said as Panda dipped his paw in and licked it.

"Doesn't taste weird. It's actually pretty good."

"Not the food. I mean this situation. Who leaves food cooking unattended like that? And why would they leave the house without locking the door?"

"I don't know, maybe it's a safe community and the pot is on a slow cook?" He replied, dipping his paw back in for some more stew.

"It just doesn't sit right with me. Let's explore the village some more...and stop eating their food," I said, slapping his paw away before he could have a third taste.

We left the small house and continued walking towards the centre of the village. The roads, if you could even call them that, were well travelled.

There were fresh-looking footprints on the ground too. Now I was no tracker, but even I could tell that something was seriously wrong with this scene.

It was so eerily quiet as we walked through the village streets. It was like we'd entered a ghost town. I half expected a tumbleweed to come gliding across the intersection ahead of us.

After a short while of walking we came across a large wooden structure. It was also a single story, but it was three times the size of the other houses.

*A town hall maybe?* I thought as we approached.

This building didn't seem to have a chimney, but there were plenty of footprints in the muddy street outside its door.

I pushed it open and we walked inside.

The interior was once again a single room, but this one was much larger. It had long rows of benches laid out with a podium at the far end.

It was like a primitive church or a meeting place of some kind. It was deserted just like the rest of town. However, there was a thick, leatherbound book left open on the podium itself.

I walked towards it and realised that I could read the language. My *Speak English Damnit!* Skill was so useful. I mentally thanked the system as I skimmed through the page it was open to.

*Meeting Notes:*
*Athenile 347-35*

*Agenda:*
*Discuss the castle that appeared in town.*
*Plan the harvest market.*
*Open discussion to the floor.*

It was a simple agenda for a village meeting. Though it confirmed one thing. The castle wasn't normally part of the village.

It seemed that it had just appeared for some reason. I wondered why. Perhaps that had something to do with the missing villagers.

Also, there was something else.

"Panda, what does Athenile 347-35 mean?" I asked, struggling to pronounce the foreign word.

It had been translated into a familiar alphabet, but I had no idea what the word meant. Therefore, it must have been something specific to this world. Something that couldn't be translated into English.

"It's a date. Yesterday's date to be exact. It seems that this village follows the Athena calendar," he mused, waddling towards me, and taking a look at the book for himself.

"The Athena calendar?" I asked.

"Yeah, she's one of the major gods in Celestia. She's quite popular. Major gods like her sometimes have their own calendars. It can get a little complicated honestly.

"Though the only real difference is the name that appears before the number. The numbers always coincide," he answered absently as he flicked through the book.

"I think Chrysus mentioned her before you know," I said, racking my brain to try and remember. I knew she was a Greek god back in my world but I doubted there was any correlation.

Though if there was. Did that mean some ancient Greek's had been isekaied here once before and managed to get home?

It stood to reason that they'd bring their religion back with them if they'd been in Celestia a while. If that was the case maybe I *could* bring Layla here one day.

Of course, that was all just postulation. If I really wanted to know I'd have to try and talk to this Athena myself.

CRASH.

My head snapped towards the door as I heard a loud crashing sound outside. It seemed someone was here after all.

# Chapter 60
# Your Name Is Literally Your Species

I heard a loud crash from outside the building and my neck snapped towards the door.

*Someone's here.* I thought, summoning my bow, and walking steadily towards the door.

Panda followed at my heels as I nocked an arrow and stepped deliberately into the doorway. I checked up and down the street but there was nothing there.

The village looked just as deserted as it had before.

"Look kid, there's a broken barrel over there," Panda said pointing towards the remains of a wooden water barrel.

It was barely a few feet away from our position. Whoever broke it must have been watching us. If I wanted to find out who they were I'd have to take a chance.

"Show yourself. We won't hurt you," I announced loudly, stepping out into the street and unequipping my bow.

I moved my hands out to the side, showing my palms in the least threatening pose I could think of. This also served a second purpose.

If someone attacked I could easily summon both daggers and enter melee with little effort on my part. Of course, archery was what I was best at, but I didn't feel comfortable enough to leave myself entirely defenceless.

I waited a few moments as Panda clung to the door frame, watching from relative safety.

I heard a few light footsteps and turned towards an alleyway between two houses opposite the meeting hall we'd just been in.

What looked like a child, took a nervous step out of the shadows towards me.

She looked terrified, moreover, she was a creature I'd never seen before.

She was small in stature, wearing a brown garment that almost looked like a kimono. Her hair was wild and forest green, it seemed to defy gravity as it floated ominously around her. Her skin was the colour, and seemingly the texture, of bark.

I focused on her and a notification popped up.

**You have discovered a new race:**
***Dryad***

**The *Dryad* are a peaceful, minority race. They are often found in remote forest locations, which makes sense since they're basically just evolved trees.
You know those huge oak trees you'd see back on Earth that are hundreds of years old? Well, once a tree reaches its thousandth year it often transforms into a *Dryad*.
When caring for your *Dryad* please remember to water it and give it lots of sunlight.
Also, these guys are technically vegan since they mostly feed through photosynthesis. However, unlike the vegans of your world, they won't mention it at every opportunity.
If you hear them say *I am Groot*, run.**

A Dryad. I think I've heard of them before in fantasy books. It's not a race I'm super familiar with though they sound pretty harmless. I thought, pushing my hood back and revealing my face.

I barely even registered the Marvel reference. I must have been growing used to the system's quirky personality.

I must have looked like a monk with the slight stubble I had growing on my head. Either that or a neo-Nazi, God I hoped the people of this world didn't have them. It's definitely not the vibe I was going for.

"Hi, my name is Kaleb and I'm an adventurer," I said softly, crouching down in an attempt to seem less intimidating.

"You look like you're trying to get a cat to come to you," Panda snickered, finally coming out from his hiding place behind the door. "Try making a puss-puss sound."

"Will you knock it off," I said irritably.

"You're the one acting like she's some lost pet. She's a dryad, they're pretty fucking intelligent."

"Watch your language!" I admonished. "She's only a child.

"Yeah, because a few naughty words are so bad when she lives in a world with killer monsters. Grow up Kaleb."

I heard a jingling sound that kind of reminded me of laughter and we stopped bickering to turn back to the dryad child.

She smiled and opened her mouth as if she was giggling, but the sound was more like little bells jingling in the wind.

She began walking towards us, still with an air of timidity, but much less frightened than before.

"You're funny mister," she said in a voice that somehow also sounded like bells jingling in the wind.

"Sorry about that, my friend here really knows how to pick his moments," I sighed, returning her smile. "His name is Panda."

"I am Treena," she replied to Panda's immediate and raucous laughter.

"She's a dryad and she's got the word tree in her name. I can't breathe," he said through gasps of air as he clutched his stomach.

"Your name is literally your species. Do you really have any room to talk?" I replied, shooting him a stern glance.

Treena laughed again with the sound of tiny, tinkling bells.

"Shall we talk inside?" I asked her softly.

She nodded and made an "mm" sound, then she walked past me towards the meeting hall and Panda and I followed.

Inside the hall I took a seat on a bench opposite her. She sat with childish abandon, leaning back on her hands, and kicking her little legs as she looked at me through big round eyes.

"Treena, can you tell us a little bit about this place? We were sent here because the big stone walls suddenly appeared. We were asked to investigate."

I purposely neglected to tell her that the Adventure Society thought it was a cultist stronghold and we were supposed to kill everyone we found.

"The wall came with the cloud castle which took my mummy and daddy," she replied.

"How did the castle take them?" I asked softly.

"The elder went into the castle and then there was this big light and everyone disappeared."

So, a strange castle and old fort walls appeared suddenly and as soon as someone went to have a look inside a light spread out and they all disappeared.

Yup, sounds like something magical alright. Not sure a guy with no mana is the best guy for the job. I thought, sighing internally.

"Do you know anything else about the castle?"

She looked at me quizzically for a moment and touched her index finger to her lips.

"Um… I know how to open the door. I could take you if you want."

I wasn't sure that taking a child into a potentially dangerous magic castle that made people disappear was a responsible idea, but I didn't have much else to go on.

"Ok, but you have to do everything I say once we're there and if anything attacks us I want you to run straight back here and lock the door ok?"

It was the best compromise I could think of. I needed to get inside the castle but I didn't want her to get hurt.

"Ok," she said chirpily, hopping down from the bench and walking towards the door.

I got up and followed her, taking care to avoid stepping on the muddy footprints Panda and I had left.

She led us a few streets over and as we rounded a building it appeared.

A small stone castle, sitting in the middle of the village centre. It looked more like a single battlement tower than a castle per se. Its architecture definitely clashed with the rustic wooden hovels that made up the rest of the dryad village.

It was surrounded by a waterless moat. So basically a pit that surrounded the stone tower castle. There was a single rope bridge leading to it.

I looked up at the angry black cloud that hovered above the castle. I wondered what that was all about. I bet it had something to do with magic.

"Kaleb, this castle has a strange magic aura. It's hard to explain but my mana senses are telling me that it's not here," Panda said, tugging on my leg to get my attention.

Treena seemed much more at ease since our initial meeting. She ran across the rope bridge, flapping her arms without a care in the world.

"Please be careful" I shouted after her as we followed at a more considered and cautious pace.

The bridge creaked as we crossed it, it certainly felt real to me.

As we reached the other side, I breathed out a sigh of relief. I'd looked over the side of the rope bridge as we crossed and the moat chasm seemed to drop into the very depths of hell itself.

I couldn't even see the bottom. A fall like that would have been the end of me.

On the other side of the bridge we caught up to Treena who bounced up and down on the balls of her feet as she waited.

Behind her was a large wooden door with metal bolts around the frame, and no handle.

"So, how do we open it Treena?" I asked nicely.

"You have to give it the password, but it's spoken in ancient orcish so you won't be able to do it. I know the words though," she practically sang towards the end of the sentence.

"Orcish? Ok, can you open it for us then."

She nodded and opened her mouth. A horrid noise that sounded like a series of harsh pig squeals came out. It was a far cry from the sound of tiny bells.

I certainly didn't expect to see a dryad perform black metal today. I thought as she screamed.

I had to cover my ears, it literally hurt to listen to the noise. It was so loud.

As she finished the door creaked for a moment before falling inwards with a loud, echoed crash. It fell like a drawbridge, definitely not how doors were usually designed to open.

The inside was pitch black. Luckily, I had just the item to light the way. I summoned the Eternal Torch of Communist Supremacy out of my inventory and held it out in front of us.

The torch cut through the darkness like a blade, casting eerie shadows up and down the stone walls. The castle itself looked more like a museum though, as I stepped inside.

It was a circular room with a winding, stone spiral staircase skirting the wall. Around the base of the wall was a bunch of glass cases.

I moved towards the first one and brushed the dust away as it swirled in a cyclone, catching in a ray of light. Inside there was a collection of Spanish looking armour.

Namely, one of those helmets they wore in the 1600's that curved funnily. It seemed out of place in Celestia.

"What is all this stuff?" I muttered to myself as I moved from case to case finding more armour and some rusted old swords and a polearm.

"It's from the war," Treena answered darkly.

"What war?" I asked, turning towards her. Her childish attitude seemed to have vanished as she stared up at me with a thousand-yard stare. I got a sinking feeling at the sudden change in her demeanour.

"The war with the Orcs," she replied solemnly. "It was a long time ago. That book can tell you more." She pointed towards a podium in the middle of the room.

I looked towards it and saw a large black book, similar to the one in the village hall.

Unlike the weapons and armour, it looked brand new. There wasn't a speck of dust on it.

"Kaleb, maybe take a minute before you open that. Its mana is off the charts," Panda said shakily from beside me.

I barely heard him as I looked towards it, mesmerized. It felt like it was calling to me. I walked towards it slowly, unable to control my body as my mind felt fuzzy.

"Forgive me brave adventurer. I'll be praying for your success," Treena said gravely from somewhere behind me.

I barely registered her words. My mind was focused on the book. I'd never wanted anything else as much as I wanted to read that book.

My mind and body were overcome with an overwhelming desire as I closed in on it, dropping the torch to the ground.

I placed both hands on the book and heard it whisper to me. The words weren't words as such, but I could tell. It wanted me to open it and I wanted nothing more than to obey.

Carefully I opened the first page and was blinded by an all-encompassing flash of light.

# Chapter 61
# The Axe Came Down

The light disappeared in a flash less than a second after I'd opened the book. I slammed it shut and took a step back.

"Well, that was anti-climactic," Panda said, relighting his bamboo pipe.

I turned around to see that we were still in the same room, nothing looked any different. What was that light?

"Hey Treena, what did that book even do?" I asked, wandering absently towards another weapons case.

There was no response.

I turned towards the door but she was no longer there. Then I heard the screams.

From outside a shrill scream echoed across the stone walls of the castle. There were quieter screams as well in the background, the clash of iron and the faint smell of burning wood joined them.

*What the hell?* I thought, rushing towards the fallen door.

Hell was right.

The ghost town we'd walked through was alive with the sound of violence. Houses were set ablaze and a thick, black smog filled the sky around us.

The smoke stung my eyes, it was so thick I could taste it. Worse though, was the stench of death and an aura so fearsome it made my eyes water – though I guess that could have also been caused by the thick smoke.

Treena ran across the bridge wailing. Her voice no longer sounded like tinkling bells. It was a guttural, erratic wail.

"Treena, wait!" I cried, rushing towards her.

My heart skipped a beat as she ran recklessly into the fray. Battle raged all around her as tusked creatures in full plate armour cut down fleeing dryads.

A notification appeared on my HUD.

### New Quest:
### *Nobody Expects the Orcish Inquisition*

### What the shit?

### Objectives:
### *Follow Treena 0/1*

### Rewards: *There's no time for that now! Catch her!*

It seemed that the system was as confused as I was. Well, either that or it was messing with me. It didn't matter either way.

I was planning on catching Treena anyway. There was no way I was going to leave a child to wander a warzone. Though first I'd have to clear a path.

I summoned my bow and used *Soul Shot* against the nearest creature. It was a large, bipedal boar wearing full plate armour and a morion helmet. The helmet itself reminded me of a deep bedpan with a ridge on the top.

My arrow smashed through the plate armour and the bipedal boar turned towards me. It looked pissed.

It snorted and glared at me for a moment before charging towards me. I panic fired a second arrow that bounced off the armour harmlessly.

*Crap, I need Soul Shot to pierce it.*

I didn't have time to channel the skill a second time before the boar reached me. I nocked another arrow and pulled back the string.

I held off firing for an extra half second. The boar skidded to a halt before me and raised a double-sided axe above its head.

Then I fired.

From point blank range I shot the arrow through the boar's eye. It squealed, and I mean that literally considering it was a huge pig.

I pulled my bow back into my inventory and swapped it for my new daggers. I stabbed one of them into the other eyeball and yanked downwards.

Then I pierced the pig's gullet with my second dagger and ripped it across its throat. Blood sprayed out like a water hose and splattered my face and eyes.

The boar dropped to the floor with a clank, gagging slightly and clutching at its torn neck. It let out a long, horrifying gasp and then it was still.

"What the hell was that thing?" I muttered to myself, focusing on its corpse.

**You have discovered a new race:**
**Conquista-Orc**

**A foot solider in the Orcish Inquisition, the Conquista-**
**Orc is a fierce fighter. What they lack in brain power,**
**they make up for with strength and tenacity.**
**They are trained from birth for a single purpose: to**
**stamp out heresy.**
**They are most well known for their war with the**
**Dryads. When I say well know, I mean infamous. They**

**committed numerous atrocities all over the world as
they rooted out and slaughtered thousands of *Dryads* –
a task they took to like a pig in muck.**

"I wish they'd *leaf* those poor dryads alone," Panda said as he tiptoed across the bridge behind me.

"Not the time," I growled.

"But the system gets to do it." He protested in a whiny, child-like tone.

I ignored him.

Treena had already disappeared into the suffocating smoke. She couldn't have gotten too far though, and I was sure I knew where she was going.

I'd told her to run back to the meeting hall if there was trouble. I was willing to bet that's where she'd be.

*I'd* told her to do that. Those were *my* words. My orders caused her to run headlong into this nightmare. I had to find her.

I raced into the smoke, not even stopping to loot my kill. As I ran, I pulled my hood back up. It hid my aura, and though I wasn't certain what that meant, it might be enough to keep attention off me.

Just in case I tried to activate the new armour set effect which made me invisible for a time dictated by my intelligence stat.

I felt strange for a few seconds and then the feeling disappeared. I wondered if a few seconds was the extent of my ability at the moment.

It would make sense considering my lacking points in the intelligence skill. I didn't have time to properly think about it though as I ran past screaming dryads and murderous orcs clashing in the street.

I didn't like the idea of leaving the dryads to face the Conquista-Orcs alone, but at least they were adults. Treena was a child. Defenceless and afraid.

It was difficult trying to run through the all-encompassing black smoke. My eyes stung and watered and my throat was on fire.

I fought for breath with every step. Worse, my vision was so severely impaired that I risked bumping into someone with every step.

The battle raged around me. Iron clashed, civilians screamed and cried and through it all I heard snorting laughs.

*Those sadistic swine. They're actually enjoying this.* I thought, clenching my teeth as I ran towards the hall.

I wanted nothing more than to cut them to shreds. A ball of rage deep in my gut told me to join the fray, that I could somehow turn the tide on the pig bastards.

I knew that wasn't true. There were too many of them and they were strong. Even with my acid arrows and daggers the last one still took effort to kill.

I wasn't certain of my chances against more than one at once.

No, I just needed to save one person: Treena.

I could figure out a plan after I got her to safety. Maybe I could climb onto a house and provide covering fire. I was an archer after all.

If I wanted to dance around the battlefield I'd have picked a sword. My daggers were a backup option, not my main weapon, even if slicing at these fucks up close and personal would be more satisfying.

I raced down the street, dodging stray axe swings and trying to drown out the terrified and pained screams from the villagers.

The shadow of a large building began to take shape through the smoke, a looming beacon of despair.

I reached the door and crashed through it. Treena had to be inside, she just had to be.

This was our meeting place. I just hoped it wasn't too...

I hit my shin on a bench and stumbled over it.

"No please!" Treena breathed, hopelessly.

I looked up, thankful that she was there, until I saw the horrific scene playing out in front of me.

A monstrous orc stood in front of the platform at the back of the hall. It was twice as tall as the orc I'd killed, and much wider.

It held an oversized, two-headed axe above its head and sneered as it looked down its snout at the glowing woman kneeling in front of it.

She was a stunning dryad with bark-like skin and flowing green hair, just like Treena's. Something about her gave me a warm feeling, it was comforting, like everything was going to be ok.

She glanced towards Treena and smiled as the orc brought his axe down, cracking her head like an egg. Her brain fluid flowed from the wound like a runny, bloody yolk.

"NO!" Treena screamed.

The woman's body stayed upright for a moment before faceplanting the floor at the orc's feet. Next to her laid a headless man.

As she hit the floor the ephemeral green glow that surrounded her flickered out and the warmth I'd felt was gone.

The orc tipped its head back and laughed heartily. One of its tusks was missing and a nasty scar bisected its left eye.

Treena staggered towards the woman. Her shoulders slumped and her hair dropped, its gravity defying mysticism gone. She dropped to her knees and patted the woman's shoulder.

"Mommy... wake up," she said softly as she patted her again. "Mommy please." She patted her a little harder this time and the body shook slightly.

I could barely watch, yet I couldn't turn away. My eyes blurred and burned; I wiped them with the back of my hand.

The room flashed and flickered and I saw visions from the horrible nightmare I'd had during the goblin king coronation.

The scene flickered between Treena hopelessly trying to rouse her mother and Laya laying there instead with a spear through her gut as Treena tried to wake her.

I didn't know what was happening. I felt sick and angry. Why was this happening?

"Mum...please don't leave me," Treena whimpered as she devolved into violently shaking the corpse of her mother.

Of course nothing happened. Her head had split open, she was gone, she was just...gone. Layla was just...gone her stomach torn open by the spear resting inside it.

I wanted to go to Treena, to hold her and let her know that she wasn't alone.

I wanted to...help. But I couldn't move. I was glued to the spot, my legs refused to listen to me as I watched helplessly from the sidelines: a helpless spectator to her tragedy.

*To my tragedy. My wife, my poor Layla.*

She stopped speaking and her head fell onto her mother's back. She shook silently, her slight frame bobbing up and down, a branch adrift on a stormy sea.

The orc was still laughing, towering above Treena and her mother. It'd scarcely seemed to notice that she was even there. Spittle flew from its mouth as the oversized axe dripped blood from over his shoulder.

I wanted to be angry as I watched the scene before me. I wanted to feel the rage like I knew I should, shoot the orc in its dumb face and take revenge for the orphan it had created.

I wanted to do this, but I felt cold. My body was numb and I stared ahead emptily as Treena sobbed frantically into her mother's still warm corpse.

*Or was it Layla's?* I couldn't tell anymore as the flickering images distorted my mind. I didn't know what was real anymore.

"Don't cry little one," the orc said, ceasing its laughter. It sounded almost...kind. "Your mother was a heretic. I have saved her from the wrath of God. Now she can rest in the afterlife. It is a mercy."

His voice was gruff yet sincere, but his eyes told another story. They were cold, heartless as they looked at the grieving child.

The anger I'd wanted so badly to feel started to bubble as I clenched my bow and summoned an arrow into my hand.

My frozen body began to thaw ever so slightly as I gazed into the uncaring eyes that hid behind that faux empathy.

Treena didn't react. She laid there, sobbing silently as her own green glow dimmed slightly.

"Do you not hear me little one? Cease your tears," it said a little less softly this time.

As I glared at the orc's eyes, it almost looked confused. Like it couldn't comprehend the sadness of the child before it. Did it really not understand the tragedy playing out in front of us? Could It not empathise with a child grieving over the murder of her mother?

Its face contorted as Treena continued to ignore it.

"This is pathetic. I have had enough," he said coldly in a soft but stern gruff.

It raised its axe slowly above its head and I tried to dash towards it. My legs wouldn't listen. My body was frozen. I strained as I tried to reach her.

I pulled with every fibre of my being but I was frozen to the spot. My body simply wouldn't listen to me no matter how much I struggled against it.

Was this magic or was something wrong with me? I'd heard of people freezing from trauma but I'd always assumed that was their brains not processing what was happening.

Though that could be the case. I couldn't even tell if the corpse before me belonged to Treena's mother or my wife. I was confused, sad, and rooted to the spot.

Despite all that, my brain knew exactly what it wanted to do. I had to do something. I couldn't watch this. I couldn't let this happen. I dug deep, using every fibre of my being and with consorted effort I managed to move my mouth.

"Treena move!" I cried.

The axe came down.

# Chapter 62
# My Turn Bitch

It seemed to happen in slow motion before me. Treena laid on top of her mother's body, trembling as it flashed back and forth between her and my wife Layla.

The orc snarled as froth sprayed from the side of his mouth with the broken tusk.

I heard a voice shouting for Treena to move. I knew it was my own, but it sounded like the voice of another man. It was almost as if I was experiencing it from across the room.

The oversized, double-sided axe arced through the air towards her. I tried desperately to move. If I could just get to her. If I could just save her.

But I couldn't move. My body was obstinate in its refusal to obey me. I felt so powerless as I watched the scene from the worst seat in the house.

I felt hopeless as the axe travelled through the air, inching closer to the small and frail child before me. She was defenceless, she was in pain and there was nothing I could do to help.

I was forced to watched as the axe moved at an agonisingly slow rate, yet I never gave up.

Despite my uncooperating body, I pushed with all my mental might. I would move. I had to move.

I had to save her, because if I couldn't protect her right here and now, how would I ever be able to trust myself to protect my own child in the future?

*I had to avenge Layla.*

My brain stopped for a moment, like a mental blink as that thought reverberated around my skull.

*Protect her? Isn't she still on earth?*

Then time sped back up.

The axe sliced into Treena's neck and within a fraction of a second she was gone. Her head rolled down the side of her mother's torso, stopping upright and facing me.

Her eyes held a lingering sadness. They were puffy and red and they looked straight into mine and said: "how could you let this happen? You said you'd protect me."

The accusatory glare was right and that truth hit me like a truck. My heart pounded, I couldn't catch my breath and my stomach twisted with the knot of self-loathing.

Blood gushed from her little body like a fountain. It ran down her mother's back like a rushing river.

And then the light went out.

Those eyes that had been so full of life, joy, childish wonder and in the end, sadness, turned to glass.

I dropped to my knees and stared open mouthed, unable to comprehend what had happened. Unable to live with my failure as an adventurer, as a human being, as a soon-to-be father.

My brain simply wouldn't function properly as I struggled to comprehend the scene. Had I just witnessed the tragedy of Treena losing her mother and then her own life. Or was it Layla that had been laying there on the ground.

What was happening to me? Why wasn't my mind able to tell the difference. It didn't make sense. It was…painful.

I couldn't tell if time had slowed down again or if my thoughts were just racing too thick and fast to process properly. As I stared at the dead child in front of me, I felt like...

The orc let out a bemused snort.

"Tiny heretic." It spat, the phlegm landing on her face.

And that was when the damn finally broke. The floodgates opened and my despair was consumed by a burning, pulsing rage.

It shot up from the pit of my stomach like an erupting volcano and my vision turned a deep crimson.

I felt numb, I couldn't feel my fingers as I summoned my daggers and charged.

Crashing into the Orc was like hitting a brick wall as he looked down at me like I was an annoying fly buzzing around him.

A bemused expression twinged on his lips, an expression that didn't reach his hateful eyes. I arced my left arm around in a bladed hook and slashed at his naval.

It barely left a scratch.

His skin was so tough and had I been in my right mind I would have disengaged and found a smarter approach. Instead, I continued slashing. I slashed and stabbed like a man possessed. I gritted my teeth so hard I felt a tooth crack.

I didn't feel the pain though, just a numb sensation of cracking enamel in my mouth.

The Orc laughed at my futile attempt to harm him as my daggers bounced off his skin in quick succession. His laugher stoked the flame of my rage and I stopped my futile assault.

I glared up at him, seething.

"Puny human," he chortled, tipping his head back.

*We'll see.* I thought as I saw myself ripping him apart in my mind's eyes.

The image was so overwhelming it burned into the back of my retina. I wanted to murder him, I wanted to hurt him and make him pay.

It was a primal feeling, a calling of the reptilian brain and at that moment my entire body merged into one. It was as if my anger had become a living, breathing thing.

I was no longer Kaleb the ex-truck driver, Kaleb the adventurer, Kaleb the...human.

I was Kaleb the living embodiment of vengeful rage.

I became connected to myself in a way I didn't even know was possible. It felt like when I mediated, it was almost peaceful, but it was a perversion of that feeling.

I knew it was wrong, but it felt so right.

I forced my soul, my very being out of my body. I pushed with every fibre of my being and at the same time I grabbed onto something else.

A power not born within me, it didn't belong to me, but I grabbed it anyway with both hands and I refused to let go.

Somewhere outside of myself I heard a guttural, terrified scream and then, I felt it.

The Orc's soul.

It was a tiny black orb. It looked sickly, twisted. I felt myself smile as I grabbed it and squeezed.

*It's my turn bitch.*

My eyes flew open and I was both back in the room and inside my meditation space at the same time. I could feel his soul, mould it and yet I could also control my body and see the world through my own eyes.

The Orc backed up and tripped over a bench. He landed on his back and scrabbled away.

He stared up at me with wide eyes, his lips trembled. I grinned as I walked towards him, twisting, and tearing at his soul.

"This is for Treena and Layla, you sick bastard," I growled.

He looked back at me with a fearful blankness in his eyes. He looked confused and terrified.

"I don't even know who that is!" He whimpered pleadingly.

He opened his mouth again to scream as I pulled on his soul but I put a stop to it. I don't know how, but I willed him into silence and he was helpless against me.

I wouldn't allow him the release of screaming. I needed him to be present in the room, to feel every bit of the pain I was about to inflict on him.

I had no idea how I was doing it, but in the moment I didn't care. I would avenge them both. I'd make him suffer.

"Kaleb, stop!" A familiar voice shouted in the distance. It barely registered.

I looked at the Orc and saw only red, a waterfall of scarlet ran through my vision. I willed him to feel pain and his face twisted in agony.

He was still unable to scream, though he clenched his toes and dug his nails into the floorboards. His eyes stared up at me, pleading with me to stop.

*Not yet, I want you to beg me to let you die.* I thought in a voice that sounded far different to my own.

"Kaleb please, you'll die!" the faraway voice screamed.

I pulled at the Orc's soul as he screamed silently. It felt tangible in my hands, though my hands were by my sides the whole time.

The more I pulled the worse he looked. His skin went pale, blood poured from his eyes. He'd already ripped his fingernails off as he contorted on the floor, gripping the floorboards and writhing in an agony worse than any physical torture.

*I need more.*

I pulled harder, tugging on his soul like it was a rope. He'd already given up fighting back. I had complete control.

"Kaleb!"

A sharp pain bit into my thigh and I reflexively gripped down hard on the Orc's soul which burst like a water balloon in my hands.

*No! I wanted more!*

Blood oozed from his mouth; his body withered before my eyes. It dried up until there was nothing left but a skeletal, mummified figure.

I looked down towards the source of the pain in my thigh. A dagger was stuck in my leg...*my dagger.*

Panda held it, he was shaking as he stared at me with watery eyes. Then there was a flash of white light and my scarlet tinted world turned black.

***

"What was that?" Director Lucas said breathlessly.

He had goose bumps and a cold sweat chilling him to the bone as he floated hight in the clouds above the island.

He had been instructed to watch Kaleb as he navigated his new quest. It had been tedious for the most part – a huge waste of his valuable time.

Until it wasn't.

A powerful aura had exploded out from the building the noob adventurer had entered. It felt malicious, evil even. It hit him like a shockwave and the gold ranked adventurer, the most powerful man in Havar, trembled.

*This pleases me greatly. He has surpassed my expectations.* Diako said into Lucas's mind.

He had felt the god's presence from the moment he left Havar. He was using him as a vessel, seeing through his eyes, experiencing things through his skin.

It was an uncomfortably intimate process and Lucas hated it. But what choice did he have? This was his god after all.

"I don't understand, My Lord, what was that?"

*You tell me. What did it feel like to you?* The god replied in a playfully amused tone.

Lucas hadn't heard him this happy since…well, ever. He'd never heard him sound this pleased before.

"It felt like indomitable power… it reminded me of my father," Lucas replied, shuddering at the thought of a phase two exuding power comparable to his tyrannical father.

*Exactly. Isn't it incredible? To unlock* that *so early in his development.* The god trailed off, as if he was biting his tongue before he revealed too much to his subject.

"Is this the thing I'm missing?" Lucas asked quietly.

He'd been told that he was missing something. A key ingredient to breaking through the level cap. It was the source of his father's greatest shame. The reason he had been exiled to Havar.

*It is.*

He shook with a sudden burst of rage as his fists closed into tightened balls. His fingernails cut into his palms and tiny droplets of blood rained down onto the burning village below.

How could a mere phase two have access to a power that he, a gold ranked adventurer, could never obtain. It was an outrage, a scandal, it was…terrifying.

Using his advanced perception he quickly scouted the village. He could only see two signs of life, both within the village hall. One of them was faint, barely clinging to existence.

A moment ago the village had been full of life. There was so much emotion in the mana, fear, hatred, bloodlust as the Orcs hunted and executed the dryad population.

Now though, after that single blast of aura, there was nothing.

The village lay still.

"Tell me one thing, why did you order me to tell him it was a cultist fort?" Lucas asked, loosening his grip on his palms.

*To test him. I wanted to see how he'd react, I wanted to prime him for...this. Emotional manipulation is a subtle but powerful art.*

*And it worked beautifully. The boy has awakened. He has the potential to be useful to me.*

*Now, I need you to make sure that he doesn't use it again.*

*Not until he's ready.*

# Chapter 63
# The Desert Samurai's Godly Duel

The Samurai stood triumphantly over the bodies of the weak cultists. Their leader's severed body bled at her feet as she sheathed her sword and grinned.

"Your turn," she said, gazing up at the huge golden throne before her.

A voice in her head had appeared when she'd entered the temple and it had claimed to be a god. Naturally she had told it she would kill it.

*Oh, alright then, I guess you've earned a face-to-face meeting.* The voice sighed in her mind, like the act of fighting her was a bothersome task. He'd grow to regret dismissing her like that.

She felt a presence and looked to see a handsome man sitting relaxed on the golden throne. He had his head rested on his hand like it was just another boring day.

That really pissed The Samurai off.

He had a large scar across his chest and scales on his cheeks. He was oddly handsome with piercing yellow eyes but his lackadaisical approach to a warrior like her issuing a challenge showed a deep personality flaw that she just couldn't overlook.

"Well done, that was quite the show you put on," he said in a cheery, playful voice.

"I did tell you I would kill your followers and I always keep my promises," the Samurai replied in a stoic voice.

"Ooh aren't you scary. I love that."

"Mock me at your own peril," she replied, she wasn't quite sure when she'd started talking with such confidence, but she liked it.

"What is it with outworlders and a lack of respect for the divine?" The god mused. "You're the second one I've spoken to this month who lacked respect. I shit you not, the last guy looked me dead in the eyes and told me he was an atheist.

"Can you believe that? I was like dude; I am right in front of you. A living, breathing God. Honestly," he said, shaking his head in disbelief.

"So, go on then, tell me what *your* problem is with divine beings," he sighed, sinking his scaled cheek even further into his hand.

"I hold respect for power. So far, all you have shown me are weaklings," The Samurai replied, keeping her hand on the hilt of her sword just in case.

"Ah ok, is that all you want, a show of power? I can do that, but first let's make a little deal," he replied, finally taking his hand off his head as he sat forward slightly and grinned. "You wanted to challenge me, correct?

"Well, just this once, I will allow it. Never say I didn't do anything for you. You get one strike; I will stand still and take your most powerful hit.

"If you can leave even the faintest scratch on me then I will allow you to take my head and the experience that comes with that – which believe me is a metric fuck tonne more than you'd need to reach the level cap.

"However, if you fail to leave a scratch then you will become one of my vassals, you will work for me and you will denounce all other gods in this world, forever. How does that sound?" He asked with a gleam in his yellow eyes.

The man was obviously deluded. No one could take a hit from her most powerful attack without it even scratching them.

She wasn't fond of the idea of not getting to fight this man child. However, a samurai never backs down from a challenge.

"I accept," she said after a moment's consideration.

She could have said more, she could have asked questions or tried to goad him into a real fight, but she decided to let her blade do the talking.

After all, the man before her had set the terms himself. If he wanted to die so badly, she would gladly help him with that.

"Perfect," he hissed, standing up from his seat.

He dropped to the ground before her, his green cloak billowing out behind him, and spread his arms wide in a Jesus pose.

"Whenever you're ready," he said, gazing at her with a slight air of bemusement.

He would regret that.

She had the perfect attack to use on him. It was a skill that, though only common in rarity, was super powerful.

She'd used it once already in this temple, it was her bread and butter, go to skill. Why mess with the classics?

### Midnight Slash (common)

**Unsheathe your blade in an instant 10-foot leap to slash through foes. This skill imbues the wielder's blade with dark mana.**
**Activating this skill has a medium mana cost.**

She leant forward, placing her dominant hand on the hilt of her blade. One leg was pushed out behind her, bent only slightly. Her forward leg was bent into a deep squat.

She lowered herself to the ground, feeling the tension rise within her thighs. She squatted lower until her front leg became a coiled spring, until the tension was so great that it was harder to hold the position than it would be to unleash the kinetic energy in her quadricep and leap forward.

Then she focused. She reached out with her mana senses, sensing everything around her. The mana was stained with blood, the blood she had spilled when she'd massacred the cultists inside the temple.

It was the perfect mana for her attack.

She focused on pulling it inside herself, she let it build and pool in the very tip of her blade until it was overflowing with her power.

Then she focused on her internal mana as she held it there. It was swirling in her core and she pushed it, forcing it to flow and concentrate in two specific places.

The first was her front leg, the second was her sword arm. This all took place in less than a second as she readied her attack, allowing the system to guide her through the skill.

Then, all at once, she unleashed that energy and slashed the stomach of the overconfident god standing before her. His overconfidence would be his downfall.

Her movement was instantaneous. One moment she was charging the skill, the next she was in front of the self-proclaimed god with her blade running across his naval.

The walls shook as it happened, the magic in the air pulsed with a terrified condensed feeling of power.

It was a physical force; much more powerful than the version she'd used to kill the cultist leader. The corpses on the ground shook with her power.

As her blade made contact with the man, it snapped.

She stopped moving, a shiver went down her spine as a momentary cold sweat tickled her skin.

She looked down.

"How?" she said, aghast at the sight of her precious weapon shattered on the floor.

She looked up and saw that not only had her blade not scratched the god, it hadn't even ruffled the bandages he had wrapped around his stomach.

*What kind of power is this?* She wondered, stepping back, and looking the god in the eyes.

He stared back impassively for a moment, still in his Jesus pose with his arms spread wide.

"It'll show you," he said in a sudden and very serious voice.

Then she understood.

He unleashed a fraction of his mana for less than a second and the image shocked her. She had the ability to sense a person's power when she looked at them.

She could see the strength of their mana in the form of a semi-visible aura that surrounded them.

When she'd first spoken to him, the god didn't have any aura surrounding him. She had taken that for weakness, but it was clear now that he held a level of control over his own power that was far above her comprehension.

As his power was unleashed for that fraction of a second. What she saw blinded her senses.

His aura was fully visible, tangible even. It oozed out of him casting a shadow larger than the massive throne behind him. It blotted out everything else in her vision.

It was terrifying. It was magnificent. It was... everything she'd ever wanted.

"I understand now," she said, after taking a moment to compose herself. She took a knee and bowed her head. "You have bested me and as we agreed, I will become your vassal and denounce all other gods in this world."

"Yeah, I know you will," he replied, changing back to his playful and carefree voice. "You should stand up though, I don't really care for all that ceremonious crap."

She did as he instructed and looked at the god as if they were equals, though she knew she was far from being able to call herself that.

"I'm Chrysus by the way," he said, offering out his hand.

She paused a moment and then shook it. She felt a tremble of his power as their skin touched. It was incredible.

"So, now we've got that out of the way I have a job for you. I actually offered this to the last outworlder I met but sadly, he turned me down... oh well, his loss is your gain I guess.

"I take it you've heard of The Celestial Map? Well, I want it. I am the god of wealth for a reason and since no one really knows what the map is, it means I want it. It is my right to own everything of value in this world.

"You're going to help me get it. I'll explain the specifics some other time, but for now the main thing you need to know is that I am currently without a high priest.

"I know!" He continued in faux surprise. "Me, a god of over-whelming power with no priest to call his own. I have a tournament starting soon to choose a new one. You're going to enter it and if you win you get to be my new right hand.

"How does that sound? Promoted from vassal to right hand in a matter of months. It's like when a guy's parents tell him he'll be *running the company soon* when he gets his first job.

"Except I'm not just blowing smoke. You win this and I will reward you with a serious power boost. Oh, and you'll be needing these."

He held out his hand and the pieces of her broken blade re-formed in the air. It was like rewinding the video on their fight as the sword fragments merged back together.

The completed katana floated gently back into its sheath. She welcomed the feeling of the sword's weight at her hip.

Then he floated a small piece of paper towards her which she plucked out of the air and opened.

*You have been granted the honour of being allowed to compete in the high priest's tournament.*
*The winner will become the next right hand of Chrysus, God of Wealth.*
*The tournament will take place in six months' time.*

*Do you accept?*
*Y/N*

"Good luck. I'd advise you to gain some more levels between now and then," Chrysus said casually, and then he disappeared without fanfare.

A new notification popped up on her interface which she couldn't ignore.

**Quest Complete:**
***Red Robe, Brown Pants***

**The Adventure Society has received reports of cultist sightings in the nearby southern oasis.**
**Traverse the Kalhatchi Desert and investigate.**
**P.S. Investigate is code for mass murder.**

**Objectives:**
*Locate the cultist lair 1/1*
*Eliminate all cultists 1/1*
*Defeat the cultist leader 1/1*

**Reward:** *Honour is the only reward a samurai needs*

*Only joking, it's really a weapon rarity upgrade token.*

She smiled as she read the notification and pulled the invitation into her inventory.

"Well, Pocco, looks like we've got a new goal."

The wolf familiar cocked its head to the side as its blood covered ear twitched slightly.

# Chapter 64
# Hysterical Mana

As my consciousness slowly returned, I stared at the glowing red light which shone through my eyelids and felt the warmth of the sun beaming down on me.

I felt something soft and slightly moist on my hands, like grass in a summer haze. A smell wafted over me: the pungent burning of lit bamboo.

My body felt tired and something inside me felt... off. I tried to delve into meditation but an intangible pain forced me out of the state before I could form any kind of visualisation.

My eyes blinked open and I gasped as the pain lingered deep in my gut. I squinted as the powerful sun above shone directly into my eyes.

There wasn't a cloud in the sky and the thick black smoke of battle was gone. I pushed myself into a sitting position with some discomfort and saw Panda sitting to the side of me, smoking his pipe.

He looked over the rim of his book, eyeing me up carefully.

"You're not gonna rip my soul out, are you?" he asked, squinting at my face.

"What?"

The last thing I remembered was running through the town. Fires were burning everywhere, dryads were crying and screaming as blades clashed all around me.

"Looks like you made it back kid," he said, his face softening as he closed his black book and placed it on the grass.

"What happened?" I asked meekly, "...and where are we?"

He regaled me with the tale of my missing memories and it all came flooding back in detailed flashbacks as he spoke.

I remembered watching Treena die as I stood helplessly, I remembered being unable to tell if the woman lying dead on the ground was Treena's mother, or my wife. I remembered losing myself to an anger, the like of which I've never felt before. I remembered holding the soul of the orc in my hands and crushing it.

Was I really capable of hurting someone's soul? That sounded like something straight out of a fantasy novel. It sounded like the kind of power a villain would have.

"... and once the orc died there was this bright flash of white light and we were here in this meadow. The walls, the village, the castle. It just... vanished," Panda finished, pulling me out of my nightmarish daze.

I stared at him at a loss for words. How do you reply to someone who's just told you that you literally killed a guy by crushing his soul?

"What about the rest of the dryads?" I asked, stumbling through my words as my mouth tried to keep up with my gushing thoughts.

"That's another, much weirder story," he sighed, picking up the black book. "You should read this; you'll understand once you read the last page."

He held out the black book to me, it was old and battered. It felt familiar somehow but I didn't know why.

Wordlessly I took it and flicked to the last page. It was blank. I flicked back through the book and found the last entry. It seemed to be a diary.

*Atheline 347-36*

*The Elder still hasn't returned.*

*He entered the castle yesterday but hasn't come out. I heard some of the villagers say he had to speak orcish to open the door.*

*I memorised the words. I'll write them after this entry so I don't forget them.*

*My mommy and papa are leading a rescue team to go find the elder. I'm scared, what if they don't come back either?*

*I don't want to be left all alone.*

*I overheard papa saying something about the orcish inquisition. I didn't really understand it but he said something about how they hunt dryads and other forest folk.*

*He said that they think we're heretical. I don't know what that word means but it sounds bad.*

*I'm sure they'll be ok though. They're strong, especially mommy. I know they'll come back to me, and when this is all over we can play again.*

I stared at the pages for a long time. My heart thumped loudly and slowly. My stomach churned and it wasn't just because my core was still suffering from the soul attack I'd used.

I couldn't read the orcish that was written at the bottom of the page. I guess my translation skill doesn't work on everything – or maybe it was spelled wrong.

It didn't matter.

After a long moment, I spoke.

"This is the book I touched inside the castle, isn't it?" I asked sombrely.

"Yes," Panda replied.

"It's Treena's diary, isn't it?"

"I think so kid, yeah."

The backs of my eyes felt hot. I didn't understand at first, but the pieces slowly began to come together. Panda didn't let me sit in silence mulling it over for long before he explained his own theory.

"You were out for a while kid, I read through the whole thing," he began, his voice was uncharacteristically sincere. "Do you remember when you asked me about the date in that book in the meeting hall? It said Atheline 347-35. I thought it must have been written wrong or something at the time.

"You see Atheline is the calendar name for the god Athena like I said before. The next number is the year 347 and the number after the dash is the day in that year: 35.

"I thought it was written wrong because we're currently in the year 20347. I figured they'd just missed the first two numbers off like a shorthand or something.

"I don't think that anymore," he took a deep breath. "I used my sage ability to research the orcish inquisition. I'd never heard of it before, but I found something.

"It was a massacre. Orcs killed dryads and other forest folk by the thousands. It was a religious thing, a feud between Athena and the orc god.

"The thing is...the reason I'd never heard of it before is because it all happened over 20,000 years ago. I'm no spring chicken, but I'm not *that* old," he sighed and slowly took a long drag on his bamboo pipe.

*20,000 years ago?* I thought.

How could that be possible? We'd spoken to Treena; I'd ripped the orc's soul out and I'd shot another one. How could that be?

I looked at Panda and tried to ask but my mouth wouldn't form the words. My brain was in overdrive, it felt like a restart on a computer. My brain simply wouldn't brain. He seemed to get the gist though and answered me anyway.

"I know, I couldn't believe it either. I think...I think Treena tapped into some kind of memory magic when she died. Strong emotions can unlock weird, and in your case creepy, powers.

"It's rare but you're living proof that it does happen. They call it hysterical mana. Like when a mother blows up a forest looking for their lost child.

"Most people can't do that normally. But sometimes, in extreme situations, people can control external mana and use it. I think that's what Treena tapped in to."

I looked up from the book, my head hurt. I couldn't organise my thoughts properly. It was all so surreal. I'd gotten so angry, so furious, over something that happened that long ago? It wasn't even real.

*That doesn't explain why I saw Layla there.* I thought, and there was something else that didn't make sense either.

"You're wrong," I said quietly. "What *I* did couldn't have been hysterical mana. I don't have any mana at all, remember?"

"You might be right there, kid," he sighed, letting small plumes of wispy grey smoke out of his mouth. "All the same though, I think that's how the village and those walls came to be. They appeared on the island suddenly, remember?

"I think Treena's anguish and grief lived in those pages. Hell, it probably happened on this same island. I don't know why they appeared now, but I could hazard a guess as to why they vanished."

"Because it played out the same way again," I said dryly. "Because I couldn't save her. I froze, I just cou—"

"No, you idiot," Panda interrupted. I looked up at him with a furrowed brow. "What part of *memory* don't you get? That already happened. You can't change the past dipshit…no…I think that when you went all apeshit psycho killer on that orc it meant something to Treena, or at least to her memory.

"I think, somehow, your anger on her behalf soothed her soul. I think she was trapped in a cycle, reliving that memory over and over and somehow when she saw you literally rip a dude's soul out of his chest on her behalf, it finally put her spirit to rest."

I wasn't sure what to say. Had my enraged reaction really helped her? Did that make my soul ripping ability a good thing? I wasn't so sure. At the time I wasn't even sure if I was angry on Treena's behalf, or angry because my deluded mind thought Layla was the one lying on the ground dead.

It felt like an evil power to have. Surely destroying a person's soul is much worse than just killing them? It's not just ending a life; it's warping and breaking everything that they are.

I could feel the memory so clearly. It felt like I was ripping apart the orc's very sense of self. Worse than that, I enjoyed it. What kind of person gets off on that level of torturous pain?

Panda watched me curiously as he quietly puffed on his pipe. He looked concerned, his brow was furrowed slightly and in that moment his eyes looked…old.

For the first time since I'd met him, he actually looked sagely.

"Kid, don't use that power again," he said solemnly.

"So, it is evil?" I asked, my heart sinking in my chest as my fears were confirmed.

"Not exactly," he answered. "No power or skill is inherently good or evil. It's more about how you use it. Soul attacks are taboo in this world because they cause irreparable damage that transcends death.

"But they *are* powerful. It's a rare ability and personal power is important in this world. You shouldn't use it because you're not powerful enough to control it. It will kill you at your level.

"Moreover, if anyone finds out you have it, *they* will kill you. Powerful people don't like noobs gaining power that they shouldn't have. It's that simple."

So, it wasn't evil? From what he said the power itself didn't have an innate morality. No, the evil deeds that came about from using it were entirely my own. I sat in silence, staring at nothing as that horrifying revelation began to sink in.

"Kid," Panda began, still speaking in a quiet and solemn tone. "Who's Layla?"

My stomach flopped. I looked up at him, feeling myself tremble. I'd never told him about her before. I was never sure if he knew my past simply by being my familiar.

I knew that he saw flashes of my time in Celestia before I summoned him, but not if he knew about my life on earth as well.

"She's my wife," I replied slowly, unable to look him in the eye. "She was pregnant when I was isekaied here."

He stared at me for a moment. I could feel his gaze even though I couldn't bear to look at him as my eyes felt hot. He didn't say anything. Instead, he leant back, stretching out, before smiling and standing up.

"Anyway," he began. "Enough of all this. You should check your notifications and then we should go back to the boat. I'm starving." His voice changed into its usual playfulness.

My mind was reeling. I had so much new information to sort through. But I was glad he didn't ask anything else. I knew he'd lost his previous summoner, maybe he knew how hard it was to talk about those things. Besides, he was right. There would be time for that later, when we were both ready.

I checked the notifications tab on my HUD. It looked like I had a couple.

### Quest Complete:
### *Nobody Expects the Orcish Inquisition*

### What the shit?

### Objectives:
### *Follow Treena 1/1*
### *Rewards: Gain level x1*

A new level was always useful, couldn't argue with that. Though I noticed an absence of *you have defeated* notifications.

I decided that it must have been because the orcs weren't there. They were long dead memories rather than living, breathing creatures. Thinking back, I didn't take any damage either.

I guess it made sense that I wouldn't get experience for killing them even if that big orc was probably a high level.

Also, the reward had changed. Originally it had said something like *you don't have time for rewards.* Did that mean the system could change its mind about what rewards it gave out, or was it simply a hidden one that had been decided from the start?

I had so many questions, but system fuckery was the least of them at the time so I pushed the thought aside and checked my other notification.

### Achievement Unlocked!
### *Kali Ma*

**You're shaping up to be an evil little prick, aren't you?**
**You fight with acid, mass murder goblins and now**
**you're ripping people's souls out.**
**A man after my own heart. Who doesn't love a good**
**villain?**
**You have tapped into the power of your soul and used**
**it to negatively affect another creature.**
**This kind of power is coveted by the most powerful**
**people in Celestia. You go girl!**

**Reward:** *Someone with your propensity for truly*
*despicable acts doesn't need a reward.*

Even the system thought ripping souls out of people's bodies was evil. I didn't need it of all things to tell me how despicable I was. Panda was right, I needed to keep this power to myself and not use it.

"Don't listen to it kid, the system is always a dick." Panda said, placing his soft paw on my head.

I smiled sadly and placed my hand on top of his. Though a part of me, the curious part, kinda wanted to experiment with soul power a little more. Maybe it was something I could work on during meditation.

I tried to push all of this business out of my mind. It would do me no good to dwell on it. Besides, I had my adventurer exam to look forward to. I didn't have the luxury of wallowing in self-pity. I needed to keep getting stronger and pushing forward.

I'd just completed my third and final trial quest. Once I handed it in, it was exam time.

I couldn't help but grin as I thought about finally being a full-time adventurer with a real rank. This journey was only just beginning.

I picked myself up off the floor, dusted myself off and headed back to the yacht. I had an exam to ace.

# Chapter 65
# Jack The Reaper – A Propensity for Violence

Jack walked calmly through the large crowd, slinking past the angry people there. He'd been busy since joining the Organisation and accepting the class: *The Reaper*.

Diako was a slave driver, but he liked that. He wasn't the type to enjoy relaxation. The god had offered him power and he was willing to work for it.

Though he hadn't worked outside of Britania yet, his work had been quite varied. Mostly it involved quests to take out major players in Britanian politics.

He'd assassinated mayors, business owners, nobles and even received a quest to infiltrate the high society and report on their activities.

As part of his new class he'd received the *Faceless Man* skill. It had come in handy during the infiltration as it quite literally allowed him to change his facial appearance.

He hoped that with time and practice he'd even be able to change his race eventually. It would be useful to be able to change into an elf or an orc or something.

No doubt, he'd one day be assassinating them as well. So far though, his targets had been exclusively limited to humans.

It was whilst wearing another person's face that he found himself slinking ominously through a large crowd. Diako's end goal, as far as Jack could tell, was to destabilise the city and incite a revolution.

Jack had no idea why, but he didn't care for politics anyway. He was a tool to be used and he was happy with that.

It had been a month since he'd first met Diako and in that month the city's people had turned from placid, subservient workers, to angry and violent protestors.

That was the crowd he found himself slinking through: a protest. They were crowded outside the main government building in their thousands. It was truly a sight to behold.

It was the perfect cover to aid his infiltration.

### New Quest:
### Gunpowder Plot

**The sparks of revolution have ignited the flame of the people's will. Now it's time to stoke that flame into a full-blown slaughter fest.**
**During the Russian revolution in your world, the people dragged the Romanov royal family out of the winter palace and executed them all... the women and the children too.**
**It was a truly gruesome reaction to years of poverty and a failure of leadership.**
**Right now, the leaders of Britania are holed up in the government building with the big clock on it. Let's make their deaths a little more palatable.**
**Your mission, should you choose to accept it, is to blow the building sky high and end their reign.**

### Objectives:
*Blow up the government building 0/1*

**Reward: *You get to blow up a building, isn't that***
***enough? Oh fine, I guess you can have a weapon***
***upgrade token as well.***

***\*Upon the successful completion of your mission, report***
***to The Organisation to claim your reward\****

Though it wouldn't be his first time using explosives for a mission, it wasn't exactly his area of expertise either. He was more of a long-distance killer.

Still, he had a propensity for violence and he understood the basic principles behind explosives. That was why he carried a large box in his inventory.

He was quite pleased with the design if he did say so himself. Using his knowledge of industrial explosives, he'd created a metal box with a V shape inside of it.

The V shape acted as a thick cone that would channel the blast in a single direction. Without this, the explosion would be omnidirectional which would waste a large amount of the explosive energy.

He'd filled the box with mana infused explosive material. He'd likened it to a plastic explosive in that the material itself wasn't inherently dangerous.

But, run a current – or in this case concentrated mana – through it and it'd kick out a big old boom.

He was very satisfied with his creation and he felt oddly superior as he reached the edge of the crowd and dropped down into the sewer system.

His previous infiltration mission had gleaned him some useful information which was vital for the completion of his new quest.

The sewer was made of rusty coloured bricks and he had to crouch to get through. It was a tight fit, but not the tightest sewer he'd ever been in. There was this one time in Columbia where he'd…actually, never mind. It wasn't important.

He made his way through the sewer which ran directly under the crowd and, of course, under the government building.

The crowd roared with outrage above as Jack worked his way under them. He soon came out into a wider, but squat, cistern.

The crowd was muffled in this area and he knew from the intelligence he'd gathered that this was the right place.

There was a single column in the middle of the cistern. It was made of similar bricks to the sewer itself but it had the feel of strong magic enchantments surrounding it.

*It's a good job I designed a mana infused bomb.* He snickered in his own head as he pulled out the large crate he'd designed.

He placed the crate on its side so that the direction of the blast would, in theory, punch straight through the column. Next came the risky part.

In order to set off the explosive, he needed to channel mana into it, but if he did that he'd be stood right next to it when it went kaboom.

That obviously wasn't a good idea.

Jack had realised this flaw in his design early on and had worked on a potential work around. It was risky though.

As he worked his way back through the sewer to reach the entry point he'd dropped down earlier, his heart was bouncing around in his chest.

He was nervous. He *never* got nervous.

When he was crouched directly under the entrance to the sewer system, he turned around and took his sniper rifle out of his inventory. He faced the cistern and activated his sight skill that allowed him to see through the dark for a long distance.

He could just about make out the crate bomb he'd planted. It was the size of a peanut in his vision. This wasn't going to be easy.

He trained his rifle's sights on the bomb and concentrated on filling the barrel with as much mana as possible. Theoretically, as long as the mana hit the charge, it should react similarly to channelling mana into it by hand.

It was still *his* mana after all.

Jack was a good shot, but hitting a peanut sized target was never easy. The distance alone wasn't that big of a deal, but the size of the target only shrank the further away he'd gotten.

He took aim, let out his breath part way, concentrated on lowering his heart rate and then, between heartbeats, he squeezed the trigger.

The magic bullet punched into the crate bomb and Jack jumped.

As he flew into the air and back out onto the street, the excess explosive force blasted through the tight sewer system, following him in a mass of flame.

It pushed him even higher into the air and just as he was above the crowd, many of whom had been blow onto the floor by the sudden explosion, he saw it.

The government building seemed to implode as walls collapsed and the roof began caving it. The entire thing fell inwards and plumes of smoke and dust covered the shocked crowd in the square.

He'd planted his bomb on the underground structural support and now his mission was complete.

***

Jack appeared in the dark temple where he had first met Diako. It was his first time being transported there since he'd joined The Organisation.

He was slightly disoriented, but only for a moment. One minute he'd been soaring through the air as he got the best seat in the house to admire his handywork.

The next he was stood before his new god in a calm and foreboding place. He had expected to have to exfiltrate the area and meet his handler at a predetermined location.

That's how it usually went. He completed the mission, he left the area, met his handler, and received his reward and new instructions.

He was fast at adapting to new situations, so as he faced his new god, he dropped to one knee in reverence. He'd never been a religious man, but Diako had been good to him and he held the upmost respect for him.

"You have completed your mission, Reaper?" Diako asked, though Jack was certain he already knew.

"Yes, My Lord," he replied.

Part of his induction into The Organisation included a crash course in correct etiquette when speaking to the god.

Most gods didn't speak with their subordinates often, but Diako was an exception to that. He was even known to speak directly into minds and share senses with some of his more trusted and prominent people.

"Good. I'm taking you off this project for a while, something has come up and I want you to handle it." Diako said, he sounded different from the last time they'd spoken. He seemed... distracted.

"Of course, My Lord," Jack replied. "What is it you would have me do."

"In a few months' time another god is holding a tournament to decide who his new high priest will be." Diako began, rage poked at his well-controlled aura, Jack could feel it like a ticking time bomb. "That god has issued me a challenge that I simply cannot refuse. I need you to win that tournament."

"You...want me to become someone else's high priest My Lord?" Jack asked, confusion clouding his mind.

"No. I want you to win because Chrysus has the audacity to threaten to oust my agents!" Diako roared and Jack fell backwards. He wasn't exactly scared, but he got the inescapable feeling that Diako's aura might kill him by accident in its unruly state.

"That impertinent upstart has issued me a direct challenge," Diako continued, reigning his aura in slightly, but still seething. "He has claimed that my activities of late have destabilised the economy of Britania, he says that as the god of wealth anything pertaining to economy is his domain.

"As I have taken action to change the economy of Britania, I have spat in his face. The little brat has threatened to leak the information of Organisation members worldwide if I don't send someone specific to attend his little tournament.

"I've already arranged for that, but I'm sending you as well. I won't let that insolent cur get away with insulting me. If I win, he won't take further action. So, *you* must win Reaper, or die trying."

# Chapter 66
# Well, Shit

I sat alone in my room at the *Sleeping Giant Inn.* I'd spent most of the journey home meditating. It was painful but eventually I managed to break through and visualise my insides.

I decided to call it my soul view. Partly because that's what it was, at least to my rudimentary understanding, but also because of how it had changed.

The place was a mess when I'd finally gotten back in. My stamina coil and health rope were alright. It didn't take long to get them back into top form.

The issue was with the orb in my core, my soul. It had been tinged green previously, it was small and always just out of reach. That had changed.

It felt different now, bigger. The blue and green orb of swirling, almost tangible energy seemed to take up half of my core.

I still couldn't touch it, not really. But I could brush it with the tips of my fingers as it swirled, an incomprehensible void, in the pit of my stomach.

I'd spent hours trying to understand it but I didn't really seem to get anywhere.

It was frustrating but there was nothing I could do about it. I'd dropped out of meditation and tried to cheer myself up by assigning my free stat points into intelligence.

It almost seemed wasteful, but it was my lowest stat and I figured the ability to turn invisible could be invaluable if I could use it for long enough.

Nothing else of note happened for the rest of the trip. Panda had sipped cocktails and engaged in a one-sided conversation with the barman. And I had spent most of my time meditating.

Once the boat returned us to Havar we made a beeline for the Adventure Society. Lucy was as happy as ever but when she gave me the report form to fill out, I froze up.

How was I supposed to put into words all that had transpired on the island? I could barely understand it myself.

In the end she allowed me to take the form away with me to fill out in my own time. She seemed concerned but I couldn't open up to her about the changing nature of my soul.

I couldn't talk to anyone about it. They wouldn't understand. It was just another reason to put me down like a rabid dog and with the map fragment on my back, they already had more reasons to kill me than not.

So, I took the form back to the inn and began trying to fill it out. I needed to explain what happened but I also had to omit exactly how it happened.

I settled on telling the Adventure Society that once we'd watched the scene play out, the memory ended. I falsely speculated that all Treena's memory spirit wanted was for someone to see her tragic story.

Even if they thought that was bullshit, they could hardly blame a temp for not understanding the intricate innerworkings of an ancient and complex magic.

Once I'd finally written it up, I was pretty happy with my work. It would hopefully protect me from scrutiny and investigations whilst also showing that I completed the quest satisfactorily.

I was pretty drained by the time I'd finished the report and I laid back on the comfortable bed and delved into my HUD.

I still had two quests I'd barely even started yet. The first was the Morningstar Hotel and Spa quest. A place that I knew was basically a crime syndicate hang out.

I was interested in it for sure, but these were dangerous people and I was only a phase two. I batted the quest notification away as I decided to leave it for later.

Then I saw the other quest, one I'd received right back at the beginning when I'd first arrived in this world and been captured by a cult who wanted to skin me.

My stomach did a summersault as I read through it. I'd forgotten the quest even existed. I'd barely been in this world for two months but it felt like an eternity.

**New Quest:** *The Celestial Map*

**Collect all the pieces of the Celestial Map. Upon completion of this quest you will unlock another quest.**

**Objectives:**
**Map pieces collected 2/10,000**

**Reward: V ast Cosmic Power**

*Vast Cosmic Power?* I wondered what that meant. It was so ominous and it reminded me of something from a book I'd read once.

Collecting all the pieces of the Celestial Map would involve murdering 10,000 people. It wasn't a quest I ever intended to complete.

It was sickening that the system had even given it to me in the first place. I'd learnt accidentally that I could adsorb the tattoos of the map fragments form the dead bodies of outworlders.

I'd accidentally killed a guy called Brad who'd been in the cell with me when I threw a cultist into a vat of acid. Shortly afterwards I'd adsorbed his tattoo. It still sat next to my own on my back.

The whole idea of it all gave me the shivers.

I jumped up out of bed, grabbed my completed report and left the inn. I needed to get my reward and start the next step in my journey to power. I needed a distraction from my swirling and spiralling thoughts.

I had to keep getting stronger so I could one day protect my family. Not that I had any idea how to bring them into this world, or if it was even possible. But if 10,000 other people from earth could be brought here on a whim.

Then there must be a way for me to bring my family across. I had no delusions about going home. For all I knew it was a one-way trip anyway.

Not to mention that despite the horrors of this world, it was still more exciting than a dead-end job and paying taxes back on Earth.

I knew that Layla wasn't present during the last quest. It must have been magic, either that or my mind was decaying. It was a scary thought, losing one's sense of self, but I couldn't dwell on it any longer.

I wasn't going to get stronger by moping around in my room.

I strolled down the street and entered the Adventure Society foyer. Lucy smiled up at me from behind the reception desk.

She had always been so nice to me; though I guess it was her job. She was probably like that with everyone.

Panda sat idly on the desk, smoking his pipe. From the looks of things he hadn't moved from there since I'd left an hour earlier to fill out my report at home.

"Sorry about that, I'm done now," I said, handing Lucy the report."

She nodded, took it from me, and began reading through it. She didn't seem overly shocked as she read it. I'd expected more of a reaction in all honesty.

"Thank you for your report, Mr Akabane. I can now officially call this quest complete. I'll need to file the report and get your reward if you'll wait here please," she said professionally before walking off somewhere behind the reception.

"You already told her, didn't you?" I asked Panda after Lucy had left.

"Do you really think that the only thing I have to talk about with women is whatever hairbrained crap you've been up to?" He admonished, shaking his head. "Because in this case you'd be absolutely right. Now, check your quest log."

I laughed and opened the new notification on my HUD.

### Quest Complete:
### *I've Been Expecting You, Mr Akabane*

**A mysterious new structure has appeared on an uninhabited island just off the coast of Havar. I'm getting some serious evil villain's lair vibes from this one.**
**If there's a mountain shaped like a skull, you know what to do.**
**After exploring the island you came across a dryad girl and decided to help her like the overly trusting idiot you are. Honestly, how you're not dead yet is beyond me.**

Helping the dryad girl turned out to be a trap. Big surprise there. You found yourself in the middle of an inquisition and blatantly ignored the plethora of war crimes to chase after one small girl.
After catching up to her, she died. Big deal, am I right? But you took it oddly personally and went absolute high school shooter on the orc who killed her.
I guess there were no cultists after all.

Objectives:
*Kill all the inhabitants on the island 0/1*
*Or*
*Spare the inhabitants and report your reasoning 0/1*
*Or*
*Investigate the island and report back 1/1*

Reward: *500 gold coins and admittance onto the next Adventurer exam.*

*Speak to the Adventure Society to claim your reward. Reward payable upon the successful completion of the above objectives*

I read through the system's rather rude play by play account of what happened on the island.

It seemed that the objective I had completed was the investigate and report back one. The others were to kill or spare the inhabitants and I hadn't reported on my soul killing to the society. They were memories after all, so the term *killing* didn't even really apply to them.

I thought back to my last encounter with Director Lucas where he'd told me that the information the Adventure Society received was often wrong.

I guessed he was right. They'd certainly dropped the ball on this one. I'd gotten angry at him the last time we spoke. I'd felt like they omitted information on purpose and were unprofessionally trying to get me killed.

But maybe he was right. Perhaps it was just part of the job to expect the unexpected and be able to adapt to different situations.

I mean, how could they have possibly known about Treena and the orcish inquisition being trapped inside a memory that happened 20,000 years ago. Cultists setting up a base made much more sense when you thought about it.

Adventuring was a hard job. In a world full of magic anything could happen. Though it wouldn't kill them to verify their facts every once in a while.

"Here you go Mr Akabane. Five hundred gold coins as promised." Lucy said chirpily as she entered the reception area with a large coin purse in hand.

I took it into my inventory and thanked her.

"So, do I qualify to take the adventurer exam now?" I asked hopefully.

"Of course," She smiled, patting Panda on the head as he looked at her, seemingly as interested as I was. "As per the agreement, you have now completed three quests for us and thus, qualify to take part in the next adventurer exam."

"That's great news!" I replied, practically bursting with excitement.

Being an adventurer was the best way I knew to gain levels and one day achieve my goal. Taking the exam was the first step towards that.

If I passed I'd be able to take on more quests and fight harder enemies. I hated to admit it, but I was a little excited about that.

"I'm glad to see you're so happy Mr Akabane. The next exam starts in twenty minutes if you want to make your way to the waiting room where the other examinees will be," Lucy replied, gesturing towards hallway on the left.

"Wait…what?" I asked, dumbstruck.

I'd hoped it would be soon but I didn't realise it was going to start immediately. I wasn't prepared. I'd only just returned from the last quest.

"Please make your way to the waiting room Mr Akabane. It's just over there," she smiled patiently.

"Isn't there one I can take in a few days? I haven't even slept since I got back," I asked meekly.

"I'm really sorry Mr Akabane but as was outlined in your quest rewards for the one you just handed in. Completion allows you to take part in the *next* exam. If you decline to take part, you'll need to complete three more temp quests before you can take another exam. Those are the rules."

"So, the exam starts now?" I asked.

"The exam starts now," she replied.

"Well shit."

### Achievement Unlocked:
### *In A While, Bibliophile*

Congratulations, you have reached the end of this book.
I guess it was *bound* to happen eventually.
Now is the perfect time to leave a <u>rating</u> or <u>review</u>
(pretty please?) In all seriousness it really helps trick the
algorithm into showing this book to other people,
which is a really *novel* idea.
All hail the algorithm.
Reward: -2 *Intelligence Points*

# Acknowledgements

Thank you to my wife, Leah, for putting up with me during my hyperfocus days when all I want to talk about is books, writing and numbers going up. I love you and I'm thankful that you never get *too* annoyed with me for this. Big thanks to my mum who is always the first person to read these books and help me correct the copious typos that I always make. And, of course, a shout out to my friends and other family members who have always supported me in my creative endeavours. Lastly, this publication would not have been possible without the help and support from the team at Level Up Publishing. Cheers for taking a chance on this novel, hopefully it was worth it.

The Part Where I Shout Out Facebook Groups So They'll Let Me Spam Their Members:

LitRPG Books – This is the perfect group to get recommendations and talk to other, likeminded people about the genre. I comment on a lot of posts here, so feel free to say hello some time.

LitRPG and Gamelit Readers – Another awesome group for like-minded people to chat about their favourite books and Royal Road fictions.

LitRPG Legends – A hangout spot for all things LitRPG and Game-lit related, they also have a discord server.

Cullen Spurr (known as Panda Sage on Royal Road) is a British novelist and web serial writer of series you've probably never heard of, such as: ODINSALL, The Crimson Cage and The Celestial Map.

(Side effects of Cullen Spurr novels may include but are not limited to: sudden dizziness, loss of reflection, an unexplainable aversion to garlic, craving bacon in the middle of the night when you don't have any in the fridge, and insomnia.)

If you find that you are experiencing any of the above then please do not hesitate to contact him in one of the following ways:

Facebook: @cullenspurrauthor

Instagram: @cullenspurr

Patreon: @PandaSageWebNovels

Join the Discord server

Or, you could attempt to summon him by chanting his name three times into a mirror, downing a shot of flaming tequila and shedding a single tear – no more, no less.

**Also by Cullen Spurr:**

ODINSALL Saga:

In a bid to save their descendants from an impending apocalypse, the Norse Gods spirit a group of teenagers away to their realm and enrol them into a school where death lurks around every corner.

The Crimson Cage Series:

A vampire, an elf, a succubus and a dwarf rob a museum.

For more Level Up books, please visit:
https://www.levelup.pub/books

From there you can sign up to be an ARC reader for our books, find out about new releases, apply to join in the WhatsApp group and read dozens of features about LitRPG.

www.ingramcontent.com/pod-product-compliance
Lightning Source LLC
Chambersburg PA
CBHW030844030726
47495CB00005B/1361